DIARY OF A
SERIAL KILLER

By

Shawn William Davis

SECOND EDITION

shawndavis6712@yahoo.com

PRINTED IN THE
UNITED STATES
OF AMERICA

CHAPTER 1

The teenage girl is absolutely stunning; she's at least 5'8," well-toned, and has tantalizing curves like an hourglass. It's hard to believe I've discovered a young woman of such high quality at a mall. If she was older, I would say she worked out, but at her age it must be all natural.

The beauty's oval-shaped face resembles a blossoming supermodel. Her long, straight, brown hair flows down to her shoulders. She has a gorgeous tan that was obviously produced by nature – not a tanning machine.

She wears ordinary clothing: a white t-shirt – with the name of an obscure rock band on it – and tight, cut-off jean shorts hug her hips and ass. I estimate that she is about seventeen years old. It's a shame I have to kill her.

It's a shame, but that's how I get *the rush*. It's a *rush* like no other. Nothing compares to it. No drug, no food, no product on earth can produce the euphoria that comes with *the rush*.

I'm sitting at a table at the Food Court in front of a cheap, fast-food Thai restaurant, eating a delicious combo meal consisting of General Gau's Chicken, Orange Chicken, and fried rice. Every now and then I take a break from eating to sip Coke through a straw. The sweet carbonation tingles on my tongue.

I'm careful to steal discreet glances at my gorgeous prey. She is seated three tables away in front of Regina Pizza talking to a less attractive blonde, who is also oblivious to my presence. I count myself lucky to have an unremarkable, nondescript appearance: medium-height, black hair, plain features. My appearance keeps me from being noticed, which is very important when you do what I do.

I spotted my target at an Old Navy store on the first level about forty minutes ago. She was shopping for clothes with her chubby blonde friend. I watched her buy a trendy light blue blouse, which is now contained in a bag at her feet. The friend is nothing special; she's a slightly overweight teenager with a pudgy face and red-spotted cheeks.

It's the brunette I'm interested in. Her sleekness is attractive, yet her curves also entice. She has an easy, natural smile. Right now she's facing her pudgy friend across the table, laughing at what must be a funny joke.

For some unexplainable reason, her laughter makes me angry. I have to look away to focus on a mother with two young children at an adjacent table. When I turn back toward my target, she isn't laughing anymore, so my rage evaporates like mist.

This girl is top-of-the-line; she is what popular culture would refer to as a "10." I'm mesmerized by her soft, firm breasts protruding from her white t-shirt. I imagine what she would look like without the shirt. Her tight jean shorts hug the curves of her ass and I have to look away so I don't salivate.

Her beauty tempts me to keep her like a child keeps a pet. However, that isn't practical. Eventually, I would be caught. Obviously, I can't allow that to happen, so I will probably end up killing her shortly after I snatch her.

This statement might seem shocking to many, but it's standard operating procedure when you do what I do. Recently, I've decided to write down my thoughts and feelings in this journal, so that future generations can read it and realize that I'm not a monster. I'm an artist. Before the moment of her death, I preserve a woman's beauty for all eternity.

As an artist, I appreciate beauty more than ordinary people, especially the beauty of women. Unlike most brain-dead drones that go through life half-asleep, I have a passion for visual art. I create art from the young women I snatch, and it is an exquisite process.

Like any young artist, I study all the old masters: Bundy, Gein, Manson, Dahmer, Gacy, Pickton, and Rader. Every day I learn new techniques through my research.

But now I have to concentrate. It looks like the girls are ready to leave. The brunette is picking up her purse. Time to go.

CHAPTER 2

A shiver of excitement runs down my spine as I watch the girl stand up and bend over to pick up her shopping bag.

My hand trembles as I hold my plastic cup; I can feel the Coke swishing around inside. It's difficult not to get up, go over to her, and run my hands all over her body. I force myself to take another bite of chicken as I watch her and her plain friend walk away. My throat feels as dry as sand, so I gulp down more Coke to help swallow the processed meat stuck in my mouth.

Stalking is a precise art; you can't become overenthusiastic. If you get too close to your victim, you could spook her. I've done it before and the results are disastrous. If she notices you, the element of surprise is ruined and your prey gets away. There's no way I'm going to jeopardize snatching this one; I have to add her to my art collection.

The rush is kicking in already. I can feel my heart beating hard within my chest like a jackhammer. My palms are sweaty. I wait until the teenage girls leave the Food Court before I stand up. I don't bother to throw away my leftover food. Someone gets paid to do that.

I feel a pang of fear as the girl walks behind a store wall out of sight. Sprinting past the Food Court tables, I relax when I see her again and let out a deep breath.

I follow her at a safe distance – about a hundred feet away. It's a Thursday night so the mall isn't too crowded. I've tried snatching these little bitches on the weekend when there are more targets available, but there were too many people and I was almost caught. Weekdays are better. There are just enough people at the mall so I can blend into the crowd, but not so many that I will be noticed when I make my move.

It's 8:45 PM and the mall closes at 9:30, so I only have to follow her around for another forty-five minutes. If I'm lucky, she's on her way to the exit right now. I hope she parked in a spot secluded enough for me to make my move; it's better not to have witnesses.

I try to act casual as I walk with the flow of pedestrians on the upper level of the mall. I ignore the clothing stores that I pass; they all look the same to me. I find it ridiculous that there are so many varieties; clothes are clothes.

I keep my eyes focused on the rear of my target. Did I mention what a great ass she has? Occasionally, a pedestrian gets in my way or blocks my view, but I easily sidestep them. A group of teenagers leaving a video game store force me over to the railing overlooking the lower level to keep my target in view. Looking down on all the brain-dead sheep shopping beneath me makes me sick.

It looks like I might be in luck; she's heading toward the exit leading to the upper level of the parking garage. I say "she," but it's really "them." Her chubby friend is still with her. To me, the friend is a nobody. She's just someone in my way. I won't have a problem getting rid of her. Actually, it could be enjoyable.

I feel adrenaline kicking in, but I have to remain calm until the right moment. I have to save my energy. A middle-aged woman and her ten-year-old brat get in my way, so I sidestep them to keep my target in view. I watch the beauty push an exterior glass door open and hold it open for her friend. How polite.

It's dark outside; the upper level of the parking garage is open to the sky, and the streetlights are spaced far apart - leaving plenty of dark areas. Large clouds block out the moon and stars. Perfect.

I follow my unsuspecting targets through the vestibule into the cool October air, watching as they huddle together. I imagine the beauty's breasts perking up as the cool night air caresses her bare nipples. I can barely contain myself.

I close the distance between us as the girls cross the parking lot. There is a single row of cars parked against a shoulder-high barrier to my right and multiple rows of cars and the exit to my left. This could get tricky because my car is parked in the lower level. It won't matter; I know what I have to do.

I reach into the right pocket of my jeans to wrap my fingers around the metal bottle of pepper spray that I purchased from a private seller on Craigslist. I reach my other hand into my left pocket to touch the handle of my ultra-sharp folding knife. Finally, I check the steel handcuffs in my inner jacket pocket. I have everything I need, so I increase my pace to a fast walk.

As they near the end of a row of cars, I see the beauty taking car keys out of her tight jeans pocket. I start to sprint. I try to minimize the impact of my sneakers on the pavement as much as possible.

They are heading toward a gray Toyota Camry that is parked second-to-last in the long row of vehicles. The beauty veers toward the driver's side of the Camry while her pudgy blonde friend heads for the passenger side. I go for the beauty first.

With trembling fingers, I pull out the bottle of pepper spray as I close in on her. I'm only a few feet away, but she still hasn't seen me yet. As I reach her, she must sense a slight disturbance in the air because she turns toward me, startled. I shove the bottle of pepper spray into her face and pull the trigger. She screams as her hands instinctively fly up to cover her scorching skin.

Looking over the car roof, I see her pudgy friend's eyes widen like a deer in headlights. I spin the beauty around and snap the handcuffs on her wrists. There is a jingling sound as she drops her car keys to the pavement. While her back is still turned to me, I reach down and scoop up the keys.

I seize my victim's wrist with my left hand while I unlock the car door with my right. Swinging the door open, I shove the beauty inside. Glancing up, I notice the pudgy girl is still frozen on the other side of the car. With my prize safely stowed in the car, I sprint around the front of the car to confront the useless blonde.

This time, I take out my knife and snap it open. I lunge. The blonde's left palm is impaled on the blade as she raises her hand to block my thrust. She screams shrilly as I pull the knife out of the wound. Blood spurts. She clutches at the gash, which leaves her neck exposed. I plunge the knife into her carotid artery; blood shoots out like a geyser. Ducking, I pull out the knife so the red fountain misses my face and sprays my right shoulder.

Checking the car, I see the beauty in the driver's seat with her eyes closed; she appears to be crying. Judging by the direct hit with the pepper spray, it must be too painful to open her eyes. Good. She hasn't seen my handiwork.

I watch the blonde collapse like a marionette with cut

strings. As her body hits the pavement, blood continues to shoot from her punctured throat like water bursting from a fire hose. I avoid the blood by stepping over her legs and circle around the hood of the car until I reach the other side.

"Hey! What the fuck are you doing?" a voice shouts.

A tall, middle-aged man is running toward me from the mall exit. It's a Good Samaritan, and he looks like he's physically fit. My blood turns to ice. However, I have time because he's still more than a hundred feet away.

Adrenaline pumping, I have to act. I pull open the driver's side door and drag the beauty out. I don't bother to glance toward the sprinting man. I forcefully escort my prize to the passenger side. I can hear footfalls against the pavement getting louder.

Avoiding the dead body, I shove the beauty in the passenger seat and slam the door. I circle around the front of the car toward the open driver's side. The tall man is closing in from twenty feet away; I can hear his labored breathing as I slide into the seat. I slam the door shut as the man's hands smash against the driver's window. Inserting the key in the ignition, I turn on the engine. The man pounds on the window with his fists.

I calmly place the car in reverse and step on the gas pedal. The tires squeal as the driver's-side rearview mirror strikes the man's hand. I don't bother to see what he's doing as I turn the steering wheel sharply toward the exit. Shifting from reverse to drive, I step on the gas and listen to the tires shriek like a tortured animal.

CHAPTER 3

There's a loud thump on the front-right quarter-panel of the Toyota as the body of the Good Samaritan rolls off the hood; the hero had the unfortunate timing to jump in front of the car as I hit the gas. The squealing tires drown out the sound of his body crashing into the pavement.

As I near the end of the aisle, I slow down to observe the terrified expressions of a middle-aged woman and a pre-teen girl, who the hero apparently left behind at the mall doors.

Their anguished faces become a blur as I regain speed and head for the exit. When I reach the exit, I halt at an intersection and look both ways. No traffic coming either way. Turning right, I barrel down an incline toward the main parking lot and parking garage.

The tires screech again as I steer toward the entrance to the parking garage. I slow just enough to avoid striking a group of pedestrians leaving the nearby movie theatre.

I pull into the parking garage, but it's the wrong aisle; my car is parked several aisles down. The beauty is sobbing quietly in the passenger seat. She tries to open her eyes several times, but the burning makes it difficult. Finally, her tears cleanse enough of the spray away so she can open her eyes – with difficulty – to look at me.

"Where are you taking me?" she asks.

"Don't worry. If you cooperate, I won't hurt you," I lie.

I try to estimate where my car is parked and turn into the second-to-last aisle in front of the movie theatre. I have to slow down as more pedestrians step out in front of my car. It takes all my self-control not to run them down.

Finally, I reach my car, but there are still patrons walking in the vicinity. I park close to my vehicle with just enough space to pull out after I make the transfer. Tapping my fingers impatiently on the steering wheel, I wait for the annoying brain-dead sheep from the theatre to reach their cars.

The next step is tricky; I must escort the beauty to the passenger side of my vehicle. I've taken great care to make sure my car isn't traced by putting stolen plates on the front and back of the vehicle. Once inside my car, I can put distance between myself and the crime scene, change plates in a remote area, and be on my way. Staying in the Toyota, I run the risk of my victim's would-be hero reporting the license or make and model of the car to the police. That I can't have, not after taking such care to acquire such a prize.

There are still sporadic groups of pedestrians in the area, but I can't wait any longer; the wails of police sirens are becoming louder. As the foot traffic around me appears to thin out, I make my move. I get out of the stolen car and go to to the passenger door. Opening it, I lean close to the beauty's chemically-scorched face.

"Do exactly as I say and you won't get hurt. Do you understand?" I say.

The girl only nods in response as she stares at me with bloodshot eyes.

I seize the beauty by her right arm and drag her out of the passenger seat; it's difficult because the handcuffs compromise her balance. After several awkward moments, she's standing next to me. Keeping a tight grip on her right triceps muscle, I escort her toward my car.

Glancing over my shoulder to check for witnesses, I continue to usher the beauty toward s my black Honda Civic. More bad luck. A muscle-bound college-age kid in a black leather jacket is escorting his hot blonde girlfriend to a nearby car. Maybe they won't notice me.

We reach the passenger door. Planning ahead, the door is unlocked, so it only takes a second to pull it open and shove my prize inside.

Glancing behind me again, I see the muscle-bound kid talking and laughing with his girlfriend. They never even looked in my direction.

I circle around the front of the car to the driver's side. Opening the door, I slide smoothly into the seat, fire the engine, and put it in reverse.

Tires squeal like a stuck pig as I hit the gas. Shifting into drive, I press the gas pedal again. Smoke kicks up as I shoot down the aisle. What a *rush*.

As I drive away, I notice passersby are drawn to my screeching tires and abrupt departure. I'm not worried because an element of risk makes the game more fun.

I slow down as flashing blue lights approach from the far side of the parking lot; the lights are heading away from me in the direction of the parking garage's upper level. Halting at the end of the aisle, I wait for them to pass before pulling out of the garage.

I assume the cops are responding to the original report of a kidnapping and assault on the upper level. When I see the lights disappear up the incline, I take a left toward the mall exit.

CHAPTER 4

Reaching the mall exit, I halt at a stop sign. Looking up, I see the flashing blue lights of the cop cars stationary on the upper-level of the parking garage, and drive down the road leading to the highway. I drive the speed limit as I follow a line of cars. Two stoplights later, I take a left toward the highway.

"What are you going to do with me?" the beauty asks.

Despite the burning spray on her face, her eyes are wide with terror.

"I'm not going to hurt you, if that's what you're worried about," I say. "I'm just going to take some pictures of you."

"What kind of pictures?" she asks without missing a beat.

I find her question annoying.

"Don't be naïve," I say. "You must know how hot you are. You're going to model for me. I even bought lingerie for you to wear. I'll let you go when we're done creating your portfolio."

"Where are you taking me?"

"Some place private."

"Look, if you let me go, I promise I won't tell anyone about you," she says.

I feel a violent rage building inside me like explosives lit by a short fuse.

"You're starting to make me angry," I tell her. "I still have the knife I used to stab your friend in my pocket. I need you to be quiet for the rest of the trip or you could get hurt. No more questions."

She's an intelligent girl; she falls quiet and stares ahead at the road. In my peripheral vision, I see tears trickling from her eyes, but she doesn't become hysterical again. Her body shivers as if I stuck her in a walk-in freezer.

Red strobe lights move toward me from the opposite lane, but I'm not worried; I assume they're heading to the parking garage to join the first cruiser. As the lights draw closer, I realize they belong to an ambulance. I smile as I think about the futility of sending an ambulance to treat a girl with a geyser of blood spewing from her neck; I hope they brought a body-bag.

I turn onto the on-ramp and steer around a sharp curve until I reach the highway: Route 290 East. I stay under the speed limit. Less than ten minutes later, I'm on route 495 North heading toward New Hampshire – the direction of my family's cabin in the Great North Woods. It's truly going to be a great time.

Fifteen minutes later, I pull off at the Boxboro exit and travel down route 42 until I reach a maze of back-roads that lead to a secluded lake. Near the lake, I drive to a remote spot in the woods between two houses that are spaced far apart: it's the hiding place where I stashed my real license plates.

First, I take off my blood-stained shirt and retrieve a fresh one from the suitcase in the back seat. I hold on to the shirt so I can toss it on the ground. Then, I reach across the girl's lap to grab a screwdriver out of the glove compartment. She flinches, but I don't blame her. She is intimidated by me. Knowing the power I have over her causes a stiffness in my jeans.

Leaving the car, I walk over to the tree concealing my real license plates. I toss the bloody shirt on the ground and kick some leaves over it. I'm not really trying to hide it; I want the cops to find it. It makes the game more exciting.

Reaching behind the tree, I feel cold metal. It only takes a few minutes to unscrew the stolen plates from my car and attach the real ones. I return to the driver's seat and replace the screwdriver in the glove compartment.

The beauty glances anxiously at me, but doesn't say anything. Like I said before, she's an intelligent girl; she 's too smart to activate my temper by saying something stupid. Her body continues to tremble as if she's having a seizure. I enjoy watching the fear take over her and contort her body in ways she has yet to discover.

I return to 495 North. Again, driving the speed limit in the middle lane. Now that I'm on the highway heading to my destination, I can finally relax. I start to come down from *the rush*, but it's all right because it allows me to conserve my energy for the fun part. I turn on the radio and hear classic rock music blast out from my favorite radio station; AC DC's *Highway to Hell* is playing – fittingly.

The sudden noise startles my prize. I don't turn the radio up because I want the girl to remain calm. Or, at least reasonably calm. Her body is still quivering from head-to-toe.

I have nothing to worry about from the girl. Her hands are fastened securely behind her back and even if she did pull a Houdini and somehow got free, I rigged the passenger door so it only opens from the outside. Either way, she's trapped.

I reach into my jacket pocket for a pack of Marlboro lights

and shake one out of the package. I take out my silver lighter, emblazoned with a black skull and crossbones, and light up. Rolling the window down a couple inches, I inhale deeply and blow out a stream of smoke. The smoke gets sucked out the crack in the window like mist dissipating in a strong wind.

"Do you want a drag?" I ask, holding the cigarette in front of her lips.

"No thank you," the beauty replies quietly, staring straight ahead at the oncoming highway as if she's in a trance.

How polite. Such a smart girl.

"That's good. These things will kill you," I say, laughing.

I concentrate on smoking my cigarette and listening to rock music. It turns out there's an AC DC marathon; the next song is *Shoot to Thrill*. It would be more fitting if the song was titled *Stab to Thrill* because I didn't bring a gun with me on this excursion; firearms are too noisy. I prefer a knife for stealth and the face-to-face intimacy it provides.

After driving for several hours, the beauty finally succumbs to exhaustion; she leans back awkwardly against the seat with her cuffed hands facing the passenger door, closes her eyes, and starts to nod off. I turn down the radio so I won't wake her up. I wonder if she would still be asleep if she knew what I was going do to her.

CHAPTER 5

Sergeant Jim Conrad was patrolling the south side of town when the radio call came in from the police dispatcher; a teenage girl had been kidnapped, and another one murdered on the upper level of the Westfield Pond Mall parking garage.

Conrad flipped on the cruiser's flashing lights and sped toward the mall, turning on the siren when the lights weren't enough to persuade drivers to get out of the way. Being the closest unit, he assumed he would be the first on the scene.

Conrad took a right onto the mall road and hit the siren again when he found his way blocked by traffic.

"Come on, get out of the way," the sergeant muttered as the cars took their time pulling over.

Conrad was unnerved because this was the third violent attack/kidnapping to be reported in the town within the past year. Nine months ago, a sixteen-year-old disappeared from the Westfield High School parking lot after a school play. Two months later, her decomposing body – punctured with multiple stab wounds – was discovered by a hunter in a shallow grave hidden in Westfield's heavily wooded Conservation Land.

Five months ago, another teenager disappeared from the parking lot of a 24-hour convenience store in a Westfield neighborhood. A nationwide Amber Alert had been put out to no avail. She was still missing.

Now, there was another stabbing and kidnapping. It was becoming an epidemic.

To Conrad, it wasn't rocket science; there was a serial killer/kidnapper on the loose. Despite the fact that his Chief kept saying, "It couldn't happen here in our small town," it was looking more and more like Westfield and the surrounding area had a serious problem on their hands. Thinking about it, Conrad became angry.

When the murder occurred last December, Conrad told the Westfield Chief and the female lead detective that the incident might be related to the murders and disappearances occurring in various towns in the surrounding area.

Westfield wasn't the only town in the Metrowest area of Massachusetts experiencing an unusual run of bad luck involving missing or dead teenage girls. Last year, a teenage girl had disappeared from a mall two towns to the east in Farmington and the body of another teenager had been discovered three towns to the south in a wooded area in the small town of Holliston. The year before, a teenage girl had disappeared from a restaurant parking lot in Marlboro – only two towns to the north. The bodies of the kidnap victims had never been found.

In addition to accusing Conrad of suffering from an overactive imagination, Chief Willard and Detective Lombardi had accused him of overstepping his authority as the second shift sergeant. Who was he to tell them how to do their jobs? How could he, a mere sergeant, determine there was a pattern when no one else saw one? The Chief told him to stop thinking above his pay-grade and the detective told him to leave the investigating to professionals. Conrad wondered if they would listen to him now. Assholes.

"Get out of the damn way!" he shouted at the windshield, as he switched the siren to "wail" and left it running.

More cars pulled out of his way, but they didn't hurry. Conrad tapped the wheel impatiently while he waited for the final stragglers to give him room to pass. Over the next rise, the mall came into view. The parking garage was on the left side. With the siren going full blast, Conrad blew through the next red traffic light.

Finally, the drivers smartened up and began to pull over before Conrad's cruiser reached them. The sergeant swung left into the mall parking lot and watched panicked pedestrians and vehicles scrambling to get out of his way as he drove toward the parking garage ramp.

As he passed the lower level of the garage, he noticed a number of people exiting the movie theatre into the parking lot. There appeared to be some kind of commotion occurring in the lower level of the garage; a small crowd had gathered there, but Conrad didn't have time to investigate. Dispatch had informed him that the kidnapping and assault happened on the upper level of the garage.

Conrad slowed down as the female dispatcher's voice came over the radio: "Westfield Control to all officers. New information just in: witnesses at the scene report the kidnapping suspect is a white male in his mid-to-late twenties, medium height and weight, black hair, wearing a black windbreaker jacket and blue-jeans. The suspect is believed to be driving the victim's vehicle: a gray 2008 Toyota Camry, Massachusetts registration 7797 GW."

Conrad waited for the town's other two patrol officers to respond to the dispatcher's radio message and then picked up his radio mike as he pulled his cruiser onto the top level of the garage.

"Nine-thirty-five to Westfield Control," Conrad spoke into the receiver.

"This is Westfield Control," the dispatcher replied.

"You can put me off at the upper level of the Westfield Mall parking garage. There appears to be a crowd gathered in the last aisle across from the mall entrance."

"Westfield Control receives at 21:08," the female dispatcher replied.

Conrad slowed to go over a pair of speed-bumps. He drove straight down the main aisle toward the last row of cars across from the mall entrance. The crowd had gathered at the far edge of the parking area.

Conrad took a left and kept the lights and siren going as he approached the crowd. The crowd must have been fascinated by something because they failed to clear the way as the cruiser approached.

Conrad hit the air horn several times and that did the trick; the crowd finally parted to let him pass like the Red Sea parted for the Israelites. As the spectators moved out of the way, he saw the object of their attention: a female body lying on its back in an empty parking space in an expanding puddle of blood.

Considering the amount of blood, Conrad guessed the female victim was deceased, so he wasn't happy to see a Good Samaritan attempting to give first aid to the victim by applying pressure to her throat with a blood-drenched cloth.

Conrad placed the cruiser in park and turned off the siren, but kept the lights going. He got out of the car and approached the crowd that was circling the body like vultures attracted to a corpse.

The police sergeant was in his mid-thirties, medium height, and had well-developed muscles from regular gym attendance. He had short-clipped black hair and blue eyes that held a steady gaze. In short, he was a fairly intimidating figure in a police uniform.

As he drew closer, Conrad gestured for the crowd to stand back so he could reach the female Samaritan. The Samaritan was a blonde, middle-aged woman wearing a black skirt and a white blouse with spots of blood on it. The rest of the crowd continued to stand around gawking, so Conrad stepped in and began to physically push them back.

"I need everyone who is not a witness to get back!" Conrad shouted as he lightly shoved the closest observers rearward.

A tall, middle-aged man with a bloody forehead, who was holding his left arm tight against his ribs, stepped forward.

"Officer, I saw the whole thing," he said.

CHAPTER 6

A woman in her early forties and a pre-teen girl stepped out of the crowd to stand by the male witness's side. So far, the man with the bloody forehead was the only spectator to volunteer any information.

"Everyone else needs to step back!" Conrad shouted, using his best drill sergeant imitation. "This is a crime scene and I will arrest anyone who remains that is not a witness!"

Conrad's new approach motivated the crowd to back off enough to give him twenty feet of additional breathing room.

"Anyone else who saw what happened needs to come forward!" the sergeant shouted into the crowd.

When there was no response from the wide-eyed spectators, Conrad addressed the man who came forward.

"How did you become injured?" Conrad asked.

"The attacker hit me with his vehicle."

Conrad raised his eyebrows. "Sir, I need you to stand aside in order to ask you some questions, but I have to check the victim first. All right?"

"No problem," the man said.

Conrad retrieved plastic surgical gloves from a leather

pouch on his belt and pulled them on. He approached the female Samaritan holding a blood-soaked rag against the victim's neck.

"Ma'am, I appreciate your help, but I need to take over now," Conrad said, adjusting his plastic gloves as he stood over the woman and the corpse.

"Officer, I'm only a lawyer, but I took a First Aid course. I tried to apply pressure to the wound, but I think she's lost too much blood."

The lawyer wasn't giving up her patient easily, so Conrad took a moment to check the other bystanders again.

"Did anyone else see what happened?" Conrad repeated to the spectators.

They shook their heads again.

"Then I need everyone to move farther back!" Conrad shouted, lifting his palms in the air and making a pushing gesture.

Some members of the crowd complied by walking away, while others backed off – but continued to loiter in the vicinity. Conrad didn't have time to go up to each person individually and ask him or her to disperse; he needed to prioritize.

"Ma'am, I appreciate your help," the sergeant said, as he took a notepad and a pen out of the upper left pocket of his dark blue uniform shirt. "But I need to get your information now."

"I'm Susan Callahan," the woman said, continuing to hold pressure on the blood-soaked cloth over the victim's wound.

Can't she see that the victim is dead? Conrad thought. *She must be traumatized by the violent scene.*

"Ms. Callahan, I need to see your ID. Would you please stand up and show it to me?" Conrad asked, hoping to lure the lawyer away from the body so she stopped contaminating the crime scene.

It wasn't a complete ruse because he needed her personal information for the subsequent incident report.

"Okay," Callahan said, releasing the blood-soaked rag and standing.

"Is that your purse on the ground?" the sergeant asked, pointing to a black bag on the hardtop near the corpse's feet.

"Oh, yes, thank you," the lawyer said, bending down to pick up the purse.

While she searched for her ID in her purse, Conrad sidestepped her and bent over the body to check the victim's pulse. He was certain she was deceased, but he went through the motions to follow protocol. The police sergeant pressed his index and middle finger against the side of the inert teenager's neck opposite the wound. Not surprisingly, there was no pulse; the traumatized lawyer had been wasting her time.

Conrad examined the blood-soaked cloth more closely and realized it was a crumpled gray suit jacket, probably the lawyer's. He lifted the item of clothing to check the neck wound; it was vicious and deep, but only a trickle of blood came out of it now. Most of her blood was pooling on the pavement. The policeman quickly re-covered the wound and left the improvised bandage in place to keep away prurient spectators.

Conrad stood up and peeled off his bloody gloves. He placed them in a plastic evidence bag and shoved it in his pocket. The Good Samaritan stood by the corpse's feet, holding out an ID in her blood-spattered hand.

"You used your jacket to cover the wound?" Conrad asked to give himself time to reach into his side pouch for a pair of back-up gloves.

"Yes, it was all I had to use," Callahan said.

"You put in a valiant effort, but unfortunately, the victim is deceased," Conrad said. "There's no pulse."

The lawyer buried her face in her bloody hand.

"I thought she was dead, officer, but I didn't want to let up placing pressure on the wound to check for a pulse."

"I understand, Ma'am."

Conrad took out his back-up gloves and pulled them on. There was no way he was going to touch this woman's ID after she contaminated it with blood; it was standard operating procedure to avoid blood-borne pathogens. After adjusting his gloves, the sergeant took the lawyer's ID, recorded her information on his notepad, and handed it back.

"Ms. Callahan, did you see what happened?" Conrad asked.

"No, I came after," she replied.

Conrad saw a handprint-shaped red stain on the left side of her face where she had touched herself.

"I was leaving the mall when I heard people screaming and ran over to see what was happening," she continued. "I found a crowd standing around this young woman. Blood was spurting out of her neck, so I tried to stop it."

"Ms. Callahan, you certainly went above and beyond the call of duty tonight. Can you stick around for a short while to speak to the detective when she arrives?"

"Certainly, officer," Callahan replied.

"I need you to step over by the cruiser so I can secure the crime scene. The detective will be arriving any minute to ask you some questions."

"Sure," the lawyer said, glancing back at the body one last time before trudging toward the police car.

Conrad saw lights flashing and heard a siren blaring in the parking lot below; he recognized the lights and siren as ambulance equipment. Obviously, it was too late for the EMTs to do anything for the female victim, but they could at least check the witness who was struck by the perp's vehicle. At this point, Conrad wasn't planning to let the EMTs anywhere near the body until the crime scene was fully processed. Where was his back-up?

Conrad returned to the cruiser and obtained road flares from the trunk. The edge of the parking garage provided a natural barrier to spectators in two directions, but Conrad needed to cordon off the open area where spectators were lining up to stare at the bloody corpse. The police sergeant lit two flares and placed them strategically at opposing points about fifty feet away from the cadaver in front of the gathering crowd.

"I need everyone to step back beyond the flares!" Conrad shouted to the curious bystanders.

Most of the spectators complied, but he had to physically push several stragglers past the flare line.

"If anyone crosses that line, they will be arrested!" Conrad barked.

After containing the crime scene as best he could, Conrad returned to the male witness, who was still standing several feet away from the teenage girl's body with his wife and daughter. The sergeant led the family over to the cruiser.

"I need to see your ID," Conrad said.

The man reached into his pocket, took out his wallet, and fumbled through it for several seconds before pulling out his ID. Conrad took out his notepad as the man handed it to him. The sergeant took a minute to copy the information and then handed the ID back. The witness's name was Stephen Jones.

"Mr. Jones, how did you become involved in the incident?"

Conrad was interrupted by the arrival of the ambulance; its flashing red lights brightened as it reached the top of the ramp and entered the parking area. Mercifully, the EMT driving the vehicle had turned off the annoying siren as it approached.

"Hold on, sir, I have to deal with this," Conrad said, stepping toward the rear of the cruiser.

The sergeant waved the ambulance over and directed the driver to park behind the police car. The driver complied and seconds later two blue-uniformed EMTs emerged from the back.

"Don't go any farther," Conrad said, holding up his hand as the EMTs reached the cruiser. "I don't want you contaminating the crime scene."

"Then why did you call us?" a thirty-something blonde woman wearing an EMT uniform asked.

"First of all, I didn't call you," Conrad replied, trying to keep his temper in check.

"Secondly, I need you to check out this gentleman when I'm done questioning him. Relax for a few seconds and I'll hand him over to you."

The blonde EMT let out a deep sigh of frustration as she

crossed her arms. Her partner, a prematurely balding man in his early twenties, stood by holding a medical bag like a loyal St. Bernard carrying a whiskey barrel. Conrad returned to Mr. Jones by the front of the cruiser to resume questioning him.

"Mr. Jones, I'm sorry for the interruption. Do you recall what I asked you before?"

"Yes, sir, I do," Jones replied. "I was leaving the mall with my family when I heard screaming coming from this side of the parking lot. I saw a woman being attacked, so I told my wife and daughter to wait by the doors while I ran toward the scene. The son-of-a-bitch was quick enough to get in the driver's seat and lock the car door by the time I reached him. He took off and hit me with the vehicle as he sped away."

"Can you give me a description of the perpetrator?" Conrad asked.

"He was a white male, skinny-but-wiry, about 5-foot-ten, black hair – slicked back with gel, wearing a black windbreaker and blue-jeans."

"That's a good description," Conrad commented, as he wrote down the information. "Did he have any other distinguishing characteristics?"

"Not that I can think of."

"What about the girl he grabbed? Can you describe her?"

"I only saw her from far away, but I can give it a try. She was a brunette, medium height and weight, wearing a white and black shirt and jean shorts. That's all I can recall."

"Westfield Control to nine-thirty-five," the voice of the female police dispatcher spoke suddenly from Conrad's portable radio.

CHAPTER 7

"Go ahead, Control," the sergeant said, keying his shoulder mike.

The dispatcher spoke quickly: "Sarge, I just received a report of a multi-car accident on route 10 East near the junction of route 135 with serious multiple injuries. Westfield Fire is responding, but they asked if our department could assist."

"Received Control. Send nine-twenty-eight to assist with the accident while Nine-twenty responds to assist me with the murder scene. I also have an ambulance with me. The witness's injuries are not serious, so I'll send it down."

"Received nine-thirty-five."

Conrad walked briskly over to the impatient EMTs.

"There's been a multi-car accident on route 10 near the 135 junction with serious injuries. This witness just has some bumps and bruises. He can wait for the next ambulance. Go help the crash victims."

"Okay, we're on it," the blonde EMT said, gesturing for her loyal, canine-like companion to follow her.

The blonde EMT sent her partner around back while she climbed into the passenger section of the cab and gave instructions to the driver. Conrad watched the ambulance back up and do an expert three-point turn until it was facing away. The siren sounded and the tires screeched as it peeled out. Conrad returned to the witness.

"Mr. Jones, there's been a serious multi-car accident on route 10 with serious injuries involved. Unfortunately, you're going to have to wait for the next ambulance to arrive to get checked out."

"No problem, officer," Jones replied. "My injuries certainly aren't life threatening."

Conrad didn't bother to correct him that he was a sergeant – not an officer.

"Hang tight while I make sure one of my officers responds to the accident scene," Conrad said, keying his mike again. "Nine-thirty-five to nine-twenty-eight."

"Go ahead, Sarge," a male voice answered from the radio.

"Nine-twenty-eight, did you copy that last transmission from dispatch?"

"Yes, I did, Sarge. I'm on my way to the accident on route 10."

Conrad could hear sirens going in the background as Officer Tannen replied, which indicated he was already on his way to the scene at a high rate of speed.

"Thank you, nine-twenty-eight," Conrad said.

"No problem, Sarge."

Conrad keyed the mike again. "Nine-thirty-five to nine-twenty."

"Go ahead," a different male voice replied.

"I still need you at the upper level to assist me. Are you almost here?"

"I'm right around the corner."

"Received."

Conrad released the button on his shoulder mike as he spotted several teenage spectators crossing the flare line – probably trying to get a better look at the body. The sergeant made eye contact with the witness, raised his index finger in a "one moment" gesture, and jogged toward the improvised flare perimeter, veering on an intercept course with a group of six teenagers approaching the body.

"Hey! What do you think you're doing!" Conrad shouted.

The teenagers froze like a half-dozen deer caught in headlights as the sergeant bore down on them.

"Did you miss the flare back there?" Conrad asked, breathing hard as he reached the young people.

"What flare?" one of the teenagers – a skinny, long-haired member of Generation Z – asked in his best Fast-Times-at-Ridgemont-High imitation.

"Get behind that flare! Move!" Conrad shouted in the young man's face, utilizing his loudest drill sergeant's voice as he pointed toward the burning light on the ground.

The teenagers finally got the point and backed away toward the invisible line.

"If I have to come back here, someone's going to jail!" Conrad shouted over his shoulder as he headed back toward the cruiser.

He circled widely around the corpse so he wouldn't further contaminate the crime scene, and approached the witness and his family. Suddenly, in his peripheral vision, Conrad saw flashing blue lights closing in from across the parking lot. His back-up had finally arrived. It was about time.

"Mr. Jones, can you hang tight for a couple minutes until the detective arrives to question you?" Conrad asked the witness.

"Honey, we have to leave. It's a school night," Jones's wife said, as she placed her arm on the pre-teen girl's shoulder.

"Officer, she's right. It's getting late, we have to go home now." Jones said.

"Your wife and daughter don't have to stay," Conrad said. "But I need you to stick around to get your injuries checked."

Jones turned to his wife. "Okay, honey, why don't you take Stephanie home now and I'll catch up with you later,"

Jones placed his arms around the shoulders of his wife and daughter, and led them away.

Officer Rick Malloy parked his cruiser behind Sergeant Conrad's vehicle. Like Conrad, Malloy kept his lights flashing as he exited the cruiser. Malloy was six-foot-three, in his early twenties, and cut an impressive figure in his dark blue police uniform. He reminded Conrad of a poster-boy for police recruitment.

"I established a perimeter with flares," Conrad said to Malloy. "Position yourself by the flares to make sure no one crosses the line to contaminate the crime scene any more than it's already been contaminated."

"No problem, Sarge," Malloy replied, heading toward the perimeter.

Now that he felt the crime scene was truly secure, Conrad surveyed the area: the body of the teenage girl lay in an empty space between two empty spaces in the nearest parking row. In the next row over, three adjacent spots were also devoid of cars. Cars were spaced intermittently throughout the rest of the rows like pieces in an incomplete jigsaw puzzle. The closest vehicle was parked two spaces over to the left – next to Malloy's cruiser.

Conrad checked his watch and saw it was 22:13 or 10:13 PM civilian time. It was hard to believe that only fifteen minutes had elapsed since he arrived at the crime scene. The mall closed at 22:00, so Conrad assumed that most of the remaining cars belonged to staff working late. Of course, some of the vehicles must also belong to the crowd of mall patrons that had gathered around the improvised perimeter. Luckily, he now had an officer to keep them out of the way. But where was the detective?

Conrad gazed over the four-foot wall surrounding the edge of the upper parking level and saw a line of flashing blue lights approaching on the mall road: the state police. He thought it didn't look good that the state police were here, but the Westfield detective still hadn't shown up.

Conrad wasn't surprised that Detective Lombardi was a no-show; two years ago, he had competed with her for the detective job and he never believed the best person won.

According to his view at the time, Officer Lombardi's political connections had won out over his competence and experience. Now, Detective Marilyn Lombardi was taking her sweet time getting here.

By the time Detective Lombardi showed up a half-hour later, the state police crime technicians had already gathered all the evidence and thoroughly analyzed the crime scene. Shaking his head with chagrin, Sergeant Conrad recognized Detective Lombardi's unmarked blue sedan as she parked behind a state police cruiser. Despite his dislike of the woman, Conrad went over to meet her.

CHAPTER 8

Sergeant Conrad approached Detective Lombardi as she stepped out from the driver's side of her unmarked police car.

He thought she looked disheveled: her fashionable white blouse and black skirt were wrinkled as if she had just engaged in a wrestling match. Her usually perfectly-combed, medium-length auburn hair was mussed up as if she just rolled out of bed. She had a haggard expression on her pretty face that made her look ten years older than her twenty-eight years.

Supposedly, her youth was one of the ostensible reasons why she received the Detective promotion over Conrad, who was almost ten years older. The Chief supposedly wanted "New Blood" for the Detective Division.

However, Conrad believed the real reason he didn't get the job was because Marilyn was the daughter of the Chief's best friend, Lieutenant Fred Lombardi, a veteran of the Westfield Police force. The Chief and the Lieutenant had worked their way up through the ranks after starting as patrolmen over twenty years ago; they were tight. It was only natural they would promote the lieutenant's daughter over a competitor.

Conrad and Lombardi had similar educational levels – they

each had a Bachelor's Degree in Criminal Justice – but Conrad had more experience; he had been working in the police field for fifteen years while Lombardi had only been on the force for five years. Also, Lombardi's Criminal Justice Degree had a concentration in Administration, whereas Conrad's degree had a concentration in Criminal Investigation. Obviously, Conrad's degree was more suited to a detective position.

Conrad worked for the Farmington Police Department for seven years before transferring over to Westfield. Farmington was a large town with an extensive immigrant population that kept the department busy.

During his time at Farmington, Conrad had responded to calls for shootings, stabbings, drug dealing, overdoses, domestics, and many other inner city type calls. Transferring to Westfield was like taking a vacation. By contrast, Lombardi only had five years of experience working in the relatively quiet town of Westfield where the most challenging calls were usually DUI's or other misdemeanors. It wasn't fair, but Conrad tried to take it in stride.

"The state police are here already?" Detective Lombardi's eyes darted anxiously around the crime scene.

"They got here a half hour ago," Conrad said, grinning sardonically as he observed her anxious demeanor.

He fought down the urge to gloat about her irresponsibility and maintained his professionalism. He wished the Chief was here so he could tell him, "I told you so."

"Oh fuck," Lombardi said. "I was at my boyfriend's house in Farmington when I got the call. I got here as fast as I could."

Conrad knew that Farmington was only a twenty minute drive at the most, so he wasn't sure why it took Lombardi almost an hour to reach the crime scene.

"That's okay, I'll update you as we go," Conrad said. "There are two witnesses to the crime; one of them is waiting over by the cruiser."

"Who are they?" Lombardi asked, as she followed Conrad toward the police car.

"The female witness waiting by the cruiser is a lawyer who attempted to render First Aid to the female victim after she was already deceased," Conrad explained, as he halted before he reached the witness. "The male witness attempted to intervene in the kidnapping of one of the female victims, but he was too late. The perp commandeered the victim's vehicle and struck the witness as he drove away. The male witness was injured in the accident and was taken to the hospital." Conrad decided he had to stick it to the detective a little, so he added, "I had the male witness wait as long as possible so you could interview him, but the EMTs got impatient and demanded to take him to the ER."

Detective Lombardi rolled her eyes as she ran her fingers through her already mussed hair.

"Fuck," she said, glancing toward the impatient-looking female lawyer standing by the cruiser. "At least one of the witnesses stuck around."

Conrad took a moment to enjoy her nervous reaction before taking out his notepad and handing it to her. "The information for each witness is in the notebook."

"Where are the state police crime scene techs?" Lombardi asked, as she glanced around and only saw one state police officer guarding the perimeter.

"The techs have moved on to the accident scene on route 10. Apparently, there were several fatalities and they need to do a forensics sweep," Conrad explained, noting the detective didn't even glance down at the notepad he handed her.

"What accident scene?" Lombardi asked, widening her eyes.

Conrad raised his eyebrows. "You were never informed about it?"

"No, the Chief called me on my cell phone to report an assault and kidnapping on the upper level of the mall parking garage."

"There was a multi-car accident on route 10 East near route 135. I just got word there were several fatalities. Officer Tannen responded to that incident while Malloy and I responded here. Tannen informed me the accident scene is under control; the vehicles have been towed and the victims are en route to the hospital. He's on his way here to assist if we need it."

"Did the state police crime scene techs find anything?" Lombardi asked.

"They discovered a partial sneaker print in the female victim's blood."

"Is it a good print?"

"The techs told me they should be able to identify the make of the sneaker. But if the perp ditches his sneakers, that information will be useless."

Conrad escorted Lombardi to his parked cruiser and introduced the female witness to the detective. "Ms. Callahan, this is Detective Lombardi. She needs to ask you a few questions and then you can leave."

"Nice to meet you," Lombardi said, offering her hand.

"Hello," Ms. Callahan said, rolling her eyes as she shook it.

"While you finish up here, I'm heading back to the station to start my report."

"Okay, great," Lombardi replied. "I appreciate all your help, Jimmy."

"No problem, I'll catch up with you," Conrad said, forcing a smile for the detective.

She smiled back, checked her pockets, and appeared to realize something. "Jimmy, can I borrow your pen? I forgot to bring one."

Unable to suppress a grin, Conrad reached into his shirt pocket and handed a silver pen to Lombardi. "Here you go."

Conrad noticed Lombardi flush slightly as she took the pen before returning her attention to the witness.

The sergeant sidestepped around the lawyer and opened his cruiser door. He got in, started it up, and pulled out.

An hour later, Detective Lombardi met Sergeant Conrad back at the station. Conrad was at a desk finishing up his report on a computer as she walked into the report-writing room.

"I didn't get anything new from the lawyer," Lombardi said, as she handed Conrad's notebook back to him.

"One thing's for sure. Our perp likes to get up close and personal," Conrad said.

"I guess so," Lombardi replied, face pale.

Conrad thought Lombardi appeared dazed as if she never expected a murder and kidnapping to happen in their small town.

Get used to it because this perp's here to stay until he gets caught, Conrad thought.

"When you get a free moment, we need to talk about strategy," Conrad said, narrowing his eyes.

Lombardi glanced away momentarily and returned her gaze to the sergeant. "I think I may owe you an apology. It's looking more and more like we have a serial killer/kidnapper on our hands."

"I know, but I have some ideas about how to catch him."

CHAPTER 9

We're almost there. After driving for four-and-a-half hours due north on route 495, we've arrived at the northernmost edge of the White Mountains; my parents' snowmobile cabin is nestled deep within the vast, mountainous forest terrain. The cabin is isolated; our nearest neighbor is more than a mile away. In order to reach the cabin, we have to travel through a maze of crude dirt roads that service our cabin and our closest neighbor.

Our neighbor is a wealthy hunter who keeps the dirt roads clear of debris in the Fall and excessive snow in the Winter. It's not yet Hunting Season, which is one of the reasons why I chose today to execute my plan.

I pull into the breakdown lane three miles before I reach the Dolebrook town exit; the town's paved roads lead to the dirt trails traveling up the side of the mountain to the cabin. I have to blindfold the beauty at this point in the trip; I can't allow her to see the next road-sign with the name of the town where the cabin is located.

The teenager trembles as I wrap a thick black cloth around her head. Not too tight. I don't want her to be TOO uncomfortable. In the unlikely event that the beauty is able to escape from my clutches, I can't allow her to know anything about the area, so she won't be able to lead the police back to the cabin. If the police find out about the cabin, it won't be long before they track me down. I always have a contingency plan in case things go awry. Things have gone bad before and my back-up plans have always saved me from disaster.

When I'm satisfied that my prisoner can't see a thing, I click on my left blinker, check the rearview mirror, notice the road is clear, and pull out. I'm careful to drive the speed limit; I am nothing if not cautious. I smile when I spot the sign for the town of Dolebrook, NH. Checking the dashboard clock, I notice that it's 2:30 AM; I should be tired, but I'm too excited to be tired.

I drive the speed limit through Dolebrook's pathetic little downtown area where the largest business is a Rite-Aid pharmacy. Passing a BP gas station, I reach a section containing tightly-packed, two-story working class houses. As I drive farther, the houses become larger and more spread out.

Glancing at my prisoner, I notice she is as still as death. She sits quietly in the seat, unmoving. I find her composure unnerving. She was trembling before, but now she's stopped. She should be afraid, but she doesn't look afraid. Maybe she's just exhausted at this point. I need to be patient. Fear will come soon enough.

The road begins to slope gradually upwards. After another ten minutes of driving, the straight road becomes sinuous with twists and turns. I am surrounded by vast open spaces interspersed with farmhouses. The shadowy mountains loom beyond.

The forest begins to intrude upon the open spaces like a stealthy enemy invading new territory as I continue along the twisting road. I slow to take a left onto a dirt road leading up the mountain. The road becomes bumpy as I leave the pavement.

The beauty beside me transforms into a sleek silhouette as

the forest closes in and the road becomes darker. I switch on the high beams as the upwards incline becomes steeper. I become annoyed as I feel every jolt from every bump and small rock in the road. The beauty doesn't seem to notice the rougher terrain as she remains silent in the passenger seat.

I spot artificial lights through the trees ahead and realize I am approaching my closest neighbor's hunting cabin. Switching off the headlights, I cruise past the cabin, while tapping the gas pedal so I don't make a lot of noise. I don't think anyone is home, but you can never be too careful.

The hunter's cabin is larger than the one owned by my family; it's two stories and about twice as long. Like my parents' cabin, there's a separate, barn-like structure to the left containing a two-car garage. The only lights are the front porch light and the overhead garage light; they must be on a timer. There are no cars in the driveway. I breathe a sigh of relief as the forest engulfs the open space around the cabin and it disappears from sight. I switch the car lights back on.

My prisoner and I continue driving along the bumpy road for another fifty yards before I turn left into our driveway. A NO TRESPASSING sign is staked to a tree by the entrance. The driveway becomes as black as pitch as overhanging trees loom over the trail, but I can see light at the end of the tunnel; it's the clearing where our cabin is located.

As we reach the clearing, I feel a rush of adrenaline as the headlights illuminate the front door. Soon, the game will begin.

To the left of the cabin is the one-car garage/storage shed containing three snowmobiles, one for each member of the family.

The driveway travels to the roll-up door of the garage/shed to the left, but I halt next to the front door of the cabin. I feel my body trembling as I turn off the engine. It's hard to believe it's almost time to begin another work of art. After playing with my prey for a while like a cat toying with a mouse, I will create yet another masterpiece.

The girl remains completely still after the engine goes silent. She leans forward, expectantly, as if awaiting a command. I have trained her well. I was wrong before; her body is still trembling – just less noticeably.

I don't say anything as I open the driver's side door. Getting out, I slam the door and circle around to the passenger side. I stare down at my victim through the glass; she is completely helpless. I open the door.

"Get up. We're here," I say, as I reach down to grab her right bicep.

She responds as if coming out of a daze.

"Come on," I say, pulling on her arm.

As she struggles to rise, I pull on her arm while I place my other hand over the top of her head – like a police officer guiding a prisoner out of the rear cage in a cruiser so she doesn't bump her skull against the top of the door jam. I don't want her to be injured before I start the game. That will come later. I will leave the blindfold on until we're inside.

"Excuse me, can I ask a question?" the girl asks me.

"Sure, go ahead," I say.

"I have to use the bathroom."

"That's not a question. That's a statement," I say, enjoying her discomfort.

"What I meant was, may I use a bathroom?"

"Certainly. When we get inside. I'm not a savage," I reply.

"Thank you."

"Keep quiet until I say you can speak again," I tell her.

She sways unsteadily as I guide her up a short paved walk-way to the front door. Holding her by the arm, I take out my house-key with my free hand and insert it in the door lock. Pushing the door open, I peer inside. It 's dark within, but I know the layout of the entryway, so I guide her in easily. Reaching over to the wall, I flip on the light switch to illu-minate the hanging bulb.

We're in the small "mud-room," which acts as a portico where we hang our snowsuits on wall pegs and leave our wet boots on a wooden shelf beneath. A spare, light-blue snow-suit hangs on a peg on the right wall above a pair of black boots. I guide the girl up a pair of steps to the inner door. The door is unlocked, so I lead my captive into the cabin.

I flip a switch on the wall that lights up a small kitchen area to the right. To the left is the large dining room table with a mini-chandelier suspended above it. A glass hutch contain-ing expensive Chinaware rests in the corner.

Beyond the dining room is the living room, which contains a recliner chair placed next to a large couch and coffee table facing a widescreen television. The left wall consists mainly of two sliding glass doors looking out on a porch. A stairwell on the far side of the living room leads to the second floor bedrooms.

To the right, a short hallway leads from the kitchen to the first floor bedroom and bathroom. The door at the end of the hall leads down to the basement where I do most of my art work. The cabin is small, but comfortable.

I halt in the kitchen and remove the girl's blindfold. She

blinks as her eyes adjust to the dim kitchen light. I lead her across the kitchen to the hallway and then to the bathroom. There's one window above the toilet that 's too small to accommodate a human being, so I know it's safe to leave her alone. Even if she could squeeze through it, it would be impossible to maneuver with her hands cuffed behind her back.

Pushing her in, I shut the door behind her. She will have to make due as best she can with her hands cuffed behind her back. There's no way I'm going to take off the cuffs. At least, not yet.

Bodily functions disgust me, so I wait in the kitchen. My parents always keep the fridge packed with bottled waters, so I grab one and drink it while I wait. I freeze mid-sip and feel a rush of excitement when I hear the bathroom door creak open. Time to play.

CHAPTER 10

I hear footsteps in the hallway; the teenager's silhouette gains detail as she emerges from the darkness into the dim light of the kitchen. I congratulate myself on my discerning taste; her face is flawless, her hourglass figure perfect. She looks helpless as she moves, tentatively, toward me with her hands cuffed securely behind her back. She is completely under my power.

I grab her firmly by her bicep and lead her into the living room. She's smart enough to stay silent, so I don't have to hit her. Holding her shoulders, I point her toward the banister.

"Don't move," I say.

I reach into my pocket for the keychain that holds my car keys, house keys, and handcuff key. The handcuff key is very small because it has to fit into a tiny slot in the metal shackles.

Holding the girl's left wrist, I insert the key into the lock and slide open the metal pincer. Seizing the chain, I pull her wrist toward the banister and lock the cuff tightly around a wooden support so her right wrist is secured.

Now I can retrieve supplies.

I leave the house through the mud room, go to the car, and get my suitcase from the trunk. Returning to the house, I place the suitcase on the dining room table and open it.

I only packed enough clothing for a few days, so it's easy to sift through the items to find the skimpy red lingerie hidden at the bottom. I ordered the lingerie on-line from the Victoria's Secret website. I run my fingers over the silky one-piece combination of bra and panties. I can't wait to see her in it.

The girl remains facing the banister, unmoving. I approach stealthily behind her, dangling the lingerie outfit in my right hand. With my free hand, I reach into my jeans pocket, take out my knife, and flip it open. She shudders as she hears the click.

"Listen to me very carefully," I whisper softly in her ear. "This is the knife that killed your whore friend."

She shudders again as I press the tip of the blade into her lower back. I press it hard enough to rip through her t-shirt and draw blood.

"Do exactly what I say or I'll slice you into little pieces," I growl at her through gritted teeth. "I'm going to release you from the handcuffs temporarily. If you try anything, I'll kill you slowly. Do you understand?"

"Yes, I understand," she replies, trembling.

I move the knife away from her lower back and observe a red drop on the tip. Flipping the knife shut, I return it to my pocket and exchange it for the key-ring. Her body is still trembling, so I assume I've made my point.

I insert the handcuff key into the tiny slot in the metal restraint and turn it. There's a click as the cuff snaps open. Exchanging the key-ring for the knife, I flip it open and return the knife tip to the girl's lower back.

"You're going to wear this." I say as I shove the silky garment into her open hand as she continues to face the banister. I pull the knife away. "Back a foot away from the banister and do exactly what I say. Do you understand?"

"Y-yes," She replies, stammering with fear.

I smile with satisfaction. "Take off all your clothing and drop it on the floor. "Hesitate, and I'll press this knife through you like butter. Start with your shirt."

Hesitantly, she follows my orders. With her back still facing me, she strips off her shirt and drops it. Unclipping her bra from the front, she slides it off her shoulders. I hear a snap as she unbuckles her belt and then a zip as she pulls down her shorts. She yanks her jean shorts down around her ankles and steps out of them. Then, she pulls down her panties. Now, she is completely bare. I feel my groin stiffening.

"Take your time putting on the lingerie. I want it done right," I tell her.

Naked and trembling, she holds the lingerie in front of her like a shopper examining a dress from a retail rack. After a brief scan of the garment, she lowers her arms and lifts her left leg so it slides into the lower portion of the garment. Holding the garment low, she steps into it with her other leg. She pulls the garment up so it covers her buttocks and then slides her arms through the bra portion.

"Don't move. I'll fasten the back," I say, stepping forward.

Keeping the knife aimed at her lower back, I click the bra straps together. Then, I step away.

"Turn around," I order her.

She turns to face me and I feel my heart beating hard in my chest as I scan her body. Her firm breasts fill the bra perfectly. Her smooth, tan midriff rises above the panties like a flat, polished mahogany surface. She truly resembles one of the models on the Victoria's Secret web site.

"Don't move," I say as I sidestep toward the kitchen table.

Reaching out, I drag the suitcase to the edge of the table and reach into a compartment for the camera case. I open the protective case and lift out the camera. All the while I keep an eye on the teenager with my peripheral vision. She hasn't moved a muscle. I strip off the lens cap and point the camera at her.

"Strike a pose," I say. "Any pose."

At first, she remains still. Then, she places her hands on her hips. I focus and take a picture. I feel like a famous photographer for a fashion magazine. A rush of adrenaline permeates my brain as I realize I am in complete control.

I switch on a table lamp to obtain more light. The added illumination creates interesting shadows on her body.

"Lift your arms and place your hands behind your head," I order her.

She complies and she's red-hot; she could be a supermodel.

I become the role; I pretend I'm a famous high-fashion photographer. I order her to assume a variety of poses that I've seen in fashion magazines. She's hesitant, but she does it anyway. She knows I am not fooling around. I'm building an extensive portfolio that I will continue to enjoy long after she is gone.

I have a combination safe at my apartment where I store my best photographs. Not all of the pictures I take make the cut; I'm very discriminating. I only place the very finest photos in the safe. There are numerous photographs of beautiful young women contained in meticulously labeled envelopes within my secure steel box.

Although the women in the safe are no longer alive, they live on in my art; they are immortal. At the bottom of the pile, I keep my "special art," the art I create with violence. Soon, I will obtain the chainsaw from the storage shed and begin creating my special art with this smooth, young canvas.

I become so involved in the role of photographer that I lose track of time. I'm changing the roll of film in the camera when she makes a break for it; she bolts for the door to the mud room. She's fast, but I have excellent reflexes. I sprint after her.

She dodges around the kitchen island countertop and reaches the door. As I circle around the dining table to cut her off, I place the camera down next to the suitcase.

The teenager fumbles with the doorknob, but she has to flip open the dead-bolt to open the door. When she finally figures it out and reaches for the dead-bolt lock, it's too late.

Lunging, I grab her and drag her down to the wood-paneled floor like a lion taking down a gazelle. Wrapping my hands around her throat, I squeeze. Her eyes bulge as her face reddens and gradually starts to turn purple. I don't want to kill her yet. I still haven't used her body as a canvas to create my special art. I release her throat and she gasps for air.

I leave her on the floor, gasping, as I retrieve the handcuffs from the banister. She's going nowhere. It will be a while before she catches her breath. I return to her and flip her onto her stomach. I re-cuff her hands behind her back and drag her to her feet. She's still breathing heavily, trying to recover.

"Don't ever do that again," I whisper in her ear. "Next time I won't stop squeezing."

I smile as a tremor shudders through her body.

"Come on," I say, pulling on her arm.

She continues to breathe in deep gasps as I lead her up the stairs. When we reach the master bedroom, I force her to lie down on the floor and handcuff her to one of the lower bed legs. She lies on her back and stares up at me with wide doe eyes as she begins to breathe normally again. I smile down at her and go into the hallway.

Descending the stairs, I cut through the kitchen and grab my coat off the wall peg by the door. Checking the digital clock on the stove, I notice it's after four in the morning. No wonder I'm starting to feel tired. All this excitement has made my adrenaline flow so hard that I haven't noticed the time.

Putting on my coat, I leave the cabin through the mud room. It's cold and dark outside. I estimate that it's below forty degrees. The towering black silhouettes of magnificent evergreen trees surround the clearing like fortress battlements.

Walking past the parked car, I follow the driveway to the storage shed. I use my key to enter through the side door. Circling around the snowmobiles, I reach the tool bench and see the mini-chainsaw on the top shelf. I reach up for it reverently.

Ostensibly, the chainsaw is used for cutting wood for the living room fire-place, but I use it to create art. I believe that a woman is more beautiful when she is helpless. That's why women are more attractive without arms and legs.

CHAPTER 11

A blast of cold air hits me as I leave the storage shed with my gas-powered art tool. I feel more confident now that I have it.

Over the years, I've refined my artistic techniques; the first time I hacked off a girl's limbs, she died immediately. I applied an improvised tourniquet made of plastic medical tubing to her stumps, so she wouldn't bleed out, but she died from shock anyway. I was sloppy then, but I'm more careful now.

Over the past several years, I've built up a formidable supply of Oxycontin that I stole from my parents' medicine cabinet. My mother is a chronic hypochondriac who has been addicted to the medication for years. Supposedly, she has an excruciatingly painful slipped disc in her back, but I don't believe her. I think she's just faking it to obtain the medication.

I try to steal a pill every other week when I visit the clueless geriatrics for dinner. I've already collected over twenty pills, which is absolutely essential if my living art is going to survive the delicate creative process.

The next time, I made the teenager swallow three Oxycontins and the operation was successful. She lived. She was unconscious when I sliced off her arms at the elbows and her legs at the knees. Sadly, she didn't feel a thing because of all the Oxy's I gave her, but no plan is perfect. The elastic tourniquets kept her alive, so I can go to work with a blow-torch I purchased on E-bay.

The intense heat of the blow-torch cauterizes and seals off the wounds more effectively than a bandage ever could. There's no time to fool around after I chop off their limbs; I have to cauterize the stumps quickly or they'll bleed out - despite the elastic tourniquets.

I store the blow-torch in a waterproof suitcase in the trunk of my car to keep it safe. It's surprisingly easy to use, but I need to wear safety goggles so I don't damage my eyes by staring directly at the flame. The art-work I do has to be precise, so it's necessary to take precautions.

I have no choice but to to keep the girls heavily-drugged so they're unconscious as I slice off their limbs. If they were conscious, they might die from shock like my first victim, so that option is out of the question. My favorite part of the process is when they become conscious and notice they don't have any hands or feet. The expressions on their beautiful, terrified faces is thrilling to see.

Unfortunately, I have to kill them quickly with my combat knife after they wake up to see they have no limbs because they won't stop screaming. Their high-pitched screeching is enough to drive a person crazy. I make it quick by stabbing their hearts and slicing their throats.

As an artist, I always try to add a dramatic touch. Before I kidnap a victim, I buy five white roses, wrap them carefully, and place them in the trunk of my car. The roses symbolize the dullness of my beautiful, but ordinary human canvases before I turn them into art.

I place the roses around the girls' bodies as I go to work with my tools. It doesn't take long for the plain white roses to change to brilliant red. After dismembering the body, I bury the gorgeous, blood-red roses with each body part.

The chainsaw cost me two hundred dollars on amazon.com – not including shipping. The blowtorch cost me eighty bucks on Ebay. The terrified expressions on the teenagers' faces when they discover all their limbs are gone: priceless! Who says serial killers don't have a sense of humor?

I need to stop fooling around because I have art to create. I carry my mechanical brush through the mud-room into the kitchen, but I halt for a second to glance at the digital clock on the stove. It's almost five AM and I'm feeling exhausted after a busy day. Maybe I should wait until tomorrow to start working. If I do it when I'm tired, I could make a mistake and kill her. I want her to be alive throughout the process in order to heighten my enjoyment.

It's too bad that I can't have sex with them after I cut off their arms and legs and they become conscious. As I mentioned before, their high-pitched shrieking would drive me mad.

It's no fun having sex with a dead body. I'm not one of those sick necrophiliacs.

The only way I can have sex with my victims is if I do it before I bring them to the basement and start slicing. I like to be fresh and wide-awake in order to truly enjoy it.

I cut through the kitchen into the back hallway until I reach the doorway leading to the basement. I flick on the stairwell light-switch and descend the wooden staircase.

The basement is nothing special. There's a large furnace in the far right corner and next to that is a storage area with boxes containing extra blankets, cleaning supplies, and who knows what else my parents keep there. A large freezer rests in the opposite corner like an oversized, rectangular white coffin. It's perfect for putting body parts on ice.

The left side of the basement is my workspace. A tool bench set against the back wall provides the wooden supports I use to attach cuffs to my victims' wrists. A pipe running along the bottom of the left cement wall is ideal for securing the right leg with a rope, while the steel support post in the center of the basement secures the left leg. Until the legs come off at least.

I usually spread an old sleeping bag or blanket on the floor and cover it with a plastic painter's sheet. The cement floor slopes down imperceptibly from the walls to a large drain in the center that keeps the cellar from flooding. The drain is also ideal for catching all the blood that inevitably flows off the plastic canvas.

The drain is connected to an underground pipe that spits the water (and blood) out into a ditch behind the cabin; the ditch travels down the slope for several hundred feet until it reaches a stream. Occasionally, blood spatter reaches the walls or the uncovered concrete floor, but it's easy to wipe it away and mop it into the drain. I never leave any evidence behind; I'm always careful.

Placing the chainsaw on the tool bench, I rummage through one of the boxes in the storage area until I find an adequate moldy blanket. I spread the blanket out on the floor next to the tool bench. I position it so it's also near the drain. Then, I realize that I forgot the plastic painter's sheet in the trunk of my car. It's no big deal. I'll just get it in the morning before I start work.

Now that my preparations are ready, I begin to come down from my adrenaline high. I need to get some rest if I'm going to be fresh for my project tomorrow. Yawning, I climb the stairs and shut off the basement light. I retrieve another bottled water from the fridge before going upstairs.

Entering the bedroom, I notice my victim appears to be curled asleep in a fetal position at the foot of the bed. However, looks can be deceiving. As I enter the room, her body shudders as a floor board creaks.

So much for being asleep. The bitch is probably biding her time waiting for an opportunity to try to escape again, but that won't happen.

I nudge her bare shoulder-blade with the tip of my boot, causing another shudder. Fear can be such a rush. She turns to face me, hesitantly, as if she is turning to face her executioner, which is actually not far off from the truth. I bend down and offer her some water to drink. After all, I'm not cruel, I'm an artist.

She leans awkwardly on her elbows so her lips can reach the bottle and takes several deep gulps. Modeling must be thirsty work. After she drains half the bottle, I pull it away from her lips and take a sip myself. The greedy bitch can't have it all.

Looking down at her, I feel like a giant gazing down at a town he is about to destroy. She seems so puny on the floor at the foot of the bed. In order to look up at me, she has to crane her neck in an awkward position that I know can't be comfortable. Her long brown hair flows across the floor in all directions like a hand-held Chinese fan.

"I'm going to bed now," I tell her. "I suggest you get some rest too because we're going to have a busy day tomorrow. I need you to be quiet for the next few hours while I sleep, and I don't want to hear so much as a peep out of you. If you do what I say, you won't get hurt. Do you understand?"

After telling her my typical lie, her eyes become wide as she nods at me without making a sound. I knew she was an intelligent girl. I'm about to step past her when I notice the enticing curves of her body. Even lying on the wooden floor, she still looks hot in the skimpy red lingerie.

I turn my head away because I need to wait until tomorrow to have my fun. I want to be wide awake so I can enjoy my time with her; there will be plenty of time to play.

I don't bother to set the alarm on the clock radio on the night-table next to the bed. Why should I? I can get up when-ever I want. I already called in sick for work tomorrow be-fore I went to the mall. I will probably have to call in sick again tomorrow for the following day's shift if I'm able to drag this thing out successfully. I'll just have to go with the flow of blood.

I make myself comfortable under the covers, flip my pillow over to the cold side, and switch off the lamp on the night table. My key-ring digs into my skin from its location in my jeans pocket. Fumbling, I take it out and place it on the night-table next to the alarm clock. Free of annoyances, I savor the darkness and the silence as I drift to sleep.

Following my orders, my victim doesn't make a sound. I pre-dict I will have good dreams.

I am right. As I sleep, I dream about my third creative project. By that time, I had refined my technique almost to perfec-tion. With every victim, I got better at what I did.

The third victim was a fighter and she defied me every step of the way. I had to admit that it made the process more ex-citing; I had to get physical with her to get her to do what I wanted. I must be smiling in my dream as I administer a severe beating to my victim in the living room of the cabin.

Suddenly, I feel anxious as I imagine one of my middle school beatings – when I was the victim. I see an image of myself lying on the ground – being struck from all sides by fists

DIARY OF A SERIAL KILLER

and feet – in a school hallway; it fills my mind like poison; the hideous mental picture intrudes on my dream like a deranged thief breaking into a house and slaughtering the family.

I have to switch gears. At least I'm not on the receiving end this time. The image fades and changes back to my fists striking the rebellious teenager. I think about all the little bitches who laughed at me when I was being brutally assaulted by middle school jocks. Now, all the girls who laughed at me are getting their comeuppance.

The image in my dream changes to a view of a clear painter's sheet on the basement floor. I see my hand holding a mini-chainsaw as it descends toward the little slut's elbow. I imagine the rush I feel as I watch her blood flow from the severed stump like a red river. The image is so vivid that I feel blood sprinkling my face like warm rain-drops. Dreams like this are what make sleeping worthwhile. I can't wait to wake up and make my dream a reality.

CHAPTER 12

There are few things better than waking up in the morning feeling refreshed after a night of inspiring dreams. The only thing that's better than dreaming about cutting off a girl's arms and legs is the act itself.

Checking my alarm clock, I see it's 12:42 PM. Technically, I fell asleep at five in the morning, so it's the afternoon now. Wow, I slept for more than seven hours; I must have been tired from all of yesterday's high-energy activities. Now I'm ready for more. Today, the real entertainment will begin. I feel myself getting hard just thinking about it.

Sliding to the edge of the bed, I stand up. Suddenly, I feel a twinge of anxiety when I don't see anyone lying at the foot of the bed. Did she escape? After taking several steps, I realize I'm panicking needlessly; I see her long, supple legs stretched out on the floor beyond the edge of the mattress.

It reminds me of the beautiful pair of trophies I'm going to have later. I'll put them on ice for a while in the basement freezer before I dispose of them in the woods. I'll place them next to her head and arms.

Continuing toward her, I observe my victim in her glory; her full breasts and hourglass figure fill out the lingerie perfectly. She looks so good, I have to sample the goods now.

As I said before, I like to initiate carnal pleasure with my victims before the art. As I feel a stirring in my groin, I realize it's going to happen right away. I want her now.

"Wake up," I say to her.

Her eyes fly open and she looks around, anxiously, as if she doesn't know where she is.

Wow, she actually fell asleep. I didn't think she'd get a wink. I hope she enjoyed her rest because it's probably the last time she's ever going to sleep soundly.

Feeling my groin getting stiffer by the second, I return to the night-table to retrieve my key-ring for the handcuff key. If I'm going to be comfortable during the act, we have to move onto the bed. But, I must be careful. In order for her to lie on her back, I have to handcuff her hands in front, which allows her increased mobility and the potential for her to fight back.

But what am I worried about? Compared to me, she's a weakling. As a male, I can dominate her easily. I've done it before with the others.

Leaning down, I unfasten the cuff attached to the bed leg and drag the girl up by the chain. She moans as the metal digs into her skin. I pull her hands in front of her, reattach the cuffs, and pull her toward the bed. Guiding her to the head of the bed, I force her to sit down.

"Lie down," I command her.

She hesitates for a few seconds, but then complies. She looks worried; a little crease has formed between her perfectly-shaped eyebrows as they press together. She should be worried.

"Don't move," I say as I begin peeling off my shirt.

Her body starts to tremble as if she's very cold. She must

know what's coming.

Dropping my shirt on the floor, I begin to unbuckle my pants. The more scared she looks, the harder I get. She closes her eyes – maybe so she won't see me disrobing. Fucking bitch. I pull down my pants and underwear. I am at full mast and ready to go. She lies completely helpless before me. What a *rush*.

I scan her body again before climbing onto the bed with her. The lingerie is slightly askew after a night of sleeping on the floor, but that doesn't matter. It will be coming off soon enough. I forcefully spread her legs as I kneel in front of her.

Frowning, she keeps her eyes closed tight, as if I'm about to strike her. Reaching down, I grasp the panty portion of the lingerie and rip it off. Her entire body shudders with dread. I toss the scrap of red fabric aside like trash, although I paid good money for it.

Seizing her arms by the wrists, I push them above her head so I can see all of her body. She looks so helpless beneath me with her legs spread and arms stretched above her head. She keeps her eyes closed as I begin to slide into her. I have to force my way in because she is so dry. Stupid bitch, I'll show her.

As I start to move, her beautiful face contorts into a pained expression, which makes me angry. I force myself in deeper and move faster. The fucking bitch still looks pained as if she isn't enjoying it like I am. I ignore the expression on her face by reaching down to grab her breasts.

Squeezing her breasts harder than necessary, I move faster. She must be starting to like it because she is stretching her arms fully above her head. I close my eyes so I can concentrate on my thrusts.

Suddenly, there's a sharp, fierce pain in my forehead. I try to ignore it and concentrate on what I'm doing, but then I feel another thud on the front of my skull. Metal digs into skin and I realize too late that it's the handcuff chain; her cuffed fists are striking me. Opening my eyes, I see her fists shoot toward me. I try to duck out of the way, but I'm trapped into position.

The girl's image becomes blurry as I feel another stabbing pain in my forehead. I realize I have to back off. As I pull out, she begins to scoot away. Rage takes over; I move forward on my knees as she rolls her body away from me. She stretches out her arms as if she's reaching for something. What's she going for? Is it the lamp on the night-table? I can't let her get it.

Aiming at her beautiful face, I pull back my right fist to strike her, but suddenly I spot a blur moving toward me fast. A sharp pain blasts through my skull as a hard metal object strikes the left side of my head. That fucking bitch! I swing wildly at her, but the pain in my head is excruciating and I can't concentrate. I feel like I'm going to pass out as warm blood streams down through my hair.

I try to pull away, but my vision blurs as I'm struck again in the skull with what I guess is the base of the metal table lamp. Blood flows from the gash in my head as I collapse onto the mattress. Another blow comes at me, but I block it with my left forearm. Pain shoots through the muscle in my arm, but I figure it's better than through my skull.

Rolling my body away, the painful blows come to a halt, but the next moment I feel myself falling through space and then a hard thump as I hit the floor. I see the white plaster ceiling spinning above me like a whirlpool. Reaching up, I feel blood pouring out of my skull. The blood flow slows as I apply pressure to the wound. That fucking bitch! Where is she? Blinking rapidly, I try to focus, but the ceiling is still spinning above me.

Closing my eyes to concentrate, I hear keys jingling. The fucking bitch has found the key-ring with the handcuff key on it! I lean on my elbows in an effort to rise, but I feel dizzy and my head drops. Another sharp pain shoots through the back of my skull as my head strikes the floorboards. I have to concentrate. I can't let her get away.

Closing my eyes, I apply more pressure to the blood gushing out of my head. I can hear bare feet slapping against the wooden floor and I worry that she's coming for me again, but then I hear her moving into the hallway. I hear footfalls on the stairs. The fucking bitch is getting away!

Concentrating, I'm finally able to sit up. The room spins around me, but I can focus. I stand up, shakily, and the room spins again.

Keeping pressure against my head wound with my left hand, I stumble toward the door. I have to move faster. I hear the sound of glass shattering downstairs. What's she doing? It sounds like she's breaking out a window.

I make it into the hallway, keeping my hand pressed hard against the bloody gash as my free palm slides along the wall to stabilize me. I hear more glass shattering as I lean against the right wall to guide my descent.

Is she breaking into the gun cabinet? I'm worried for a moment, but then I remember the guns aren't loaded. That stupid bitch!

Getting excited, I descend faster. I reach the bottom of the stairs and see her standing next to the smashed gun cabinet pointing the barrel of a hunting rifle at my face. I hear a click. The triumphant expression on her face evaporates; her eyes widen with fear as she realizes there's no ammunition in the gun!

Taking my hand away from the gash in my skull, I reach out to grab the gun. I try to snatch the barrel, but she pulls it away from me. I feel blood gush, so I return my left hand to apply pressure to the wound, but I can still use my right hand to smash her face in. Lunging toward her, I take a swing.

Suddenly, there's an intense pain in my right cheek as something hard strikes my face; the rifle stock connects with my cheekbone as she swings the rifle like a baseball bat. Losing my balance, I collapse to the floor. A sharp pain rips into my shoulder as I hit the hard wood.

Raising my arms to defend myself, I see the rifle stock descending on me again and again. My forearms ache as she strikes me repeatedly, but at least she can't reach my body or head.

Adrenaline kicks in and lets me focus, so I reach out to grab the rifle stock the next time it descends. Using all of my strength, I seize the wooden stock as it comes toward me. Now, there's a violent tug-of-war for the rifle.

Her lips contort into a snarl as if she's an enraged animal while we jostle back and forth for the rifle. She's in a better position than I am because she's standing and I'm on the ground, but I'm stronger. I use the rifle stock as leverage to pull myself to my feet.

Suddenly, my body flies backward into the banister as she releases her grip on the rifle. My back strikes the wall and I slide down to a sitting position. I have the rifle in my grip, but I'm down and the room is spinning.

I hear bare feet slapping against floorboards. Trying to focus, the couch and TV wavers in my vision like a blurred picture. I try to use the rifle as a crutch to push myself up, but I slip and collapse again.

Focusing all my energy, I finally succeed at getting to my knees. I can no longer hear feet slapping against floorboards. She must have made it to the mud room already! I can't let her get away!

Concentrating with all my might, I use the rifle as a cane to push myself to my feet. The room spins as my eyes search anxiously for the girl. I panic when I realize she's nowhere to be found. She's gone.

Using the rifle like a cane, I stumble forward. I have to catch her. As I move, I keep steady pressure against my head wound. I don't dare to take my hand away because I'm afraid I will lose too much blood. I move maddeningly slowly across the living room floor.

Finally, I reach the dining room table and the rifle clatters to the floor as I lean on the table for support. The room continues spinning, but the pinwheel effect begins to slow as I take deep breaths. I can't stay here. I have to move.

My left hand has become soaked with blood as I press it against my skull, but I have to use all my remaining will to move my legs across the kitchen floor toward the mud room. Gaining momentum, I reach the door. Reaching down with my free hand, I seize the door handle and turn it. I begin to focus more clearly as I pull the door open.

Descending the steps of the mud room, I freeze as I reach the outer door. Glancing down at the wall peg, I realize the spare snowsuit and boots are missing. The bitch took them!

I didn't think she would get far in the woods naked, but with the snowsuit and boots, all bets are off! She could easily make it far through the cold, inhospitable forest - equipped with warm clothing and footwear. I have to stop her before she reaches the shelter of the trees.

Emerging into the cold morning air, I scan the clearing. A tremor of fear shivers through my body as I realize she's nowhere in sight. Heading for my car, I figure I can use the spare key under the seat to start it up and give chase. I'll run the bitch down.

CHAPTER 13

Tracey Randall was a born optimist, but as she lay on the cold floor at the foot of a bed with her wrist cuffed to the bed-leg, she thought she was going to die. The sociopath who had kidnapped her said he wasn't going to hurt her, but the psychotic gleam in his eyes and the sadistic half-smile on his lips told her differently.

Later, when the psycho woke up, un-cuffed her from the bed leg, and secured her hands in front of her, she thought she might finally have a chance to fight back. With her hands cuffed in front, she could hit hard with her fists, and she would do whatever she had to do to get away.

When the psycho began taking off his clothes, she wanted to throw up, but held it back. As the rape began, the only thing that got her through was waiting to take him out the moment he became distracted. As soon as she saw him zoning out, she gathered her strength and smashed him on his forehead with both fists. The fucker didn't even know what hit him.

She hit him again and again until he finally got off her. She was able to roll away, reach out, and grab the neck of the metal table lamp on the bedside table with both hands. Swinging it like a baseball bat, she heard a sharp crack as it connected with the side of his skull.

That did it. It looked like he was going to pass out. Another swing, another crack, and he hit the floor. She didn't waste any time while he was down.

Tracey slid off the bed and went straight for the key-ring on the night table. She felt a moment of panic when she didn't see the ring where the psycho had left it, but then realized she must have knocked the ring onto the floor when she grabbed the lamp.

Reaching down, she picked up the keys and went through the ring quickly until she found the tiny handcuff key. In a moment, she was free. She didn't know how badly he was injured, so she didn't waste time looking at him.

She remembered seeing a gun cabinet in the living room downstairs when the psycho was getting his rocks off taking photos of her. At the time, she had imagined smashing the cabinet, grabbing a rifle, and blowing him away.

Tracey went down the stairs, two-at-a-time, until she reached the lower floor. She darted across the living room to pick up a chair from the dining room table. She returned to the gun cabinet and smashed the glass with the chair legs.

Her heart raced as she heard the kidnapper's feet pounding against the floorboards in the room above. Reaching into the cabinet, she grabbed the biggest hunting rifle she could find and took it out. Apparently, she did it just in time because she could see the psycho coming down the stairs in her peripheral vision. He appeared to be severely injured as he tried to hold his brains in with his hand as he descended.

Tracey felt immense satisfaction as she aimed the barrel of the rifle at the kidnapper's head as he reached the base of the stairs. Her euphoria dampened when he didn't appear to be intimidated. She thought he was bluffing, so she pulled the trigger, but nothing happened. Still, she wasn't about to give up yet.

As he came toward her, Tracey switched her grip on the rifle and pulled it back over her shoulder like a baseball bat. The psycho didn't know what hit him as she struck him in the face with the rifle stock. As he went down, she saw an opportunity to finish him off.

A rush of adrenaline shot through her as she smashed him repeatedly with the rifle. He held up his arms to block the blows, but she continued to pummel him with everything she had.

Then somehow, the sick bastard got lucky and grabbed the rifle as she brought the stock down on him. There was a brief struggle for the weapon and she decided to let it go. As she released it, the creep's momentum sent him flying into the stairwell banister and he went down.

Tracey decided to cut her losses and sprint for the door to the mud room. Reaching it, an image of a blue snowsuit hanging on a peg flashed through her mind as she pulled the door open. There it was on the wall. Descending, she took it down, held it out, and wriggled her body into it. It was too big, but she wasn't complaining.

Tracey pulled on the snowsuit, zipped it up, and reached for the boots on the shelf below. The boots were also too big, but it was better than going barefoot. Thus equipped to handle the outside environment, she flew out the door.

Tracey checked the car to see if the kidnapper had left a spare key in the ignition, but didn't find one. She also checked under the sun visor, but had no luck. Leaving the car, she ran down the driveway as fast as the over-large boots would allow. It was awkward running in the footwear, but she could do it.

Tracey glanced back as she turned a corner in the driveway,

but the woods blocked her view of the cabin. She didn't even know what it looked like from the outside. Still, that wouldn't matter unless she moved fast. She planned to head for the main road, flag down a car, ask them to drive to the closest police station, and bring the police back to the cabin.

Suddenly, her heart froze in her chest as she heard the rumble of a car engine firing up behind her. The psycho was going to pursue her in his car and run her down! Without hesitation, she veered toward the woods and held her arms in front of her face as she crashed through a thick tangle of tree branches at the edge of the road. Sharp wood scratched her cheeks and forehead, but she was able to protect her eyes.

Tracey continued sprinting, dodging from side-to-side to avoid massive tree trunks, as if she was running an obstacle course. As the car engine got louder, she scrambled behind a thick trunk and dropped to the ground. Peering around the tree, she saw the psycho's black Honda barreling recklessly down the driveway until it disappeared from sight behind the trees.

If the creep was hunting for her with his vehicle, then reaching the main road from the driveway was out. She would have to cut through the woods and hope she came out at a road. As the sound of the car engine faded away, Tracey stood up, turned, and plunged deeper into the forest.

****

Driving through downtown Westfield toward the police station, Jim Conrad checked the digital clock on his Toyota's dashboard; it was 1:15 PM. Despite the fact that he hadn't gone to sleep until after three am last night, he was still going in to work early for his three-to-eleven shift. He was anxious to start the investigation. He figured Lombardi would need all the help she could get.

Conrad had been so keyed up from the previous night's events, he was lucky to get any sleep. The adrenaline rush from the murder/kidnapping eventually fizzled out sometime after three in the morning and he was finally able catch some Z's.

It was another mild day for late October, so Conrad cracked the window to let in some fresh air. Most of the leaves on the trees had already turned a bright shade of red, orange, or yellow. The colors exploded like fireworks from the forest bordering the highway. The sky was a bright, crystalline blue. There were fewer trees in the downtown area, so there was a lot less color, and a lot more traffic.

Conrad stopped behind a short line of cars at a traffic light at the town's main intersection. He tapped his fingers impatiently on the steering wheel as he waited for the red light to turn green. He was anxious to start the investigation and any delay seemed intolerable. There was no way a psychopath was going to get away with a murder and kidnapping in his town. Not if he could help it.

Once Conrad set his sights on something, he was like a bulldog going for a bone; nothing could stop him. This situation was even more intense than usual because the stakes were so high; a young woman's life was at risk. He had to track down the killer before he had another body on his hands.

Conrad got a sick feeling in the pit of his stomach as he thought about the blonde girl with the slashed throat. The killer had taken her out for absolutely no reason. He could have escaped with his victim without murdering the blonde, but he must have done it for the thrill. That was a very bad sign; it meant they were dealing with a bona-fide sadistic killer.

As he drove, Conrad racked his brain about what the next

step should be in the investigation. It had been several years since he took a criminal investigation or forensics course, and the minor incidents in town over the years certainly hadn't prepared him for the current crisis.

Last night, he secured the crime scene for the state police techs and interviewed the relevant witnesses. Also, he had taken some decent pictures with his cell phone, which he included with his report.

After meeting with Lombardi at the station last night, he had finished writing a detailed incident report. So far, he had done everything right. But what about today? How should he proceed now?

Although he wasn't a detective, Conrad decided that he had to think like one. He would listen to any ideas Detective Lombardi might have, but he couldn't count on her to plan a detailed investigation because she had never dealt with an incident of this magnitude.

She was used to dealing with breaking and entering, embezzlement, and credit card thefts. Would she know what to do in a kidnapping and murder investigation? If she didn't, he hoped she would at least listen to his ideas.

As Conrad pulled into the station parking lot, he thought about the most effective way to start. Lombardi would want to re-interview the eyewitnesses, but he didn't think they would learn anything new or helpful from them.

What they needed to do was put together a geographical profile of the perp's activities in Westfield and the surrounding towns. Serial rapists and killers rarely traveled far to hunt for victims. They usually lived in the same area as their crimes. Also, a geographical profile could help them predict where the killer would strike next.

He needed to make phone calls to other police departments

in the area to find out the precise locations of previous crimes where there was the same method of operation – known in law enforcement as Modus Operandi. Once he confirmed the locations, he could begin mapping the areas of the perpetrator's suspected activities. Then, they could narrow down the areas where he might strike again.

Conrad parked his car behind the station, got out, and headed for the back door. He was feeling more confident now that he had a plan. He didn't have any time to waste if he was going to apprehend the psychopath before he killed his victim or struck again.

CHAPTER 14

I yank the car door open and collapse into the driver's seat. Reaching under the seat, I panic when I can't find the spare key. The search is difficult because I have to keep one hand pressed against the gaping wound in the side of my skull, while my free one rummages around.

Finally, my fingers brush against cold steel. In my agitation, I fumble for several awkward seconds until I grasp the spare key between my thumb and forefinger. Hands trembling, I pick up the key and attempt to jab it into the ignition twice before it goes in. Breathing a sigh of relief, the Honda's engine rumbles to life as I turn the key.

In my mind, I can see the little bitch sprinting down the dirt driveway in her stolen blue snowsuit. My face flushes red-hot as a wave of nausea flows through my stomach like sewer water. While I'm fumbling like a rookie, she's getting away.

Rage threatens to crash through my mind like a large body of water pushing against a cracked dam. The dam hasn't broken yet, but water is trickling out from more and more holes in the façade; I will have to to poke virtual fingers into the dike like the famous little Dutch-boy in the clichéd children's story. If I don't suppress my anger, I'll never catch the deceitful little bitch.

Leaning back in the seat, I take deep breaths. My rage diminishes as I focus on my breathing. I need to forget about the bitch's duplicity. I have to stop dwelling on how she attacked me and got away.

Opening my eyes, I focus on the dirt driveway leading to the garage door of the snowmobile storage shed. Looking up, I see the forest trees reaching high into the clear blue sky like giant green fingers. My mind clears.

Turning the wheel sharply, I press down on the gas pedal. Tires grind against dirt and pebbles as the car jolts to the left.

I have to slam the brakes to avoid striking a tree trunk at the edge of the driveway. Then, I switch to reverse and back up. When I'm facing down the slope toward the driveway exit, I press the gas pedal again. Dirt and pebbles kick up behind the rear tires as the car launches ahead like a rocket.

I keep my eyes peeled for any sign of movement at the edge of the forest as my Honda barrels down the incline. If I'm lucky, the bitch is running headlong down the dirt road in a panic and I will catch up with her and crush her with my tires. I plan to run over her mangled body several times to make sure she's dead. She has caused me far more trouble than I anticipated, and I have no choice but to abort my art project and bide my time until I can snatch a more docile victim.

Scanning the edges of the road, I steer the car down a twisting incline in the long, dirt driveway. Traveling too fast, I almost strike a cluster of trees as I slide around a curve. When I reach the end of the driveway, my foot presses on the brake and a cloud of dust rises around the car. I glance both ways down the intersection.

A left-turn leads to a dead-end where our wealthy neighbor dumps leaves, brush, branches, and grass that he clears from the road and his property, while the right-turn leads past our neighbor's house to the main road. I only have a split second to make a decision, so I turn left toward the dead-end; it's less than a half-mile to the cul-de-sac, so I can get there quickly.

I scan the tree-line for movement as I steer around the twists and turns. It isn't until I start to shiver that I realize I'm still in the buff. I was in such a rush to catch the runaway that I didn't have time to grab clothing.

I notice the heat is set on low, so I turn it up. My shivering abates as the heat intensifies on my bare legs. Turning a corner, I spot the end of the road; large piles of leaves, brush, and branches fill a large clearing. The road widens as it expands into the clearing, so it's easy to slow down and turn around.

Clearly, the bitch didn't go this way, so I need to check the other way. The Honda's engine roars as I press down on the gas pedal and slide precariously around corners – narrowly avoiding trees at the edge of the road. I don't' have any time to waste. If she reaches the main road and flags down a car, I'm finished.

Passing the driveway leading to my parents' cabin, I continue toward my neighbor's house. The Honda jolts me in my seat as it rolls over small rocks and potholes. I lift my foot on the gas pedal as I approach my neighbor's house.

I don't think anyone is home, but I can't be too careful. Eyeing the large cabin, I drive past it at a moderate speed. As the cabin disappears behind a line of trees, I hit the gas pedal again.

Reaching a long straightaway leading down a hill, I increase pressure on the gas pedal and watch the Honda's rear tires kick up a trail of dust in the rearview mirror. The forest opens up into fields on either side as I increase my velocity down the steep incline. I feel like I'm on a rollercoaster as I descend into a deep trough and ride up and down a series of small hills. The ground flattens and the forest closes in as I approach the paved road. I have to slow down around several sharp curves to keep from sliding into trees.

I'm still steering with one hand, which makes driving treacherous. Again, I almost lose control and wrap the front of my Honda around a tree trunk. I slow down as I approach the intersection with the paved road.

Halting at a stop sign, I look both ways down the blacktop. Which way should I go? Could she have made it this far? I don't think so. If she made it this far, I would be able to see her from this vantage point. She must have taken to the woods. That fucking bitch!

Cursing inwardly, I check for traffic and see no cars coming. I do a 180-degree turn on the paved road so I return to the dirt trail leading to the cabins. There's no need for speed now, so I drive cautiously. My face is hot and my hand is clammy on the steering wheel. This situation is becoming a disaster. What will I do if the bitch reaches a main road, flags down a car, and asks the driver to take her to a police station?

It's a big worry, but the forest is vast and nearly impenetrable. Maybe she will get lost and starve to death in the woods. I can only hope that she chooses to go in the wrong direction and finds herself deeper in the forest and collapses from exhaustion. It's possible that if she travels in the wrong direction long enough, she will never find civilization again. The thought makes me smile.

CHAPTER 15

After running for what felt like miles, Tracey Randall felt hungry, thirsty, and tired. She had expended a lot of energy and still hadn't encountered any signs of civilization. The over-sized boots didn't help her progress; she estimated that she was using twice her normal energy to move in the awkward footwear.

Breathing heavily, Tracey sat down and leaned against a tree trunk. It was a cool morning – maybe fifty degrees – but she was sweating profusely under the heavy snowsuit, which was also slightly over-sized. She unzipped the front down to her belly. The fresh, cool air felt good on her skin. She closed her eyes and concentrated on breathing deeply and evenly; she could make it through this.

She just needed to make a plan. So far, she had been running blindly into the dense forest. Her priority had been to avoid the kidnapper who was hunting for her in his car. She realized that her strategy up to this point consisted of staying away from any roads the psycho could be driving on, and yet, roads and civilization were her only chance to contact help and save herself.

Analyzing her location, Tracey realized the forest sloped gradually downwards in one direction and upwards in the opposite direction. So far, she had been running parallel to the slope in neither an upwards or downwards direction.

Upwards would take her to the top of the cold, inhospitable mountain, so that was out. Her only choice was going downwards. She had to reach a road or a town eventually, didn't she? It didn't help that she had been blindfolded on her way in and had no idea where she was.

Her stomach was growling because she hadn't eaten anything since visiting the Food Court at the Mall yesterday, and all she ate at that time was a slice of pepperoni pizza. The only liquid she drank since then was a few sips from the water bottle that the psycho was generous enough to offer her. She didn't know how long she could keep going with limited fuel. Maybe she needed to slow down and conserve her energy, and yet time seemed to be of the essence.

Tracey continued to focus on her breathing as she rested her body. She didn't know how much farther she needed to go to reach civilization. It could be miles for all she knew.

Glancing up through the trees, Tracey tried to estimate where the sun was located. The thick green canopy blocked out all but a few stray rays of sunlight. The tiny gaps in the upper foliage were too small to determine where the light was coming from. Maybe she would get lucky and the forest would open up at some point in her journey.

Back at the cabin, she had searched desperately for a weapon to use as she lay on her back being assaulted by the creep; she spotted the table lamp on the night table and the digital clock next to it; the clock read 1:13 pm. She estimated that she had been running through the woods for about an hour, which meant it was still early afternoon. She did not want to be caught in the woods at night with wild animals prowling around; she had to find a road or cabin before it got dark.

Thinking about the inevitable darkness that would soon descend on the mountain, she stood up and began making her way downhill. This time, she moved at a fast walk rather than a run. The slope was gradual enough so she had no problem with her footing. Not surprisingly, she found it was a lot easier to make progress going downhill than running parallel to the incline. Thank God for small favors.

Actually, she needed to thank God for big favors – for giving her the strength to fight back against the rapist as he assaulted her. She remembered drawing her arms back over her head and concentrating all her rage into the first swift strike and every subsequent strike after that. Thank God it had been enough to knock the sadistic scumbag off her.

As she lay on the hard wood floor, Tracey swore to herself that if she ever made it out of this situation alive, she would stop skipping Church on Sundays. For the past month, she had found excuses not to go. Now, she would do anything for the chance to go to Church, sit on an uncomfortable wooden pew alongside her family, and listen to a boring sermon for an hour or more. Spending time with her family seemed more important than ever - now that her life was threatened. It was amazing how you took your loved ones for granted when everything was going your way.

Tracey continued her downward journey, pausing at times to circle around clusters of tree trunks or push her way through thick tangles of branches. She made sure to cover her face to protect her eyes from sharp, protruding branches, and yet her cheeks, forehead, and chin always seemed to get scratched anyway.

At times, the bushes at her feet became so thick that she felt as if she was trudging through several feet of snow. Occasionally, the forest opened up and the going was easier, but she still couldn't determine the precise location of the sun.

Finally, the forest cleared enough so she could feel the glorious sun shining down on her. The light on her skin felt like the hand of God touching her face. The sun beamed down its comforting warmth from almost directly above her.

The sun rose in the east and set in the west, so she figured it must be halfway through its journey at this point. Not knowing which direction it was traveling, she would have to wait to determine if she was moving southwards toward civilization. Either way, going downhill seemed like a strategy that would eventually pay off.

As she traveled, she passed through terrain that alternated between thick tangles of bushes, branches, and tree trunks, and open spaces. She breathed a sigh of relief every time the forest opened up and allowed sunlight into the interior. The next time she saw the sun clearly, it was above her and to the right, which meant she was traveling in the right direction: southward.

As she trudged inexorably downhill, Tracey's mouth and throat began to feel as dry as sandpaper. The growling in her stomach subsided and was replaced by random sharp pains in her abdomen. She felt an uncomfortable pressure in her belly as if her empty stomach was steadily filling with air.

Tracey began to feel lightheaded as if she was floating downhill rather than walking. She needed to reach help soon before she collapsed from hunger, thirst, and exhaustion. She prayed to God to ask Him to guide her in the right direction.

****

Conrad entered the police station through the back door and passed by the secure evidence locker and armory as he made his way down the rear corridor. Soon, he reached the open door of the locker room on the left.

Entering, he took a left down the first aisle between two short rows of lockers. Reaching his locker in the back, he used his index finger and thumb to spin the combination lock in the proper sequence. Opening the steel door, he put away his leather jacket and picked up his ceramic coffee cup from the top shelf. He cut across the hall to the break room – heading straight for the coffeemaker.

Conrad guessed the coffee had been sitting in the pot for a while, but at least it was still warm. The sound of liquid energy filling his cup was music to his ears after a long night at the crime scene. He grabbed some sugar packets from a small basket on the counter, tore open the tops, and added them to the cup. Sliding to the end of the counter, he opened the fridge and retrieved two tiny French Vanilla-flavored packets of cream from the bottom salad drawer.

Conrad turned when he heard someone enter the break room; it was the detective's father, Lieutenant Lombardi.

"Sergeant Conrad, you did a good job at the crime scene last night," Lombardi said.

Lombardi was a fit, sixty-year-old with thick gray hair and a matching moustache. The gold badge on his chest gleamed in the bright overhead lights.

"Thank you, lieutenant," Conrad said, as he tore open a packet of cream and poured it into his tepid coffee.

"My daughter and the Chief are meeting with the victim's parents in the Chief's office."

"Which victim?" Conrad asked.

"The kidnapping victim."

"Are they locals?"

"Yes, Mr. and Mrs. Randall of 126 Highland Street."

"They must be pretty upset," Conrad said, taking a sip of coffee.

"They're taking it better than the deceased girl's parents did.

When we told the girl's mother the news last night, she had a nervous breakdown and had to be hospitalized."

Sgt. Conrad and Lt. Lombardi turned toward the doorway when they heard muffled shouts emanate from the corridor. Conrad was the first to react. He continued to stir his coffee as he walked briskly past Lombardi and entered the hallway, heading in the direction of the noise.

The shouting was coming from behind the door to the large conference room at the end of the hall. It was a deep male voice. The words became clearer as Conrad approached the door; "What kind of half-assed operation are you running here?" the voice shouted.

Conrad knocked twice and entered without waiting for a reply.

Lombardi looked miserable as she sat hunched in front of a pile of paperwork at the end of the table. Her pale skin accentuated the dark bags under her eyes. She looked like she had been awake all night.

A middle-aged woman sat to Lombardi's left. To the right of the woman was a balding, fifty-year-old man, who was standing and pointing across the table at the Chief, who was also standing with hands raised in supplication. The Chief only stood 5'8," so the six-foot Randall appeared to tower over him as he shouted and gestured wildly.

"You people are useless!" Randall shouted. "You don't even have a plan! You don't know what the fuck you're doing!"

Conrad circled the conference table and approached Randall.

"Sir, I need you to calm down and explain to me what's wrong," Conrad said, placing his hand on Randall's shoulder.

Randall's head spun around and his fierce blue eyes focused

on Conrad's face like twin spotlights.

"What's the problem?" Randall asked. "Some piece of shit grabs my daughter at the mall in front of two-dozen witnesses and your moronic department doesn't even have a plan to find her!"

"No, sir, you're wrong. We do have a plan," Conrad said, meeting Randall's frenzied blue eyes. "If you calm down, I'll tell you what it is."

Randall let out a deep breath as if he was expelling all the tension from his body. He looked Conrad up and down and appeared to be impressed at the sight of his perfectly pressed, dark-blue police uniform.

Randall sighed deeply again, and sat down at the table. Conrad circled around to the other side and sat down directly across from the distraught father. He addressed Randall only, ignoring everyone else at the table.

"First, we're going to review the surveillance cameras at the mall to see if we can identify this creep," Conrad said, leaning forward intently. "Once identified, we can find out where he lives and bring him in. I'm going to contact all the local police departments in the surrounding towns to see if any similar crimes have occurred. From there, we will create a geographic profile, which will further help us track the suspect down. We'll form a task force with other police agencies, including the state police, so we can utilize all available resources." Conrad leaned back in his chair and paused to let the information sink in. "As soon as the forensic evidence is available, we'll run any DNA we find through a national database and attempt to match it with known offenders on record. Rest assured, sir, that we are going to do everything in our power to find your daughter."

Conrad's detailed explanation appeared to assuage the older

man's anxiety. Randall's body relaxed as he leaned his elbows on the table.

"Do you really think we have a chance of finding her?" he asked.

"A very good chance," Conrad stated as he glared into the older man's eyes.

"Now tell me about your daughter. What's she like? Is she resourceful? Will she fight back?"

CHAPTER 16

I feel hot – as if I'm sitting in front of a raging fire – as I pull my vehicle in front of the cabin. My sweaty hand slips on the steering wheel. My body feels like an overheating car engine that's about to blow a rod. This could be bad. This could be very bad. I shudder with dread as the image of the girl pointing the barrel of a hunting rifle at my face fills my mind.

I have to think of a plan, a way out of this. I feel a cauldron of rage boiling in my brain as I imagine the little bitch running through the woods in her stolen blue snowsuit.

Pounding my right fist against the dashboard, I don't stop until my hand is sore. Suddenly, my vision blurs and I feel like I'm about to pass out. I still have to press my left hand against the bloody wound in the side of my skull to keep my brains from spilling out. I'm exaggerating slightly, but I'm afraid that if I take my hand away, a river of blood will gush out.

Leaning back in the seat, I breathe deeply as I try to calm down. Now, more than ever, I need to focus. What am I going to do now?

As I breathe, my mind clears. I still feel like I'm burning up with fever, but at least now I can concentrate. The first thing I need to do is attend to this wound; there's a first aid kit on the wall next to the medicine cabinet in the bathroom.

Hands trembling, I turn off the car engine. With my palm pressed firmly against my skull, I cross my free arm over my body to open the driver's door. I get out with difficulty and stumble toward the cabin. My heart feels like it's beating a thousand beats per minute; I'm sure it's going to explode like a blood-filled grenade. My head feels like an anvil being pounded by a steel hammer. I need to calm down.

Focusing on the dirt driveway beneath my bare feet, I make my way toward the cabin. A blast of cold air hits my naked body and I can't stop shivering. I feel like nature itself is trying to add to my humiliation. To add insult to injury, I howl with pain as I stub my toe ascending the mud room steps. Someone deserves to die for this, and they will. Soon.

Placing the keys on the kitchen counter, I make my way to the bathroom. I unsnap the metal latch on the first aid kit and open it up. I grab the largest, thickest bandage I can find, but there's no way to open the package with only one hand. I try ripping the plastic with my teeth, but it's too sturdy.

Swearing, I return to the kitchen and pick up a sharp knife from the drawer. Awkwardly, I hold the package down on the counter with my left elbow so I can keep putting pressure on my head wound. Using my free hand, I slice open the plastic around the bandage. I cut about a quarter of the bandage away, but there's still enough left to cover the laceration.

Returning to the bathroom, I look in the mirror. I look like hell. My normally pale face is flushed red like an apple.

Turning my head slightly, I remove my left hand from my skull to check the gash. As soon as the pressure stops on the wound, blood trickles out in a steady stream. The sight of my own blood makes me sick, so I switch the bandage to my left hand and press it hard against the gash.

Returning to the first aid kit, I rummage around until I find white medical tape. I try peeling off a strip, but it's impossible to do with one hand, so I go back to the kitchen, attach a piece of tape to my finger, and fling the roll down like a yo-yo. A ten-inch strip opens up, so I place the roll on the counter and slice off the strip with the knife.

Maneuvering one-handed, I cover the bandage with the tape as I continue to apply pressure. I try to pin the ends of the tape to my skull, but it's difficult because my hand is shaking. Finally, the tape sticks to my hair and my left hand is free.

Sighing with relief, I return to the bathroom with the medical tape. I use the mirror to tape the bandage into place perfectly. I probably need stitches, but there's no way I'm going to a local hospital. The chances that the little bitch will escape and bring the police back to the cabin are great enough as they are.

But will she be able to do it? I blindfolded her on the way in, and there's no telling how far she will stumble through the woods before she reaches a road. There are numerous cabins built on the slopes of the northern mountains, and maybe she didn't even look at the cabin's exterior as she ran away. Will she be able to find it? I think not.

If she contacts the local police, they could make a list of all the cabins in the area and visit each one, but the girl would have to inspect the interiors of each cabin, personally, in order to identify it. Besides, there are hundreds of cabins in this area, maybe even thousands. After all, this is a big ski, snowmobile, four-wheeler, and hunting area. Maybe I will make it out of this situation after all.

When I'm convinced the bandage is on tight enough, I go upstairs to the bedroom and put my clothes on.

I need to formulate a plan to fix this situation. The girl's actions have infuriated me, but I need to concentrate on what I'm doing if I'm going to stop her. What if I find her on the road before the police do? It's worth a try at least.

Sliding on my black windbreaker, I make sure my cigarette pack and lighter are secure in the right pocket. Then, I grab a bottled water and a package of pop-tarts from the kitchen before going to my vehicle. I place the items down on the passenger seat, but then I realize I forgot something far more important. Returning to the kitchen, I pick out the sharpest steak-knife I can find in the drawers. I bring it to the car and place it in the glove compartment.

Relaxing in the driver's seat, I reach for the pop tarts and rip open the package with my teeth. I tear a hunk out of the sweet pastry, and gobble up the treat as if I haven't eaten in weeks. Then, I wash it down with a swig of water.

Starting the engine, I back out of the driveway. I'm nervous, but I feel better now that I have a plan. I will scour all the local roads and find the girl before she can find help. The only help she will find is a sharp knife across her soft throat.

The rearview mirror shows a dust-cloud forming behind my car as I press down on the accelerator. The Honda barrels down the dirt driveway like a boulder in an avalanche. More dust kicks up as I'm jolted by the rocks and potholes in the driveway.

My parents really ought to fill in some of those potholes and remove the larger rocks. I'm certainly not going to do it. I have too much going on to bother with those mundane details.

I take a left at the end of the driveway and re-check the cul-de-sac that I checked before – just to be thorough. Who knows, maybe the bitch backtracked and ended up there. No go – it's just the usual piles of leaves and branches in the clearing. No bitch.

I do a three-pointer and head in the opposite direction.

I slow down as I drive past my neighbor's house. It's not for any rational reason, but out of a kind of superstitious dread. When my neighbor is home, I always slow down, so anytime I drive by, I slow down – even when he's not home. It's a habit I haven't been able to break. If I don't slow down, I feel anxious.

After passing the house, I press down on the accelerator again and race down an incline that has rollercoaster dips at the bottom. I feel my stomach drop as I fly over the small hills and troughs. Sure, it's fun, but it's nothing like doing my art.

I start to feel anxious as I think about the unfinished canvas, the one that escaped. One way or another, I need to complete the project. If I can't find the slut, then I need to find a suitable substitute. However, I can't think negatively. I will find her.

When I reach the main road, I have a dilemma. Should I go left and travel deeper into the mountain range or go right toward town? I better check the route going to town first just in case the bitch made it this far. I can't let her find help. After ruling out the town, I can scour the mountain roads until I find her. I am nothing, if not relentless. I will find her and kill her.

I don't find her in town, so I do an about-face. For several hours, I travel the mountain back-roads hunting my prey. I can cover a lot more ground by car than she can on foot. I know the area well, so I re-trace my route down the roads she is most likely to emerge on.

As I turn each corner on the winding mountain road, I imagine I will see her on the other side of the bend and run her down. At this point, I can't take any chances. I can't afford to kill her slowly like the others. I will do the second best thing and bring her mangled body back to the basement where I'll create a less satisfying piece of art. Actually, pieces of art.

It's not as satisfying when the victim is dead, but I will get something out of it. As I drive, I'm feeling more anxious. My heart is pounding like a bass drum, and my hands are slippery on the wheel. I hope I find the slut around the next corner.

CHAPTER 17

Running headlong through the forest, Tracey's legs suddenly gave out and she collapsed into a pile of leaves. As she went down, she had the presence of mind to brace her fall with her elbows to minimize potential injuries.

She found herself lying on a soft pile of dried leaves, staring up through intersecting tree branches. Tiny cracks of sunlight shone through the green canopy above. Tracey remained flat on her back until the world stopped spinning, and then sat up and looked around.

As she glanced around, her vision blurred; she was assailed by dizziness. The world spun around her like a pinwheel and she was forced to let her head drop back down into the soft leaves. Closing her eyes, the spinning sensation ceased. Tracey took a moment to savor the peaceful sensation of lying perfectly still. She felt like she could fall asleep and not wake up for weeks.

A sharp pain in her gut caused her to groan. Her stomach was empty, but it felt as if it was being pumped full of air. It was then that she noticed her mouth felt as dry as beach-sand. As she licked her lips, she felt hardly any moisture at all.

Tracey experienced a sensation like floating on an air current, but when she opened her eyes, she saw she was still lying flat on her back looking up through the trees. The cracks of light between the leaves felt too bright, so she closed her eyes again.

Her tongue felt as dry as an unused sponge in her parched mouth. She would do anything for even a tiny sip of water. Tracey imagined a waterfall cascading over rocks into a tropical pool. The image became so vivid that she imagined she could actually hear the sound of moving water.

Tracey thought she must be losing her mind because suddenly she was sure she could hear the sound of water splashing against rocks. She was almost positive it was the faint, unmistakable tinkling sound of water trickling in a stream. Feeling a surge of hope, she opened her eyes.

Tracey stared up through the trees until her head stopped spinning. Then, she pushed herself up on her elbows and sat up. The world spun around her, slowed, and then stopped. She could see the thick black bases of tree trunks surrounding her.

Tracey leaned forward, got on her knees, and pressed her hands against the hard, yet slightly yielding, gray bark of a tree. She held herself immobile against the tree until she felt she had the energy to try to stand. She attempted to get up, but her legs gave out and she collapsed into a sitting position. Still, she was sure she heard the sound of water. Sure of it.

Tracey began to painstakingly crawl through piles of dried leaves in the direction she thought she heard trickling water. Her head was heavy and her body weak but she willed herself to keep moving her hands and knees over the ground. The trickling sounds were becoming louder. Was it her imagination producing the sound, or was it real?

Suddenly, the ground sloped steeply and her body slid down a bed of soft, slippery leaves. Collapsing flat on her stomach, she stretched her arms in front of her like a diver plunging into a pool of water. She let herself slide down the incline until she found herself on level ground. The sound of trickling water was louder than ever. Crawling forward several more feet, she saw a dazzling, shimmering light ahead; it was the sun gleaming on a stream of clear, cascading water.

She had reached the edge of a wide stream plunging down the side of the mountain in a series of swirling rapids.

Crawling onto a flat rock, she moved to the edge of the stream above the water. She lowered her arms over the edge, scooped up a double-handful of water, and brought it to her lips. The wet sensation on her tongue felt intoxicating. The cool, wet life-force moistened her mouth and slid down her throat like a healing elixir. She scooped up more water, lapping it up like a thirsty dog drinking from a puddle of water. Her mouth and tongue began to feel moist again, and she felt a surge of energy.

Tracey paused to raise her hands out of the water. She crossed her arms in front of her and lay down on them like a pillow. *Thank you, God,* she thought. *Thank you for saving me.* Then, she felt herself drift into unconsciousness as she listened to the hypnotic sound of water lapping against rocks.

Tracey didn't know how long she slept at the edge of the stream, but she felt hopeful when she awoke. As she returned to consciousness, she dipped her hands into the stream and luxuriated in the cold, wet feel of it. She brought a handful to her mouth and drank it in as if it was the most exotic drink in the world.

She pushed herself to a sitting, and then a standing position. Her head felt light, but she was no longer dizzy. She stared down at the mesmerizing swirls of clear water cascading down the hillside. White foam curled around gray rocks in bubbly patches. The sound of flowing water was like natural music.

Gazing up the mountainside, Tracey saw the wide stream descending a gradual slope toward her. Her eyes followed the swirling water upwards until the stream disappeared into the trees. Gazing down the mountainside, she saw the flowing water descending the hill in a winding, snake-like pattern among the trees.

Tracey stepped off the rock and returned to solid ground at the edge of the stream. She had to be careful because the forest shadows were darkening; twilight was approaching. She followed the stream as it made its way toward the base of the mountain.

Occasionally, she had to skirt around a tree growing close to the edge of the stream, but mostly it was smooth and easy. When she encountered a flat rock at the water's edge, she lay down on it, like she had before, and scooped water into her mouth until she was satisfied. She continued her routine as she made her way steadily down the mountainside.

It was now fully dark, but Tracey felt a rush of elation as the ground leveled out and the forest opened up to reveal a man-made structure; she saw the stream meandering beneath a metal bridge connecting two sides of a road. She caught her breath as she heard the sound of a car rumble over the bridge. A steep embankment led up to the road, but she thought she could make it.

Tracey began the challenging climb with a light heart. She grabbed hold of protruding rocks, roots, or whatever she could find as she inexorably pulled herself up the steep slope. She was able to find handholds and footholds in strategic places during her journey until she finally reached the top.

She was out of breath, but that didn't stop her from climbing over the rise into the breakdown lane next to the road. She stood, breathing heavily, but feeling triumphant.

Glancing right, she saw the road traveled up a gradual slope until it disappeared around a bend marked by a cluster of trees. Looking left, she saw the bridge led to a straightaway, which disappeared into the distance with mountains on either side. The thick forest fenced in the road like an interminable green wall.

Tracey was disappointed there were no residences in sight, but the discovery of the road was an important step toward rescue. Unfortunately, she saw no cars coming from either direction.

Glancing both ways, she decided she would have a better chance of finding civilization if she turned right at the bridge and headed up the slope toward the bend in the road. After hours of trudging through the forest, her improvised mental map instinctively chose this direction as the most likely route to the nearest town.

Tracey realized she was sweating heavily under the thick snowsuit as she made her way up the incline in the breakdown lane. She wanted to unzip the front to get some air, but she didn't want to flash any drivers coming her way; she thought it might send the wrong impression. She shuddered as she thought about the liberties the kidnapper had taken with her back at the cabin.

Tracey felt a rush of excitement as she heard the roar of a car engine approaching from the other side of the bend in the road. She couldn't see the car because it was blocked by trees, but she could hear the engine getting louder.

She began waving her arms before she even saw the car, but then she had a sudden dark thought. What if it was the killer? What if he was hunting her down on the roads? She froze like a frightened deer as bright headlights swung around the corner and headed toward her.

CHAPTER 18

My pulse races as I turn a corner in the road and see a figure in blue walking in the left-hand breakdown lane. It must be her. Without even checking for oncoming traffic, I gun the accelerator and swerve into the opposite lane, heading for the figure. I feel a surge of adrenaline as I pull into the breakdown lane and close in on my target.

At the last second, the blue silhouette tries to dive out of the way, but it's too late. I smash into it and feel a jolt as my left tire crushes the body into the pavement.

The sound of screeching tires fills my ears as I hit the brakes. checking the rearview mirror, I see a red-stained pile of clothing lying in the breakdown lane. I have to make sure.

I shift into reverse and hear the tires screech again as I press on the accelerator. There is another jolt as both tires run over the body. Hitting the brakes again, I observe the bloody pile in front of me; the corpse is twisted into an unnatural position; its arms and legs are splayed out at impossible angles like a disassembled mannequin. For the first time since she escaped, I smile. I killed the fucking bitch.

My hands shake as I place the car in park and reach for the door-handle. The handle clicks and I get out, trembling. Suddenly, I feel a superstitious dread and I don't want to look at the body. What if it isn't her? No, it has to be her; the figure is dressed in blue; she was wearing a blue snowsuit.

My entire body quakes as I approach the mangled blue-and-red pile in the road. As I draw closer, I feel a sharp stab in the pit of my stomach. It isn't her. It's just some random male wearing torn blue-jeans and a ripped blue winter jacket.

Standing over the body, I observe the mangled figure has greasy hair, an unkempt beard, and disheveled secondhand clothing that was obviously dirty before I ran him over; it's just my luck to run over a homeless guy. A ripped plastic trash-bag with old clothing spilling out of a torn gap lies on the pavement next to the body; it's more proof that I wasted my time and energy by running down a nobody.

An immense wave of rage crashes through my brain and I feel slightly dizzy as if I'm being pounded by intense surf. I have to find her and kill her.

Trembling like an addict, I return to my vehicle and start the engine. I've been lucky that no traffic has approached from either direction, but it's only a matter of time before my luck runs out. I have to get out of here. Pronto.

I back up to avoid running over the body again. Then, I look both ways and pull out into the road. I'm just in time because headlights are coming from the opposite direction. I gun it and race past a red truck as it drives toward the corpse in the breakdown lane.

Checking my rearview mirror, I see the truck's brake-lights come on; the driver must have noticed my bloody handiwork and stopped to investigate. However, it's too late now because I'm long gone. A moment later, the truck disappears from view in my rearview mirror as I steer around a sharp curve.

I need to be more vigilant. I have to retrace my route and

cover all the possible roads that she could end up on. It will take time, but I've heard patience is a virtue and I don't have anything better to do.

I notice my hands are still shaking on the steering wheel, so I reach into my jacket pocket and take out my cigarette pack. Shaking one out, I put it in my mouth and reach for my lighter. Grinning at the sight of the black skull engraved onto the face of the silver lighter, I light the tip of my cigarette and take a deep drag. As the nicotine enters my system, I begin to relax.

I can do this. I can cover all the roads, track her down like an animal, and slaughter her. I also need to be careful; I can't exceed the speed limit. I probably have blood on my hood and fender; I can't get pulled over by a cop.

It's difficult to slow down and drive carefully when I know the slut is out there somewhere trying to find help. Sweat breaks out on my forehead and my hands begin to quake again as I imagine the slut going to the police and describing what I look like. If she was able to see anything out of the sides of the blindfold I put on her, I could be in trouble.

After a fruitless hour of searching, I finally decide to give up. I'm starting to get burned out from being on an adrenaline-high for too long. I need to return to the cabin and cover-up what I've done; I have to hose the blood off my car and burn all the bitch's possessions. No evidence can remain. I've seen that show CSI and I know what the authorities can do with technology.

I return to the cabin in a justifiably foul mood. Parking near the storage shed, I go around to the back to grab a water hose. I fit a high-pressure nozzle onto the end and spray down the front of my Honda to wash off all the blood spilled from the homeless cretin. Then, I meticulously gather up all the bitch's clothing and possessions, and carry them outside to the fire pit behind the cabin. I toss the items in the pit, spray them with accelerant, and throw a match on the pile.

I like to watch things burn.

When I'm satisfied that all the bitch's belongings are incinerated, I return to the cabin to clean up the glass from the broken gun cabinet. I sweep the shards into a dustbin and place them in the trash. I will have to make up a story about how the glass was broken to tell my parents

The only high point of the day was when I ran down the homeless man. Sure, he wasn't my intended target, but it felt good anyway. Someone had to pay for the bitch's duplicitous escape. I feel a thrill shiver through my body as I imagine the sight of my hood and fender striking the man. Then, I imagine the jolting sensation as my tire crushed him into the pavement.

Killing the cretin is the only thing that has kept me sane after a day of vicious setbacks. It makes me realize what I have to do; I must go on a rampage. No more extensive plans and long waits. I need to release my tension ASAP. My body starts to have another mini-seizure as I imagine running down a teenage girl in a mall parking lot.

CHAPTER 19

Tracey held her breath as the headlights turned the corner and approached her. The glare from the car's high-beams blinded her momentarily, so she used her hand to shield her eyes. She prepared to dash into the woods if the car swerved toward her.

Tracey watched as the car sped by her and raced toward the bridge. The driver was in a rush and didn't even notice her. How was she going to find help if all the drivers sped by? Maybe she would have to try to flag one down. She mentally prepared herself to flag down the next one.

Tracey followed the inner line of the breakdown lane up the hill and around a curve. Her only light was from a bright crescent moon and surrounding stars. The trees around her appeared shadowy and ominous. She hoped another car would come by soon.

Tracey shivered, despite being wrapped in a thick snowsuit. As the darkness deepened, it became colder. She didn't even know what time it was. The last car went by twenty minutes ago. Where were all the cars?

Tracey reached an open section of the road that appeared to continue straight into the distance until it reached the ominous black shapes of mountains on the horizon. She eyed the dark woods beyond the breakdown lane, and a tremor ran through her body. Anyone or anything could be lurking in there – preparing to strike – and she wouldn't know it.

Finally, she spotted headlights on the distant horizon again. At first, they were just tiny pinpoints of white light, but they grew steadily larger as a vehicle drew closer.

Tracey began to wave her arms frantically before the driver was even remotely close enough to see her. She realized that the driver approaching in the opposite lane might not be able to see her across the street, so she ran to the other side and resumed her activity in the breakdown lane closer to the car's trajectory.

Tracey felt a rush of excitement as the car finally drove within range; she could see a male silhouette hunched behind the wheel. There was no way the driver could miss her arms moving in the air.

The car did not appear to be slowing down, so Tracey stepped into the actual road, mere feet away from the approaching vehicle. It still did not slow down. Tracey felt sick to her stomach as the car sped past her. She saw the driver glance at her and then look ahead as he kept going. What was wrong with people?

Sighing, Tracey continued her journey toward the distant dark horizon. Despite all the water she drank at the stream earlier, she was beginning to feel thirsty again. She felt as if she should be seeing some signs of human settlement by now, but there was still nothing.

Tracey continued slogging ahead despite her growing thirst and fatigue. After another twenty minutes of trudging down the endless straightaway, she saw headlights on the horizon. Tracey felt a surge of hope and then a sinking feeling as she remembered how she felt when the last vehicle sped by. There was no way in hell she was going to let this one get by her.

As the headlights drew closer, Tracey saw they belonged to a huge tractor-trailer truck. One way or another, this truck driver was going to stop for her.

Steeling her courage, Tracey stepped into the middle of the road and waved her arms. She flinched as the truck's air-horn blasted her ears. The truck wasn't slowing down, but there was no way she was letting it get by.

She stepped directly into the path of the oncoming behemoth and continued to wave her arms. Tracey's eyes narrowed as the truck blasted its air-horn again as it continued to barrel toward her at full speed. If this was it, then she could at least say she tried. At least she wouldn't die slowly at the hands of her demented captor; the truck would kill her quick.

Finally, as the truck approached to within five-hundred feet, the driver hit the brakes and began slowing down. Tracey was blinded as the powerful headlights closed in on her, but she still wasn't going to move. He would have to run her down.

The huge truck continued slowing and then halted directly in front of her. Tracey shielded her eyes from the headlight glare as she heard the driver cursing within the cab. She stepped toward the center line to get out of the main glare of the headlights. Mercifully, the driver turned down the high-beams before stepping out of the cab.

"What the fuck are you doing in the middle of the road!" a gruff male voice shouted as a hulking silhouette moved toward her from the truck cab.

Tracey felt a shudder of fear as the large man approached. Surely, this trucker wasn't another dangerous psychopath. She prayed to God that he was a normal human being and not another killer or rapist.

The headlight glare obscured some of the stocky trucker's features as he moved toward her. She could make out that he was tall, heavy, balding, and wearing a plaid red-and-black shirt with blue-jeans.

"Are you deaf, or something? I asked what you are doing standing in the middle of the road!"

As the loud, bellowing voice grated her ears, Tracey's resolve gave out and she began to cry softly to herself.

"Oh my, you're just a baby," the trucker said, lowering his voice as he observed Tracey's face in the glow of the headlights.

"I need your help. I was attacked," Tracey said between sobs.

"Attacked? By who?"

"By a kidnapper who raped me and then tried to kill me."

"My God," the trucker said, wiping sweat from his brow. "You better come with me and I'll take you to the police."

Tracey forced herself to stop crying as she realized that she had to trust someone eventually if she was ever going to find help.

"Young lady, I'm sorry for scaring you," the trucker said, as he raised his hands in the air to show that he meant no harm. As Tracey stood with her arms crossed in front of her, the trucker appeared to realize what the problem was; she was still afraid of him. "Listen, I have two young daughters myself, so I'm not going to hurt you. My thirteen-year-old daughter must be close to your age."

"I'm seventeen," Tracey said, uncrossing her arms.

"It looks like you've been through a lot. You need to come with me so I can take you to the police," the trucker said, turning and gesturing for her to follow him toward the cab.

Tracey relented and circled around to the passenger side of the truck. The door flung open as the trucker pushed it from the inside. Tracey clutched the inner door handle for balance and lifted her leg onto the truck's high step. She stepped up, climbed into the cab, and shut the door.

CHAPTER 20

As I enter the kitchen from the mudroom, I notice my hands are still shaking. I need something to take the edge off. Is there any booze in the house? Normally, I don't drink alcohol because I need my mind to be sharp, but I can't stop these annoying tremors. As I try to hold my right hand steady in front of me, it jerks and quivers as if I'm having an epileptic fit. The bitch's escape has really affected me, and I need to calm down.

I check all the kitchen cabinets for alcohol and curse when I can't find any. Why couldn't my parents be alcoholics? The absence of alcohol makes me shake even harder. I'm not allowed to smoke in the house, but I grab my cigarette pack and lighter out of my pocket anyway and try to hold a cigarette steady enough to light it.

My lack of coordination is disturbing. It takes me three tries to line the lighter up with the tip of the butt. The first time, I line it up perfectly and have trouble flicking the lighter and by the time I get a flame, my fingers jerk away. The second time I get a flame right away, but the lighter almost slips from my grasp. Finally, on the third attempt, it lights. I inhale deeply and blow out a cloud of gray smoke. Damn, I need to at least open a window.

I open the kitchen window next to the mudroom, lean on the sill, and blow the smoke through the screen. The time on the wall-clock is 10:28 PM. What a miserable day. Leaning on the windowsill is uncomfortable, so I figure I'll just go outside. It's dark, but that doesn't matter because there's no one around. Bears usually don't approach the house unless there's food left out.

I go outside and shiver as a cool breeze chills my body. Staring into the black depths of the forest, I contemplate my failure. I smoke quickly without really enjoying it. I'm still shaking badly. What will it take to stop this trembling?

I smoke the cigarette down to the filter, throw it on the gravel walkway, and crush it with my heel. Holding my hand in front of me, I realize my fingers are still jerking like an epileptic in the throes of a grand mal seizure.

A rush of fury overcomes me and I have the sudden urge to destroy everything in my path. Glancing around, I search for an object to vent my wrath on. My eyes focus on the thick wall of trees ahead. I'll tear them all down like matchsticks!

Feeling a burst of furious energy, I dash through the mudroom, cut through the kitchen, and plunge recklessly down the stairs into the basement. Somehow, I flick the light switch on my way down. My eyes focus on the spot on the floor where my victim was supposed to be tied down, and it makes me want to pour gasoline over the floor and light the whole place up. Instead, I focus on the chainsaw resting on the hardware table. The next thing I know, I'm holding the chainsaw in a death-grip and ascending the stairs. I fight the urge to activate the rotating blade right away and enjoy its mechanical music. I can't risk destroying anything in my parents' cabin.

I feel like I'm moving in slow-motion as I go through the house and descend the steps of the mudroom. The outer door is slightly ajar, so I kick it open. Glancing at my parked car, I have the overwhelming urge to smash it to pieces. The thought of what a cop would do if they saw my damaged car cruising on a local road causes me to change my mind. I dash across the side lawn toward the woods.

I can't cut down any of the trees on the periphery because it'll be too obvious, so I plunge into the forest interior. Total darkness envelops me and I can't see a thing, which explains what happens next. I feel a sharp pain in my forehead as I run headlong into a thick, low-lying branch. My feet slip out from under me and I hit the ground like a rock. I'm lying on my back, staring up through the darkness. Despite this setback, my right hand is still clamped firmly around the handle of the chainsaw.

I reach for the bandage taped to the left side of my head, and find that it's wet. Not good. I don't know whether the sudden blow to my head from the tree branch opened the wound up again, or if it's been bleeding progressively. My humiliation is complete; I can't even hack up inanimate objects to vent my fury.

I feel dizzy as I push myself unsteadily to my feet. My head is still spinning – even in the absolute darkness – so I grab a tree branch, possibly even the same one I ran into, for support. I wait until I can focus clearly again and make my way toward the lighter area beyond the trees.

Heading toward the yard, I can see well enough to avoid knocking myself out again. I reach the open space around the cabin and take a deep breath as I instinctively search for a target. My eyes focus on the picnic table in the clearing behind the cabin. Checking the bandage, I realize it's moist, but not leaking. Good enough.

I let rage flow through my brain like a poison river, as I pull on the metal chain and hear the roar of the chainsaw firing up. I hold the vibrating metal beast in a two-handed grip like an executioner holding an axe, and stalk toward the rear of the cabin. I watch the chainsaw descend on one of the wooden benches as if someone else is operating it.

As the saw bites into the wood, I imagine the screams of past victims and picture the rotating blade slicing through muscle, tendon, ligaments, and bone. I close my eyes and let the enjoyable image to wash over me as the blade plunges through the barrier and strikes the ground. Lifting the blade, I sweep it to the left so it bites into one of the wooden supports, slicing through it like butter. There goes an arm. Another sweep to the right and the table collapses onto its side as it loses another support. There goes a leg.

I luxuriate in the roar of the chainsaw as I circle around the table and bring the blade down on whatever remains. The rotating saw hacks slowly through the wood as if it's ripping through a femur bone. Inevitably, it cuts through all the way and I imagine a geyser of blood shooting from an arm severed at the elbow

Now for the coup de gras – I plunge the blade into the center of the table-top as if it's a woman's torso. As the blade rips through the wood, I imagine a screaming victim being sliced at the waist. I finish the job and the table collapses. Now for the real fun – disassembling whatever's left. I hack the remaining wood to splinters as if I'm taking apart a body.

When not a single shard remains larger than six-inches, I finally stop, breathing heavily. The silence feels absolute as the roar of the blade ceases. Nothing remains on the ground but a chaotic jumble of splintered wood. I imagine that the wood is a bloody pile of body parts and a feeling of immense satisfaction comes over me.

Letting the chainsaw fall to the ground, I enter the cabin to obtain matches and lighter fluid. I find them in a cabinet and return to the backyard. I toss the splintered pieces of wood into the fire pit and douse the pile with flammable liquid.

Throwing a match onto the jumble, I step back as bright flames leap from the wood. In moments, the pile is consumed in a furious conflagration. I enjoy watching the pile burn. Lifting my hand in front of my face, I smile when I realize it's steady.

CHAPTER 21

Sgt. Conrad worked the camera controls until the screen zoomed in on a tall, pale man with dark hair. He leaned forward until his face was only inches from the video screen.

"I got you now, fucker," Conrad whispered. "I know what you look like."

After several hours of painstakingly reviewing surveillance footage, Conrad had hit pay-dirt on the mall security camera. He found a close-up of the perp as the perp exited the glass doors of the mall – only seconds before he initiated the attack. The camera was positioned above the doors directly in his path, he hadn't bothered to look up to check for cameras while he pursued his target. The perp wasn't as smart or careful as he thought he was; this image was going to be his doom.

But when? So far, they had very little to go on. Conrad hoped some new information would come to light soon.

He leaned back in the office chair and sighed deeply. It was 11:30 PM and his shift had been over for a half hour, but he still felt keyed up. He had the nagging sensation that there was still something he had to do, but he couldn't put his finger on it. He glanced over at the security guard seated next to him at the console.

"Is there a way to get a copy of this image?" Conrad asked the guard.

"Sure, I'll save the screen to the hard drive and print it for you."

"I appreciate that. The clearer you can make it, the better."

"Eight-by-eleven is the largest it will print."

"Okay, good enough."

The security guard went to work on the keyboard below the flat computer screen at the center of the bank of monitoring screens. Conrad leaned farther back in the flexible chair as he listened to the guard's fingers clicking the keys.

Before visiting the mall, Conrad had spent the day calling all the area police departments that were investigating missing local teenage girls. From the information he obtained, a clear pattern had emerged: the kidnapper chose his victim in a public place, stalked her, and waited until she was in a remote area to attack. All the kidnappings occurred between 8:15 PM and shortly before midnight and they all happened on weekdays.

Yesterday's fatality was the first time the perpetrator had murdered an acquaintance of the kidnap victim. In all of the previous cases, the victim had either been alone or the acquaintance had been incapacitated without being mortally wounded.

The fact that there was a second fatality of an innocent bystander at yesterday's incident showed a disturbing pattern: the killer's violent behavior was escalating. He had lost any compunction about murdering anyone who got in his way at the scene.

Conrad believed the perp had actually gone out of his way to kill the kidnap victim's friend, Diane LaSalle. From the evidence at the scene and the testimony of the eyewitnesses, the perpetrator did not have to resort to deadly force to make a getaway, which meant it was a thrill kill. A bonus to the kidnapping. That sick fucker. Conrad hoped to God the kidnap victim was still alive, but as he compiled facts from other departments, the chance of her survival was looking less and less probable.

The body of the teenage homicide victim, which had been discovered about nine months ago in the Westfield Conservation Land, did not help Conrad's optimism. The female victim had been identified as Linda Florentine, a student who had been kidnapped several months earlier from the Westfield High School parking lot.

Conrad's theory was that the perpetrator tried to abduct the student in the parking lot as she walked alone to her car, which was parked in a remote area of the lot, and the student had fought back. According to Conrad's theory, the student had given the kidnapper the slip and escaped into the woods behind the school. If she had run in the opposite direction, toward the school, she would have had a better chance of survival. As it was, the perpetrator had caught her in the woods and stabbed her half-a dozen times in the chest and abdomen.

In Conrad's opinion, the homicide was an intended kidnapping gone awry. Unfortunately, no one else in the department agreed with him. The Westfield Chief and Lieutenant surmised that the stabbing was the result of a domestic argument or attempted sexual assault by someone the victim knew. Therefore, they directed Detective Lombardi in that direction.

The female victim, Florentine, had recently broken up with a boyfriend who attended high school with her. She had begun dating another boy from the same school at the time of her murder. The victim's ex-boyfriend had a reputation for getting into trouble, so the spotlight was focused on him.

To Conrad, this was an obvious mistake. It was clear from the evidence at the scene that a chase and a struggle had occurred, which indicated the victim did not know her attacker. Not surprisingly, interviews with both boyfriends yielded no results. For one thing, they had ironclad alibis.

Conrad believed the murder fit with other area kidnappings. In early April, a sixteen-year-old had disappeared from the parking lot of a 24-hour convenience store in a Westfield neighborhood. A nationwide Amber Alert had been put out to no avail. She was still missing. Last year, a teenage girl had disappeared from a shopping mall – similar in size and setup to the Westfield Mall – two towns to the east in Farmington. She was still missing.

Two years ago, the body of another teenager had been discovered three towns to the south in the small town of Holliston in a wooded area. The body was that of a teenage student who had been reported kidnapped hours earlier from a mini-mall in the next town over, Ashland. Conrad theorized that she had fought back, escaped into the woods, and been murdered when caught. Her body had also been stabbed multiple times.

About three years ago, a teenage girl had disappeared from a restaurant parking lot in Marlboro – only two towns to the north. She was also still missing. Coincidence? Hell no. Any idiot could see it was all connected. Unfortunately, the idiots that worked for the Westfield Police Department were the type to delude themselves into thinking there was no deadly pattern when to Conrad it was obvious. They were afraid to admit that a serial killer/kidnapper was stalking female teenagers in the towns of Metrowest Massachusetts because it might cause a panic.

Conrad thought a panic was exactly what was needed. Then,

the affected towns could combine resources and bring in the state police. As long as no pattern was identified and each murder was being investigated separately, the killer was free to roam and kill. The police sergeant had to work hard to suppress the fury building at the thought of the monumental incompetence of his department.

It wasn't until he felt someone tugging on his sleeve that he realized the security guard was trying to get his attention.

"Sergeant, here's the picture you wanted," the guard said, handing Conrad an eight-by-eleven color copy close-up of the perp's face.

Conrad took the photocopy and scrutinized it. The picture wasn't perfect – it was partially pixilated due to the low quality of the mall camera – but it was enough to use to identify suspects. It was a good start, and that was more than Conrad could say of the other investigations.

Conrad was slightly startled when a voice came over his portable radio: "Westfield Control to Sergeant."

"This is the Sergeant," Conrad replied, speaking into his shoulder-mike.

"The Chief wants you to return to the station immediately."

The Chief? What the hell was he doing up at this time of night? It was after midnight.

"What's this about, Control?" Conrad asked as he keyed his mike.

"Sarge, you're not going to believe this, but a trucker just picked up our missing kidnap victim, Tracey Randall, on a highway in northern New Hampshire."

CHAPTER 22

I find myself chain-smoking as I drive South on route 495. The destruction of my parent's picnic table has alleviated some of the stress caused by the slut's escape, but not all of it. I feel tension building again. I have to do something about it soon. As I drive, I hold my free hand in front of my face and only notice an occasional tremor.

Lighting another cigarette, I turn up the volume on the radio. Metallica's *Enter Sandman* is blasting from the speakers.

I try to concentrate on the road, but images of the slut's escape invade my mind. I imagine her fists striking my head and then the coup-de-gras when she smashes the lamp into my head. I recall the dizzy sensation as I tumbled off the bed and the pain in my back when I struck the floor. Then, I remember seeing her naked back as she darted out the bedroom door.

The image of the slut pointing the rifle at me would have held more terror if I hadn't known the gun wasn't loaded. I remember trying to grab the gun out of her hands, but she was tough and fought back harder than I could have imagined. My only consolation is that I won't let it happen again.

By the time I reach my apartment in Westfield, I'm out of

cigarettes and I'm too exhausted to buy a new pack. Besides, I need some rest, I have to be at work tomorrow by 3 PM. It's already after 5 AM according to my dashboard clock.

I park my car in the designated space in front of the building and follow the walkway to the front glass doors. Ascending several steps, I pull open the unlocked wooden exterior door, enter the vestibule, and open the interior glass door with my key. I climb the stairs to the second floor and use my other key to open apartment number five. Entering the dark living room, I re-secure the deadbolt.

The bitch escaped, but at least I made it back to my apartment without getting caught. If only those idiotic cops knew that I was living right here in Westfield under their noses.

****

Conrad returned to the police station and met with the Chief and Lieutenant. The Chief was seated at his desk and the Lieutenant was in one of the interview chairs. Despite the late hour, both appeared tense and alert. Conrad remained standing. Detective Lombardi was conspicuously absent.

"Where's the girl?" Conrad asked.

"Safe and sound in a New Hampshire police station," Lieutenant Lombardi replied.

"In what town?" the sergeant asked.

"It's a sleepy mountain town called East Brookfield."

"East Brookfield – never heard of it. What part of New Hampshire is it in?"

"It's located in the Great North Woods," the Chief replied.

"So, North," Conrad said. "Do we know what happened yet?"

"We know she got away," the lieutenant said, unhelpfully.

"Where did he take her?"

"The East Brookfield cops said the perp took her to a snow-mobiling cabin. At some point during the kidnapping, she fought back and escaped," the Chief explained.

"Can we get a listing of all the cabins in East Brookfield?" Conrad asked.

"Slow down a bit, Jimmy," the Lieutenant said, condescend-ingly. "She wasn't found in East Brookfield. She was found by a trucker on a highway in West Brookfield, one town over. The trucker dropped her off at the East Brookfield Police Sta-tion because it was on his way to wherever he was going."

"I need to get up to East Brookfield right away," Conrad said.

"The girl left the police station," the lieutenant said, sighing as if the sergeant exasperated him. "They took her to the closest hospital thirty minutes away in a town called Graf-ton."

"I'm not sure if the young lady will be ready for an interview yet," Conrad said, raising his eyebrow. "It could be days be-fore she recovers psychologically. However, I want to speak to the trucker who found her and the police who spoke with her. I also want to read the police report."

"And you will – first thing in the morning," the Chief said, leaning forward on his desk.

"Why not now?" the sergeant asked.

"I want you to go up to East Brookfield in the afternoon with Detective Lombardi," the Chief said. "After you speak with the police there, I need you to go to the hospital and see if you can get any information from the girl."

"It might be too soon to speak to her, but we'll check out the situation." Conrad glanced at his watch and saw it was 11:45 PM. "What time is the Detective going to be in?" he asked.

"She'll be here at the start of your three-to-eleven shift tomorrow," the Chief said.

"Why not earlier?" Conrad asked.

"Detective Lombardi isn't feeling well and she can't make it in until three tomorrow. Be here at three, sergeant," the Lieutenant said, scowling.

"Okay, I'll see you at three then," the sergeant said, nodding at the Chief and Lieutenant before leaving the office.

CHAPTER 23

In my dream, I'm dismembering the slut in the basement of my parent's snowmobile cabin. It's going great until I hear a sound like a fire alarm blasting my ears. Opening my eyes, I discover the origin of the alarm is my piece-of-crap alarm-clock on the night-table next to the bed. It's 1:30 PM: time to get ready for work. I know it's foolish, but I can't resist ripping the clock out of the wall and smashing it on the floor. It will cost me, but at least it makes me feel better at the moment.

I pick my crumpled jeans off the floor and rummage through the pockets for my pack of cigarettes. I find the pack, but it's empty, so I swear vigorously. I forgot I finished them off last night. I pick up the smashed alarm clock from the floor and hurl it into a wall, shattering it into smaller pieces. Despite the stench wafting up from the fabric, I pull on my crumpled jeans so I can go to the store to pick up cigarettes. Holding my right hand in front of my face, I notice it is only trembling slightly.

My head is sore and I have a slight headache, but otherwise I feel all right. The bandage has come loose, but my wound has stopped bleeding.

I make a quick run to the convenience store and return to my apartment. We're not supposed to smoke indoors, but I light up anyway without bothering to open a window. Fuck them. The nicotine calms me a little, but suddenly I feel hungry. I pour myself a bowl of cereal and alternate between taking a bite from my mini-wheats and taking a drag off my cigarette. I impress myself with my multi-tasking. I didn't bring an ashtray with me to the kitchen, so I flick the ashes on the floor and stamp out the cigarette on the white tiles. Fuck it. I'm renting.

I'm already feeling jittery, so there's no way I'm brewing up a pot of coffee – although I'm feeling slightly tired from my busy day yesterday. Sitting at my desk in the corner of my room, I open my laptop computer. It's time to update the diary. Someday I will be famous. Readers all over the world will be impressed by my cleverness and artistic sensibilities.

Ten minutes later, I begin to question whether it was a good idea to update my diary so soon because I become angry when I reach the part when the slut escapes. I have to rush through it to get to the destruction of the picnic table, which cheers me up. It will be funny when my parents notice it missing and I pretend I don't know anything about it. Sorry, Mom and Dad, I guess somebody stole it!

My parents are losers anyway. They never cared about me, so why should I care about their possessions? They're as rich as the Trumps, but as miserly as the Scrooges. You would think I would have a better apartment than this cheap piece-of-shit I live in, but they don't lift a finger to help me with expenses.

My father cut me off after I was kicked out of college for allegedly assaulting a co-ed. I hardly even touched the bitch. I don't know what he thought was worse: being charged with assault and battery or not getting a degree. Probably, not getting a degree. He said I disgraced the family with my behavior.

The family, what a joke. I hardly ever saw my parents grow-ing up. My father thinks he's a big-shot because he runs a multi-million-dollar company, and my mother thinks she's a bigger-shot because she's a successful corporate lawyer. Both of them worked twelve hour days and were never around when I was a kid.

A nanny watched me after school from age eight-to -twelve; I rarely saw my parents on a school day. Come to think of it, I saw them even less on the weekends. They flew down to their vacation home in West Palm Beach just about every weekend.

Usually, they left on Friday afternoons and came back Mon-day afternoons, so they could enjoy a three-day weekend. I guess if you're rich, you can get away with taking long week-ends whenever you want. Sometimes my weekday nanny watched me on weekends, and sometimes they hired baby-sitters. If I was lucky, they would take me with them to West Palm Beach twice a year.

My father is the ultimate hypocrite for lecturing me about being violent. After all, I've overheard my mother and him going at it on plenty of occasions late at night; I've heard yelling, things breaking, and lots of crying after they arrived home on weekdays, usually between nine and ten at night. I even saw my father strike my mother in the face with a closed fist. She used to wear sunglasses to cover her black eyes.

When I was a kid, I was supposed to be in my room at nine o'clock and asleep by ten, but I rarely ever fell asleep that early. I used to sneak downstairs and spy on them while they drank and fought like cats and dogs. Usually, they just argued a lot and yelled at each other.

Although I miss some of the amenities I had while living in the Big House, I'm thankful to be living in my own apartment. If I'm lucky, I might talk to them on the phone once a month and visit them for dinner twice a year. If I'm unlucky, I might see them twice as often. Of course, when I talk to them or visit, I pretend it's a privilege and put on my most charming persona. After all, I want their money when they die. Being an only child, I can't imagine what else they'd do with it.

It's difficult to imagine all the havoc I could wreak if I possessed unlimited funds. If my parents were dead, I could take over the Big House and set up a secret dungeon in the extensive basement. I could put up a false wall – like in a Poe story – so only I knew the secret chambers existed. Then, I could have multiple captives and make art projects last for weeks, maybe even months.

However, that's a dream that will have to wait. As far as I know, the geriatrics are in perfect health. I'd kill them myself if it wasn't for the elaborate security systems at the Big House, and the ability of modern forensics to analyze trace evidence.

After typing my diary on the laptop and saving it, I take a shower because I'm starting to smell pretty ripe. While shampooing my hair, my fingers touch the bandage on my skull, which I had almost forgotten about. A brief sting of pain reminds me. I'm concerned because the bandage is soaked with water and hanging loose.

Gently, I peel it off and touch the wound lightly. It's tender, but it has finally stopped bleeding. It's a good sign because if I'm careful, I can wear an unobtrusive band-aid that I will paint black to blend in with my hair. A large, white bandage on my skull would look suspicious.

After showering, I shave, brush my teeth, and put some gel in my hair. I'm careful to avoid touching the wound for fear of opening it again. I could care less what I look like, but I have to make certain annoying concessions to fit in and not call attention to myself.

Retrieving the small first-aid kit from the mirrored cabinet above the bathroom sink, I carry it to the kitchen and place it on the table. This isn't the first time a slut has hurt me during a snatch-and-grab. After my first bad experience, I visited a local pharmacy and purchased a basic kit with bandages.

Spreading out some old *Fangoria* horror magazines on the table, I head down to my car to get a can of black spray paint from the trunk. Returning, I spray a handful of band-aids black to blot out the flesh-color.

I pick out a clean uniform from my closet and put it on. I feel a slight rush of power when I'm fully dressed. Maybe something interesting will happen today at work to take my mind off the slut's escape. Then again, maybe looking at all the hot bitches walking around will make me even angrier. Fuck! I need to concentrate on the job. For now, at least.

I try to follow the rule that says, "You shouldn't shit where you eat," but I broke it once when I saw a super-hot babe and decided I had to have her. It was a risky move, but I got lucky that time and it worked out. I brought her up to the snow-mobile cabin and we had a little party. Afterwards, I scattered pieces of her throughout the Great North Woods.

That was the first and last time I mixed art and work. Since then, I've cleverly struck out at a number of locations in the area. Twice, I didn't plan well enough and the sluts got away and ran into the woods. Luckily, I caught them both. I was able to stab them each a bunch of times, but I didn't have time to enjoy it. I would have liked to bring them up north, but you can't succeed every time.

I started making art about the same time I started getting picked on in Middle School. It all began in the sixth grade.

As daily beatings and humiliations occurred in the corridors outside the classroom, I resorted to drawing ultra-violent pictures in class when the teachers weren't looking. I guess it was a coping mechanism.

I only know egg-head terms like "coping mechanism" because of my extensive research into the field of psychology. After reading biographies about my hero, Ted Bundy, I was inspired to read psychology textbooks to learn more about my urges. After all, Bundy had a Bachelor's degree in psychology, and that enabled him to be a more efficient killer.

To hide my drawings, I utilized a covert system that took advantage of my reflexes; when a teacher glanced my way, I slid my drawing under my book or whatever paperwork was on the desk. I could do this in a split-second – undetected.

At first my drawings were nothing great; they were a little better than stick figures, but not much. After the second beating in the hallway by the school jocks, I needed something to keep myself sane, so I drew my first detailed picture in Pre-algebra class. In the picture, a dark figure moved among a crowd of jocks, swinging a samurai sword in glittering figure-eight arcs. Heads and limbs flew through the air like detritus tossed about by a hurricane. Compared to my later work, the picture lacked detail and resembled a roughly-drawn cartoon.

That's when I began to study drawing so I could portray more realistic scenes. I started by copying violent comic book art from graphic novels like *The Walking Dead* and *Aliens vs. Predator.* By the eighth grade, I could draw realistic scenes featuring bloody decapitations, hideous impalements, spurting wounds, and innovative tortures.

My skills continued to improve until my drawings began to take on a realistic photographic quality. Instead of using comic books for inspiration, I turned to the works of fantasy artists like Boris Valejo and Frank Frazetta. The colors brought out all the details of the blood and gore.

In the tenth grade, I began studying anatomy and forensic textbooks to add realism. I progressed steadily until I was eventually drawing realistic killings and mutilations like the ones found on the pages of *Fangoria,* the ultimate high-blood-content movie-horror magazine. By my senior year, I was creating detailed sculptures of human beings in various states of disassembly. I didn't start working on human canvases until several months after I was kicked out of college.

I check the band-aids and find they're dry. It takes two to cover up my wound. Using a mirror, I push a clump of hair out of the way and apply the sticky parts as close to the skin as possible. When I'm done, my hair falls back into place and covers most of the black plastic. Turning my head to the side, I notice the black band-aids up close, but when I move a few feet away from the mirror, they're not as visible. Good enough.

Before leaving my apartment, I perform my daily ritual. In my room, I have a single shelf of books that line an entire wall; they are novels and textbooks that have inspired me to be an efficient killer.

The first book on the shelf is my How-to Manual: *The Stranger Beside Me* by Anne Rule. This engrossing novel details the ingenious crimes of my hero and idol, Ted Bundy. Apparently, Ms. Rule actually knew this great artist and "master of deception!"

Next on the shelf is the complete works of Edgar Allen Poe. I've always wanted to kill women by using the various methods in his stories, but it would take more time, energy, and resources than I currently have.

Next, there's a line of psychology textbooks. I use them to get inside people's heads so I can break down their inner defenses, and also to put up a convincing facade to the public. After, a line of anatomy textbooks. Not surprisingly, I use them as a guide to make art.

Finally, at the end, I keep a line of books detailing the crimes of lesser artists like Gacy, Rader, and Dahmer. However, they will never ascend to the level of the quintessential artist working with human canvases, Theodore Robert Bundy. Truly, he is my mentor and inspiration.

I lightly touch each book spine with my fingers as if the knowledge contained within is filling me with power. After, I imagine an electric current flowing through my body that makes me unstoppable. I do this so I never forget that the key to my unusual success as a killer and artist is intellect.

Passion inspires me, but it's intellect that keeps me from getting caught.

As I leave the building, I light another cigarette and continue smoking as I start up my car. It's only a twenty-minute drive to my place of work in Farmington. Parking in my usual spot, I check my looks in the rearview mirror. I practice a disarming smile. Nothing to see here, folks. Just a happy employee earning a buck.

Leaving my car, I smoke another cigarette on my way to the service entrance. After smoking the butt down to the filter, I enter the building and traverse the long rear corridor to the office. I punch in and get a glass of water from the water bubbler in the break-room. There's one other male employee there eating a snack, so I dutifully smile and ask how he's doing – although I could care less.

I'm glad we don't have any female employees in my department because working with one could be difficult for me. It's possible that I would become distracted by thinking of the ways to make her into art. I would probably have to quit the job to stop myself from becoming obsessed and stalking her.

It's happened before.

I meet with my supervisor briefly and he assigns me a patrol sector. He's a fat, balding, middle-aged slob, but at least he leaves me alone to do my thing. As long as I keep walking around and respond to any calls on the radio, I'm free to do pretty much as I please.

I work with two other guys on the three-to-eleven shift, but they don't bother me too much either. The only time I see them is in passing or when we have to respond to an emergency call together. We're not supposed to fraternize with each other on the clock, which is perfect for me because I don't want to waste my time talking with those losers.

One of the guys is only a few years younger than me – twenty-four – and he wants to build experience here so he can put it on his resume when he applies to area police departments. The dumb bastard actually wants to be a cop. Why bother when they're so easy to outwit?

The other guy is a part-timer in his early fifties. He only works this job a couple days a week because he works full-time as a Campus Police Officer at Farmington State University. I tried to apply there once, but they rejected me when they found out I was expelled.

I thought about visiting Farmington State to find victims, but discovered that security had become way too tight. When I went there as a student, I rarely saw any cops or surveillance cameras.

Since then, there have been a few violent incidents and the college has gone overboard with security. The last time I took a stroll around campus, I saw Campus Police Officers everywhere I looked – either in cruisers or on foot. Those fuckers were armed too. On top of that, I saw surveillance cameras perched on the corners of every building.

One of the campus cops even asked me for my ID when he caught me walking around. That wouldn't have worked. I told him I didn't have it on me and let him escort me off campus. Rule number one is to never let them know your identity. That was the first and last time I thought about going to a college to hunt for victims.

I've discovered that parking lots at night are the best places to snatch victims. Parking lots at malls, stores, and high schools usually don't have surveillance cameras. Camera systems are expensive, and the managers that run those places are too cheap to implement their use. Their loss is my gain.

I'm assigned to the West side, so I ascend to the upper level and head toward the Food Court. The cereal I had for breakfast didn't quite cut it, so I'm still hungry. I buy a donut and Power-aid drink at Dunkin Donuts and then make all the usual checks in the area as I munch and sip.

The back corridor and the bathrooms are clear of loitering teenagers, so I move on. A couple times I caught the little fuckers having sex in the handicapped bathroom. I called for back-up and kicked the little bastards out of the building. Sometimes my job can be fun.

I saunter past the stores on the upper level, nodding at some of the employees working inside when they notice me. I have a good reputation for responding quickly when there's trouble, and then being able to handle it. The employees like me because I'm known for being aggressive with shoplifters or loiterers. Of course, I'm never so aggressive that I call attention to myself. I wait to unleash that side when I'm off duty.

Our mall has a zero tolerance policy for shoplifters, so my strategy is basically to distract them long enough until back-up arrives, pat them down for stolen merchandise, and

DIARY OF A SERIAL KILLER

forcefully escort them off the premises. I have a pair of hand-cuffs on my belt, but I rarely need to use them because most shoplifters who get caught are cooperative. When I do use the cuffs, I make sure they're tight enough to cut off circulation.

All in all, working as a mall security guard isn't a bad job. The pay isn't great, but there's no heavy lifting and once in a while I get a chance to grab a shoplifter or two and rough them up. Women shoppers are sometimes a distraction, but like I mentioned before, I try not to shit where I eat. Except for that one time, I've been able to maintain my self-control and wait until I leave work to hunt.

CHAPTER 24

At three PM, Sergeant Conrad met Detective Lombardi in her office at the station. He sat in a hard folding chair placed across from the detective's desk and watched with only slight annoyance as she reclined in a comfortable, padded executive chair.

"Feeling better?" Conrad asked, raising an eyebrow.

"I still have a little bit of a cold, but I feel better than before," Lombardi said. "The Chief and the Lieutenant told me the basics of what's been going on, but they said you could update me."

Good, she didn't notice my sarcasm, Conrad thought. He gave her a quick rundown of developments and moved on.

"Hopefully, the cops in East Brookfield documented the incident well because their report could contain valuable information," Conrad said, leaning forward.

"I agree," Lombardi replied. "We need a copy of the report and we also need to track down that trucker who picked her up and interview him."

"If he lives far away, it could put a crimp in our plan," the sergeant said, narrowing his eyes.

"We would have to do a telephone interview then," Lombardi said.

"Phone interviews are usually not as effective, but I guess it's better than nothing."

"Once we get all the information from the East Brookfield cops, we'll head over to the Grafton Hospital to see if we can get any information from the girl," the detective said.

"Depending on her physical and mental condition, we may have to wait before we grill her too intensely," Conrad said. "We don't want to cause her any additional trauma. But if she appears as if she can handle it, we should go for it. The information she provides could help us to track down the perp."

"We have to find this bastard before he does it again."

"Absolutely," Conrad agreed, nodding. "Are you ready to go?"

"I'm ready when you are," Lombardi said.

"Okay, let's go."

They left the station by the back door and cut across the rear parking lot to Detective Lombardi's blue unmarked cruiser. Lombardi took the driver's seat while Conrad sat in the passenger side. They drove out of the parking lot and headed for Route 495 North.

After traveling several familiar back-roads, they pulled onto the highway. Despite the 65-mph speed limit, Lombardi immediately brought the speed of the car to 85 mph. She was depending on her detective status to get her out of any potential speeding tickets from state troopers.

Conrad was silent as he brooded over their next move. Whatever action he and Lombardi took today would depend in part on the quality of the information they could obtain from the East Brookfield Police Department. Not to mention, the quality of the information they could get from the victim. If she had been able to catch a glimpse of the perp's license plate or house address, that would end things quickly.

However, that scenario wasn't realistic; the perp would have taken precautions to prevent that. Realistically, the sergeant predicted they might be able to obtain enough information to send them in the right direction, but there would be no quick resolution.

Conrad tried to imagine the psychological state of the victim and whether she had the presence of mind to provide them with information to help find the killer. The reality was the teenager might be too traumatized to effectively vocalize what had happened to her.

He had seen victims go into temporary states of shock; suppressing the painful memories related to a traumatic experience. As a defense mechanism, they were able to wipe their mental slate clean and replace all the negative memories with a tabula rasa.

Sometimes, only hypnosis could reveal the details of what had happened during a victim's ordeal, and hypnosis was an arduous and time-consuming process. Not all psychologists could do it effectively, and those that could often charged outrageous prices. Also, it wasn't 100% reliable or admissible in court. Conrad hated to rely on shrinks to get information from victims. Hopefully, it would not be necessary.

Conrad tried to imagine what the killer was doing right now. Was he at home? Did he have a job? Did he live in an apartment or a house? The only facts he knew for sure was that the perp appeared to be in his mid to late twenties and had access to a vehicle and a vacation cabin. Was the killer actually homeless and had broken into a random cabin in the woods? Conrad didn't think so. His actions were too methodical to depend on random decisions.

This guy was a planner. Conrad was disturbed by the killer's precision; it meant that he would probably be difficult to catch. Although a few of the perp's kidnapping attempts had failed, he appeared to learn from his mistakes and become more efficient with each new try. Conrad needed the guy to break down, lose control, and do something stupid. Maybe the fact that the teenager escaped would cause him to crack.

But what made him tick? What was his motivation for kidnapping teenage girls? Did he kill them right away or hold them prisoner for a while? The fact that the last victim escaped pointed to the fact that he at least kept his victims alive for a period of time. The killer had revealed his deadly potential to commit murder when he stabbed the victims who tried to escape. In addition to a probable sexual motivation, Conrad thought the killer's violent acts demonstrated a massive amount of rage.

But what causes a level of rage so overpowering that it consumes a person and leads to murder? Was this psychopath able to hold a job or did he live at home with his parents? If he lived at home, why did his parents not notice his disappearance for days at a time so he could bring his victims to a remote cabin? Was he picked on or abused as a child? Probably. Most of the serial killers Conrad had studied had been beaten or bullied by parents or someone close to them.

Another question: how was the killer able to conceal his rage so he didn't draw attention to himself, only to release it periodically? What the hell was going through his mind? The fact that the victims were attractive teenage girls pointed to an obvious sexual component. The precision of the crimes showed a need to manipulate and control. But how much control did he have?

Conrad tried to wrap his mind around the fact that a human being could be filled with so much rage and yet maintain a calm façade most of the time to avoid being caught. It made him think of the infamous serial killer, Ted Bundy, who was the ultimate "master of deception." Bundy showed one smiling face to the world and another darker one to his victims.

The ability to put up a normal façade most of the time made this psychopath as dangerous as Bundy. Not to mention the calm and meticulous preparations that went into planning and perpetrating the crimes. Conrad knew he needed to get inside the killer's head to figure out his next move.

Lombardi's voice broke his deep rumination.

"Sarge, our exit is coming up next. We're almost there," the detective said.

Conrad snapped to attention as if awakened from a deep slumber. He had become so consumed by his thoughts that he had entered a trance-like state.

"We're here already? How long have we been driving?" Conrad asked, gazing out at the mountainous terrain surrounding the highway.

Lombardi gave him a strange look.

"Sarge, it's been over three hours."

Three hours? Where had all the time gone? Conrad wondered.

"I've been trying to predict this sick puppy's next move by attempting to get inside his head, and it hasn't been easy," Conrad said.

"Don't try too hard or you're liable to drive yourself crazy," Lombardi said, raising her eyebrow.

"I need to know what he thinks, so I know what he'll do."

"Like I said, Sarge. He who fights with monsters....."

".....must be careful lest he thereby becomes one," Conrad finished the quote. "I didn't know you read Nietzsche."

He was impressed.

"I think that quote should be a requirement for everyone in our field," Lombardi said, flashing a half-grin. "Hopefully, we'll get some good information from the cops and the victim."

"Hopefully," Conrad agreed, as they turned onto the East Brookfield exit.

CHAPTER 25

This shift has been a nightmare so far; I can't stop my hands from shaking; my uniform is soaked with sweat; I feel like I'm about to pass out and my heart is slamming in my chest like a jackhammer. Every woman I see in the mall has her face. I don't know why they all look like her, but they do. I see her everywhere: in the Food Court, the stores, the walkways. Everywhere I turn.

My vision blurs as I walk down the Food Court Aisle toward the Dunkin Donuts stand. Concentrating, I force my eyes to come back into focus. I take one step after another. My mouth feels as dry as sandpaper. I'm trembling all over. But how noticeable is it? Can other people see it?

I notice a few strange looks from passersby, but I ignore them as I focus on my goal: Dunkin Donuts. The skinny, long-haired teenager behind the cash register studies me with narrowed eyes as I approach.

"Hey, dude, are you all right? Your face is red and you're sweating."

Tell me something I don't know, you little prick. I feel like I'm burning up.

"I may be getting sick. Could be a fever," I say, as I lean on the counter for support.

"Like, you don't look so good, man," the teenager says, continuing to stare at me with the same stupid expression.

It takes all my self-control not to reach across the counter and strangle the scrawny bastard.

"Get me a Power-aid," I say as I pull my wallet out of my pants pocket. My hand trembles noticeably as I do so.

"Hey, your hands are even shaking," he says as he observes the wallet quake in my sweaty grip.

I feel a wave of pure rage flow through me as I glare at the teenager.

"Just get me the fucking drink," I say, gritting my teeth.

As the rage takes over, the trembling subsides. The teenager's eyes widen as he scurries over to the refrigerator containing the cold beverages. If I get a chance to let all my rage out, maybe I can control the symptoms afflicting me.

I imagine smashing the teenager in the back of the head with a closed fist as he opens the glass door of the fridge and takes out a blue Power-aid bottle. As he returns to the counter and places the bottle in front of me, I imagine punching him in his skinny, pale forehead. I hand him a ten-dollar bill, and my hand barely trembles. If I had met this kid under different circumstances, I'd open his throat from ear-to-ear.

The little fucker hands me my change and I stuff it into my wallet without counting it. I unscrew the cap from the bottle and take a massive swig. The sandpaper feeling in my mouth diminishes.

As I walk away, the teenager can't help but offer a parting shot at me: "I hope you feel better," he says.

I don't dare turn around despite my desire to tell him to "fuck off." Someone could overhear.

I feel a little better as I continue to sip the drink. Although I'm not supposed to (except on my break), I sit down at a table near the edge of the Food Court to drink in peace. I feel my forehead and there's still sweat on it. Holding my hand in front of my face, it continues to tremble slightly.

I make the mistake of turning my gaze to check out a pair of attractive teenagers walking by. They are wearing skin-tight mini-skirts that hug their asses – leaving little to the imagination. Of course, the image sparks my imagination anyway.

As soon as I focus on them, I start to tremble again. One of them is a brunette like the one that escaped. Her body is fuller, but her hair is about the same length. That fucking bitch! I have to kill her; slice and dice her. That will make me feel better.

But how? I don't even know where she is. Only that's not true. I really do. I have a way to find her quite easily. I burned her belongings in the fire pit, but I keep their drivers' licenses as trophies.

Taking out my wallet, I reach under my license to get to hers. I slide it out and stare at her insipid grin. My eyes focus on her street address: 147 Highland Street, Westfield, MA. Perfect. I can still make up for letting her get away. I'll hunt the bitch down. Then, we'll have a party worth remembering.

I barely make it through the rest of the shift. The only thing that keeps me from having a nervous breakdown is the thought of re-capturing the bitch and bringing her to my northern retreat – where I can do all the things that I wanted to do before.

I seem to be running hot – I buy two more Power-aids and down them both before my shift ends. This time, I go to the convenience store on the first level, so I don't have to see the scrawny teenager again. I can't be responsible for my actions if he says one more thing to me.

The liquid keeps me from passing out, but my face is still hot and my forehead is dotted with sweat. Not to mention the unsteadiness of my hands. One of my moronic co-workers makes a comment that I don't look good. I tell him I must be coming down with something, which insures that I will call in sick tomorrow.

If I call in, I will have the entire day to myself. I can track down where my little escapee lives and stake out her house. When she returns, I'll wait for the right moment and grab her. I'll follow her to the edge of Hell if I have to. There's no way I can let her live after the humiliation she has caused me.

There's no smoking in the mall, so I light up as soon as I leave the building. Inhaling, I blow out miniature jet-streams of smoke as I walk to my car.

I become increasingly excited as I contemplate my plans. I'm good at stakeouts; I don't get nervous and I keep a clear head in the field. I always get a rush of excitement, but it doesn't get in the way. So far, there's been no trembling or sweating when I'm on a stakeout. I should be able to maintain my composure on this one.

Unlocking my car door, I slide into the driver's seat. Instinctively, I check the glove compartment to make sure my knife is still under the registration. I feel reassured as my fingers close around the handle.

Suddenly, I have an inspiration. I usually work with a knife, but why not use something that will give me more bang for the buck? I think back to my experience at the cabin. If I had a loaded firearm then, I could have blown the bitch away as she tried to run. Before I go on my stakeout tomorrow morning, I'll look up the Westfield Police web site on the Internet and find out what I have to do to apply for an LTC – a License To Carry. It shouldn't be a problem because I have a clean criminal record; I was never officially charged for that thing I did in college.

Turning the key in the ignition, I listen to the engine fire up. Now I have something to look forward to. Unhurried, I pull out of my parking space and cruise down the aisle toward the mall exit. As I drive, I hold my hand in front of my face and notice it has stopped trembling.

CHAPTER 26

The ride from the highway exit to the East Brookfield Police station seemed to take forever, as Conrad and Lombardi followed a long, twisting road that snaked its way between mountains like a meandering boa constrictor. Conrad kept expecting to see the police station around the next corner, but all he saw were more trees. Lombardi had informed Conrad that the police station was on the same road they were traveling, route 64.

They passed a large open lot containing trucks and construction equipment on the right called Burton Construction. After the construction lot, the forest opened up into expansive farmlands on both sides of the road with the forest and mountains looming beyond. Conrad didn't realize he was obsessively tapping the palm of his hand against his knee until Lombardi gave him a strange look. He stopped doing it.

The farmlands eventually faded away to be replaced by middle class homes spaced intermittently throughout a wooded area. Soon, they passed a gas station/convenience store at an intersection with a sign containing an arrow pointing right: DOWNTOWN – THIS WAY.

It was hard for Conrad to imagine that East Brookfield had a significant "downtown." It was probably no more than four or five buildings: a post office, library, town hall, and maybe one or two private businesses.

Conrad was about to give up and concede they were never going to arrive when they finally turned a corner and saw an unimpressive, one-story building with a separate two-car garage come into view over the next rise. A faded sign near the road read "East Brookfield Police."

Conrad breathed a sigh of relief; the trip from the highway to the station was no more than thirty minutes, but it had felt like hours. He needed to slow down; impatience could lead to mistakes, and this stage in the investigation was too crucial.

Lombardi pulled into one of the open spaces in front of the station's double glass doors. The next spot over was occupied by a red-and-black East Brookfield cruiser, an old Crown Victoria dating back to the early 2000's. Conrad saw another cruiser parked in one of the open garage bays. Was anyone out patrolling? He wondered. He hoped this was not a bad sign.

They got out of the unmarked cruiser and headed for the double glass doors. Conrad held one of the doors open so Lombardi could enter first. He followed her in as they approached a long front counter that separated a waiting area equipped with uncomfortable-looking plastic chairs from a dispatch console and a pair of desks.

Three individuals were seated casually around the desk at the center of the office: a young, overweight blonde woman, dressed inappropriately in cut-off jeans and a form-fitting red tube-top, and two police officers. They appeared to be eating a late dinner, as Chinese food boxes were spread across an otherwise bare desk; they were shoveling piles of food into their mouths with plastic utensils.

One of the policemen wore a gold badge, so Conrad guessed that he was the Chief, or at least the person in charge. He appeared to be in his sixties, had a shiny bald head, a double chin, and seventies-style sideburns that Conrad hadn't seen since watching the original Dirty Harry movie. The younger cop was as thin as Popeye's Olive Oil with bad teeth, a crew-cut, and a brown mustache that looked like an over-sized caterpillar on his narrow face.

None of the trio looked up from their dinner as Lombardi and Conrad stood waiting at the counter. The sergeant glanced at his watch and saw it was 7:15 PM; they didn't have any time to waste. He felt nauseous watching the diners shove mystery meat and fried rice down their throats like savages. Didn't they have a break room to eat in?

Finally, the twenty-something, puffy-cheeked blonde turned to face Conrad and Lombardi as she chewed. Her eyes widened.

"Can I help you?" she asked through a mouthful of food.

Conrad glanced at his partner and realized she was too stunned by the scene to answer.

"I'm Sergeant Conrad and this is Detective Lombardi from the Westfield Police Department in Massachusetts. We're here to get a copy of an incident report that was written last night."

The older officer wearing the gold badge elbowed the blonde in the shoulder, as he continued to cram Chinese into his mouth. The blonde got up reluctantly from her meal and waddled over to the dispatch console.

Leaning over the console, she began typing on the computer keyboard. Both Conrad and Lombardi were subjected to a view that revealed more of the overweight blonde's anatomy than they would have cared to see.

Conrad couldn't help but smile at the ridiculous scene; it was like something out of a bad cop-comedy-movie. His smile widened as he glanced at Lombardi and saw that she still wore an expression of utter shock on her face. As Lombardi turned to Conrad, he wiped the smile off his face so he could nod reassuringly to let her know that he would deal with the situation.

Conrad turned away from the dispatch console as the blonde continued to type commands into the keyboard. The police officer, who was not wearing the gold badge, locked eyes with him briefly before returning his gaze to the pile of meat and fried rice on his plate. Conrad thought the cop looked like "Cletus" from the old Dukes of Hazard show. Not knowing what else to do, the sergeant scanned the office to avoid meeting the gaze of his partner, which he thought might cause him to smile inappropriately again.

He saw a pair of beat-up, gray, metal filing cabinets in the corner, which appeared to date back to the the 1950s, placed next to a decrepit, rusted water bubbler. To the right of the enthusiastic diners, an open doorway led into the unlit depths of a hallway. A rectangular gold sign – with words that were too small to make out – hung on a wooden door in the back. He assumed it was the door to the Chief's office. Norman Rockwell's famous picture of a burly police officer leaning toward a youth, who was seated next to him at a diner, was hung askew on the wall above a computer printer desk.

Conrad was surprised they actually had a computer at the dispatch console. From the look of the place, it appeared they were still doing handwritten duty logs. The dispatch radio was connected to an oversized, hand-held speaker microphone that would have looked at home in the hand of Edward R. Murrow on his 1950's news program.

After an uncomfortably long time, the sergeant heard the sound of the electronic printer doing its magic. Several seconds later, the blonde went over to the printer table beneath the Norman Rockwell picture and ripped off a sheet of paper.

Waddling back to the counter, she handed the sheet to Conrad without meeting his eyes. Not missing a beat, she returned to the desk with the food and picked up where she left off stuffing her face.

Conrad glanced down at the report in his hand, depressed when he saw it was only seven lines long. He should have known what was coming from the look of the place, but he felt letdown. He skimmed quickly over the short narrative:

AT 22:42 DISPATCHER CONLAN RECEIVED A CALL FROM A TRUCK DRIVER, NICHOLAS TURNER. HE SAID HE PICKED UP A FEMALE HITCHHIKER ON ROUTE 64, BUT HE WAS UNSURE OF THE TOWN. HE THOUGHT IT WAS EITHER PAXTON OR WEST BROOKFIELD. MR. TURNER SAID THE GIRL TOLD HIM SHE HAD BEEN KIDNAPPED AND HE WAS ON THE WAY TO THE STATION WITH HER. HE SAID THE GIRL WAS PRETTY SHAKEN UP, SHE HAD SCRATCHES ON HER FACE AND BODY, HE SUGGESTED AN AMBULANCE. I, OFFICER BLAKE, CALLED THE GRAFTON HOSPITAL TO ASK THEM TO SEND AN AMBULANCE TO THE STATION. ABOUT TWENTY MINUTES LATER, MR. TURNER SHOWED UP WITH THE GIRL. HE SAID HE WAS IN A RUSH, SO HE GAVE US HIS CONTACT INFORMATION (358 STONEWALL DRIVE, PHOENIX, ARIZONA, 02394, 762-948-3321) AND THEN LEFT. AT 23:28 THE AMBULANCE ARRIVED AND PICKED UP THE GIRL (TRACEY RANDALL, 147 HIGHLAND ST, WESTFIELD, MA, 01622, 508-429-2104) END OF REPORT.

Conrad didn't know whether to laugh or cry. The only information that was of any use was the truck driver's name, address, and phone number – assuming they were correct. Rarely, had he seen a more half-assed report.

When he worked as a campus police officer at Farmington State University years ago, the reports were more professional. The campus cops at Farmington never would have been brazen enough to hand in an unfinished piece-of-crap like this one. Conrad was disgusted. Below his feeling of disgust, a reservoir of rage began to build.

Handing the report to Lombardi, Conrad kept his eyes focused on the balding policeman wearing the gold badge. The policeman stared back impassively as he continued to eat. If Conrad could have killed him with a stare, he would have.

"What the fuck....." Conrad heard Lombardi whisper beside him.

"Are you the Chief?" Conrad asked the bald cop.

"Chief Robert Graham. You got questions about the report?" the balding man asked with his mouth still full. He stopped shoveling food into his mouth long enough to make this statement, and then resumed packing it in.

"Yes, I have a few questions, Chief," Conrad said, raising an eyebrow. "The name on this report is Officer Blake. Is he around?"

"That would be me," the skinny cop wearing the silver badge interjected as he took a break in his own caloric intake.

"Perfect, then I'll direct my questions to you," Conrad said. "In the report, the truck driver said he thought he might be in the town of Paxton or West Brookfield. Where are these towns in relation to East Brookfield?"

"Both towns are west of us," Chief Graham interrupted.

"How sure are you that she was found in one of these towns? Did you interview the truck driver thoroughly?"

"Look here, son," the Chief interrupted again. "That's what he told us. He was in a rush to get out of here and make his delivery. We're not about to hold up a working man from getting paid. Besides, she looked like she needed medical attention, so we made that our priority."

"Did you happen to get a chance to ask the young lady any questions?" Lombardi asked the officer without any attempt to disguise her sarcasm.

"Like I said, we were focused on getting the young lady medical attention. We didn't want to upset her while she was resting in the lobby," the Chief blurted.

Lombardi frowned as she glanced at the uncomfortable-looking plastic chairs in the lobby.

"Were you able to get ANY information at all from the young lady?" Lombardi asked, rolling her eyes.

"Just what you see in the report," Officer Blake said.

"So you didn't think it was important to ask the victim what had happened to her?" Conrad demanded. He leaned across the counter as if he wanted to reach over and strangle the officer and the Chief.

Chief Graham's face turned red as he dropped his fork, stood up, and charged toward the counter.

"Look, sergeant, we don't need you flat-landers coming up here and telling us how to do our job," the old man said, raising his voice as he pointed a finger at Conrad. "All the information you need is in the report. The truck driver's address is there and the girl's address is there. If you have any more questions you can ask them yourself!"

"No problem, Chief, that's what we'll do," Conrad said, taking a deep breath as he straightened up from his leaning position.

Turning to Lombardi, he held out his hand for the report. As she handed the paper to him, he spoke to her in a soft voice – just above a whisper: "The only information we don't already have is the truck driver's address and phone number.

If we can talk to him, maybe we can get him to pin down a more exact location of where he found the girl. I memorized his info, so as far as I'm concerned, we're all set here. Do you need to ask them anything else?"

"Yes, one more thing," Lombardi said, turning toward the Chief, who stood by the counter with his hands on his hips. Conrad thought he looked ridiculous with a basketball-sized pot-belly protruding from an otherwise slim physique. "Is it possible the trucker was mistaken and found the girl in a town other than Paxton or West Brookfield?" the detective asked.

"Of course it's possible," the Chief said, scowling at her.

Lombardi turned toward the officer, who was still seated at the table. He appeared to have finished eating, and was now lounging back in his office chair as if he was at the beach.

"Officer Blake, did the trucker or the victim describe the landscape where the girl was picked up?"

"They said they were surrounded by forests and mountains."

"They never described any signs of houses or civilization?"

"Nope."

"Okay, then we're finished here," Lombardi said, raising an eyebrow.

"You can have your report back now," Conrad said.

With a dramatic flourish, he held the paper up with both hands and ripped it to pieces. He tossed the scraps over the counter, did an about-face, and headed for the door.

Lombardi hesitated for a moment to enjoy the contorted, incredulous expression on the Chief's red face.

"Gentlemen, we truly appreciate ALL the effort you exerted to help us," Lombardi said, smiling and winking at each cop before turning away.

CHAPTER 27

"Those morons are an embarrassment to the police profession," Conrad muttered to Lombardi as they left the police station and headed for the unmarked cruiser.

"I wrote better reports when I was working as a corporate security guard," the detective replied as she opened the driver's side door.

"I would have been fired if I handed in a report like that when I worked campus police at Farmington State," Conrad said, pulling open the passenger door when he heard a click.

Glancing at his wristwatch, he saw it was almost 7:30 PM.

"That's fifteen minutes of our lives we can never get back," he said, grinning at the detective over the roof of the car. She returned his smile before ducking to enter.

Sliding into the driver's seat, Lombardi started the engine while Conrad slid in beside her.

"I don't know about you, but I'm going to have nightmares about those people," Lombardi commented, as she backed out of the parking space.

"It's a setback, but we can turn it around," Conrad said as they drove to the edge of the parking lot.

The detective stopped at the road and looked both ways before proceeding in the direction they came from.

"I agree," Lombardi replied. "We can turn it around when we interview the victim."

"I just hope to God that she's not too traumatized to give us any information."

"It can't get any worse than what we just dealt with."

Twenty minutes later, they reached the highway and pulled onto route 495 South; the Grafton exit was two exits ahead. Soon, they were headed down another road that resembled an asphalt rollercoaster.

They drove past more farmland interspersed with long stretches of forest. Eventually, houses appeared in the open spaces between forest stretches and later, commercial businesses. Finally, the forest faded away as they drove through an actual downtown area with two and three-story buildings lining the sidewalks. There was even some mild vehicle traffic.

Taking a right at an intersection, they spotted a blue hospital sign with a pointing arrow. Soon, the commercial buildings became more spread out and merged with a series of narrow, closely-packed, two-story houses. They continued to follow the signs for the hospital.

Conrad checked the dashboard clock and saw it was almost eight o'clock; visiting hours ended at 8:30 PM at most hospitals, so they were cutting it close. Maybe the hospital staff would give them some extra time because they were cops.

Finally, they spotted a sign marking the hospital entrance ahead and Lombardi pulled onto a curving roadway that led up a slope to a large parking lot set in front of a modest, four-story hospital building. Only about a quarter of the lot was filled with cars. They found an open spot near the main entrance and parked. Getting out, they headed for a pair of glass doors.

The automatic doors slid open at their approach and they entered the main lobby. Lombardi took the lead as Conrad followed her to the reception desk.

"We're looking for a patient, Tracey Randall," the detective said to a middle-aged female desk attendant.

The attendant punched keys on a computer keyboard and checked the screen.

"Are you family?" she asked.

Lombardi took out her wallet and flashed her badge. The attendant didn't look impressed.

"Visiting hours are over in twenty-five minutes," the woman at the desk said with apparent relish.

"That still gives us some time," the detective said. "Where's the room?"

The attendant frowned as she glanced down at her computer screen. "She's in room 328."

"Thank you," Lombardi replied, as she hurried toward the elevator.

Conrad had to jog to keep up with her. The detective pressed the "up" button and the doors opened a moment later. As they boarded, Lombardi pressed the button for level three. As the elevator ascended, the detective glanced upward as if she could see through the ceiling to the floors above.

Conrad thought she appeared anxious, which was okay because it might give her an edge during the interview. As long as she didn't panic and they worked together, it should work out fine. He was planning on letting her take the lead and only stepping in when necessary. He had done interrogations with her before, and she had always done a decent job.

They stepped off the elevator as the doors opened on the third floor. Conrad followed Lombardi to a Nurse's Station down the hall where she asked for directions; Tracey's room was two doors down on the right. The detective turned toward the sergeant and raised her eyebrows as if to say, "Are you ready?" and Conrad responded with a barely perceptible nod.

After a short walk down the hall, Lombardi knocked on the closed door of room 328. A middle-aged woman opened the door a crack and peered furtively out at the detective and sergeant. Her eyes widened as she focused on Conrad's police uniform; she opened the door without asking questions.

Lombardi and Conrad entered to find Tracey sitting up in an adjustable hospital bed – apparently healthy and relaxed – while her father sat next to her reading a magazine. Tracey perked up and placed a paperback book on her lap when she saw Conrad's uniform.

"I was wondering when you guys would show up," Tracey said, flashing them a half-smile.

Conrad couldn't help but smile back. Lombardi was all business.

"Do you mind if we ask you some questions?" the detective asked as she approached the bed.

"Of course I don't mind," Tracey replied. "I've been waiting for cops to show up to question me since I got here late last night. Just to let you know – you're late."

Conrad cracked a smile again as he stood by Lombardi's side looking down at the vivacious young woman. Other than the IV tube embedded in her arm, she appeared healthy.

Tracey's father stood up and shook Lombardi's hand, then Conrad's.

"Thank you for coming, officers," he said. "This thing has been stressful as hell and we were wondering when someone from law enforcement was going to show up."

"Sir, I apologize that we're the first officers you've met so far," the detective said.

"I'm just glad you're here now, ma'am," Mr. Randall said.

"Sir, would you and your wife mind leaving the room for a short while so we can ask your daughter some questions about what happened?"

"No problem. We'll be right outside, honey," Tracey's dad said, as he led his wife out of the hospital room, and closed the door behind him.

The detective sat in the plastic chair where Tracey's father had been seated at the foot of the bed, and turned it so she was facing Tracey. Conrad circled the hospital bed, picked up the chair on the other side, carried it back, and sat down near the head of the bed so he had a clear line-of-sight with Tracey without blocking Lombardi's view.

"Tracey, I realize this has been a traumatic experience for you, but we need to know the details about what happened in order to catch the perpetrator who did this," Lombardi said, leaning forward in her chair.

"I understand," Tracey said, raising an eyebrow. "I've seen plenty of cop shows so I know the routine. I'll do my best to remember everything."

Tracey continued to surprise Conrad; he had expected her to be more reticent about re-living the painful details of her kidnapping. He thought it was a good sign that she was so clear-headed and cooperative because it could only help in the long run.

Lombardi didn't seem sure what to say next, so Conrad took the lead.

"Tracey, we would like you to tell us exactly what happened from the beginning. We'll try not to interrupt you unless we need clarification."

"From the beginning," Tracey said, staring off into space as if gazing at an object far away. She hesitated as she appeared to go back in time. Then, she snapped herself out of her trance and began to speak, animatedly.

Tracey described the details of her ordinary trip to the mall with her friend without appearing noticeably upset. Conrad saw her face turn pale as she drew closer to the part of the story where she and her friend were attacked in the parking lot. When she came to the actual attack, her demeanor underwent a visible transformation; she sat up straight, her body became as rigid as a board; she crossed her arms in front of her as her face went from pale to ghost-white.

Conrad leaned forward as she described her attacker.

"He was close to six feet tall," Tracey began. "Maybe one-hundred-seventy pounds, short dark hair – almost black – lightly gelled and combed back, dark eyes – probably brown but maybe dark green, not exactly a tan complexion – but not pale either. He had a confident, relaxed demeanor, and he always had a half-smile – more like a smirk actually – except when he got angry. When he got angry, he looked like he was possessed. His eyes got this wild look in them and his face scrunched up and turned red as if he was about to blow a fuse.

Tracey paused as she stared off into space as if she was looking at the psychopath's face at this moment.

"Do you remember what he was wearing?" Conrad asked, in an effort to snap her out of her trance.

"Sure, he was dressed in a black windbreaker jacket, black t-shirt, blue-jeans, and wore dark-blue New Balance sneakers. He had a circular tattoo on his left forearm that was colored in half-black and half-white. I think it was the Yin-Yang symbol His voice was calm, but with an edge to it as if he could go off at any time. That's why I didn't say anything. He had a typical New England accent – he didn't pronounce his "R's." All in all, he was an average-looking guy. The only time you could see something was clearly "off" with him was when he lost his temper. Then, he was scary as hell."

CHAPTER 28

Conrad took detailed notes as Tracey described the killer. He noticed that Lombardi listened without writing anything down. That was typical. She usually relied on him to take notes during interviews. It was okay with Conrad because she might catch a detail he missed while he was scribbling in his notebook.

It took a full hour for Tracey to tell her harrowing story. The more Conrad heard, the more he was impressed with her fortitude. He respected that she was a fighter and didn't give up. Instead of saying to herself, "Poor me, I'm doomed," she always thought positively and planned her next move.

At one point in her story, Tracey's eyebrows creased into a determined frown as if she were gathering her energy to fight back against the killer. Instead of breaking under pressure, she hardened like steel.

Conrad felt physically sick as Tracey described the rape. His daughter was twelve years old, and it terrified him to think that she could encounter a monster like this one. He also had an eight-year-old son, and it was disconcerting to think that he was also vulnerable to human predators. Conrad vowed never to let his kids out of sight until they were both twenty-years-old, and only after he had taught them how to shoot a gun.

"He would have killed me," Tracey said in a matter-of-fact tone that sent a chill down Conrad's spine. "I could see it in his eyes. I saw a sick gleam in them that told me that after he had his kicks with my body for who-knows-how-long, he was going to murder me.

Conrad and Lombardi knew better than to argue with Tracey's intuition; they accepted what she said and waited for her to continue. When Tracey remained silent, Conrad asked, "Is there anything else you can think of that could help us catch this guy?

Tracey stared off into the distance as she bit her lower lip.

When she didn't reply, Conrad nodded at Lombardi to let her know she was all set to ask the first question.

"Tracey, did you notice anything at the kidnapper's cabin or car that might help us to identify him?"

Tracey appeared to be in deep thought as her eyebrows knitted together in an expression of intense concentration. Conrad held his pen poised over his notebook.

"I don't know," she said. "I think I told you everything that mattered."

Conrad waited several seconds to give Lombardi the opportunity to ask more questions, and then spoke up when the detective remained silent.

"Tracey, do you remember what brand of cigarettes the kidnapper smoked?"

"Marlboro Lights," Tracey replied. "I saw them on the dresser after I smashed the lamp against his head."

"Tracey, do you remember what possessions you had with you at the Mall?" the sergeant asked, leaning forward in his chair next to the bed.

"Just the usual stuff you would take shopping," Tracey said, biting her lower lip and looking up at the ceiling. "The clothes I was wearing, my wallet, and my car keys."

Conrad gave her a few seconds to add anything else and then asked, "Tracey, can you remember what you had in your wallet?"

Tracey looked up at the ceiling again as she appeared to think about the question and then said, "I think I had about eighteen dollars in cash, two credit cards, my library card, and my driver's license."

After mentioning her driver's license, Tracey's body stiffened and her eyes widened.

"Do you think he still has my wallet?" she asked.

"If he's smart, he won't keep it," Conrad said, dreading what he had to say next. "However, we have to assume that he's seen your driver's license and knows your home address."

Tracey's face turned pale.

"Will he try to get me?" she asked.

Conrad saw she was trying to maintain her composure, but her body was trembling.

"He would be stupid to try to contact you again; that's the most likely way for him to get caught," Conrad said. "The important thing is that you are always aware of your environment and don't place yourself in any situation where you are alone and potentially vulnerable."

"I thought it was over, but it's not," Tracey whispered as her green eyes became watery.

"We can't assume that your assailant will be reckless and try to contact you again, but we also can't bury our heads in the sand and assume he won't," Conrad said. "If Detective Lombardi has no further questions, I'm going to call your parents into the room."

The sergeant glanced at Lombardi and she shook her head. Conrad went to the door, opened it, and waved to Tracey's parents, who were waiting in chairs next to the nurse's station.

They hurried over and Conrad held the door for them as they entered.

Lombardi stood and offered her chair to Mrs. Randall, as Conrad placed his hand on Mr. Randall's shoulder and gestured to his own chair.

"Please sit down, Mr. and Mrs. Randall," Conrad said, as Lombardi stood beside him with her arms crossed in a show of solidarity. "I don't want to frighten you, but we need to talk about how to protect you and your daughter in case the kidnapper attempts to contact her again."

"Is she still at risk?" Mrs. Randall's green eyes widened, as her daughter's had earlier. Conrad noticed a striking resemblance.

"We can't be sure of anything, Mrs. Randall, but I want you and your family to take precautions."

"Is he going to come after her again?" Mr. Randall asked, his face turning ashen.

"Mr. Randall, we can't assume that anything bad is going to happen, but there are some basic things you can do to keep your family safe."

Conrad glanced at Tracey and was surprised to see that her eyebrows were knitted together and her forehead creased into an expression of determined concentration. She didn't look scared anymore; she looked angry and resolved to fight.

"I thought this was over," Mrs. Randall said, sobbing.

Mr. Randall stood up, went to his wife, and placed his hands on her shoulders.

"Mom and Dad, please pay attention to him, we have to listen to what he has to say," Tracey said.

As if Tracey was the parent, Mr. and Mrs. Randall obediently focused their attention on Conrad.

"First, the obvious suggestion: always lock all the doors and windows of your house," Conrad said. "Also consider getting a home security system. They're expensive, but worth it for the peace of mind. Is there any place that Tracey could stay for a while until we catch this guy?"

"She could stay at my sister's house in Rhode Island," Mrs. Randall said, hopefully.

"Mom, I'm not going to hide from this creep," Tracey interjected. "We don't know how long it's going to take to catch him or even if they're going to catch him. I'm not going to change anything in my life because of what that loser did."

Conrad couldn't help but smile at the teenager's verve.

"Tracey, from the way you dealt with your kidnapper, I have no doubt that you can take care of yourself. But please follow these precautions just to be safe. First, make sure your house is secure at all times. Second, always be aware of your environment and avoid situations where you are alone outside the home. Travel in groups whenever possible; never go out by yourself; always go out with friends, preferably more than one. Stay in public places whenever possible. Be aware of the cars and people in your neighborhood such as a jogger who doesn't belong or a vehicle that drives around aimlessly." Conrad paused as he considered. "I would suggest always carrying mace or pepper spray. Take a self-defense course if you can. I'm not trying to scare you; I just want you to be safe." Conrad paused to take a deep breath. "I'm going to see if we can place a police detail on your street for at least a couple days in case the kidnapper becomes reckless enough to try his luck. The detail should scare him away in the short run, but you can't always depend on it."

Lombardi gave Tracey her business card.

"Call me if you remember anything else or feel unsafe at any-time," the detective said, handing Tracey the card. Tracey appeared to be reassured as she took it.

"Don't hesitate to call us if you see anything unusual or feel that someone or something is out of place," Conrad said. "When are you planning to return home?"

"The doctor told us she's going to be released tomorrow morning," Mr. Randall said.

"Okay, I'll have a detail in place on your street when you get there," the sergeant said. "Tracey, you stated earlier that the kidnapper drove a black sedan, but you weren't sure of the make?"

"Yes, it looked like a Japanese-made car; it could have been a Honda, Toyota, or Hyundai."

"At least that narrows it down," Conrad said. "We'll inform the detail officers to look out for a black, possibly Japanese-manufactured sedan in the neighborhood.

"What does this detail consist of?" Mr. Randall asked.

"One officer in a cruiser," Lombardi said. "We can't guarantee how long we can keep him/her there, but it will scare the hell out of the suspect if he decides to visit your neighbor-hood."

"How can I get mace or pepper spray to protect myself?" Tracey asked.

"They changed the law recently in Massachusetts so you no longer need an FID card to purchase it, so you should be able to find it any sporting goods store."

"Officers, I appreciate your help," Tracey said. "Thank you for looking out for me."

"No problem," Conrad replied. "Call us if you need anything. You have Detective Lombardi's card, but you can also call the station anytime for any reason. Just say the word and we'll send a car out to you. Hang in there. You're a tough young lady and you're going to be just fine. Do you need anything else?"

Mr. Randall stood up and shook Conrad's hand, "Thank you for all your help, sergeant."

Mr. Randall then offered his hand to Lombardi. "Thank you for your help, detective."

"No problem." Lombardi replied, taking his hand. "Call us if you need anything."

"We will," Mrs. Randall said, standing and placing her arm around her husband's waist.

"Be safe," Conrad said, nodding at each member of the family before heading toward the door. He felt reassured when Tracey flashed him what appeared to be a genuine smile. Conrad thought it was important to Tracey for someone to finally hear her story, and now that she had told it, she appeared more confident and at ease.

CHAPTER 29

I don't know what time it is when I wake up because I smashed my alarm clock yesterday. Pieces of it are scattered across the worn gray carpet of my bedroom floor. Cracks of light shine in from the edges of my window shade, so I know it's daytime. Morning or afternoon I couldn't say.

I had a difficult time sleeping last night because of my heightened excitement; imagining the intimate details of my revenge kept me up until the wee hours of the morning. I had to drink a quarter of a bottle of Jack Daniels just to fall asleep.

When I finally fell asleep, I had a horrific nightmare. Or more accurately, it was a vivid flashback to something that happened when I was eight-years-old; my parents had just hired a new nanny to watch me after school while they worked late. The nanny was great at first – she played with me and acted like she was my friend. She was young and pretty – a curvy brunette. She couldn't have been any older than twenty.

But after a few weeks, she changed. I don't know if she was bored with me or if I was an especially annoying child, but she lost all patience with me. She became irritated by everything I did.

She brought me to the Big Den, parked me in a recliner in

front of the 60-inch television screen, and handed me the remote control. She told me to watch TV while she did work for my mom and dad. I asked what kind of work she was doing, but she frowned at me and said she would punish me if I kept asking questions.

My natural childish curiosity got the better of me. As I sat flipping through the channels with the remote control – lingering periodically on scary movies – I began to wonder what my nanny was doing. What project was she working on for my mom and dad? It kept bothering me.

I made a thorough search of the house starting with the ground floor. First, I checked the indoor pool/ locker room, billiard room, indoor movie theatre, and game room in case she was having fun without including me. Then, I checked the front hall, dining room, kitchen, living room, library, small den, study, and even the walk-in freezer. It took me an hour to search all the rooms on the first floor and when I didn't find her, I went upstairs.

Upstairs, I checked all the offices, guest bedrooms, and bathrooms. I still couldn't find her until I headed toward my parents' bedroom. As I approached the room, I heard strange muffled sounds emanating from behind the closed door. Being a stupid eight-year-old, I had no idea what was going on.

I crept to the door and turned the knob. Opening the door just wide enough to see in, I peered inside.

At the time, I couldn't make sense of what I was seeing. My nanny wasn't wearing any clothes and it looked like she was wrestling with a man on the bed. It seemed like she was losing because she was making strange noises. I became worried because I thought the boy was hurting her. I was thinking about sneaking away and dialing 9-1-1 when my nanny happened to turn her head in my direction and locked eyes with me.

Her eyes widened with shock at first and then an expression of fury contorted her formerly pretty features into an evil mask of rage.

"John, get the fuck off me," she said. "Look!"

She pointed at me and the man's eyes widened as he turned.

"I thought you said you were keeping him busy," John said.

"I thought I was. Get the fuck off!"

I saw my nanny push the man off her, spring up from the bed, and stalk toward me with that same scary expression of rage distorting her formerly attractive features. I got scared, so I shut the door and ran down the hallway.

I only got about twenty feet when a shrill voice screamed at me, "Get back here you little freak!"

Terrified, I stopped dead in my tracks. I was too scared to move, so I just stood there and heard her heavy-footed thumping advancing down the hall. I felt hands grab my shoulders so hard it hurt. She spun me around and slapped me in the face so hard that it felt like a swarm of bees had stung my cheek. I remember I was shaking as she bent down and held her index finger inches away from my face.

"You've been a bad, bad boy! I told you to stay in the den and watch movies! I told you not to leave! Why did you leave?"

She still wasn't wearing any clothes, and I had no idea what I was seeing, but I guessed it was bad because my mom told me to always wear clothes. I stared at her breasts and curves as if they were part of an alien landscape. I started crying, but it didn't soften her. She grabbed me by the scruff of my neck and dragged me to my bedroom.

"Now I have to punish you," she said, as she shoved me into

my room.

Hauling me to the closet like a piece of luggage, she pushed me in and slammed the door shut. I stood there in the dark with hanging clothes draped over my face and shoulders. I heard scraping noises outside and then something was shoved against the door. I tried to turn the knob, but it didn't move. Later, I realized she had wedged the chair from my desk against the doorknob. I was trapped. I don't know how long I stayed there, but it seemed like a very long time – many hours. I sat down and cried until I dozed off.

When the door finally opened an indeterminate amount of time later, my nanny was wearing clothes again.

"If you tell your parents anything, I will lock you in the closet and never let you out!" she threatened me with a harsh whisper that reminded me of a snake's hiss. "Do you understand?"

I think I just nodded at her.

She brought me back to the big den, sat me in front of the entertainment center, and handed me the remote again.

"If you leave here, I'll make you sorry you did," she said.

After that, I was too scared to leave. I only got up from the recliner to go to the bathroom and get snacks from the kitchen. I never told my parents because I believed her, and I didn't want to get locked in the closet forever.

After that, TV became my babysitter and I learned about life by watching endless movies. At first, I was fascinated by horror movies because I liked monsters and being scared, but as I grew older, I naturally became interested in the plethora of soft-core pornography that infested cable TV like a plague.

I became fascinated by the naked bodies on the screen, and it didn't take me long to figure out what my nanny was doing with the man on my parents' bed. She was doing something bad, and I would be punished for it if I watched her do it again. I never left the den after that.

Body trembling, I return to the present. I realize it wasn't a nightmare, but a vivid flashback. I'm covered in sweat and shivering. The memory has made me feel powerless and vulnerable.

I'm hesitant to stand up from my bed because I'm afraid my head will pound like it's being struck by a sledgehammer.

Finally, I bite the bullet and stand. I feel a little woozy, but at least my head isn't pounding. Not yet at least.

I update my diary on my laptop and trudge to the kitchen to consume a bowl of cereal. It helps to calm my stomach. I only drink water because I want to be clear-headed for today's stalking mission. I need to keep my mind sharp so I can focus on grabbing the slut. As soon as I get the opportunity, I'll pull a snatch and grab. I'll take her up north again and continue where I left off. This time, I will show her no mercy.

I push the empty bowl of cereal away without bothering to clear it from the table. The place is becoming a mess; dirty dishes are scattered across the counter-tops and cigarette butts litter the white plastic tiles. Usually, I'm a clean-freak, but lately I've been slacking.

I light a cigarette at the kitchen table, smoke it down to the filter, and crush it out on the floor with the others. Black patches of ash are strewn over the white surface beneath my feet like bomb craters on a miniature arctic landscape.

I'm starting to feel a headache coming on, which is bad because I have a lot of work to do today. Maybe a small dose of caffeine might help my hangover. I pour a glass of Mountain Dew and swill it down in several gulps. Holding my right hand in front of my face, I feel anxious when I notice it trembling slightly. No more caffeine.

I take three extra-strength Tylenol tablets with a glass of water, return to the bedroom, sit down at my computer desk, and log onto the Internet while I wait for the tablets to work. While waiting, I check the band-aids on the side of my head. One of them peeled off during the night, but I was planning to replace them both anyway.

I Google the Westfield Police web-site and search for the application for a License to Carry. After scrolling through the site, I find it and print it out.

I fill out the LTC form carefully. When I reach the references section, I write down the name and phone number of my supervisor at work, and the names and numbers of some of my parents' friends who will vouch for me out of loyalty. My supervisor at the mall thinks I'm a good worker because I rarely call out sick, never complain, and do whatever he asks me to do. Sucker.

I don't worry too much when I reach the section of the application requesting information about a criminal record because I don't have one. Not even a misdemeanor. Charges were never filed against me for the supposed assault in college.

The Westfield Police web site states that I have to make an appointment to apply for a License to Carry. No problem. I'll do that now. I pick up my cell phone, dial information, talk to an operator, and obtain the Westfield Police business number.

I'm about to start dialing the number when the hand that is holding the phone starts to tremble violently. In a few seconds, I'm shaking so badly that the phone almost slips out of my grasp. What if I call and make a mistake and say the wrong thing? What if I accidentally say something stupid that makes the police realize who I am? The faint tremor in my hands spreads across my arms and throughout my whole body.

I reach for my cigarettes and lighter in my jeans pockets and pull them out with quivering fingers. I place the skull-and-crossbones lighter on the computer desk while I take out a cigarette. The cigarette wavers in my hand as I place it in my mouth. Picking up the lighter, I have to concentrate to get it to line up with the cigarette. As soon as the tobacco lights, I suck the nicotine-laced smoke down my throat, hold it for a few seconds, and blow it out.

I have to get a hold of myself. Why am I freaking out about making a simple phone call? Maybe my mind is rebelling against the idea of having any interaction with the police. After all, they're the same people who are trying to hunt me down and put me in prison for life. I was never afraid of the police before, but then again, no one ever escaped from me before. This is a whole new situation. Someone can identify me.

I am tempted to go to the kitchen and reach into the cabinet above the stove to retrieve the half-bottle of Jack Daniels that's left over from last night. But if I do that, my breath will smell like alcohol, and I don't want to be memorable. Besides, I don't want to lose my edge while I do my first recon of the bitch's neighborhood. I have to find a way to calm down.

Glancing around the bedroom, I look for an object to vent my wrath on. Unfortunately, every object I see is something I need. I'm not going to smash my computer because I need it to hunt for my victims' personal information, to do research, and to write my diary. If I smash the lamp on my night table, I'll inconvenience myself when it's dark. I want to punch a wall, but I'm afraid that a neighbor will hear the loud crash and report me to the landlord.

My eyes focus on the corner where my black-light poster of

the Grim Reaper hangs. It's a cool-as-hell poster of a hooded figure sweeping a vicious-looking scythe toward the viewer with lightning flashing in a dark background. I found the poster in one of those swinging racks in the back of Spencer's Gifts. I imagined that it was my reinvented self beneath the dark robe holding the scythe.

My eyes focus on the curtains and window-shade. If I rip those to pieces, I won't be able to sleep during the day. Many of my activities are performed at night, so this would be unacceptable.

Fuck it. The poster has to go. I spring up from my seat and the next thing I know I'm tearing the poster off the wall and ripping it to shreds. Scattering the strips across the floor, I feel a little better, but when I hold my hand in front of my face, it's still trembling.

There's nothing else that I can destroy in the room without causing me a major inconvenience, so I stalk over to the living room. There's a couch, recliner, coffee table, television stand, flat-screen television, cable box, DVD player, side-table, table lamp, and clock on the wall. The clock reads 9:28 AM; there's still plenty of time to go on a recon mission in the bitch's neighborhood.

I don't need to know what time it is when I'm watching horror movies on cable in the living room, and I figure I rarely ever use the table lamp, so I make the logical decision to pull the cheap plastic clock off its hook in the wall and break it apart with my bare hands. The clock's white plastic shell cracks open like an egg and tiny mechanical pieces spill out of it like metal guts. I drop it on the floor and I'm about to stomp on it when I realize I'm not wearing anything on my feet.

I stride over to the side table, rip the shade off the lamp, and attempt to tear it apart, but it's made of some kind of sturdy material that won't rip easily, so I drop it on the floor and crush it under my bare heel. I pick up the lamp, tear the cord out of its socket, and smash the bare bulb into the wall; I enjoy the sound of shattering glass. I twist off the metal casing that surrounds the shattered bulb and hurl what remains of the structure into the wall, putting a sizable dent in the plaster. So much for not making any noise.

Looking around for more materials to destroy, I focus on the curtains and shade hanging on the living room window. Since I don't ever sleep in this room, I don't need window accoutrements, so I pull the shade out of its socket, unravel it, and throw it into the hallway with one hand, while tearing down the curtains with the other. The curtains are thick, so there's not much I can do to them but toss them on the floor.

Breathing hard, I hold my hand in front of my face. It trembles ever so slightly, but I doubt it would be noticeable to anyone else. Good enough, I'm ready to make the call.

I have no problem lighting a cigarette on my way to the bedroom to get my cell-phone. Placing the lit butt in my mouth, I pick up the phone and the scrap of paper next to it on the desk. I dial the number and take a drag from my cigarette as I wait for someone to pick up.

"Westfield Police, this call is recorded," a young male voice answers.

I go into social mode: "Hi, my name is Eric Blackburn and I would like to set up an appointment to apply for an LTC."

"Okay, no problem. I'll check with the secretary," the dispatcher replies.

I take another drag off my cigarette and pace across the room while I wait.

"Sir, when would you like to make your appointment?"

"As soon as possible," I say.

"Can you come in today at 2:00 o'clock?" the dispatcher asks.

"Sure, no problem," I say, grinning. "Do you know how long it takes to process the application?"

"It usually takes about a month," the dispatcher replies, "and just to let you know, there's a hundred dollar fee."

Even the mention of the money can't dampen my excitement.

"Sure, do you prefer check or cash?" I ask.

"Either one is fine. When you arrive, just ask for the secretary, Diane."

"Okay, I'll see you at two."

"Goodbye, sir."

A Cheshire-cat smile spreads across my face as I click the "off" button on my phone. In one month, I will be able to upgrade my weapon of choice from a knife to a handgun, and then blast a hole in the slut if she tries to escape from me again.

CHAPTER 30

Jim Conrad hardly slept the night after interviewing Tracey Randall. Tossing and turning, he had nightmares that his own twelve-year-old daughter had been kidnapped by the psychopath stalking the community. Tracey Randall was still in danger, and this made the situation hit home with brutal force.

Until last night, he had been able to create some distance between his emotions and the investigation, but now it was becoming increasingly difficult – if not impossible. He found himself alternating between worrying about the safety of Tracey Randall and his own daughter, Jessica Conrad.

Conrad's wife, Laurie, had noticed him tossing and turning during the night, and asked him if something was wrong. He didn't want to tell her the truth for fear of worrying her. He told her he was having trouble sleeping because he was coming down with a cold.

Laurie was an English teacher at Westfield High School and she worried enough about his occupation. If he let slip any of the sordid details pertaining to his investigation, she might also start to lose sleep and that wouldn't do anyone any good.

Laurie knew about the murder and kidnapping at the mall,

but she thought Detective Lombardi was conducting the investigation. How could she know that Lombardi needed all the help she could get with the case?

When Laurie left for work at 6:15 AM, Jim kissed her goodbye and told her he loved her – as if nothing was wrong. But if nothing was wrong, then why couldn't he return to bed to catch up on his lost sleep?

Last night, he and Detective Lombardi didn't return to the station from their interview with Tracey Randall until after midnight. It was only a fifteen-minute drive from the station to his home in the adjacent town of Holliston, but when he arrived, it had taken him another two hours to unwind and by then it was after 2 AM.

Conrad faked a cheerful demeanor as he encountered his thirteen-year-old daughter in the upstairs hallway. He figured that his facial expression probably didn't matter anyway because she barely nodded her head as she trudged past him toward the bathroom. She rarely became fully alert until after she had taken a shower, but it didn't hurt to be careful.

Conrad knew that after Jessica took a shower, she was more energetic and liked to chat, but this time he avoided her by going into the study while she was eating breakfast alone in the kitchen. Normally, he would have asked her how she was doing and started a conversation.

When Jessica left the house to go to school, Jim stood by the living room window and watched her while she waited for the bus. She was standing with another neighborhood kid, a big-for-his-age, fourteen-year-old football player who could probably handle himself against an attacker, but Jim still felt better when three additional neighborhood girls and two boys showed up.

Jim paced back and forth in the living room as he glanced out the front window from time to time to check on the teenagers. He breathed a sigh of relief when he finally saw them board the bus safely.

Since he couldn't sleep, Jim decided to go to the station to try to get some work done. After showering and dressing, he prepared extra-strong coffee. He took a large gulp as he went out the front door and headed toward his red Camry parked in the driveway. Placing his coffee thermos in a cup-holder, he slid into the driver's seat. He took another gulp before turning the key in the ignition.

Conrad drove to work as if he was on autopilot as his sleep-deprived, over-taxed mind tried to brainstorm how to catch the psychopath before he struck again.

It was a beautiful, cloudless, sunny fall day, but the bright weather didn't help quell a sick feeling in the pit of his stomach. He wondered if he would feel like this until the killer was caught. He certainly hoped not.

Jim tried to alleviate his depression by taking another titanic swig of his coffee. He felt it gave him an energy surge, but he couldn't be sure if it wasn't just a placebo effect.

He slowed down as he approached a flashing yellow light in front of the retirement complex, made sure no one needed to cross the street, and proceeded toward the police station. He passed the Westfield Historical Society on the right as he approached the station on the left.

Jim pulled into the station entranceway and cut through the front parking lot to the narrow lane running along the side of the building to the back parking lot. He was surprised when he saw Lombardi's blue unmarked vehicle in one of the spots next to a black-and-white. He parked in the open space next to it, got out, and headed for the back door of the station.

What was Lombardi doing here so early? Maybe she couldn't sleep either. This was the type of case that gnawed at your psyche like a grave-robbing ghoul feeding on a corpse.

Jim entered the back corridor and passed the evidence locker, break room, and locker-room. He entered the main cubicle area where the report-writing desks were located. He didn't have his own desk, so he had a choice of using three generic "Officers' Desks" equipped with computers linked to the main police system.

Jim walked past the empty desks and headed for the dispatch control center at the front of the building. He poked his head in and spoke to the twenty-six-year old, cop-wannabe dispatcher, Jack Reynolds.

"Hey, Jack, how's it going?"

"Hey, Sarge, you're in early today," Jack said, glancing at the clock on the wall, which read 7:15 AM.

"I just wanted to check and make sure a patrol car was stationed outside Tracey Randall's house," Jim said, crossing his arms as he leaned against the frame of the dispatch doorway.

"Yep, it's all set," the dispatcher said, checking his computer screen. "The lieutenant set up a detail based on Detective Lombardi's call last night."

"Do you know who's working it?" Jim asked.

"Rob Gregory is working it, Sarge."

Gregory was a twenty-four-year-old rookie fresh out of the Police Academy, but he seemed competent enough.

"Does he know what to look for?" Jim asked.

"The lieutenant told him to keep a look-out for any cars or people that don't belong in the neighborhood."

"How would he know who belongs or doesn't belong in the neighborhood?" Jim asked without expecting an answer from the dispatcher, who raised his eyebrows at him. "He should be on the lookout for any vehicle driven by a dark-haired man in his early to late twenties. The suspect could be driving a black Japanese-made sedan or some other rented vehicle. Can you get this information to him?"

"No problem, Sarge. I'll do it right away," the dispatcher said, keying the mike on the radio. "Westfield Control to 924."

"Twenty-four's on," Gregory replied from his cruiser radio.

"The Sarge says to be on the lookout for a dark-haired man in his mid-to-late-twenties driving around the neighborhood in a black, possibly Japanese-manufactured sedan or another rented vehicle of unknown description."

"What does he want me to do if I see someone who matches the description?" Gregory's voice spoke from the microphone.

The dispatcher glanced up at the sergeant leaning against the door frame.

"Tell him to pull him over, check his ID, and find out his reason for being in the neighborhood," Jim said, impatiently.

"The Sarge wants you to pull him over and check his Identification," Jack said, as he pressed down on the mike.

"Received, Control," Gregory replied.

"All set, Sarge?" the dispatcher asked, glancing up at Jim leaning in the doorway.

"All set for now," Jim said, frowning. "I'll let you know when I get any further information for the detail officer."

"Okay, Sarge."

Jim left the dispatch center and cut across the spacious cubicle room to the side hallway where the chief, lieutenant, and detective's offices were located.

CHAPTER 31

I feel better after making the phone call to set up my LTC appointment. In about a month's time, I'll have official permission from my local police department to carry a concealed firearm. Then I can kidnap, torture, and dismember the slut without worrying about her escaping again.

However, right now I need to formulate a plan to recon the bitch's neighborhood. I can't risk taking my car because she may remember what it looks like. That means I have to use a rental to conduct surveillance, which means I have to raid my emergency money stash that I tucked away in a small safe in my closet. I hate to use my emergency funds, but making sure that I don't get caught and sent to prison for life qualifies as an emergency in my book.

I feel a rush as I enter the bedroom and head toward the closet. The safe is also where I keep my most intimate treasures: the pictures of my victims in various states of disassembly. Sliding open the closet door, I bend down to reach the safe on the floor. I sit, Indian-style, on the floor so I can concentrate. My hand trembles slightly as I reach for the combination lock, but I don't feel badly about it, I know the tremors are caused by excitement rather than nervousness.

The first time I try to open the lock, I dial the numbers incorrectly and nothing happens. I'm successful on the second try; I start to salivate as soon as I hear the click. Obtaining my slush fund is the perfect excuse to look at my art collection. As a rule, I try not to look too often because it's addictive and distracting. While I'm grabbing the money, I'll take a quick look.

Reaching into the safe, I wrap my fingers around a thick envelope. Opening the envelope, I count out twenty fifty-dollar bills; it should be enough to get me started. After placing the money in my wallet, I reach for the folder at the bottom of the pile.

Sweat breaks out on my forehead as I feel my heart beat fast within my chest. As my fingers close around the folder, I feel my groin stiffening. Opening the folder, a rush of excitement blasts through my brain as I gaze upon the first picture: an unconscious, naked teenage girl lying spread-eagled on a clear plastic sheet on the cellar floor of my parent's cabin – her arms amputated at the elbows and her legs at the knees. At that point, I had cauterized her wounds with a blowtorch and soaked up most of the blood from the sheet. The picture is truly a work of art; I should have been a professional photographer. Her complete helplessness turns me on.

Savoring her vulnerability, I move on to the next picture: another girl who is mostly intact with the exception of a missing left forearm. I haven't cauterized the wound yet, so blood is still spraying out of the red stump as if it's being shot from a high-powered hose.

Unfortunately, she's unconscious so she doesn't feel a thing, but that couldn't be helped because of the screaming I mentioned earlier. My plaything would have died from shock if I hadn't softened her up with enough Oxycontin to sedate a grown man.

Inflicting pain on people who deserve it can be such a rush. The "deserving" category includes attractive women of all ages, but especially attractive teenage girls. They're the ones who laughed at me in middle school.

A flash-back image forms in my head of two attractive teenage girls laughing as one of their boyfriends holds my shoulders down, while the other one stands behind me and uses all his strength to pull my underwear upward until the band almost reaches my shoulders. The girls' laughter penetrates like knives as it overlaps with the sound of my ripping underwear. To make matters worse, the sight of the girls' teenage bodies and the pressure on my groin gives me a hard-on. When the girls see my erection, they laugh even harder.

Apparently, the sight of my erection makes the boys angry because they begin to beat me with their fists and call me a "pervert" and a "freak." The girls' laughing subsides as they join in with the boys by hissing comments like "he's sick" and "kick his ass." I fall down and the girls start kicking me. As pain wracks my body, I remember thinking that I would get them back for what they were doing.

As my mind returns to the present, I realize that my hands have clenched into fists and I've crumpled the picture I was holding into a ball. I didn't realize that I was destroying the art work in my hands. I try to smooth out the wrinkled picture, but it's irretrievably damaged, which is unfortunate. Every picture is a special piece of art.

I feel the rage building. The vicious flashback has caused the old feelings of shame and humiliation to return. The only way I can beat down these emotions is to overpower them with rage or to get off. Since there are no objects around to vent my rage on, I decide on the latter.

Sitting on the floor by the closet, I flip through the pictures to find the perfect one to calm my torment. I find a particularly good one consisting of a hot, naked blonde missing her left hand. I remember that I wanted to make the experience last, so I cut off her hand first, and after I had milked all the enjoyment I could out of it, I sliced off her forearm at the elbow. Boy, that bitch had a lot of blood in her. I only wish she could have felt it.

In the picture, her hand had just been severed, so it was resting beside the gory stump of her wrist. Blood was shooting out from the stump like one of those Vegas fountains that reach fifty feet in the air.

I feel myself getting hard again.

I bring the picture over to the bed, drop my pants, and go to work. It's over in less than a minute and I have to retrieve a towel from the bathroom to mop up the mess. When I recover, I place the picture back with the other works of art and re-secure the safe. Now I can concentrate on what I must do.

I use my laptop to log onto Map-quest. I punch in my address, and the address on the bitch's driver's license. The directions to her house pop up on the screen like magic. I hook up the laptop to my printer and click the mouse on the "print" option. Seconds later, I have a hardcopy in my hands. Folding the paper, I place it in my jeans pocket next to my bottle of pepper spray.

I leave my apartment and light a cigarette on my way to the elevator. Reaching the metal double-doors, I press the "down" button and they open. A cloud of smoke hovers in the confined space as I descend.

As I walk out of the elevator, I cough and take another drag from my cigarette. Leaving the building, I cross the short walkway to my personal parking space.

I stamp my cigarette out on the asphalt before sliding into the driver's seat.

It's only a fifteen minute drive to the rental agency in Farmington. As I drive into the parking lot – stocked with a variety of unimpressive cars – I hold my hand in front of my face and notice it's steady. Must be from looking at my pictures earlier.

I park in front of the rental building, get out of the car, and open the front glass door. An attractive, brunette, twenty-something is at the front counter. Focusing on her breasts poking out under her blue sweater, I feel a surge of rage, but I suppress it by concentrating on the business at hand.

"Hi, I'd like to rent a car for a week," I say, forcing a smile.

"No problem, sir. What kind of car are you looking for?" the slut asks.

If only she knew what I would do to her if I had her at my cabin.

"Nothing fancy. Just something cheap to get me from Point A to Point B."

The brunette stares at a computer screen while she types. "We have a Ford Focus available that might meet your needs."

The only thing that will meet my needs is to separate your limbs from your body as you scream in agony. This thought causes a genuine smile to form on my face. The girl smiles back, believing I am being friendly. Stupid bitch.

I feel powerful as I reach into my wallet for a stack of fifty dollar bills, count them out, and hand them to the brunette. After handing me back my change, she asks to see my credit card and I sign all the usual paperwork.

"Would you like insurance?" she asks.

"No, I'm a very safe driver," I reply.

I'm telling the truth; I've never been in an accident – not even a fender-bender if you exclude when I ran down the home-less man a few days ago.

The brunette hands me a copy of my paperwork, which I fold and place in my pocket next to my wallet. I don't feel like forcing another fake smile, so I say "thank you" – just so I won't arouse suspicion – and leave the building.

Returning to my vehicle, I consult the map that I printed from Map-quest. It shouldn't be a problem to find the bitch's neighborhood. If I can get her alone for even a few seconds, I'll grab her and no one will ever see her again.

CHAPTER 32

As he entered the side corridor of the station, Jim Conrad heard voices from an open doorway. He stepped through the doorway to find the portly Chief Willard seated at the head of the long table, while the lieutenant and detective sat at the center.

All eyes turned toward the sergeant as he entered, and he noticed worry creases in every forehead. The Chief's pudgy face appeared redder than usual and the lieutenant's normally tanned visage was unusually pale. The dark circles under Detective Lombardi's eyes indicated she had not slept well last night either.

"Have a seat, Jim," the Chief said, wiping sweat from his forehead.

Conrad sat across from the detective and lieutenant. He rested his elbows on the table as he leaned forward intently.

"Thank you for setting up that cruiser detail at the Randall House, detective," Conrad said to Lombardi.

"No problem," Lombardi replied as she looked down at the table, shuffling the stack of paperwork in front of her.

"How long can we keep the detail going?" the sergeant asked the Chief.

The Chief glanced at the lieutenant and then returned his gaze to Conrad. "We can only afford the detail for one week."

Conrad raised his eyebrow. "Do you think we will apprehend the perpetrator by then?"

"Look, Jim, you know the recession has hit our budget hard and we're already maxed out on overtime," the lieutenant said.

"It's too bad there's no shortage of work in the killing and kidnapping business," Conrad replied, frowning.

The lieutenant's face reddened. "We don't have time to worry about how long the detail at the Randall house is going to last. We need to concentrate on our next move to catch this piece-of-shit before he strikes again."

"I can't argue with that logic, LT," Conrad said, crossing his arms as he leaned back in his chair.

"Did your interview with the Randall girl produce any leads?" the lieutenant directed his question to his daughter.

"Her description of the kidnapper matches the image that Sergeant Conrad obtained two days ago from the mall video camera," Lombardi said, closing her eyes and rubbing her temples.

Conrad thought that despite the dark circles under her eyes, Lombardi's dark Mediterranean features and raven-black hair still made her exotically attractive. He watched her pull a manila folder from the stack of papers in front of her, open it, thumb through it, take out a photo, and slide it across the table to her father.

Her father's eyes glinted as he glared at the photo of the suspect. Everything about the lieutenant from his jet-black hair to his lean, dark visage and taut, wiry frame reminded Conrad of a wolf.

"Were you able to determine from the interview which town the trucker picked up the girl in?" the Chief asked, crossing his hands over his pot belly as he sat up straight in his chair.

"We learned nothing new about the location of the pick-up from our interview," Conrad said. "The girl was completely lost, but we know from the East Brookfield police report that the driver was moving southwest on route 64. He estimated he had traveled about twenty miles after he picked up the young lady, so we can narrow it down to one or two towns to the west of the East Brookfield police station."

"Searching for the perpetrator's cabin isn't an option if we don't even know what town she was picked up in," the lieutenant interjected.

"Not necessarily," Conrad said. "It will just take more time."

"It's time we don't have," the Chief commented. "It's a long-shot and we can't waste our time with long-shots. This is the third incident that has occurred in our town within the last year, so the media will have us under a magnifying glass. We have to make observable progress quickly or we'll lose all credibility. A case like this could make or break this department."

"What about letting the media work for us for a change?" the lieutenant asked. "We could give them the picture of the suspect that Jimmy obtained from the mall surveillance camera and have them post it. Then, we could set up a hotline for people to call if they think they've seen him."

"Not a good idea," Conrad interjected with no hesitation. "There are two schools of thought when it comes to the media. One school is what you just mentioned: make them work for you. The other is 'don't let them get in the way.'

I'm for the second school. Think about it." Conrad paused as he made eye contact with each person in the room. "Do we really want the perp to know we have a picture of him? What if he gets spooked, leaves town, and starts kidnapping and killing somewhere else? I would rather have him in the dark about what we know. If he knows what we have on him, he can stay one step ahead of us."

"I agree with Jimmy on this one, Dad," Lombardi said. "We can't show our cards to this psycho. We have to keep him in the dark."

"All right, fair enough. Did the crime scene techs make any progress with the forensic evidence?" the lieutenant asked his daughter.

The detective searched through her paperwork until she found the preliminary report from the state police. "The techs analyzed the sneaker print they found in the victim's blood, and determined the perpetrator wears a size twelve-wide. The tread design on the sneaker-print belongs to a rare Massachusetts brand called Rockport. There are only two styles of this particular sneaker: one white and one black."

"I think we can rule out the white," Conrad commented. "It wouldn't work for stealth. It's more likely that he was wearing black. I know it's another long shot, but most people replace their sneakers every year or so, so we could isolate the local retailers that carry Rockport sneakers and check their sales records for the past year, if they still have them. Maybe the perp bought the sneakers with a credit card."

"That's an interesting idea, but it's another long shot," the Chief said. "We need to create an immediate plan of action that will yield results quickly so we can keep the media pacified. At this point, we can't waste our time with long shots."

Conrad remained silent to give Lombardi a chance to reply. When she didn't say anything, he spoke up.

"The first thing we need is a large map; it has to be big enough to cover an office wall," the sergeant said, making eye contact with each person at the table, starting with the Chief and ending with the detective. "Then, we need to call all the area departments and record the times and locations of the perpetrator's crimes since he began his reign of terror in this region. This will allow us to create a geographic profile that we can use to pinpoint the probable location of the killer's residence and the most likely location of his next attack."

The sergeant paused to let the information sink in.

"That sounds promising," the Chief said, turning to Lombardi. "Detective, are you all right with this plan?"

"Absolutely," Lombardi replied, nodding. "I can easily find a good map of the area on-line and print it out. Then, I'll simply enlarge it. I'll return to the station with the map and we can pin it to a wall in my office. I should be able to get it all done in less than an hour."

"All right, that's more like it. Now that we have an objective, let's get cracking," the Chief said, picking up his paperwork and standing up.

The others took the Chief's lead, stood up, and followed him out of the conference room. The Chief and lieutenant took a left down the hallway toward their offices while Conrad took a right toward the common report-writing room.

"Where are you going?" Lombardi asked.

"I'm going to grab a desk and start making phone calls," Conrad said.

"Why don't you use my office? You'll have more privacy

there," she said.

Conrad was surprised, but he went with the flow. "Okay, Marilyn," he said, doing an about-face toward her office.

"The door's open. I'll meet you there after I get the map," Lombardi said.

"That sounds like a plan," Conrad replied, nodding at Lombardi as they passed in the hallway.

Conrad felt strange being alone in Lombardi's office, but he agreed with her that it was a better place to make the phone calls. He shut the door behind him, sat down at her desk, took out his notepad, thumbed through it, and picked up the telephone. He began dialing the first number on his list.

Detective Lombardi returned less than an hour later with an impressive map. Conrad was speaking to a detective from the small town of Holliston when she entered the office carrying the map. Conrad told the detective he would call him back. He glanced down at the time on the computer and saw it was already 11:15 AM.

"Where do you want to put it?" Conrad asked.

"How about right behind you?" Lombardi replied.

Conrad looked behind him and saw the wall was mostly blank with the exception of the detective's framed copies of her degrees from Farmington State University and Anna Maria College.

"We'll have to take down your college degrees," Conrad said, cracking a half-smile.

"I think my ego will survive," Lombardi said, returning his smile as she placed the rolled-up map on her desk. She went to the back wall, took down the framed degrees, and placed them on the desk. She pulled out the hooks in the wall and tossed them in the small waste-basket by the door.

"Let's do it," she said.

Working together, they spread the map out on the wall and tacked it up. Conrad admired the map for a moment with his hands on his hips. Then, he picked up his notebook from the desk, thumbed through it, and stopped at the last page he had been writing on.

"We have to make a few more phone calls before we have all the information we need," he said.

"Give me a number and I'll go out in the hallway to make a call on my cell phone while you use my desk phone," Lombardi said.

Conrad tried not to show his surprise as he ripped a page out of his notebook and handed it to Lombardi. She left the office and shut the door, presumably to give him some privacy. He couldn't understand why she was letting him use her office while she downgraded herself to the hallway.

As he tried to recover his composure, he heard Lombardi's muffled voice behind the door asking to speak to a detective. Not wanting to lag behind, he dialed the number of the Marlboro police. The phone rang once before the dispatcher picked it up.

"Marlboro police, this call is recorded," the dispatcher said.

"This is Sergeant Conrad with the Westfield Police. I need to speak to the detective on duty."

"Hold on a second, sir, and I'll transfer you to his extension."

The phone rang twice and a male voice answered. "This is Detective Lawrence. How may I help you?"

"I'm Sergeant Jim Conrad with the Westfield Police. You may have heard about the kidnapping and murder in our town several days ago."

"Yes, I did. I was sorry to hear about it."

"I understand that you had a similar kidnapping in your town two years ago. Do you know what the date of that incident was?"

"Give me a minute to look up the file," Detective Lawrence said.

Conrad waited impatiently for several minutes while he listened to file drawers opening and closing, and paper shuffling in the background.

"You still there?" the detective asked.

"Yep, I'm here."

"Susan Anderson disappeared on June 13, 2010," Detective Lawrence said.

"Do you mind reading me the report?" Conrad asked.

"No problem. I was the investigating officer, so I can tell you what happened."

"Even better," Conrad said.

"Susan was sixteen years old. She was crossing a restaurant parking lot at about 9 PM on a Friday night with a friend," the detective began. "Her friend, Rachel Markiewicz, witnessed the kidnapping. She testified that a tall, dark-haired man wearing a black leather jacket and dark blue jeans leaped out from behind a car and hit both girls with a blast of pepper spray. While Rachel was momentarily blinded, she heard a struggle occurring between the perpetrator and her friend. Her friend screamed, but her scream was cut off as the attacker covered her mouth with his hand. Rachel stated that when she opened her eyes, she saw the assailant dragging her friend away as he kept her mouth covered."

The detective paused to take a breath, and resumed his

monologue.

"Rachel stated that she was too afraid to move until the kidnapper reached a black car that was parked a few spots away. When she saw the perpetrator place handcuffs on her friend's wrists, she ran to the back of the car to check the license plate number. Rachel said she was too afraid to intervene as she watched the kidnapper shove Susan into the passenger seat of the car, shut the door, and go around to the driver's side – all while ignoring Rachel. Rachel took a picture of the license plate with her cell phone and got out of the way just in time as the perpetrator backed out of the parking space. She watched the car race across the parking lot and take a left when it reached the road. Then, Rachel dialed 9-1-1 and gave the police the license plate. The police ran the license plate number, but it came back to plates that were stolen from a vehicle in town. We followed a number of leads since it happened, but the investigation has gone cold."

CHAPTER 33

I look both ways before I pull out of the rental car parking lot and proceed in the direction of the bitch's house. The map is on the passenger seat so I can consult it whenever I need to. My intended victim is only several miles away across town. The dashboard clock reads 11:29; I have plenty of time before I need to be at the police station at 2 o'clock for my LTC appointment.

I turn on my favorite rock station to relax during the drive. AC/DC's Runaway Train is playing. The bass guitar slams out its heavy beat, strengthening my motivation to wreak havoc. Violent images flood my head as the music blasts from the speakers; I imagine hacking off limbs and watching blood spraying.

I drive more recklessly as the images permeate my mind, so I turn down the music in order to concentrate. There's no way I can afford to get pulled over by a cop for speeding.

It's hard to be cautious when you're excited, but I have to try. Focusing on the road ahead, I drive toward a pathetic cluster of buildings that compose a quaint commercial area of Westfield. There's not much here: a gas station/convenience store, a Honey Farms connected to a nail salon, a Bertucci's restaurant, a diner, a tanning joint, a lawyers' office, a Laundromat. Small town America at its best, what a joke.

People think they are safe within their suburban enclaves, but they're not – because people like me learn to travel undetected. It all goes back to when human beings were primordial hunter/gatherers and we had to track and kill our prey to survive. Most people have forgotten their primitive roots, but not me.

I drive past a geriatric community on my left, the blinking yellow light in the road reminds me to slow down when I pass, so I don't run over some old bastard. I speed up instead, but just as fast I have to tap the brakes as I approach the police station on the left. It's ironic that I have to drive by it to reach the slut's neighborhood. I don't look at the police station as I pass, so I won't psych myself out.

I pass a back road on my right that leads to a neighborhood referred to locally as "the Kings," a planned community built in the 1970's; all the houses look the same. The builders tried to mix it up a little with maybe two or three different designs, but it didn't fool anyone.
I pass the Westfield Historical Society on the right; I can't imagine what irrelevant moldering documents are contained inside that building. The only exciting thing this town has produced is me. I smile at my reflection in the rearview mirror.

Growing up in town is an advantage. After all, I explored the area extensively as a kid. Instead of socializing after school and risk being teased and beaten up by the other kids, I explored the woods.

I reach the part of town that makes me sick: the churches. On my left, an ostentatious tower rises out of an ornately designed Catholic Church, while a large, box-like structure across the street houses the plain protestant Congregational Church. Knowing a little about history, I despise both equally.

I may hate church, but I can't deny being entertained by some of the stories in the Bible. I especially like the part in the Old Testament when Moses's commanders inform him they have defeated an enemy army and killed all the men who opposed them, but they allowed the young boys and women to survive because they weren't a threat. Moses becomes angry and tells the commanders to kill all the young boys lest they grow up to fight against them in the future.

Then, the icing on the cake. Moses tells the commanders to kill all the older women because they're too old to reproduce. The only prisoners Moses allows his soldiers to spare are the young women of child-bearing age, so the horny Israelites can have sex with them and produce more Israelite warriors. Now that's a story I can get into.

There are a lot more stories in the Old Testament like the previous one, but I don't have time to write them down in my diary. I have absolutely no interest in the stories of the New Testament where Jesus hangs out with losers like prostitutes and tax collectors, and tells people to love and help each other. Those stories make me want to puke.

Once I read about the slaughters in the Old Testament, I couldn't go back to reading the boring parts. I was hooked. I skimmed through the ancient text until I found all the violent passages that I believe truly reflect human nature.

I drive by the churches and head toward another commercial area; there's a gas station next to a mini-mall that has a small park behind it with a baseball field, tennis courts, and a basketball court. I've visited the park in my youth, unknown to the children playing in it, and spied on them from the woods. I also captured and killed many small animals there.

I take a right before I reach this pitiful little section of build-

SHAWN WILLIAM DAVIS

ings and climb a hill past the Congregational Church toward the high school. It may be that the bitch doesn't live very far from the high school; maybe I can snatch her when she walks to or from school. It's worth a shot at least.

At the top of the hill, I drive past another line of older houses with dates written on their facades until a football/soccer field comes into view in a small valley to my left. There is a large parking lot next to the field and the actual high school building beyond it.

I didn't have as bad a time in high school as in I did in middle school, but I still get a sick feeling as I gaze at the structure. I feel as if I'm about to throw up as I observe a group of teenagers running around on the sports field. I have to turn away and resist the urge to drive through the fence, and run them all over.

Finally, I make it past the school and approach an intersection going left and right. If I take a left, I'll circle back toward the commercial area, but a right will take me to the bitch's house. I stop at the stop sign, look both ways, and proceed right.

The houses on this street are large, modern colonials that appear to be more expensive. I hope she isn't a spoiled rich bitch because it will only make matters worse. If that's the case, I will have to kill her slowly.

The curving road rises to the right to an embankment embedded with trees, and sinks to the left into a valley containing colonial houses spaced intermittently throughout green fields. Soon, the forest opens on the right to form clearings sprinkled with trees, which obscure dark, mysterious houses at the ends of long private driveways. To my left, the colonials in the valley fade away and are replaced by farmland complete with an impressive red barn, a marketplace to sell vegetables, horse stables, and seemingly endless crops.

Beyond the stables and fields I see the ever-present forest lurking in the distance. I'm pretty sure the slut's road is coming up soon on the left, so it's possible she may be dwelling somewhere beyond those trees. I spot the street I'm looking for, and wait for a car going the other way to pass before I turn onto it. I follow the street as it descends steeply down a hill. The area appears rural and it's hard to believe there are houses back here, but there must be because the map says so.

A mile later, the road levels out and the forest fades away in places to reveal a typical suburban neighborhood. The houses on each side of the road are not as big as the colonials I passed, but at least there's variety here; I see capes, ranches, and split-levels.

My palms become moist as I meticulously check the street signs. I pick up the map and scrutinize it while I cruise at a leisurely thirty miles per hour. Sure enough, I see her street on the right.

As I turn onto the road, my heart thumps hard against my ribs like a bird trying to escape from a cage. I slow to twenty miles per hour as my sweaty hands tremble on the wheel. The houses on this street are mostly ranches with grassy yards that are large enough to provide minimal privacy for the residents. Strategically placed trees spaced between the properties help in this regard.

I scan the area carefully and check the house numbers as I go; I must be close. There's a wide grassy field behind the houses on the left side of the road, while a forest looms behind the houses on the right side. It would be easier to conceal myself in the woods than in the field, so I hope her house is located to the right.

Suddenly I see something that freezes the blood in my veins:

a police cruiser is parked across the street from what I now know is the bitch's house. I see one silhouette behind the windshield. My heart feels like it's going to explode in my chest as I slow to fifteen miles per hour and then ten. If I'm too slow, I may attract attention, so I speed up slightly.

Instinctively, I reach down, open the glove compartment, and grab a pair of sunglasses. I put them on just as I'm nearing the front of the cruiser. Across from the cruiser I see a ranch house with a modest yard, but I'm too nervous to study it carefully or check the number, so I stare straight ahead as I drive between the house on the right and the cruiser on the left.

As I pass, I realize the officer has his face buried deep in a newspaper. I remain calm and do nothing to arouse his suspicions in case he looks up. I sigh with relief as I drive past. The idiot never even glanced at me. Just to be safe, I look in the rearview mirror to make sure he hasn't pulled away from the curb. He's probably not even aware that I'm here.

The cruiser hasn't budged, and I take that as a good sign. I continue following the road until it curves out of view of the police car. With the police guarding her house, it's going to be difficult to snatch the bitch.

As I think about the police car parked on the side of the road, my body starts to tremble. How am I going to grab the slut if she's being guarded day and night?

CHAPTER 34

Detective Lombardi watched with rapt attention as Sergeant Conrad inserted the last red tack into the map on the wall; thirteen red tacks were imbedded within various towns, each representing a crime with a similar Modus Operandi occurring during the last three years.

The wall-size map contained the town of Westfield in the center-right area surrounded by the adjacent towns of Northfield, Southfield, Hopkinton, and Shrewsbury. To the west of Shrewsbury was the city of Worcester, where another suspicious disappearance had also occurred.

"That's the ones we know about so far," Conrad said, surveying the map.

"I hope we nail him soon so we don't have to insert any more tacks," Lombardi said, frowning at the map.

"It's possible that our perp committed crimes in other areas we don't know about, but this is a good start," Conrad said.

"What's next?" the detective asked.

"All we need now is a ruler."

"That's easy enough to get." Lombardi opened the middle drawer of her desk and rummaged through a collection of small office items. She pulled out a clear plastic ruler. "Here ya go," she said, handing it to the sergeant.

"This part is pretty basic." Conrad took the ruler and placed it between the red tack imbedded in the town of Northfield in the northwest and the town of Marlboro in the northeast. Then, he reached into his pocket, took out a pen, and used the edge of the ruler to draw a horizontal west-to-east line between them. "That's the northern border of the perp's known activities." He drew another line between the tack in Marlboro and Farmington to the southeast, and then another between Farmington and Holliston to the south. A long line went between the red tack in Holliston and the one in Worcester in the far west, and then from Worcester to Northfield. "These are the exterior borders, which indicate the limits of the area our psychopath feels comfortable operating."

Conrad stood back to survey the shape formed by the lines in the map, which resembled a rough diamond.

"Next, we draw connecting lines between the tacks in the remaining towns." Conrad used the edge of the ruler to draw more lines within the rough diamond perimeter to connect all the towns. The result was an elaborate pattern of crisscrossing lines. "Finally, we check where the lines are intersecting and shade the areas of overlapping intersections."

Conrad shaded the overlapping intersections until a dark area formed within the map; the dark area was contained completely within the town of Westfield.

"It looks like our boy is probably local," Conrad said, shaking his head as he stared at the map. "The fucker is probably living in town right under our noses."

"How accurate is the diagram?" Lombardi asked as she traced the dark area of the map with her fingers.

"It's not 100% accurate, but it does reflect mathematical probabilities, and right now the probabilities indicate that he's living in our town. That doesn't mean he's going to

DIARY OF A SERIAL KILLER

strike again in Westfield, but it's likely he's a resident here."

"Where would a young guy in his mid-to-late twenties be living in town?" Lombardi asked.

"A person in his or her twenties usually can't afford to own a house, so he's either still living with his parents, or he's living in an apartment. The fact that he has a lot of freedom to commit crimes indicates that he's probably not living with his parents; the only option left is he rents an apartment."

"The only two apartment complexes in town are the Westfield Garden Condominiums and the Westfield Commons," the detective said.

Despite his fatigue, Conrad felt a rush of excitement. "If he's living at the Westfield Gardens, then we can narrow it down even more because at least half of those apartments are condos, and it's doubtful a young man in his mid-twenties owns a condo – unless he has a job that pays well. My guess is that with all his extra-curricular activities, the perp is too distracted to work a job requiring an advanced educational level, which leads to the conclusion that he rents."

"I know the building manager at the Westfield Gardens complex," Lombardi said, widening her eyes. "We can see her right now and get a list of people who rent."

"Then, we can head over to the Westfield Commons, track down the manager, and get a list of all the renters there. When we have the complete list, we can narrow it down further to renters who are males in their mid-to-late twenties and place them under surveillance if necessary," Conrad said.

"We have this fucker now." Lombardi grinned at Conrad.

Conrad smiled back as he nodded his head.

If the geographical profile was accurate, then it was a big

step in the right direction, but Conrad thought it wasn't time to celebrate yet. The Westfield Gardens was a relatively small complex consisting of only eight buildings and possibly several hundred renters, so it would be fairly easy to check, but the Westfield Commons was a large, sprawling complex that was spread out over twenty buildings and had more than a thousand renters. It would take a lot more time to systematically check all the residents in the Commons and narrow them down to viable suspects.

Still, they might get lucky; one of the suspects could have suspicious characteristics that send up a red flag. However, in this game of life and death, Conrad didn't want to rely only on luck.

CHAPTER 35

My hands tremble on the steering wheel – worse than ever – as I try to maneuver my way out of the bitch's neighborhood without calling attention to myself. The cruiser disappears from my rearview mirror as I turn the corner and take a left at the next side street. I thought the side street would take me back to the main road, but instead it curves the wrong way and takes me deeper into the suburban sprawl.

My driving feels erratic; I take my foot off the gas too much to slow down and press down on the gas too much to move ahead. I don't want to speed, but I also don't want to be too slow.

I try to light a cigarette as I drive, but my fingers are quivering so much that I can't hold the lighter steady. Maybe I should pull over to light it, but I'm afraid it would call attention to myself.

I realize that I'm heading in the wrong direction when I encounter a sign for the town of Shrewsbury. After ten minutes of driving on unfamiliar backstreets, I reach a commercial area that I recognize and start to backtrack toward Westfield.

I pull into a parking lot in front of an Ashland liquor store so I can light a cigarette. My fingers continue to tremble, but

I manage to hold the lighter steady long enough to light the tobacco.

I feel better as I take my first deep inhalation of smoke, and blow it out. Tendrils of smoke hover in the interior of my car like a wavering mist, so I crack the window to let in some air. The quivering in my hands starts to subside as I pull out of the parking space.

I can't believe they assigned a fucking cop car to watch over the slut's house! Imagining the cop's silhouette behind the windshield of the cruiser causes me to break out in a cold sweat. I can feel liquid beading on my forehead, but my body is shivering as if the temperature in my car just dropped.

The only way to eradicate my nerves is to hunt for a new victim as soon as possible; I only feel confident and in control when I'm hunting for prey. Sure, it's a risky move with the cops looking for me, but it will be worth it if I can stop my body from trembling.

I check the dashboard clock as I pull into my parking space at my apartment building: 12:26 PM. I still have plenty of time before I have to be at my LTC appointment at the Westfield Police Station. I'll wait until I get inside to light a cigarette because smoking is more enjoyable when it's prohibited.

Sliding out of the driver's seat, I lock the car and head up the walkway toward the front door. My face feels hot and my palms are moist. Even worse – my hands are shaking so badly that it takes me three tries to insert my key into the front door. When I finally get the key in, I look around to make sure no one has seen me; I don't want to appear suspicious in case the cops come around asking questions.

After entering my apartment and locking the door, I strip my clothes off to take a shower. In the bathroom, I stand next to the shower and turn the temperature up high. I wait for the temperature to reach the right level – not too hot, but hot enough to soothe my tense muscles – and pull the curtain aside to step into the shower.

I forgot about the band-aids covering my head-wound, so they peel off as I stick my head under the shower spray. I open the curtain a few inches and toss the disgusting things on the white bathroom tiles. Touching the wound lightly, I'm pleased that it's still not bleeding. Maybe I won't need to replace the band-aids.

The shower doesn't relax me as I hoped it would. When I emerge from behind the steaming plastic curtain, I hold my hand in front of me and notice it is still trembling slightly. That's not going to work when I go to my appointment at the police station.

Suddenly, I have an inspiration. I have a stash of Oxycontin that I stole from my mother's medicine cabinet stored in a plastic baggie under my mattress. One of those should do the trick. I wash a pill down with a glass of water and smoke a cigarette while I wait for it to take effect.

Twenty minutes later, I feel more relaxed, but I still can see a very slight, but noticeable, quivering in my fingers as I try to hold my hand steady. I head to the bedroom, reach under the mattress, grab another pill out of my stash, and wash it down.

I start to dress in my best clothes as I wait for the second pill to take effect. I put on pressed black dress-pants and button up a fine gray dress-shirt. A pair of shiny black shoes completes the ensemble. I find a conservative maroon tie on my tie rack in the closet and use the mirror in the bathroom to adjust it properly.

After combing and putting gel in my hair, I look in the mirror and decide that I look like a solid, law-abiding citizen. While preening myself, I'm careful not to rub my fingers against the wound that is just starting to heal.

I decide to smoke another cigarette in the living room as I lounge back in the recliner. As I hold my free hand in front of my face, I see that it's as steady as a rock. The only problem is that I feel slightly dizzy. When I'm done with my cigarette, I stand up, but I get a head rush and feel like I'm going to pass out. Standing still for a few seconds, the feeling passes.

I feel like I'm floating on air as I walk to the kitchen. Opening the fridge, I grab a 12-liter bottle of Mountain Dew and pour myself a glass. I didn't want to drink any caffeine before, but now I believe it's necessary to even myself out. After gulping down the caffeinated soda and chasing it with a glass of water, I feel better. I'm surprised when I check the clock on the stove and see it's already 1:42 PM. My appointment is in eighteen minutes! Where did the time go?

I make sure I have my driver's license in my wallet and my application form before I leave the apartment. I feel a little dizzy as I ride the elevator down a floor, but it's nothing I can't handle. I float my way out to my rental car, slide in behind the wheel, and light another cigarette. Turning the key in the ignition, the engine rumbles to life. I back out of my reserved spot carefully and I'm on my way.

I don't bother to turn on the radio so I can concentrate on driving. It's hard enough smoking and driving without being distracted by music. Maybe I should have cut that second Oxycontin pill in half.

As I pull into the police station parking lot, my dashboard clock reads 1:55 PM; I made it with five minutes to spare. I snuff out the second cigarette I lit on my way over and get out of the car. Straightening my tie, I feel confident as I stride toward the double glass doors at the front of the Westfield police station.

CHAPTER 36

Sergeant Conrad and Detective Lombardi updated Chief Willard and Lieutenant Lombardi on their progress in the detective's office.

"How sure are you that the killer is living in Westfield?" the lieutenant asked.

"Sure enough that I'm willing to systematically check the lists of residents in the town's two apartment complexes," Conrad replied.

"Okay, then do it," Chief Willard said, glaring at the red tack on the map that was inserted into Westfield – as if he was outraged that the killer could possibly be living in his town. "Whenever you're ready you can head out and meet with the apartment managers."

"Detective?" Conrad asked, turning to Lombardi.

"I'm ready to go if you're willing to make a stop at Dunkin Donuts on the way," Lombardi said, grinning sheepishly. "I didn't sleep well last night."

"You and me both," Conrad replied. "Stopping at D and D is a great idea."

"Do whatever you have to do," the Chief said as he turned

away from the map and left the office.

"It would be cheaper to make coffee in the break room, but I don't have the patience or the talent to make it as good as the professionals," Lombardi said, flashing Jim a mischievous grin.

"I couldn't agree with your logic more," Conrad replied, smiling back. "Are we taking your car?"

"Yep, I parked out front today. I'm going to make a quick stop at the Ladies Room and then I'll meet you out there."

"I need to make a pit stop as well," Conrad said, leaving the office and heading for the locker room.

After making a stop, Conrad grabbed two bottled waters out of the fridge in the break-room for the detective and himself, and made his way toward the front of the building. As he walked, he took out his notebook and reviewed his notes. He passed the dispatch console on the right and entered the secretary's office, which was also located next to the lobby.

"How's it going, Tara?" Conrad asked the attractive, middle-aged secretary.

"Not bad, Jim. How about yourself?" she asked.

"I'm hanging in there."

Conrad opened the security door leading to the front lobby and waved to the dispatcher through the bulletproof glass barrier as walked toward the exit. He barely noticed a young man in a gray shirt and maroon tie who entered the lobby and walked past him toward Dispatch. Conrad was too busy to care what the guy wanted and he figured the dispatcher could handle whatever report or complaint he had.

Conrad stood by Lombardi's car and studied his notes as he waited for her. She arrived a few minutes later and he heard a familiar beep as she opened the locks with her key remote. He handed her a bottled water and went to the passenger side.

"Thank you," Lombardi said, taking the water. "We probably only have time to check one apartment complex. I have to be back in twenty minutes to fingerprint a kid who just applied for an LTC." She opened the driver's side door.

"While you're doing that, I'll head over to the second complex," Conrad said, ducking his head as he entered the car.

Lombardi slid into the seat beside him and started the car. She backed out of one of the front spaces reserved for customers, shifted the car into drive, and headed for the exit. She took a left toward the closest Dunkin Donuts that had a drive-through. Lombardi ordered a latte for herself and a large hot coffee with cream and sugar for her partner. She took a right out of the drive-through and headed for the Westfield Gardens condo complex.

They arrived ten minutes later and parked in front of a small, one-story building at the center of the complex that housed the manager's office. A piece of paper was taped to the inside of the door window, which read: NO CASH IS KEPT ON THE PREMESIS.

Conrad let Lombardi take the lead because she knew the apartment manager. He followed her into a short hallway and took a right through an open door into the manager's small, but tidy office. The manager was a sixtyish, slightly overweight, gray-haired woman. She was seated behind a desk looking at a computer screen. She glanced up from the screen as the sergeant and detective entered. Conrad read the nameplate on her desk: Rebecca Kirkland.

"How are you, Rebecca?" Lombardi asked.

"Not bad. How about you, Marilyn?" Kirkland replied.

"I've been better," Lombardi said. "I'm sure you've read about what we've been dealing with in the papers."

"My God, it's awful. What that poor girl must have gone through," the manager said. "Thank God she was able to get away."

"We got lucky that time, but it's not over yet," Lombardi said. "I need to ask you a favor that could make all the difference in our investigation."

"Sure, anything," Kirkland said, folding her hands on the desk.

"We need a comprehensive list of all the residents in your apartment complex, including all their accompanying information."

"Some of that information is confidential."

"Would it be possible for you black out the confidential information on a printout?"

"I guess I could do that."

"The bottom line is that this information could help us catch the killer before he strikes again," Lombardi said.

Kirkland's face turned pale. "Do you think he's living in this complex?"

"I'm not going to lie to you, Rebecca. It's a possibility. That's why we need the list."

"Oh my God," Kirkland said, mouth dropping. She took a few seconds to recover her composure and said, "In that case, I'll give you everything. I could get in trouble for this, so I'm trusting you to be discreet."

"Oh, don't worry, we'll be discreet," Lombardi said, flashing Kirkland a crooked smile. "Even more importantly, we need

YOU to be discreet. If it gets out that we're looking for this psycho in the Westfield Gardens complex, it could compromise the entire investigation. Not to mention the panic and paranoia it would create."

"Okay, fair enough. I'll get started right away," Kirkland said, typing on her computer keyboard.

"One more thing," Conrad interjected as he reached into his pocket, took out a photograph, and held it up to Kirkland. "Do you recognize this guy as one of your tenants?"

Kirkland squinted her eyes at the photo and gestured for Conrad to hand it over so she could get a closer look. She scrutinized the photo for thirty seconds before handing it back.

"No, sorry, he doesn't look like any tenants I know," Kirkland said. "Do you have a better picture? His face isn't that clear in this photograph."

"Sorry, that's the only one we have," Conrad said.

"It might take a while to print out all the info," the manager said, turning to Lombardi. "Are you going to wait or come back for it?"

Lombardi glanced at Conrad and he mouthed the words "come back" to her.

"Rebecca, we're going to come back for it if you don't mind."

"No problem at all. Anything I can do to help."

"We appreciate it," Lombardi said, turning toward the doorway.

"Any time."

Conrad followed the detective to the unmarked cruiser. As they sat down, the dispatcher's voice blurted over the cruiser radio: "Control to nine-thirty-six."

Lombardi picked up the mike and keyed it. "This is nine-thirty-six."

"Can you return to the station to fingerprint a gentleman for an LTC?" the disembodied voice asked.

"No problem," she replied, hanging up the mike.

CHAPTER 37

I enter the police station lobby and pass a tall, arrogant-looking cop going in the opposite direction. I consider myself quite strong because I can do over a hundred push-ups, but that fucker's thick arms and shoulders make me think I should sign up at a gym. He appears to be so intent on business that he hardly notices me.

I approach the bullet-proof glass encasing the dispatch center and wait for the dispatcher to look up from the console. When he does, I offer him a wide, friendly smile.

"Hi, I'm Eric Blackburn and I'm here for my LTC appointment."

"Okay, have a seat in the lobby and someone will be out to see you shortly."

"No problem."

I maintain a wide smile as I nod at him reassuringly. Then, I turn gracefully on my heel and glide over to a row of seats facing a large Plexiglas window next to the front double glass doors. I can see my rental car parked in the lot outside. My actions feel effortless as if I'm in a dream; the Oxycontin is working its magic.

I sit down, close my eyes, and lean my head back against the

SHAWN WILLIAM DAVIS

wall. I don't think I could wipe the smile off my face if I wanted to. The drugs have pushed all my pain and nervousness into the far back corner of my mind and replaced them with pleasurable images.

I imagine myself wielding a forty-four Magnum like Dirty Harry and blowing holes in anyone who gets in my way. I picture blowing a massive, bloody hole in the muscular chest of the arrogant cop who didn't even notice I existed as I passed him in the lobby. I follow up the first shot by aiming at his forehead and exploding his skull with a high-caliber bullet.

Suddenly, I feel a finger tapping my left shoulder. Opening my eyes, I look up to see a fairly good-looking, middle-aged woman wearing business attire standing next to me.

"Did you bring your application?" she asks as she holds out her hand palm upward.

"My application?" I ask, as I fumble with the stapled papers in my hand. I became so immersed in my vivid Dirty Harry scenario that I forgot why I came here in the first place. "Sure, here it is," I say, getting it together and handing it to her.

"Thank you," the lady says, taking the papers from my hand. "I'll be back in a few minutes."

As she turns and walks away, my mind is already returning to another fantasy scenario: I imagine taking a leisurely cruise through the Westfield High School parking lot in my rental car. I park in the back aisle near the tree-line, as I've done so many times before, and wait for the students to leave the building. I imagine that I check the dashboard clock and it's 2:05 PM; school gets out at two and the students should be spilling into the parking lot any minute now.

Here they come; I spot teenagers in pairs, groups, and alone as they leave the front of the building and fan out through the lot in search of their vehicles. I've seen this image so many times that I have it memorized.

At first, I try to find a female walking alone, but then my eyes focus on a group of three attractive females heading toward the rear aisle where I am parked. It looks like they are moving toward a car parked several spots down from me. Reaching over to the passenger seat, I wrap my fingers around the handle of my newly purchased, high-caliber hand-cannon. I pick up the weapon and exit the car.

The three teenage girls are giggling and laughing, annoyingly, as they approach a blue BMW convertible; they're rich bitches, even better. They stop laughing when they see me approaching with my handgun by my side. Suddenly, they are screaming in terror; the sound is music to my ears.

One of them, a fake blonde wearing black spandex pants, bolts for the driver's door while the other two turn and run away across the parking lot. I aim carefully at the bare back of a real blonde wearing a low-cut red dress and pull the trigger. Thunder explodes from the barrel of my gun as I cut her down. The other running bitch, a brunette with tight jeans, glances over her shoulder at me as I blast her too. She drops.

I hear the BMW's engine fire up as I circle around the car to the driver's side. I raise the gun as I watch the pseudo-blonde fumbling with the gearshift. As she slides it into reverse, I open fire. Glass fragments pepper her face as the side of her head caves in near her temple. Her eyes roll up in her head as she slumps forward into the steering wheel. The horn sounds, but I'm already moving away from the scene toward my car. I hear a crash as the BMW rolls into a car in the opposite aisle.

I feel fingers tapping my shoulder again, so I open my eyes and look up at the bitch who took my application.

"You forgot to fill out this box," the old bitch says with a trace of annoyance in her voice as she hands me back my application. She points to a blank box where I was supposed to write the initials of the state I live in. That stupid bitch! I wrote down the town of Westfield in the adjacent box, so it should be obvious what state I live in!

I try to control my temper as I fill out the box and hand the paper back to her. I remember the pleasant image of the teenage girl's head caving in, so I'm able to flash the old bitch a convincing smile as she takes the application and scurries off. Fucking moron. Where was I before she interrupted me?

I close my eyes and picture myself back in the high school parking lot holding my gun by my side. Everywhere I turn, I see the backs of students as they flee, screaming. I hear the sound of sirens in the distance, so I return to the car, place the gun on the passenger seat, and turn the key in the ignition. I imagine the sound of squealing tires as I put the car into drive and take off across the parking lot.

I spot a pair of teenagers running toward the street, so I swerve at them. I hear a satisfying double thump as their bodies strike the front grill and hit the pavement. I feel a jolt, as if I ran over a large bump, as my tires crush them into the asphalt. A job well done.

I open my eyes when I hear the door next to the dispatch center opening. The annoying old bitch is walking toward me yet again. I'm sick of dealing with her, but the thought of running over the two high school students is still fresh in my mind, so I'm able to force another convincing smile for her. She actually thinks my fake grin is genuine and smiles back at me.

"Your application is all set and we're conducting your background check. If you follow me, I'll take you to the fingerprint room where the detective will record your prints.

"Sure, that sounds great," I say, keeping my smile in place as I stand up and follow her across the lobby.

I hear a buzzing sound as the bitch pulls the security door open. I follow her through an office area equipped with a single secretary's desk and past the dispatch center.

We travel down a short corridor to a large room equipped with several desks, which we proceed to cut across. She takes me through a doorway on the right that leads to a side corridor.

I still feel like I'm floating on air, so I glide behind her. I don't even feel like I'm really here; I feel like a character in a movie acting out a role.

We pass by several closed doors until we reach an open doorway near the end of the hallway. I follow the old hag into a small room and she gestures for me to sit on one of a pair of chairs placed next to the doorway. In the center of the room is an impressive-looking machine with a clear glass center panel; it's located next to an ordinary table with a computer on it.

"Please remain seated and the detective will be with you."

Again, I can't wipe the smile off my face as I picture following her into the corridor and strangling her. However, instead of engaging in this risky action, I sit calmly and watch her leave. After scrutinizing the side of the machine from my seated position, I decide to get up and take a closer look at it. The sound of footsteps echoing in the corridor motivates me to return quickly to my seat.

I'm just getting comfortable when I see a gorgeous brunette wearing a gray dress-shirt and black skirt entering the room. Her firm breasts poke, alluringly, at the polyester shirt, as her wide hips press against the sides of the skirt. Is this the detective? It can't be; No detective can be that hot.

"Are you Eric?" she asks.

I remain silent as I imagine ripping off her clothes to expose the luxurious smooth, tanned skin beneath.

"You're Eric, right?" she repeats.

I pull myself out of my fantasy to answer her: "Yes, I'm Eric."

""You're in the right place," she says, smiling at me.

The smile I send back to her is genuine as I picture fondling her naked breasts.

"If you step over to the machine, we can begin the process," she says.

I feel dizzy as I stand up too quickly. Hesitating for a moment to regain my equilibrium, I approach the detective, who reminds me of a sultry, old-school actress in a film noire. I feel a rush as I stand next to her and she reaches down for my hand. She lifts my relaxed hand onto the clear platform on the machine and presses the tips of my fingers down on the glass. In close proximity, I notice that she has dark circles under her eyes. I wonder if she is the one who has been assigned to investigate my extra-curricular activities.

"Hold your hand steady," she tells me, as she works the keyboard of the computer plugged into the machine.

She has to lean over to type, which causes her shirt to open, revealing a tantalizing glimpse of cleavage. Her thin eyebrows press together as she views something that concerns her on the screen.

"This isn't working," she says. "Your prints are smudging."

It's not working? What the hell? Don't tell me I'm not going to get my LTC because of a technical problem with the fingerprinting machine!

"Don't worry, we just need to clean your fingertips," the detective says, as she picks up a small bottle and squirts some liquid on a paper towel. "Hold out your hands."

I do as she instructs and she wipes my fingertips with the soaked paper towel.

"People who sweat a lot sometimes have excess oil on their skin, which interferes with the picture," she explains to me.

People who sweat a lot? I thought the Oxycontin had me in the zone; I shouldn't be sweating.

The detective guides my hands to the clear panel and presses my fingertips against the glass again. She stares at the side monitor as she leans over to type on the keyboard. Of course, I take the opportunity to check her out again.

"Okay, that looks better," she says, smiling at me.

"My prints are okay?" I ask.

"Yep, they're fine," she says.

We repeat the process with my other hand, and it takes two attempts with additional wiping before it finally works properly.

"Okay, that's it, we're done," she says, standing erect from her leaning position.

I couldn't feel more relieved.

"Do you know how long it will take before I receive my LTC?" I ask.

"It should take about three or four weeks."

"That's not too bad."

"Not at all," she says. "There's a bathroom across the hall if you want to wash your hands."

"Sure, that sounds good," I say, staring at her ass while I follow her into the hallway.

If she only knew what I would do to her if we were alone and she was unarmed; the pistol she wears on her hip is a strong disincentive to try anything.

She waits for me in the hallway as I wash my hands. Staring at myself in the mirror, I can't believe how relaxed I appear to be; I don't think I could have done it without drugs.

I return to the hallway and follow the detective as she escorts me out. On the way, I memorize every curve of her body; first, I picture what she would look like without clothes and then I picture her without limbs. What a rush!

When we reach the lobby, I try to think of something normal to say. After some hesitation, I come up with the lame comment: "Thank you for your help."

"No problem," she replies. "It was nice to meet you, Eric."

As she shuts the security door and leaves me alone in the lobby, I realize that my mission was a stunning success; in four short weeks, I will be armed with enough firepower to keep the pretty detective working 24-hour shifts.

CHAPTER 38

Conrad borrowed Lombardi's unmarked cruiser while she was tied up with fingerprinting the LTC applicant. The sergeant traveled to the second apartment complex, Westfield Commons. Unfortunately, the police didn't have a connection there, but Conrad was prepared to be persuasive.

The Westfield Commons office was located at the center of one of its largest six-story buildings. The manager was an ex-military, thirty-something man wearing an expensive gray suit. His office was significantly larger and better furnished than Rebecca Kirkland's.

"Nice to meet you, sergeant," the manager said, shaking Conrad's hand in a firm grip. "I'm John Malloy, chief administrator of the Commons."

"Nice to meet you too," Conrad said. "However, I wish it were under better circumstances. I'm sure you've heard about the recent murder and kidnapping in town."

"Yes, I was very shocked to hear about it."

"I have a favor to ask that requires your utmost discretion. We believe the perpetrator may be living in your apartment complex."

Malloy's expression remained impassive as he appeared to process this information.

"How likely is it?"

"Very likely."

Without missing a beat, the administrator said, "I'll be happy to cooperate however I can."

"We appreciate that. We're going to need to look at the records of all your tenants."

"As you know, the records are confidential, but if you promise to be discreet about it I might be able to help you out," Malloy said.

"Discretion is not a problem," Conrad replied. "This investigation is confidential and we need you to exercise discretion on your end as well."

"As a former Marine officer, I'm used to exercising discretion," Malloy said. "I don't want this getting out any more than you do. It would be a disaster for business."

"I'm glad you understand," Conrad said. "It saves me the trouble of trying to convince you that it's necessary for public safety."

"I'm glad to help," Malloy replied. "The only thing I ask is if you discover the individual residing in our complex, you arrest him quietly. I don't want lights, sirens, or SWAT teams used."

"Mr. Malloy, I guarantee it will go down what way," Conrad said, lying for expediency.

If they traced the psycho back to this complex, they wouldn't use lights and sirens because they wouldn't want to warn him they were coming. But they sure as hell weren't coming to pick him up without a SWAT team.

"Good enough," Malloy said. "The only caveat is I have to black out all the financial information on the forms. I hope that's not a problem."

"Not a problem at all," Conrad said. "We're not interested in his finances."

It turned out that Conrad had nothing to worry about because the manager understood the situation. Conrad thought Malloy was all about the bottom line and he didn't want the word getting out that a psychopath might be living in his upscale community.

Conrad didn't blame him for blacking out his tenants' financial information; he was just covering his ass from a lawsuit in case it ever leaked out.

Conrad reached into his pocket and pulled out the photo of the perp captured by the mall security camera. He held it up in front of the manager.

"Do you recognize this guy as one of your tenants?"

Malloy's eyes narrowed as he scrutinized the picture.

"Do you mind if I take a closer look?"

"Sure," Conrad said, handing the photo over.

Malloy studied it for several seconds, shook his head, and handed it back.

"Sorry, sergeant, it's a no go."

"Thanks for checking."

"I'll have one of my employees drop off the folders containing all the residential information at the police station in a few hours," Malloy said, glancing toward the open doorway as if he was willing Conrad to leave. "Is there anything else I can do for you, sergeant?"

Conrad got the impression that the administrator was anxious for him to leave.

"No, I'm all set. Thank you for your help."

By the time Conrad returned to the station, Lombardi had finished fingerprinting the applicant. He found her in her office studying a police report documenting one of the attacks.

"How did it go?" she asked.

"Unlike your friend at Westfield Gardens, he's not handing over any financial information, but that's not our priority anyway," Conrad said. "We only need names, addresses, genders, dates of birth and general background information."

"It shouldn't take long to narrow down viable suspects from the records," the detective said.

"As long as there's not too many single, twenty-something tenants living in these complexes, we should be all right."

"Once we get a list of names, we can check their criminal records in the CJIS system. This can't be the first time this psycho has been in trouble with the law."

"It's a good thing this fucker doesn't know how close we are to nailing him," Conrad said, glaring at the red tacks imbedded in the map on the wall. "or he'd leave town in a hurry."

CHAPTER 39

I feel exultant as I drive out of the police station parking lot. I'm amazed at how easy it was to convince those morons that I'm an ordinary, law-abiding citizen. The drugs were a stroke of genius; my body didn't reveal even a faint tremor while I was there. Things couldn't have gone any smoother. In several weeks' time I'll be even deadlier than before, but for now I have to work with what I have: a knife.

I light a cigarette as I crank up the music on my favorite Heavy Metal station; *Enter Sandman* by Metallica is playing. It's fitting. The car feels like its driving itself as I head back to my apartment. A combined high caused by the Oxy and fooling the police has made my mood unusually cheerful.

Parking in my spot, I head up to the apartment. The short elevator ride to the third floor makes me slightly dizzy. I have a moment of panic when I reach my apartment and find the door unlocked. Has someone been inside? Did they find my souvenirs?

Lowering my center of gravity, I prepare for a possible encounter with an intruder. I gently push the unlocked door open, glide in, and listen for any sound of movement. Nothing. Checking the kitchen first, I find it empty. Then, the living room. Empty.

I pad stealthily into my bedroom like a jungle cat and find no one there. Sliding over to the night-table next to the bed, I take out my combat knife. Muscles tensed, I raise the knife as I enter the bathroom. No one here either. Then, why was my apartment door unlocked?

I try to remember if I locked the door before I left for the police station. I can't remember doing it. Are the drugs making me soft? I never forget to lock my door. A nosy neighbor could have entered and discovered my weapons or souvenirs.

I normally don't take drugs because they dull my senses, but I made an exception to make it through the stressful application process at the police station. My lack of caution is disturbing. What else did I forget to do?

I pace frantically around the apartment as I try to think about mistakes that could lead the police to my door. I can't think of anything, but that doesn't mean I didn't slip up somewhere. The bitch knows what the interior of my parents' cabin looks like, but I'm not sure if she got a good look at the exterior. Does she even know the location?

I'm worrying for nothing. Since I didn't find the bitch on the roads, I know she took to the woods. It's easy to lose your sense of direction in the woods. I'll bet she ended up miles away from the cabin by the time she was able to flag down a car. Besides, the local police are even more moronic than the ones in Westfield, so if she reported something, they would screw it up anyway.

My mouth feels dry, so I pour a glass of water and continue pacing as I drink. After finding my apartment door open, my good mood evaporated like a puddle on a hot day. I can't stop worrying about what other mistakes I might have made that could send me to prison. I need to do something to regain control.

Still pacing, I check the time on the lower right corner of my computer screen and see that it's only three in the afternoon. I wasn't even at the police station for a full hour. I don't feel high anymore, and I can't seem to get rid of my nervous energy.

Holding my hand, palm-down, in front of my face, it trembles slightly. The drugs are wearing off? I have to do something to regain control, but it's too early to go out looking for victims. I need to do something that will distract me.

I decide to grab the quarter-full bottle of Jack Daniels from the cabinet above the stove, and finish it off. I bring it in the living room, sit down on the recliner, and swig directly from the bottle. Lighting a cigarette, I alternate between smoking and drinking.

After finishing the bottle, my eyelids feel heavy and I have the urge to pass out in the chair. Crushing out my cigarette in the ashtray, I let myself slip into unconsciousness. Everything goes black for a while.

I wake up with a start after a vicious nightmare/flash-back about middle school.

I dreamed about a girl I met in the woods after school, and the corresponding pain and humiliation that attended that horrific event. Her name was Michelle Blakely, and it happened sometime in late April in seventh grade.

Michelle sat one desk ahead of me in Algebra class. She was gorgeous and it was hard not to spend most of the time in class staring at her. She had long, straight, dark hair and an unusually well-developed body for a seventh grader. She had large, firm breasts and a sleek, yet curvy, physique.

On that day she was wearing a tight gray sweater that could

barely contain her protruding breasts and a pair of skin-tight jeans that showcased her perfect ass. Needless to say, I tuned out the teacher and concentrated on her.

By age thirteen, I had spent countless hours in front of the 60-inch widescreen TV watching soft-core porn movies on Cinemax - in addition to my usual diet of horror movies. The nanny from hell had stopped watching me after school, but old habits die hard and by age thirteen I was thoroughly addicted to cable TV.

Not surprisingly, my frequent viewing of soft-porn movies gave me an unrealistic view of women. Despite my many shortcomings at age thirteen, I believed I actually had a chance with attractive women.

I must have gone into a trance-like state that often overcame me at that age. At times of boredom or stress, I used my imagination to retreat into a fantasy world where I was unaware of my surroundings. That must be what happened because I can't remember at what point I realized Michelle was staring back at me.

I was picturing myself kissing and fondling her on the comfortable couch in the big den at my house. Then, the next moment we locked eyes. I realized that class was over and everyone was getting up and leaving with the exception of Michelle and I.

At first, her eyebrows creased together in an expression of concern, but soon her lips curled into a mischievous half-smile. I froze in place at my desk as I watched her stand and come over to me.

"Do you like what you see?" she asked me as she maintained a playful half-smile, which in retrospect was really a smirk.

"Huh? What?" I asked.

"You seem to like me. Am I right?" she asked.

"Yeah, sure," I stammered back.

"Why don't we get together then?" she asked. "We can meet in the woods behind the baseball field. Do you know where that is?"

"Sure, I know where it is," I replied, stunned. "But isn't your boyfriend Bryan Donnelly?"

Everyone knew Michelle's boyfriend was the Town League football team's star quarterback, Bryan Donnelly. He was a monster of a seventh grader – weighing in at 180 pounds – most of it muscle.

"Bry and I broke up. I'm single now. Will you meet me?"

"Sure, I guess," I replied, unable to believe my luck.

I couldn't believe they had broken up.

"I'll see you there at three o'clock. Will you be there?" Michelle asked.

I was so stunned that all I could do was nod back. Her smile widened and she winked at me before she turned and walked away. I was a nervous kid and a loner, so my first friendly contact with an attractive woman had shocked me into complete immobility. I sat alone at my desk in the classroom staring, blankly, at the bare chalk board as I imagined her and I spending time together alone in the woods.

Feeling anxious, I couldn't concentrate on anything my teachers said for the rest of the day. I imagined a succession of romantic scenarios featuring myself and Michelle Blakely.

The rest of the day went by in a haze until the bell rang. I skipped going to my bus and went directly to the field at the back of the building. I paced around the soccer field and baseball field – checking my wristwatch every few minutes. At 2:45 I headed toward the woods.

I had never been in these particular woods before, but I knew that several miles beyond this stretch of forest was the housing development known as "The Kings." Did Michelle Blakely live in the Kings? I figured she must because why else would she choose this spot?

My heart was pounding hard as I plunged into the woods. My palms were sweaty and my mind raced. Would she really be here? It was just like one of my fantasies.

As I saw her step out from behind a large gray tree trunk, my heart went into my throat. She looked beautiful and she wore the same tight outfit from class. I took a step forward.

Then, her full red lips curled into a mocking smile and reality struck me like a battering ram as I saw Bryan Donnelly step out from behind an even larger tree trunk.

"Bry, that's the asshole who was staring at me in class!" Michelle shouted, glaring at me venomously.

"Is that true, geek?" Donnelly asked, lips curling into a sardonic smirk.

I stood, frozen, with shock for several moments, but when I saw Donnelly's muscular leg take a step toward me, I turned and ran.

Outrunning the star quarterback was a losing proposition. I didn't get more than fifty feet when he tackled me into a pile of wet leaves. I felt like I was hit by a car as his muscular frame slammed into my scrawny one-hundred-thirty-pound body. I went down hard and gasped for breath as he knocked the wind out of me.

Pain erupted from nerves all over my face and body as Donnelly pounded me with his fists. I don't know how long it lasted, but it seemed to take forever. Throughout the beating I could hear Michelle's mocking laughter in the background.

Finally, after being beaten relentlessly by countless punches and kicks, I lay quivering in pain like a pile of jelly in the wet leaves. I heard them both laughing as they walked away.

I skipped school for the rest of the week because of my bruised and swollen face. The purplish-black welts sprouting from my forehead and cheeks made me resemble a creature from a science fiction movie. My parents asked me what happened, but I refused to tell them because I thought I would only get beaten worse if Donnelly got into trouble. My parents had busy lives, so they didn't push it.

After that, I became a target. Donnelly and his friends never missed an opportunity to punch, kick, trip, or dump my books in the school hallways. Even Michelle and her popular female friends joined in on the action. The next two years became a living hell as I tried to remain vigilant to avoid my tormentors. If I saw them coming down the hall, I turned and ran the opposite way.

My strategy didn't always work as they often seemed to find me at the most inopportune moments. I watched countless numbers of milk cartons, plates, glasses, mystery meat patties, and canned vegetables scatter across the floor of the cafeteria when my lunch tray was dumped.

I became so nervous that I visibly trembled whenever I traveled through the hallways at school. This only provoked them more. They called me names like "fag" and "pussy," as they administered daily beatings and petty humiliations. As I watched my books and lunch trays scatter across the floor, I swore that someday I would have my revenge.

Contemplating the horrific memories from my middle

school days is making my head pound worse than ever. I also have a sick feeling in my stomach as if I just swallowed bloody road kill.

I need to remember that it all happened in the past. Back then, I was a defenseless victim, but now I'm the victimizer and I've already obtained my revenge ten times over. However, it still isn't enough to quell the humiliation I feel every day. It will never be enough.

Sucking on nicotine-laced smoke, I see the digital clock on the cable-box shows its seven-thirty-five; it's dark out now. Blowing the smoke out, I know what will make me feel better.

With a new sense of purpose, I spring out of the chair and head to the bedroom to get changed. I strip off the dress clothes I wore to my police station, and pull on a pair of black jeans and a dark green shirt with a collar. The shirt is preppy enough to throw off anyone who might view my dark clothes with suspicion. My black leather jacket completes the ensemble.

I check my looks in the bathroom mirror and notice that my eyes are slightly bloodshot. I splash some water on my face and squeeze some Crest onto a toothbrush. I brush my teeth and comb my hair – although there's not a lot to comb because I always keep it short.

I can feel my entire body trembling with nervous tension, but I'm not worried because I'm about to put my energy to productive use. It's time to get some payback on the evil slut that escaped.

I can't deliver the payback to her personally because of the cop staked out at her house, but I can vent my rage on those like her. I've been waiting for a moment like this since she got away. It's only a Monday night, but the mall will be open until 9 PM, so I have time.

I go to my closet, open my safe, and take out one of the stolen sets of license plates. I place the plates in a brown paper bag and bring it with me. I stuff my bottle of pepper spray in the left pocket of my leather jacket and my combat knife in its sheath in the right. I am ready to go.

My mouth feels dry, so I drink one last glass of water before leaving. By the time I go, it's eight o'clock, but there is still time before the mall closes. There are bound to be some mall rats that will leave the mall at closing time, and I'll be there waiting for them.

Lighting another cigarette, I turn the key in the ignition of my rental car and pull out of my parking space. Taking a right out of the complex, I head toward the town of Farmington. I'm feeling so confident that I want to push my luck and track prey at the same mall where I work. If I could get away with that smooth interview at the police station, I can get away with stalking sluts at my place of work.

I head toward the lake and stop at a remote parking lot. No one uses it in the Fall. I unscrew the rental car plates and replace them with the stolen ones. I throw the rental plates in the trunk. Piece of cake.

The twenty-minute drive to the mall seems to take forever. After circling the lot, I drive to the first level of the parking garage where I know there are no video cameras. It never made sense to me that they have cameras in the parking lots, but not in the parking garage. The mall's negligence is my opportunity.

I drive up the ramp to the second level and cruise around to check all the parked cars. I count twenty-four cars that are spread out. Then, I park in the back and wait.

CHAPTER 40

The dashboard clock reads 8:25 PM. The mall closes at 9 PM, so the mallrats should be arriving at the parking garage any time now. I turn off the radio so I can concentrate, and tap my fingers impatiently on the steering wheel.

I'm parked at the back of the second level at the end of an aisle lined intermittently with cars. A cluster of four cars is parked very close to me against the side wall to the left, while two more vehicles are parked slightly farther away to the right. They would be ideal targets if the owners fit my victim profile.

We are far enough away from the mall entrance to have adequate, but not perfect, privacy. I've checked this level from the vantage point of the entrance several times while I was working, and I was pleased with the results. The lighting in the rear is dim and I could only make out dark silhouettes from the mall doors.

I feel a rush when I spot two people enter the garage from the double-doors leading to the mall. From the shape of their silhouettes, I can discern that one is a man and the other a woman. As they approach closer, I see that the man is wearing a dark suit and the woman has on a white dress-shirt with a black skirt. They appear to be middle-aged business professionals.

I am so primed to kill at this point that I actually consider leaving my vehicle and sprinting full-speed toward them with my knife drawn. Of course, it's too risky. Not only are they not the proper targets, but there's a chance one of them could be armed.

Halfway down the aisle, they halt next to a black Mercedes and the woman takes a set of keys out of her purse. She unlocks the driver's side and gets in, while the man does the same on the passenger side. I'm glad I didn't risk it because the light is brighter at the center of the garage where they're parked, so there's a better chance someone could spot me.

My fingers tap on the steering wheel as I wait for more people to exit. I feel let-down when I see a group of four teenage boys enter the garage. I despise teenage boys almost as much as teenage girls, but there's no way in hell I'm taking on that many at once.

The boys walk over to a red Toyota parked within the cluster of cars only twenty feet away. They are talking among themselves and don't notice me as they clamber into their vehicle. If only they had been girls.

Suddenly, my body tenses as if I'm hit by a jolt of electricity. I spot three female shapes entering the parking garage from the mall. Two of them are wearing jeans and the one in the middle has on a short black skirt. I feel myself getting aroused.

Keep coming, bitches, I think as they head in my direction. A sick feeling permeates my stomach when I see the girls halt near a green SUV parked close to the mall entrance. They are too far away and too close to any potential witnesses. Fuck, fuck, fuck, I'm not having any luck. I feel like punching my windshield as I watch the girls get in the vehicle and drive toward the exit.

I calm down as I spot more silhouettes near the mall entrance: two teenage boys and two teenage girls. The teens are walking side-by-side, boy-girl, boy-girl. One of the couples is holding hands. Isn't that cute. It's a challenging target, but still a possibility if they get close enough.

Here they come. Details of the couples become more distinct as they approach the cars parked nearby to the right. One of the girls is an average-looking brunette, but the other one is a shapely blonde knockout. The slut is wearing a low-cut red shirt exposing her cleavage and a short black skirt showing a lot of leg. The boyfriend holding her hand is wearing blue-jeans and a red t-shirt with a collar. He is thin, but muscular; he's probably a high school jock. His buddy is shorter and stockier. Both of them look like they could put up fight. That means no go.

I slam my fist on the armrest as I watch them get into the white Acura parked a mere twenty feet away. The blonde is unbelievably hot: an ideal target. But there's no way, it's too risky.

I spot a crowd of people exiting the mall at the far end of the parking garage. There are so many; it's hard to isolate individual targets. The dashboard clock reads 8:50 PM; there are only ten minutes left until the mall closes.

My body starts to tremble as I watch the crowd disperse into smaller groups as they head toward their cars. A pair of very attractive twenty-something females walk toward a beige Hyundai parked only forty feet away to my left. They would make ideal targets if it weren't for all the other people in the vicinity. I slam my fist on dashboard as I watch a family consisting of a man, woman, and two pre-teen boys heading toward a blue SUV parked directly across from the girls' Hyundai. Too damn risky.

Sweat breaks out on my forehead as I watch the teenage girls enter the vehicle and back out of the parking space. My face feels like it's on fire, and my palms are moist as I watch them drive away. Moments later, the family follows them in the SUV. More people head toward various parked vehicles, but I don't get a chance to scrutinize them because all my attention is focused on the Hyundai driving away. I feel my eyebrows twitch as I watch a twenty-something couple get into the white Lexus parked against the wall to my left.

Time is running out. There are only three cars left in the garage and I don't see anyone else leaving the mall. That means the cars belong to employees. They could be young, attractive female employees, but there's no telling when they will be leaving. It could be in fifteen minutes or an hour. I don't have the patience to wait that long.

Fuming, I turn the key in the ignition of the rental car and press down hard on the gas. Tires squeal and a thirty-foot black mark forms in my wake as I race toward the exit ramp. More squealing as I make a sharp turn to go down the ramp.

Suddenly, I have to slam on the brakes to avoid striking a tan SUV coming in the opposite direction. As the SUV drives past, I sit stewing in my impotent rage as I try to figure out my next move. Maybe I will take one last drive through the main mall parking lot.

I leave the parking garage and head down the roadway next to the mall building; the parking lot is on my left and the mall building to my right. As I approach the main doors of Macy's, my breath catches in my throat; four attractive teenage girls are leaving through the double glass doors; they are dressed in tight jeans and short skirts. The nearest surveillance camera is on the far side of the parking lot. I stop to let them cross on the crosswalk.

The girls are in no rush as they step onto the crosswalk, so I wait until they are all in front of me and step on the gas pedal. Shrieking tires drown out their high-pitched screams.

One of them dives out of the way to the left and another to the right, but I hear a loud thump as I strike the other two head-on. Pressing on the brakes, I watch their bodies roll off the hood onto the pavement. I open the door as I curl my fingers around the handle of the combat knife resting on the passenger seat.

I am dimly aware of high-pitched screaming as I get out of the car and move toward my victims. The blonde who dove out of the way is apparently rushing to the aid of a brunette girl lying on the pavement, so I intercept her and plunge my blade deep into her gut. Her wide-eyed expression of utter incredulity is a pleasure to behold. A trickle of blood drips from her red lips as I tear the knife out and push her away. As she plummets toward the pavement, I go for the brunette on the ground.

The girl lying on the asphalt is moaning as she clutches a dislocated shoulder. I grab her by the hair, lift her head up from the pavement, and slide the knife across her throat. I hear a gurgling sound as blood spurts from the gash. Dropping her head onto the asphalt, I move on to the next one lying in front of the car.

Suddenly, I see a dirty blonde-haired girl in a black mini-skirt step in front of me. It's the other girl who dove out of the way. She's coming straight at me with her formerly pretty face contorted into an animalistic snarl.

Before I can raise the knife, sharp pain stabs my forehead and cheeks as fists strike my face. In desperation, I lift my left arm to shield my face while slashing out with my knife. I hear a soft gasp as she stops swinging and reaches down to her bloody side. I realize that I only grazed her, so I lunge the knife toward her throat.

Amazingly, she intercepts my arm with her free hand and clamps her fingers around my wrist like a vise. Her adrenaline-fueled strength is formidable, so I punch her in the side where I wounded her and try to pull my wrist out of her grasp. I hear another soft gasp as I strike her bloody wound with my fist. She lets go and I step back.

I hear loud shouts emanating from the direction of Macy's double-glass doors and see two men wearing business attire moving swiftly toward me. I turn on my heel and leap over a blood pool spreading out from the neck of one of the victims. I spot a pair of elderly women nearby – frozen like statues – as they watch me dash to my car and slide into the driver's seat. I place the bloody knife on the passenger seat and slam the door.

Suddenly, I see a silhouette outside my driver's window and feel someone pulling open the door. The door flies open and an unknown guy, who came out of nowhere, reaches for me with groping hands. The car is still running, so I step on the gas pedal and hear the tires shriek as I pull away.

The man's fingers briefly clamp onto my shirt, but are pulled off as I speed away. From the corner of my eye, I see one of the men in business attire dragging the bloody body of the girl whose throat I slashed out of the path of my vehicle.

G-forces push my body back against the seat. I make sure the way ahead is clear and then check my rearview mirror to see a crowd of people converging on the scene like vultures to a battlefield. As I drive toward the exit, the scene becomes smaller and smaller in my rearview mirror.

CHAPTER 41

As the scene of chaos diminishes in my rearview mirror, I resist the urge to press down on the gas pedal; it would only call more attention. I can feel *the rush*, but I can't let it consume me and dictate my actions.

Despite my euphoria, I force myself to halt at the stop sign at the edge of the parking lot, and take a slow right onto the road toward the rear of the mall. I cruise past the back parking lot, keeping my eyes peeled for cops. Not that I could outrun them in this car anyway.

All of a sudden it hits me: the risk I just took. I've never slaughtered bitches in full view of multiple witnesses before without fear of being caught. My body starts to tremble as I consider the multi-jurisdictional manhunt that will be underway for me. At this very moment, the cops have probably received a description of my vehicle and my license plate.

The license plate number won't help them find me because the plates are stolen. A patrol officer could recognize the number on the stolen plates and pull me over. What the hell was I thinking?

Sweat breaks out on my forehead as I try to resist the urge to drive like a maniac until I'm far from here. Instead, I use all my willpower to keep to the speed limit.

I take a left past the 14-screen movie theatre, and then a right at the stoplight on the road that runs adjacent to the nearby outdoor mall. My heart hammers against my rib cage as I spot flashing blue lights in the distance racing across Route 10 toward the mall. They're far away and heading in the opposite direction, but it causes my hands to tremble on the steering wheel.

I merge into a line of traffic and try to blend in. I see more flashing blue lights racing across the intersection ahead. Again, they are heading away from me.

I feel like my head is going to explode as I halt at a stop light behind a line of cars. My sweaty hands slide on the steering wheel. I don't even bother to try to light a cigarette because I'm shaking too badly.

I take a right at the light and follow the path of the flashing blue lights I saw only seconds earlier. But, instead of taking a right toward the mall at the next set of lights, I take a left past a Bank of America. I join a line of cars heading toward a residential area beyond the commercial district.

All the main roads will be heavily patrolled by cops, so I take the back roads home. I've driven an identical route through the residential maze many times in the past to prepare for an emergency like this one. I know the way like the back of my hand.

I join a line of traffic heading away from the commercial district, and wipe sweat from my brow as I make sure I leave two car-lengths between myself and the vehicle in front of me. I don't want to turn on the radio because my nerves are on edge as it is. Rock music would only make me jump out of my skin now. I pass a BJ's Wholesale on the left and the Farmington YMCA on the right.

Taking a right at the next stop sign, I breathe a sigh of relief when I see that I'm surrounded by unimpressive ranch homes with small yards and short driveways.

The traffic is light in the residential area as I predicted, although not so light that I'm the only car on the road. As I follow Route 126 toward the Sudbury line, I enter a section of the road with no streetlights. The only lights come from the porch lights of the small homes on either side of the road. The woods thicken around me and the trees blot out the stars as they overhang the road. I begin to relax as darkness envelops me.

After driving in complete darkness for several miles, I enter another small commercial district. I pass a combination gas station/convenience store on my right and a small pizza place/Laundromat on the left. There's a short line of traffic at the next stop light and I wait for a moment as there's a delayed reaction when the light turns green. I take a left toward the Sudbury-Farmington line.

I place my palm against my forehead and realize it's dry. My hands also feel steadier on the wheel. Finally, I feel relaxed enough to turn the radio on low. I'm only twenty minutes away from my apartment. If I can just keep my cool and drive the limit, I should be fine.

Now that I'm several miles away, my mind returns to the scene at the mall; the level of carnage I created was unprecedented even for me. What caused me to go so berserk? Usually, I stalk a single victim or a pair with the goal of snatching the hot one and taking her back to my lair where I can play with her at my leisure. This time, I just wanted to take out as many of the sluts as possible to satisfy my bloodlust.

I recall the satisfying feeling of slamming into the bodies of the two girls with the front fender of my car. The wide-eyed expressions of horror on their faces as they realized they were about to be hit were priceless. I can hear the double-thump of their bodies striking the hood as if I'm at the scene now.

CHAPTER 42

Jim Conrad was about to climb into bed when his cell-phone rang. He picked it up and pressed the green talk button.

"Hello?"

"Sarge, this is Westfield Dispatch. We need you to come back to the station."

"I just left the station," Jim replied, sighing.

"There's been another killing. A double homicide at the Farmington Mall. A third victim is in critical condition."

Jim felt a jolt of adrenaline.

"I'll get there as soon as I can."

"What do they want now?" Laurie Conrad asked, irritated.

"As usual, they want our first-born."

"What?"

"There's been another killing. A double homicide in Farmington."

"Oh my God," Laurie replied. "You hardly slept last night and now you have to go back out?"

Jim knew she was asking a rhetorical question; she knew the

drill.

"I'm afraid so."

"I'll make you some coffee," Laurie said.

"I appreciate that," Conrad said, hugging his wife.

She hugged him back tightly. Laurie broke the embrace to head to the kitchen while Jim went to the bathroom to splash water on his face.

He looked at his reflection in the mirror above the sink and almost didn't recognize the haggard face staring back at him. His face was paler than he'd ever seen it and the dark circles under his eyes made him look strangely malevolent. But that didn't matter. What mattered was to keep going. He could sleep when he was dead. Jim cracked a half-smile at this grim thought.

Jim was already wearing half his uniform because he had only started the process of undressing when he received the call. All he had to do was button up his French blue police shirt and reattach his duty belt. He hadn't even had time to take the gun out of its holster and place it in the safe in the closet.

Jim could smell fresh coffee as he entered the kitchen. His wife looked worried, but appeared resolved to be supportive.

"With all the caffeine you've been drinking, don't forget to stay hydrated," Laurie said, as she reached into the fridge for a bottle of Gator-aid, and handed it to her husband.

Jim needed his hands free to prepare his coffee so he shoved the bottle in one of his back pockets. When the coffee machine stopped making gurgling noises, he picked up the pot and poured the contents into a large travel mug. He filled the mug to the top and added five spoonfuls of sugar with a liberal dose of cream.

"Be careful, honey," Laurie said, wrapping her arms around Jim's waist as she stared into his eyes.

"Don't worry, I'm not doing anything dangerous," Jim said, trying to sound carefree. "I'll be safer at the crime scene than anywhere else because of all the cops around."

"Okay, I won't worry, honey, but come back as soon as you can and get some sleep."

"I'll be home as soon as I can."

Jim kissed his wife and headed for the kitchen's side door.

"Thanks for the coffee," he said as he left.

"No problem," he heard his wife say as he stepped through the doorway.

In his exhausted state, he slammed the door too hard and felt badly when he saw his wife's startled expression through the glass pane.

He went to his car, slid into the driver's seat, and placed his travel mug and Gator-aid in the double cup-holder on the dash. As the engine fired up, he put it in reverse and pressed down on the gas pedal.

Jim rolled his window down halfway to generate a cool breeze that he hoped would keep him awake. He also took as many large gulps of coffee from his travel mug as he could without making himself sick.

The dashboard clock showed 10:15 PM. There was very little traffic at this late hour, so he figured he could make it to the Farmington mall in less than twenty minutes. But first, he had to drop by the station to meet with Lombardi and possibly receive directives from the Chief.

Detective Lombardi was leaving through the police station's

front double-glass doors as Jim pulled into the parking lot. She spotted his car and headed in his direction. He halted in the middle of the lot when she reached his vehicle. Jim hit the door unlock button when he saw her reaching for the passenger door handle.

He noticed she was holding an extra-large Dunkin Donuts coffee in her right hand. As she slid into the seat beside him, he thought she looked exhausted. Her pale face and the dark circles under her eyes made him recall the reflection of the stranger he saw in the bathroom mirror earlier.

"We don't have time to waste. Let's go," Lombardi said.

"You got it," Conrad said, hitting the gas. "You might want to put on your seatbelt though."

Lombardi did as she was advised and strapped herself in. Conrad hesitated briefly to look both ways as he reached the edge of the parking lot, and pressed down on the gas pedal again. The tires of the red Toyota SUV shrieked like a torture victim as the car catapulted down the road.

Conrad maintained a steady speed twenty miles an hour above the posted speed limit. He didn't have flashing lights for his civilian vehicle, but he figured he wouldn't get pulled over for speeding in his own town since all the patrol officers knew him.

"How did you find out about the incident?" Jim asked.

"A Farmington detective, Ken Johnson, called the Westfield station only minutes after the murders happened," Marilyn replied. "The detective told the dispatcher that he received a call from you earlier today asking questions about an incident in Farmington that fit a similar victim pattern. He thought it was an odd coincidence that another incident happened only hours after you called. He figured that since we were already working the case, we should pool our resources and knowledge."

"It's a good thing Detective Johnson is a team player," Jim said. "Some cops would never have made the call due to territorialism over jurisdiction."

"Thank God he's smart enough to know that we have to work together to catch this psychopath."

Conrad made it to the Farmington Mall in a record thirteen minutes. He never bothered to slow down when he crossed the Westfield town line into Sudbury and then Farmington. He figured that if he was pulled over, he could talk his way out of a ticket by flashing his police ID and explaining where he was going.

Conrad felt a jolt of adrenaline as he spotted a dazzling sea of red-and-blue emergency lights flashing in the mall parking lot. As he got closer, he realized they were all clustered around the front door of Macy's.

Jim noticed Marilyn tense up as they approached the scene. A chill crawled up his spine like an icy spider as he spotted a stretcher with a black body-bag on it being wheeled toward an ambulance by a pair of EMTs. He counted four marked police cars, two unmarked vehicles, and three ambulances parked around a swathe of caution tape wrapped around a fifty-foot by fifty-foot area directly in front of Macy's front doors.

CHAPTER 43

Conrad parked his SUV behind an unmarked gray Crown Vic. He felt lightheaded from the multitude of flashing red-and-blue strobe lights beaming out from the caution-tape barricade. The confused lighting created roaming shadows, making the scene appear surreal and otherworldly.

Conrad glanced left when he heard someone tap on the driver's side window. He rolled it down.

"Hey, buddy, you can't be here." A uniformed Farmington cop stood outside the car.

"Detective Johnson told me to meet him here," Conrad replied, glancing up at the officer. "I'm Sergeant Conrad with the Westfield PD."

"Oh, sorry, sergeant, I didn't realize who you were," the cop said, stepping away from the door.

Conrad glanced at Lombardi. "I guess you can't blame him for wanting to protect the crime scene."

"Sure we can," Lombardi replied. "All he had to do was look at the patch on your police uniform."

"That's true," Conrad said, as he opened the driver's door. He heard a click as Lombardi opened her door.

"Sergeant, I can take you to the detective," the young Farmington cop said.

"I would appreciate that," Conrad replied, stepping out of the car.

Lombardi joined them.

"I'm Detective Lombardi with the Westfield Police," Lombardi said, extending her hand. The cop shook it.

Conrad and Lombardi followed the uniformed cop around a marked cruiser and an ambulance until they reached the caution tape barrier. Conrad saw three white-uniformed crime techs checking evidence within the perimeter. A female tech was bending down to examine a large puddle of blood about twenty feet from the tape. A man in his twenties wearing a gray suit stood next to the tech – talking to her. Conrad saw two more sizable blood puddles beyond the first.

"Detective, this gentleman said he was supposed to meet you here," the cop said to the man in the suit.

The detective turned to face Conrad and Lombardi. Then, he nodded at them as he moved toward the barrier. He was in his mid-forties, had short blond hair, and a fit, muscular body that filled out his suit well.

"Thanks for coming, sergeant and detective," the detective said as he ducked under the caution tape. "I'm Detective Johnson." He shook Lombardi's hand and turned to Conrad to do the same. "It's a strange coincidence that you called me looking for information about a violent killing that happened several months ago on the same day as another double-murder involving a similar weapon and victim pattern."

"It certainly is," Conrad agreed. "I'm sure you've read in the papers about what happened in Westfield two days ago at our local mall. One teenage girl was brutally stabbed and another kidnapped. The girl who was kidnapped escaped and we interviewed her last night in a New Hampshire hospital."

"Are you sure we're dealing with the same perp?" Detective Johnson asked, raising a blond eyebrow.

"I'm sure," the sergeant replied. "But, I'll admit that the perp appears to be getting desperate; this time, it looks like he didn't even bother to attempt a kidnapping. What exactly happened here?"

"It appears this bastard was trying to inflict maximum damage on the victims," Johnson said. "Four young women were using the crosswalk when the killer tried to run them down. He hit two, and they were smashed to the pavement. Then, he jumped out of the car with a knife to finish the job. If it wasn't for the brave intervention of one of the women, they would all be dead."

"So, this time he went berserk without even bothering to attempt a kidnapping," Conrad said. "The same thing happened with the serial killer, Ted Bundy, after he escaped from police custody the second time. Instead of Bundy's usual pattern of kidnapping women using subterfuge and then bringing them to a second location to do his dirty work, he went on a chaotic killing spree in a sorority house - unlike anything he had done before."

"Like Bundy, this psycho is obviously a very sick puppy," Johnson said. "Did you obtain any information when you interviewed the kidnap victim?"

"She told us that he took her to a snowmobiling cabin in the mountains of New Hampshire," the sergeant said. "He made her dress up in lingerie and took pictures of her. Then, he raped her. She fought back and escaped. She made it out of the cabin, but never saw the exterior. She escaped into the woods and traveled what she believed was many miles before she was picked up by a trucker on Route 64. The trucker took her to the East Brookfield police station and the cops there failed to do anything that approximated a meaningful investigation. However, they did call an ambulance to get her injuries checked. We interviewed her at the hospital last night and they released her this morning."

"It's unfortunate that she had to get up-close-and-personal with this creep," Johnson said. "But, I would imagine she was able to give you a good description."

"She did, and it matches a photo of the perp that I obtained from the security cameras at the Westfield Mall. I have the photo at the station if you want to see it."

"Once I get this scene wrapped up, we should meet and go over everything we have," the detective said.

"Did you find any forensic evidence?" Lombardi asked.

"Our tech, Lisa, found a clear sneaker imprint in one of the blood puddles," Johnson said.

"We also found a sneaker print at our scene in Westfield," Lombardi said. "We can compare the prints and see if they match up."

"I don't think you have to be Nostradamus to predict that the prints are going to match up perfectly," Conrad said. "When this scumbag isn't cruising local high school parking lots for victims, he feels comfortable using malls as hunting grounds. He always goes after attractive young women – usually teenagers – using a combat knife as a weapon."

"The women he attacked here were in their early twenties," Johnson said.

"Could they have been mistaken for teenagers?" Lombardi asked.

"Certainly."

"This attack appears to be a spontaneous crime of opportunity – rather than his usual meticulously planned stalking, assault, and kidnapping pattern." Conrad said.

"That sounds about right," the Farmington detective replied. "The wounded young lady, who fought successfully against the killer, told me he stopped his car to let them cross on the crosswalk and then stepped on the gas pedal without warning. There appeared to be minimal planning involved in the act, as he couldn't have anticipated the attack until he saw the females leave through the front doors and step onto the crosswalk."

"This particular attack has obviously deviated from the killer's usual MO, but the use of the combat knife, choice of victims, and the efficiency of the killings points to our boy," Conrad said. "Despite the differences, I'm sure we're dealing with the same psychopath."

"I believe you're right," Johnson agreed. "I remember reading in the paper that the killer stabbed one of the victims through the throat at the Westfield Mall attack."

"Unfortunately, he's becoming deadlier with practice," Conrad said, as he observed the female crime scene tech taking samples from the closest blood puddle.

Suddenly, Conrad felt queasy and light-headed. He could usually handle bloody crime scenes, but his recent lack of sleep was apparently making him more sensitive. He staggered and caught himself before he went down. Lombardi grabbed his right arm while Johnson held his left.

"Are you all right?" Johnson asked. "When's the last time you got any rest?"

"I got a few hours last night," Conrad said, as he tried to focus his blurry vision.

"You need to get your partner home to rest," Johnson said to Lombardi. "We can meet up and discuss the case tomorrow."

"Okay, help me guide him over to the car," Lombardi said.

As they escorted him back to the red SUV, Conrad had to stop suddenly as his vision blurred and he felt like he was about to drop. The pause enabled him to recover and they made it the rest of the way to the vehicle. Lombardi opened the passenger door and guided Conrad into the car.

The sergeant leaned back in the seat as Lombardi slammed the door shut. As he tried to get comfortable, he focused on the Gator-aid in the drink-holder that his wife had asked him to take. He unscrewed the cap and took several large gulps. He figured he must have been dehydrated from overwork and excessive caffeine intake, and should have listened to his wife and drank the Gator-aid before he went to the crime scene.

Lombardi went to the driver's side, slid into the seat, and rolled down the window as Detective Johnson approached the car.

"I'm okay now," Conrad said, turning to Lombardi. "Let's go back to the crime scene."

"Fuck that," Lombardi said, raising an eyebrow. "You're not the only one who's dragging. The detective gave us all the relevant details we need. He doesn't have anything more for us that can't wait until tomorrow."

Lombardi turned to look up at the detective, who was standing above her next to the open driver's side window. "Detective Johnson, is there anything else we need to know?"

"No, I gave you everything crucial," he replied. "However, I do want to meet you at your station tomorrow to check out that photo of the perp."

"That's fine. I should be in around 10 AM," the detective said.

"I'll give you a call tomorrow before I head over," Johnson said.

"Okay, I'll talk to you then," Lombardi replied.

"Stay safe," Johnson said, as Lombardi placed the SUV in reverse and backed away from the emergency vehicles.

CHAPTER 44

I'm hiding in the woods behind the slut's house; it's dark and I'm watching the lighted rear windows through my binoculars. There are two lit windows to the left of the back porch and one to the right. There's also a window lit in the top-half of a back door that leads onto the porch. It would be child's play to smash the window and reach through to turn the doorknob.

I estimate it's around 10:00 o'clock PM. From the looks of the cheap, one-level ranch house, I don't think they can afford an alarm system.

I scan my binoculars downward and spot a basement window in the concrete foundation beneath the porch. All I have to do is lie on the ground next to the foundation, tap out the glass with a small hammer, and crawl through to the basement. From there, I can access the rest of the house.

I feel a rush of excitement as I imagine confronting the slut in her darkened bedroom. I imagine sneaking up on her, covering her mouth with my hand to muffle her screams, and then going to work with my knife.

I wait for all the lighted windows to go dark before I make my move. I place the binoculars on the ground behind a tree trunk. From my position at the edge of the woods, I can see the roof of a neighbor's house to the left, but the rest of the structure is concealed by a wall of trees separating the yards; the trees should provide me with adequate cover. The neighbor on the right is too far away to be a concern. Considering the minimal lighting in the backyards, there's no chance I will be spotted in the dark.

Glancing left and right, I see the coast is clear and make my move. Staying low, I hurry across the darkened lawn. Fallen leaves create an uneven carpet across the grass. As I move, a light wind alters the layout by blowing clusters of leaves across the gaps. I head straight for the basement window beneath the porch.

When I reach the porch, I duck under it and lie down on my stomach next to the ground-level window. In this position, I'm concealed from view from the yard. I carefully position my small hammer next to the corner of the glass and prepare to strike. Taking a deep breath, I swing the hammer. Luckily, the sound of tinkling glass can barely be heard above the sound of leaves blowing in the wind.

My gloves protect my hands as I push in the remaining glass in the frame. I hear more tinkling as the glass shards land on a hard surface below the window. When the glass is completely cleared, I peer into the dark basement, but I can't see anything. I wait for my eyes to adjust to the darkness and see the black metal top of an oil tank beneath the window.

Pulling my head out, I turn my body around so I can place my feet on top of the oil tank as I slide in. However, there's only enough room for me to place my knees on top of it as I go through the gap. It's an old-fashioned tank that is longer horizontally than vertically, so there's enough space for me to climb on top of it.

I slide off the curved metal surface and land on the concrete floor. I wait as my eyes adjust to the dark. The shattered window provides enough light for me to move about without banging into something. An old bureau with boxes piled on it has been placed against the concrete wall across from the tank, and there's a water heater in the corner that's about half the size of the oil tank.

I spot a string dangling from a bare light-bulb on the ceiling, but I don't pull it; the window provides enough light to make my way through the cellar. I cross the basement floor, skirting around an improvised obstacle course of cardboard boxes and plastic containers.

Farther along, I reach a washer and drier placed against the wall at the base of a stairwell leading upward. At the top of the stairs I see a faint sliver of light around the perimeter of a closed door. I slide my knife out of its sheath as I ascend.

My heart hammers in my chest as my hands shake with adrenaline. I pause halfway up the stairs when one of the wooden steps creaks beneath my foot. Grasping the railing for balance, I carefully lift my foot onto the next step to minimize any further noise. I halt when I reach the door and listen for any sounds on the other side.

I don't hear anything, so I turn the knob slowly, push the door open a crack, and peek out. I sense no movement, so I push the door open a foot and wait, listening.

I am looking out at a small kitchen with a table set against the left wall and countertops above a sink and a stove to the right. A large, dark rectangular shape, which I assume is a refrigerator, looms beyond the countertops like one of the rock slabs from Stonehenge. A window above the sink lets faint blue light in from outside.

I push the door open another foot and slide through the gap into the kitchen. Treading softly across the linoleum floor, I reach an opening. There's an exterior door straight ahead on the other side of a shadowy living room equipped with a sofa, two recliners, a coffee table, and flat-screen TV. A right will take me through the living room, while a left will take me down a carpeted hallway, so I turn left.

I am wearing black walking sneakers to minimize noise and act as black camouflage to hide me in the dark. The first door on the right opens to a closet, so I pass it and continue down the dark corridor.

Advancing cautiously with my knife clenched tightly by my side, I pass a study on the left and a bathroom on the right. Finally, I reach the last two doorways in the hallway. Both doors are open several inches. People really should lock their doors when they go to sleep.

Peering through the crack to the right, I see two dark, human-sized lumps under the covers of a king-sized bed. I slide left and peek into the next room. A window on the far wall provides enough blue light to make out the dim shapes of a bed beneath it and a dresser beside it. I see my prey asleep in the twin-bed beneath the window. She looks so beautiful and peaceful that it seems almost a shame to slice her to pieces.

Carefully, I push the door open and feel relieved when it doesn't make a sound. I slip into her bedroom, and glide over to her bed like a shadow. I feel superior as I stand above her, looking down on her helpless form. I can make out all the details of her gorgeous face: her small forehead, perfect eyebrows, high cheek-bones, smooth skin, and long, flowing brown hair. I switch grips on my knife and raise it above my head.

Without warning, I rip the covers off her body and press my palm firmly over her mouth. Her eyes fly open wide and stare up at me with disbelief.

Yes, I'm here – you better believe it, bitch.

I hear her muffled voice as she tries to scream through my palm, so I clamp my hand tighter over her mouth.

The knife descends like lightning and rips open her abdomen like an earthquake tearing open a fissure. I can't see her blood, but I can feel it flowing over my hand as I rip the knife upward. I feel immense satisfaction as a gash opens in her chest as if she's a gutted fish. Her eyes roll up in her head as her body convulses in grotesque spasms.

I lean close to her face and whisper, "Did you really think you were going to get away from me, slut?"

Her body continues to convulse as I pull the knife out of her chest. I hear a sickening gurgling sound as I take my hand away from her mouth. Blood drips from her beautiful lips. She gasps once and is then still. I have won. Did she really think she could escape my wrath?

As I stare down, triumphantly, at her corpse and feel *the rush* permeate my brain, the image begins to fade. My equilibrium wavers, I fall backwards, I find myself lying on my back. Suddenly, I open my eyes and focus on the white plaster of the ceiling above my bed. It was only a dream. I feel as if a crushing weight has been placed on my chest as I breathe in quick, gasping breaths.

CHAPTER 45

My evisceration of the slut wasn't real, so I feel let down. The act of slicing her open felt incredibly vivid, so it's difficult to admit that it only stemmed from my imagination.

The knowledge that she is still running around free is humiliating and takes the glow off my accomplishments at the mall last night. The only way to end my shame is to make my dream a reality; I have to complete a list of specific tasks to capture my elusive prey.

First, I need to check my rental car for bloodstains. The bitches splashed their blood on my clothing, so some of it may have rubbed off on the driver's seat when I sat down. I also need to check the front hood and bumper. I was riding so high after my victory that I forgot to check the car when I was done.

It turns out my instincts were correct because when I leave my apartment the next morning and check the rental vehicle, I find two tiny bloodstains on the driver's seat. It will be easy to eliminate with the cleaning supplies I have stored in the cabinet under the kitchen sink.

Also, I find two minor dents in the hood where bodies impacted with it, but no blood. The dents are only noticable if you're looking for them.

I obtain the materials and go to work on the stains with elbow-grease and powerful cleaning ingredients. After an hour of scrubbing, I'm satisfied that the bloodstains on the seat are no longer visible. A crime scene tech could still detect the blood by using a chemical test, but I don't foresee that happening any time soon because I'm still way ahead of the cops.

I return the cleaning materials to the cabinet under the sink and pause to reflect. Is there anything else I need to do? I cleaned the bloodstains on the upholstery. I checked the hood for blood and damage. What next?

I know what I need to do; I need to return the rental car and trade it for another. The cops will be on the lookout for the red Ford Focus that ran over two girls at the mall last night, so I need to trade it in for a car with a different make and color. I will invent some plausible excuse such as, "I don't like the way the car handles."

Suddenly, the phone rings and I nearly jump out of my skin. The wall clock reads 9:56 AM; the only people who would be brazen enough to call me at this hour are my parents or my work. Should I answer it? Why the hell not? It could be my mother calling to change our dinner plans. I need those Oxycontins from her medicine cabinet.

I pick up the phone.

"Hello?"

"Hello, Eric. It's your father."

That's just my luck. I was hoping it was my mother. I can deal with her. HE always puts me on the spot. However, I need to adapt to the situation, so I plaster a fake smile on my face and try to get into character.

"Hi, Dad," I reply with false enthusiasm.

I can't think of anyone I'd rather not be talking to. Except maybe the police.

"Son, your mother told me you are visiting us for dinner this Sunday."

"Not this Sunday. It's the Sunday after," I reply, rolling my eyes.

"Why not this Sunday?"

"I'm working overtime."

"Are you still working the same job?"

Oh no, here it comes. Where else would I be working?

"Of course," I reply, annoyed.

"I was hoping you had moved on to bigger and better things."

"Well, sorry to disappoint you, Dad, but I'm still working the same job."

"Have you thought about returning to college and developing some skills so you can get a better job?"

It's always the same old thing with him. He wants me to take classes at Westfield Community College. It's been eight years since I was kicked out of Farmington State University during my sophomore year, and he never stops bringing it up. After what happened to me at Farmington, I don't want to ever go back. Even as a commuter. But, I can't tell him that.

"Yes, Dad, I saved up enough money to sign up for a class next semester," I lie.

"Just one class? Why not go back full-time?" he asks.

"Dad, I can't afford to pay for full-time classes."

"Son, if you return to school full-time, I'll pay for it. I'll also give you money to buy groceries and pay rent, so you won't have to worry about working full-time. You can still work part-time if you want to."

I roll my eyes again. If I'm stressing out about taking classes full-time, when am I going to engage in my extracurricular activities? When will I have the time and energy to do my stalking and killing?

"Okay, Dad, I'll think about it."

"Well, think hard, Eric. You're not going anywhere at your job. The only way for you to get ahead is to return to college."

"Okay, Dad, you've convinced me. I'll go back. It IS the only way to get ahead. Maybe we can talk about it more at dinner?" I say to placate him.

"Excellent, son," My father says with a lot more enthusiasm than before. "I'm happy to hear you've had a change of heart. I knew you wouldn't be content working THAT job forever. You are a Blackburn, after all. When Blackburn's fall, they pick themselves up."

I wish I could make you fall down permanently, you old geezer! I think. Instead of voicing this opinion, I say, "Okay, Dad. I look forward to seeing you and Mom on the Sunday after next."

"Dinner will be at five."

"Okay, Dad, that sounds good."

"We'll see you then, Eric."

"Okay, Dad, I'll see you then."

"Goodbye, Eric."

"Goodbye, Dad."

I resist the urge to hurl the phone against the wall. Instead, I take a deep breath and place it gently on the charger. I feel like I want to puke. I thought that conversation would never end. Although, I have to admit that I'm getting pretty good at playing my father.

Now where was I? Oh yes, the car rental store. The cops will be on the lookout for a red Ford, so I need to trade it in pronto. On my way there, I'll come up with a reasonable explanation for the switch to tell the bitch at the counter.

My eyes dart to the blank television screen in front of me and I have the sudden urge to turn it on and watch the news. The carnage I created at the mall last night will be all over the local media. It would be entertaining to see what the talking heads say about my work.

Many serial killers enjoy watching media stories covering their shenanigans because it makes them feel important. I have a sudden, powerful urge to switch on the TV.

However, that way of thinking goes against my philosophy. If I become obsessive about following news media reports about my activity, I could become distracted and careless. I don't want an ego-trip to get in the way of my methodical planning. If I get too excited about what the media says about me, it could affect my thinking and I could get sloppy. No, I can't give in to that urge; it's unproductive.

Leaving my apartment, I jog down the stairs and out the door toward the rental car in question. I get in and start it up. I return to the rental store, park in front of the building, and walk over to the front doors.

The same dumb blonde is behind the counter. A clock on the wall behind her reads 10:20 AM. I manufacture a smile as I approach her.

"Hi, how's it going?" I say.

"Pretty good," the girl says, looking at me warily.

Stupid bitch. Yesterday, I signed up to rent the car for a full-week, so she must think I'm here to complain about the vehicle.

"I would like to exchange my Ford Focus for a Honda if that's possible," I say to the girl.

"Is there a problem with the car?" she asks, raising an eyebrow.

I want to slap her face, but I use all my willpower not to.

"No, not at all. You see, I'm used to driving a Honda and it doesn't feel natural when I drive anything else. The bottom line is I don't feel comfortable driving this car."

"We don't have any Hondas, but we do have Toyotas," the bimbo says, as she types on a computer keyboard and then stares at a screen behind the counter.

"A Toyota will be fine," I say. "Toyotas handle the same."

The girl types in more commands and looks at me across the counter separating us.

"I have a red Toyota Corolla that's ready to go," she says.

"Do you have any other colors?" I ask.

Red won't work. The Ford was red. The cops will be on the lookout for a medium-sized red sedan that ran over two girls at the mall.

The girl's eyebrows knit together in an obvious expression of annoyance. I want to reach across the counter and grab her by the throat, but I keep my cool.

"We also have one in light green," she says. "Will that be all right?" She raises her eyebrow again.

"Sure, that's fine," I say, forcing another smile.

I want to wipe that stupid smirk off her face by giving her a permanent ear-to-ear grin with my knife.

"Okay, I'll draw up the paperwork," the girl tells me as she types on her keyboard.

A few seconds later, I hear the sound of the printer as she produces the paperwork for my rental agreement. They already have my credit card number on file, so all I have to do is provide my signature. The girl escorts me out to the back of the lot where my new puke-green Toyota is waiting. She hands me the keys and it takes all my willpower not to snatch them out of her hands and tell her to "fuck off."

Instead, I say, "Thank you."

I'm all out of smiles, so all I can manage to throw her way is a neutral expression. She doesn't seem to care one way or the other as she turns her back on me and walks away. It would be so easy to creep up on her and place her in a deadly stranglehold. It would feel so satisfying to wrap my bicep and forearm around her neck and squeeze until she stopped breathing. Maybe I'll come back for her later.

Sliding into the driver's seat, I start up my new vehicle. I have to make another trip to the bitch's neighborhood, but this time I'll be smart about it because I know where the cop car is parked and what direction it's facing.

Her street goes around the block in a circle, so I will enter the circle from the opposite direction, drive to the edge of the blind corner behind the parked cop car, check out the layout of her house, and turn around before the cop notices me.

If I do a three-point turn behind the cruiser, it will be a painfully slow process and could potentially attract the cop's attention, so instead I'll back into a neighbor's driveway – as if I belong there – and pull out and head in the opposite direction. In order to follow me, the cop would have to glance in his rearview mirror at the right moment, register my car

SHAWN WILLIAM DAVIS

as suspicious, and complete a three-point-turn in his cruiser. By then, I'll be long gone.

I pull out of the rental car lot and head in the direction of the slut's neighborhood. The dashboard clock reads 10:42 AM. I'm excited at the prospect of getting my hands on her again.

It only takes me fifteen minutes to get to her neighborhood. I drive past her street on the right and take the next right that will take me around to her house from the opposite direction. I cuise past an unimpressive variety of ranch and Cape houses that have small yards and short driveways. Glancing at the speedometer, I make sure I am traveling at a cautious 15 mph, which is slow enough to avoid running into trouble, but fast enough not to call attention to myself.

The houses spread out as the road curves around to the right. A large, gray, colonial-style house looms at the end of a long driveway on the left; it looks out of place among the ranches and Capes. Soon, the houses to my left and right give way to a stretch of lonely woods; I spot the entrance to a dirt road between a pair of pylons with a chain strung between them. A faded white sign reading "Conservation Land" hangs down on the center of the chain.

I was in such a rush to get away from the cop last time that I never even noticed this isolated section of the bitch's road. As I continue to follow the curving road to the right, the woods on the left opens up to a small yard with a Cape house at the end of a short driveway. It looks familiar. Is it the slut's neighbor? I must be getting close. I slow to a crawl as I approach the blind corner, preparing myself for the ugly sight of the black-and-white police cruiser parked next to the curb.

The speedometer reads 10mph, then 5mph, then 0 as I pause at the edge of the blind corner. Then, I give it just enough gas to coast around the corner. Where's the cruiser? Looking left, I recognize the slut's light-blue ranch house, but there's no cruiser parked across from it. Gaining confidence, I accelerate to 10 mph. There's no cruiser! It's gone!

I feel a rush as my eyes bore into the bitch's house like twin drills. Do they really think those cheap wooden walls can keep me out? One car is parked in the driveway: a dark blue Toyota Camry. Across the street is an open field. I watch her house recede in my left side mirror as I drive past.

With the cruiser gone, I can circle around and set up a stakeout behind the line of trees across from the Conservation Land entrance.

CHAPTER 46

Tracey Randall woke from a horrific nightmare, soaked with sweat. Her body trembled as if she had chills, but she also felt hot. She threw off her soaked blankets and sat up in bed.

In her dream, she was back in the cabin in New Hampshire being raped by her kidnapper. Like before, she fought back by pounding his forehead with her fists. Like before, she pushed him off the bed so he hit the floor. Like before, she made a run for it. Unlike before, there was no snowsuit hanging on a peg in the mud room, so she had to run naked into the cold. Unlike before, she could not escape.

Tracey felt like she was running at top speed, but the killer still caught her. She made it outside, but before she could reach the safety of the woods, the psycho tackled her to the hard, snowy ground. She fought back by punching him all over his body, but he pinned her to the ground. She felt his fingers constrict around her throat like a noose; the pressure choked her airway.

Tracey fought him as she gasped for air, but he was stronger than she was. She pounded him in his face with her fists, but his hand pressure was relentless; she could not get him to release his grip. She broke out in a cold sweat as she felt energy draining from her body. Her mind began to tune out like a fading radio signal as blackness closed in on her.

Tracey found herself floating in the air like a spirit, looking down at the killer with his hands clamped around her throat. Finally, the psycho must have realized she was dead because he unwrapped his fingers from her flesh. He continued to sit astride her looking down at her naked body. Then, he began fondling her breasts.

Tracey wanted to fight back, but as an ethereal being, she could only watch as the psychopath groped her cold body. She was filled with impotent rage as she watched his hands violate her pale corpse. Just when she thought she would go completely mad, the image faded to blackness and she felt herself back in her body – lying beneath the covers on her bed.

Tracey sat, trembling, on her mattress, thanking God the dream was not real. It had felt extraordinarily vivid, which made it all the more terrifying. It's not every night you dream you were violently murdered.

Tracey stood, shakily, from her bed and went to the window above her desk that looked out on the backyard. She made sure the backyard and woods beyond were clear, and checked the window lock to make sure it was secure.

Last night, she checked every window and door-lock in the house before she went to bed. Even that precaution did little to ease her worried mind. The killer was still running around loose and she was sure he still wanted to get her.

Tracey sat down at her desk and accessed the Internet on her personal computer. Since she had arrived home, she had spent a lot of time studying self-defense videos on Youtube. So far, she had watched a series of martial arts videos and one police defensive training video.

She found the police defensive training to be more practical. Mostly, it was just punches, elbows, and low kicks - whereas the martial arts videos tried to get fancy with high kicks she could never pull off. She memorized and practiced several moves that she thought might help her if she was attacked again.

Tracey was already an athletic person, which was a plus in her mind. She played on the High School tennis team and basketball team, so she already possessed a ground-work of strength, speed, and agility. She would have played on the High School softball team as well, but the program ran at the same time as tennis, so she had to prioritize.

According to her computer screen, it was 10:20 AM, so both of her parents were at work. Her mother worked as a secretary at a dental office in town and her father worked on an assembly line at a computer manufacturing plant in Farmington.

This morning, her mother had driven her father to work so Tracey could borrow her father's car: a 2010 Toyota Camry. Tracey needed it later to visit a therapist, who specialized in PTSD cases, in Farmington.

Tracey's mother said she would come home during her lunch-break at 11:45 AM to have lunch with Tracey. Mrs. Randall thought some companionship mid-way through the day would ease Tracey's anxious mind.

Tracey's father suggested that Tracey might feel better if she kept busy and returned to school to attend classes. Tracey had already decided that option was out of the question. Her face felt hot, sweat broke out on her forehead, and her hands became clammy as she contemplated leaving the house to go to school.

The high school building was wide open and there wasn't a single security guard assigned to protect it. The teachers were busy teaching classes and didn't have the time or skill to protect her. At least at home she was behind locked doors and windows. The police detail across the street was another good reason to stay home. There were no police officers assigned to the high school to watch over her. She felt safer in her house under the watchful gaze of the Westfield PD.

No, she wasn't going to school any time soon. At school, she was vulnerable.

Tracey's parents hoped that her therapy appointment today at 1 PM would help her to deal with her chronic anxiety since returning home. Tracey had been on edge since she escaped from her psychotic kidnapper and all of the usual activities that she did to relax had failed to blunt the edge. Watching action movies on DVD, playing RPG video games, reading mystery books, and listening to a mix of music on her Ipod could not distract her from her constant anxiety.

A nervous tremor stayed with her no matter what she did. Where-ever she was in the house, she felt a flutter in her stomach as if a black butterfly was flying around inside her. When she ate her favorite foods, she became nauseous. She was not the same person she was before, and she desperately wanted to get her old self back. She was coming to realize that once your innocence was lost, it was gone forever.

Tracey decided to try reading a book to distract her from her worry. Before she had been kidnapped, she was about three-quarters of the way through *The Girl With the Dragon Tattoo* by Stieg Larson.

When she returned home after her ordeal, she thought it would not be a good idea to continue reading the book because she remembered a scene where the heroine, Lisbeth Salander, had been sexually assaulted by her psychotic lawyer.

Granted, Lisbeth got back at him by blackmailing and inscribing a painful tattoo on his chest, which read something like "I am a disgusting rapist pig." Tracey would relish the chance to get back at her attacker.

Like Tracey, Lisbeth Salander, had fought back against her victimizer and gained the upper hand. Tracey fought back and escaped, but unlike Lisbeth, she did not have the upper hand. Maybe she would become inspired by reading more about Ms. Salander's heroic exploits.

Tracey picked up the book from the floor, where it had fallen next to the desk, and carried it to the living room. She sat in her favorite recliner, switched on the lamp beside her, and adjusted the seat so she was leaning back all the way. For a few brief moments, she felt safe and secure in her home as she had before the terror of the kidnapping.

As she became comfortable and had time to think, her anxiety returned. An image of the kidnapper's profile flashed into her mind as he drove her north on the highway. She shivered and opened the book to try to distract her mind from negative visions.

A short time later, Tracey became engrossed in the story and lost track of time. Her paralyzing anxiety dissipated as she escaped into a world of fiction. However, when she reached the part in the book where the serial killer captured and tortured the journalist, Michael Blomkist, her anxiety returned full-force.

Suddenly, she felt like someone was creeping up behind her. She got up and looked around. There was no one there, but she was sure that someone had broken into the house. She dropped the book and raised her arms to fend off a potential attack

CHAPTER 47

Tracey advanced cautiously toward the intersection of the living room, kitchen, and hallway. The hallway was empty, but she imagined a menacing figure emerging suddenly from one of the doorways.

Her body tensed as she approached the opening to the kitchen where an attacker might be lurking behind the wall separating the kitchen from the living room. Peering into the kitchen, she saw no one there.

Tracey walked quickly across the linoleum floor and checked the deadbolt lock on the back door that led onto the porch; the lock was secure.

Tracey began a systematic check of every door and window lock in the house. She completed a circuit of the kitchen, dining room, and living room until she reached the front door, which she also found locked. Then, she did a double-take and returned to look out the front window. She saw her blue Toyota Camry parked in the driveway, but the street was empty.

Where was the police cruiser? Panic flooded her system like a black wave. Maybe the officer was parked farther up the street? They would tell her if they were going to remove the detail, wouldn't they?

Tracey shook off her fear like a wet dog shakes off water. She returned to the hallway and prepared to go room-to-room to check every window lock.

The first door she came to in the hallway was a closet. Tracey reached for the doorknob, turned it, and leaped back in case an attacker was waiting inside to lunge at her. Instead of seeing a figure within, she only saw jackets on hangers.

Tracey advanced down the corridor; her body tensed as she approached the open bathroom doorway on the left. Pressing her back against the wall opposite the doorway, she shuffled ahead until she could see inside. She saw towels hanging on a rack and the front edge of a toilet poking out behind the sink. The room appeared empty, but what if someone was hiding in the shower?

Entering the bathroom, Tracey minimized the sound of her footsteps on the tiles as she approached the shower stall across from the toilet. The shower curtain was already half-open, so she could see there was no one lurking behind it. She breathed a sigh of relief.

Tracey re-entered the hallway and paused to listen for any signs of movement ahead; it was eerily quiet. She continued toward the guest bedroom doorway on the right, and repeated her technique of pressing her back against the opposite wall as she shuffled sideways toward the doorway. The door was open a quarter of the way, so she could see the edge of the guest bed and the night table beside it.

Tracey drew back her leg and kicked the door open the rest of the way. She jumped with fright as the door slammed into the wall; she must have applied too much force. Her adrenaline must really be pumping.

I'm scaring myself, she thought.

The guest bedroom was empty. But what about the closet? Tracey turned the corner and approached the closet. The closet door was ajar and she saw no one hiding inside. She blew out a breath.

Tracey went to the end of the hallway and checked the last two rooms; her room and her parents' room. The rooms and closets were empty. She also checked all the windows to make sure they were locked. They were. That's it then. The house was secure.

Except – she had forgotten about the basement. There was a single ground-level window built into the rear of the foundation that she needed to check. Damn. It was dark and creepy down there.

For this mission, Tracey retrieved her tennis racket, which was constructed of a mixture of titanium and plastic, from her closet and held it two-handed like a baseball bat. She knew there had to be an advantage to being on the high school tennis team: a ready-to-use makeshift weapon. She held the racket in front of her like a sword and advanced into the hallway.

Tracey felt more confident now that she had something to defend herself with. If the psychopath tried to come at her with a knife, she would smash his head in with a titanium-reinforced racket. She went to the end of the hallway and entered the kitchen. Turning right, she faced the basement door.

Tracey brought the tennis racket back over her shoulder, as if she was about to serve a ball to the opposite court, and then reached for the doorknob. She yanked the door open and observed the wooden stairwell descending into darkness.

Tracey held the racket in a ready-to-strike position as she reached around the corner to flip on the light switch. The stairwell lit up and a section of gray concrete wall and floor appeared below.

The stairwell was located at the center of the basement, so empty air surrounded her on each side. Tracey wasn't sure which way to aim her racket, so she swept it from side-to-side as she descended.

Tracey felt her heart beating hard in her chest like an overheating engine. She kept expecting a hand to reach out from under the stairs to clutch her ankle. If that happened, she thought for sure her heart would explode like a muscle-and-blood bomb.

When she reached the concrete floor, she turned to make sure no one was hiding in the space beneath the stairwell. She checked left and right. The way to the left was better lit, so she went that way.

Tracey passed by her father's tool bench and headed toward the washer and drier placed against the far wall. The only possible spot where someone could hide was behind a large metal boiler in the corner. Carefully, Tracey moved toward it with her raised racket. Her body trembled as she approached the blind spot. Steeling herself, she stared into the dark gap between the boiler and the concrete wall. No one was there.

Tracey's eyes moved upward to a beam of light shining in through a plain glass window at the top of the wall; she thought it would be easy for someone to smash the window and enter the cellar undetected. She needed to do something about that.

Tracey circled around the rear of the stairwell until she reached tall metal shelves lining the walls. It was darker on this side as the only light came from the bulb hanging from the ceiling near her father's work bench.

Four-to-five-foot stacks of plastic and cardboard boxes took up most of the floor. Only two stacks in the corner had enough space behind them where someone could crouch and hide. Tracey approached the boxes with her racket raised and checked behind them. No one. The house was secure. The only danger had existed within her mind.

Tracey closed her eyes and took a deep breath. It was all in my head, she thought. I'm cracking up, but that's okay. At least I'm safe.

Lowering the tennis racket to her side, Tracey ascended the stairs to the kitchen and shut the cellar door behind her. She went to the fridge, obtained a Power-aid drink from the shelf on the door, unscrewed the cap, and took a swig. Apparently, baseless fear makes you thirsty, she thought.

Tracey wished she could laugh at the situation, but she couldn't. A vague, formless anxiety lurked in the recesses of her mind like a wraith in a tomb.

She returned to the front window to look for the police cruiser, and felt another rush of anxiety when she didn't see it. To the right, she could see all the way to the spot where the road turned in a sharp corner, so the cruiser obviously wasn't there.

To the left, a line of trees separated her families' yard from the neighbor's yard, so her view was blocked that way. Technically, the cruiser could be parked behind those trees, but then the officer wouldn't have a clear view of the house. She felt her shoulders begin to tremble.

Tracey needed something to distract herself from her unproductive worry. She had checked every window and door lock in the house, and they were all secure. There was no rational reason to stand by the front window, quivering with fear. So the police car was gone? So what? She knew it wasn't going to be there forever anyway. However, she had thought it would be there for at least a week.

Her only option was to keep her mind busy; she returned to

the comfortable recliner where she had been reading about Lisbeth Salander's challenging exploits. She leaned her tennis racket against the side of the recliner, so it was within easy reach. Then, she placed her Power-aid bottle down on the carpet and picked up the book from the side table. She opened it to the page with the tiny dog-ear in the corner and resumed reading. Tracey continued to feel tense for several minutes until her mind escaped into the artificial world between the pages.

Tracey felt empowered when the heroine of the book, Lisbeth, rescued the journalist, Blomkvist, as he was being tortured in the serial killer's secret basement chamber. Tracey felt elated as Lisbeth smashed the serial killer in the face with a steel golf club, which was what Tracey planned to do with her tennis racket if she encountered her kidnapper again.

Tracey lost track of time again as she read about Lisbeth Salander's brilliant scam to steal billions of dollars from the corrupt businessman, Hans Wennerstrom. Lisbeth's ingenuity was inspiring, and Tracey felt that she could emulate Lisbeth's audacious behavior if she had to.

Tracey was startled when she heard a car pull into the driveway. She leaped to her feet, darted to the front window, and relaxed when she saw it was only her mother's red Honda SUV. Was it eleven-forty-five already?

Tracey had lunch with her mother, and she was happy to have the company, but she was also anxious to finish the last several pages of her book. When her mother left at 12:15 PM, she made a bee-line for the recliner and completed the last twenty pages of *The Girl with the Dragon Tattoo*.

Tracey felt badly for Lisbeth at the end of the story when Lisbeth saw Mikael with another woman, but she was sure that Lisbeth possessed the fortitude to recover from the hurtful experience. Besides, after Lisbeth's brilliant banking scam, she was a billionaire.

Tracey realized that it was time to get ready for her appointment. She changed out of her sweatpants and t-shirt into jeans and a button-down shirt. She discarded her sneakers for shoes with heels. The shoes weren't the best thing to wear for self-defense, but she couldn't imagine the kidnapper being brazen enough to come after her as she drove to or from her therapist's appointment. After the false alarm in the house, Tracey decided she was becoming unnecessarily jumpy.

Despite her slightly increased confidence, Tracey still glanced in all directions as she left through the front doorway of the house. She checked the lawn, the trees, the street, or anywhere someone could come at her. Her eyes narrowed as she thought she saw a glint of steel behind the trees at the corner of the road, but she decided it was just her imagination.

Tracey locked the front door and pressed the unlock button on her car key as she jogged toward the driver's side of the Toyota. She slid into the front seat and hit the button for the automatic locks. The click of the locks was reassuring. She started the car and glanced over her shoulder as she backed out of the driveway.

CHAPTER 48

After spending less than two hours on the stakeout, I hit pay-dirt; the bitch is walking out the front doorway of the house. I feel a rush of adrenaline as I watch her hurry to the car. Now she's mine.

Instinct compels me to start the engine and go after her right away, but I force myself to calm down. I wait until she gets in the car and shuts the driver's side door before I start my engine. My entire body is trembling with anticipation.

I felt letdown earlier when I spotted another vehicle, a red Toyota SUV, pull into the driveway behind the Camry at around 11:42 AM. I watched a middle-aged woman, who I assumed to be the slut's mother, walk on a concrete path from the SUV to the front door, and let herself in with a key. I figured that she probably left the front door open, and I could walk in if I wanted to, but two targets are more risky than one. Anyway, the middle-aged woman left by herself in the SUV about a half-hour later.

Now it's 12:30 PM and the bitch is in motion. The seconds go by excruciatingly slowly as I watch her back out of the driveway onto the street, pause for what seems like a maddeningly long time, and drive away. Again, I want to hit the gas pedal and race after her, but I have to restrain myself. I can't allow her to spot me.

I wait until she reaches the end of the street before I pull out from my hiding place behind the trees. Then, I remain motionless in my vehicle until I see her turn the corner onto the main road. Now I can move. I want to smash down on the gas pedal, but I tap it instead. I can't call any attention to myself.

Using all my available restraint, I cruise at a leisurely 20 mph down the slut's street toward the main road. As I watch her car disappear behind a line of trees, I have to fight the urge to slam down on the gas. Instead, I speed up to 30 mph as I tap my fingers impatiently on the steering wheel.

When I reach the main avenue, I look both ways for traffic and pull out after her. Breathing a sigh of relief, I spot her car ahead about a hundred yards distant.

My breath catches in my throat when her car suddenly disappears from view. Now, all my restraint is gone; I slam my foot down on the pedal and listen to the engine roar as I accelerate to 60 mph – on a road with a 35 mph speed limit. Sweat breaks out on my forehead as I climb a small hill, accelerating to 70 mph. I hit the brakes when I realize the road is about to descend ahead.

My car fishtails, but I keep it under control as I slow to 45 mph. Apparently, I did it just in time as the road descends so I spot her car only a hundred feet distant. Slowing to 25 mph, I put more distance between her and me.

I need to calm down. She doesn't know she's being followed, so she's not trying to evade me. As long as I know the direction her vehicle is headed, I don't have to panic when it disappears over a hill or around a curve. It will still be there ahead of me as I follow her.

Now that I have a hundred yards between myself and my prey, I feel more comfortable. I try to relax, but my body is quaking with adrenaline. I attempt to light a cigarette, but my hands are shaking too much to hold the cigarette and lighter steady.

Panic floods my brain as a black Lexus SUV pulls out of a side-street ahead of me, blocking my view of the slut's Toyota. I accelerate until I'm tailgating the Lexus and pull to the left to see if I can spot the Toyota. I see it several hundred feet ahead, so I back off the Lexus's bumper before I start to look suspicious.

Tapping my fingers on the steering wheel, I back off until there's a space of two car-lengths between myself and the Lexus. I want to ram the Lexus off the road so I will have a clear view of my prey, but that option is untenable with my small sedan.

Instead, I periodically swerve a few feet into the opposite lane so I can see around the Lexus. I relax when I see a glimmer of light reflecting off blue metal on what I hope is the bitch's Camry driving ahead of the Lexus.

I want to pass the Lexus, but it would be suicide on this hilly road because I wouldn't see any oncoming cars until they were up in my grill. In this situation, I have to force myself to be patient because I'm stuck here.

I need to relax because she's not going anywhere anytime soon. Tomorrow, she will still be living in an unimpressive house on a non-descript suburban lane, and she will still be living there next week, next month, and for the rest of the year as far as I know. Unsuspecting, she will continue to take road trips by herself to who-knows-where in her pathetic blue Toyota. If I lose her now, there will still be plenty of opportunities to get her in the future.

I calm down as I realize I can stakeout her house and follow her some other time – if by some chance I lose her now. I want to grab her today, but I don't HAVE to grab her today.

My revenge will taste just as sweet tomorrow or next week.

The next time I get my hands on her, I will take measures to insure she doesn't escape. I'll use my combat knife to slice the tendons in her ankles so she can't run. Then, I'll bandage the wounds so she doesn't bleed to death and play with her at my leisure. It was foolish not to incapacitate her before. I won't make that same mistake again.

Imagining the scenario of slicing her ankle tendons helps me to relax. She won't get away next time.

Sure enough, we reach a stop sign at an intersection and the black Lexus takes a right, while the blue Toyota takes a left. I pull up to the stop sign and wait for the Toyota to get some distance before I follow it.

As I shadow her, I feel more confident; she's not getting away. She doesn't even know I'm tracking her.

Now I can light a cigarette. Cracking the window, I take a pack out of my pocket, shake one out, and light up. I suck the smoke deep into my lungs and blow it out. I feel like a predator that has cornered its prey.

I tap the brakes when I see her brake lights come on. Then, her right blinker lights up and she slows to take a right onto a side street. I continue to cruise at a leisurely 30 mph. After all, the area is thickly settled and the safety of the public is always my number one concern.

Her car disappears from view, but I'm not worried. Enjoying my cigarette, I don't have a care in the world. She's not going anywhere. Taking a leisurely right onto the side road, I spot the blue Toyota about 50 yards ahead.

Soon, I have to pay attention again as the roads become more congested when we reach a commercial area on the outskirts of Farmington. With all the added traffic, I have to be careful not to lose track of her.

Cursing, I hit the brakes as a light-blue BMW convertible cuts me off from a side street. I light another cigarette as I'm stuck in a line of cars at a stoplight. No problem. I'm in no rush. I can't see her, but I know her car is just ahead.

I realize the BMW is assisting me because it's acting as camouflage. She might notice me following her if I'm right behind her.

As the traffic begins to move again, I toss my cigarette out the window. After another mile, the slut's left blinker clicks on as we near an office complex. She pulls over to the left side of the lane as she waits for traffic going the other way to pass her.

I don't want to make her suspicious, so I continue to follow the BMW as it passes her on the right and continues down the road. Glancing in my rearview mirror, I watch the Toyota pull into the parking lot in front of the office building. I wait for an opening in the oncoming traffic, click on my left blinker, and pull into the driveway of a small house.

I wait, irritably, for almost a full minute for traffic to let up so I can back out and backtrack to the office building. Finally, I catch a break and hit the gas pedal. After racing several hundred yards, I slow down as I approach the office complex.

As I near the entrance, I see the bitch's car parked four spaces away from the front glass door on the left side of the building. If she had parked closer to the door, she would have had a better chance. Unfortunately for her, there's plenty of space for me to intercept her when she returns to her vehicle.

I pull into the parking lot and halt as I can't decide whether to go left or right. Remaining stationary, I watch the slut get out of her car and hurry past the four parked cars between her and the front glass door.

There's a white sign on the wall next to the door containing a list of names. She checks the names on the sign, ascends several steps, yanks open the door, and hurries inside as if the devil himself is on her tail. She appears to be slightly paranoid as if she doesn't want to spend too much time in the open. Little good it will do her.

I cruise past the bitch's car, and back into an open spot in the opposite row where I have a good view of the glass door. I'm far enough away not to be noticed, but close enough to step on the gas pedal and strike her like a bolt of lightning when she steps into the parking lot.

I watch people come and go from the office building. The dashboard clock reads 12:55 PM. I figure she will be gone for at least a half-hour if she is at a doctor's appointment. Maybe she has a one o-clock appointment? I light a cigarette and wait.

CHAPTER 49

I chain-smoke as I wait for the bitch to reappear from the front door of the office building. My throat feels dry and sore, and I'm craving a drink of water, but I can't abandon the stakeout. She could step out at any moment.

It's 1:32 PM; over a half-hour has gone by and there's still no sign of her. Her appointment must be an hour long, which means more intolerable waiting. The problem is that if I wait longer, there's a better chance someone will see me smoking in my car and report me as suspicious to the cops.

As I sit fidgeting in the driver's seat, beads of sweat break out on my forehead and nervous tremors run through my body. I don't know if these symptoms are from the nicotine I've been ingesting or the anxiety caused by waiting. Probably both.

I can't take this much longer. I need to act and I need to act soon. I focus all my concentration on the front glass door. I feel my unused energy simmering in my brain like boiling water about to overflow from a kettle. I can't let that happen. I have to calm down. She should be leaving the building any moment now. I need to be ready.

I go over the plan in my mind. I'm parked in the row across from the row of cars against the building where the slut is parked – two spaces away diagonally from her car. Ideally, I would park in the space directly across from her car, but that space is taken. Even so, if I pull out of my space as soon as I see her exit, I will have time to intercept her as she is about to reach her car.

I have to time this perfectly, because I have to let her go far enough so she can't run back to the building, but not so far that she is able to get inside her vehicle. My best option is to incapacitate her by striking her legs with my front bumper.

Obviously, I can't hit her hard enough to kill her because I want to take her alive, but I have to hit her hard enough to knock her down. Then, I can grab her, handcuff her, throw her in the car, and slice her ankle tendons at my leisure when I have more time.

It sounds good, but I know from experience that plans don't always go the way I imagine. Sometimes, the little sluts evade me or fight back. Then, it becomes challenging. I'm hoping this will be a simple snatch and grab.

On my way to the bitch's house, I pulled over to the side of the road to change the rental license plates over to ones I stole a month ago from the mall parking lot where I work. It was a risky move because a cop could have driven by and saw what I was doing, but I figured it was a lot less risky than allowing someone to write down the license plate of my rental car as I do the snatch and grab. Snatch and grabs tend to attract more attention than pulling over to the side of the road. Usually, people drive past a car in the breakdown lane without looking too closely.

Reaching into my right pocket, I make sure my canister of pepper spray is within easy reach if I need it. Then, I reach into my left pocket to check the steel, police-issue handcuffs. I left the glove compartment open because my combat knife is tucked away under the registration and other paperwork. The handle is facing me, so all I have to do is reach over and grab it. It would be easier just to leave the knife on the passenger seat, but I can't risk anyone walking past my car and seeing it.

There she is; I watch her push open the glass door and step out. I can't see the outline of her breasts because of her baggy button-down dress shirt, but her tight jeans give me a good impression of the rest of her figure.

I feel a surge of adrenaline as I inch my car out of the parking space; I go slow so I don't call attention to myself. If she sees me and recognizes me, she will turn around and run back into the building before I can grab her.

She is completely focused on her car because she's not looking around. There are four cars between the front door and her car. I pull out a few more feet as she hurries past the first one. As she passes the second one, I turn the wheel to aim the nose of my vehicle at her. All I have to do is press down on the gas pedal.

In my peripheral vision, I see a dark gray Crown Vic enter the parking lot from the entrance. The car has a large antenna in the back and the front plate is blue, indicating that it's a state vehicle. I freeze. Crown Vics are the premiere cop vehicle and this one could be an unmarked.

As the Crown Vic turns toward me, I back slowly into my parking space. Straight ahead, the bitch is fumbling with her key in the driver's side door of her Toyota. It would be child's play to cut off the Crown Vic and run her down where she stands. Instead, the Crown Vic glides in front of me like a cruising shark, blocking my view of her. The driver has a buzz-cut and he's wearing a dark blue state police uniform. The cop glances over at me, so I reach down and fumble with paperwork in the glove compartment.

When I glance up again, the unmarked Crown Vic continues

its circuit of the parking lot to the right. Ahead, I can see the top of the bitch's head poking above the headrest of the Toyota's driver's seat. I hear her car engine start and watch her back out. I am in shock as I contemplate my bad luck.

As the slut pulls out of her spot and heads toward the entrance, the unmarked cop car disappears from view around the corner of the office building. Timing is everything and this fucking cop has just ruined all my carefully-laid plans. I can't believe this is happening. She is getting away because of blind chance. A deadly rage builds within me like the expanding funnel of a tornado.

CHAPTER 50

I'm paralyzed by shock and rage; I can't believe I'm watching the slut's green Toyota heading toward the entrance to the parking lot. How could my plan have gone so wrong? One unforeseen factor, an unmarked state trooper car, caused it all to go to hell.

As I sit in my car trying to figure out what happened, the bitch is getting away, but I'm too distracted to formulate a decent plan. Fuck it, I'll just go after her and see what happens. Maybe I'll get lucky.

Hands shaking on the wheel, I steer out of the parking space as I tap the gas pedal with a quivering leg. I use the back of my hand to wipe away rivulets of sweat streaming onto my cheeks from my saturated forehead. My dark t-shirt is already soaked.

Driving toward the entrance to the parking lot, I keep expecting the unmarked police cruiser to come up behind me at any moment with its lights flashing. That cop really fucked me over. I don't feel safe committing to any kind of plan now. Still, I have to try to salvage something out of this.

When I reach the road, it takes a long time for the traffic to let up long enough for me to pull out, and even then I have to cut off an oversized red pickup truck that honks its horn. I don't bother to flip him the bird because I'm in stealth mode; the cop is still nearby. I pull to the left to see if I can spot the slut's car ahead; it's nowhere in the line of traffic.

The traffic halts as it bottlenecks at a stoplight intersection. I wipe away the sweat streaming into my face. Though it's a cool sixty degrees outside, I turn on the air conditioning because I feel like I'm burning up.

It takes me fifteen minutes to get out of the congested downtown area that should have only taken me five minutes. At least the air conditioning dried up my sweat.

I breathe a sigh of relief as I turn onto a side street. It's one of those sickening Norman Rockwell streets lined with colonials fronted by wide, lush lawns. An attractive blonde woman is walking her small black dog on the sidewalk. She's in her twenties: way too old for me.

As I cruise through the neighborhood, I look around for prey. A group of kids are running around in the yard to my left. I'm not interested in kids. I'm no pedophile.

Then, I feel a sudden rush of adrenaline. Maybe my luck is changing. Ahead, the houses and yards give way to a long stretch of forest. Even better, the road curves so the stretch is out of view of the neighborhood. And best of all, two young girls wearing black spandex pants and skimpy cut-off shirts are walking side-by-side on the sidewalk.

I cruise past them and notice they are a little young for my taste, maybe fourteen or fifteen, but close enough. I pull over onto the sidewalk in front of the girls. Glancing in the rearview mirror, I see them hesitate as they regard the obstacle in their way. One is a blonde and the other has light brown hair. Both have small, but perky breasts poking out from their green and purple cut-off shirts.

Reaching into my right pocket, I check my can of pepper

spray. I open the driver's door and step out. The girls look tense as if they are contemplating running away, but don't want to overreact. I flash them my best disarming smile and say, "Hey girls, I'm looking for Prescott Street. Do you know where that is?"

"I don't - like - know what you're talking about," the blonde says in a bitchy voice, sarcastically accentuating the word "what."

Her eyebrows press together and the edges of her mouth turn down. Her attitude infuriates me.

"You see, I'm lost and I was told that Prescott street was nearby," I say as I approach closer.

When I reach within ten feet of them, they both start to back away – but not fast.

"Look, mister, we told you we don't know where it is, so why don't you just leave us alone?" the brunette says, brown eyes widening.

You should be scared now, I think.

"It's too late for that, bitches." I grin as I whip out the can of pepper spray like an evil magic wand.

They both turn to flee, but they're way too slow. I make a lightning-bolt lunge and tackle the blonde to the pavement. She screams, but the only other person around to hear is her friend, and she's high-tailing it down the sidewalk. I wrap my arm around the blonde's neck and squeeze. She shuts up as her air is cut off.

"You fucking slut, I'll teach you to mouth off to me," I tell her, as I loosen my grip around her neck so I can get her into position to spray her face. As the burning liquid does its work, she screams again, but it's a useless gesture because there are no houses around on this stretch of the road. I tighten my bicep muscle and she goes silent again.

I drag the sobbing blonde toward the passenger side of the rental car. It's a quiet street and so far there's been no traffic. I can't believe how lucky I am. She tries to struggle, so when I reach the car, I push her down on the sidewalk to pin her against the asphalt. Then, I grab her left arm and twist it behind her back. Reaching into my pocket, I pull out a set of metal handcuffs and slip a cuff around her wrist. I hear a comforting metallic click as it snaps shut.

Suddenly, I tense as I hear a car approaching from behind. I drag the girl further behind the car, and stand on her back as I turn toward the woods – as if I just stopped here to take a piss. My car is blocking the girl, so the driver can only see the top of my back. The bitch gasps for air as I apply my full weight on her lungs. I hear the car drive past me and turn to watch it disappear down the street. I don't want to suffocate the girl, so I step off her. I kick her in the ribs so she doesn't get any ideas about getting up.

Reaching down, I seize the cuff dangling from the girl's wrist and pull it toward her free wrist. She twists her body in an attempt to writhe out of my grasp, but she's too weak and in a bad position. I press my knee into her back, and she stops struggling. She moans softly, which makes me smile.

Grabbing her free arm, I pull it toward her cuffed wrist and snap the second cuff around her bare wrist. Now that she's shackled, I drag her to a standing position and open the passenger door. She hardly struggles as I shove her into the car like a bag of groceries, and slam the door shut.

I hear footsteps on the pavement behind me. Turning around, I only have a split second to register a large object heading straight for my face. I try to raise my arms, but it's too late. Something heavy smashes me in the forehead, and I stumble backwards as I lose my equilibrium.

Luckily, I'm able to break my fall with my left arm as I hit the pavement. Pain radiates outward from my crushed limb, but I ignore it so I can lift my free arm when I spot a tree branch descending toward my head. I block the branch with my forearm and roll my body left toward the tree-line. Pain radiates from my lower back as the branch strikes it, but I use my momentum to get to my knees and spin around.

The tree branch descends toward me again, so I raise my arms just in time to block it. My forearms become sore and raw as I continue to block blows that are aimed at my head. I'm too busy fighting for my life to see any details of the person wielding the branch.

Finally, I have the presence of mind to realize that I'm still clutching my can of pepper spray in my right hand. As I block a blow with my left arm, I lift my right arm upward and pull the trigger. I swing the can back and forth as if I'm strafing someone with a machine gun. My finger lets up on the trigger when I hear a soft gasp emanate from the figure in front of me.

Then, I have a free moment to focus on my assailant so I can find out who the hell is beating me with a tree branch. As the image clarifies, I realize it's the brunette girl who I thought had run away. Apparently, she started to run, but she came back, and picked up a fallen tree branch on the way. Fucking A – that's never happened before.

Catching my breath, I lower my center of gravity and square off against the bitch. I watch her wipe her face with the back of her hand, but I don't see an opening to lunge because she's still brandishing the heavy branch. When both of her hands are free, she resumes a two-handed grip as if she's clenching a broadsword.

"Back the fuck off, bitch, and you won't get hurt," I say,

raising my left arm to fend off a potential attack with the branch, while I take low aim with the pepper spray.

"Let her go," the brunette says in a surprisingly firm voice as I watch her try to blink the pepper spray out of her eyes. I have to admit I've never seen someone recover from the stuff so fast.

"Back the fuck off," I say, launching another stream of spray at her that gets blown toward the road by a gust of wind.

"Fuck you," the girl says, winding up like a baseball player and swinging the branch at me hard.

Intense pain shoots through my forearm as I'm hit again. Just my luck – she must be a softball player. That fucking hurt. I hope it's not broken. I shoot more spray at her, but a damn breeze is still blowing the spray away toward the road. Fuck. I drop the can and hear it clatter on the pavement as I raise my arms to defend myself. I leap backward to dodge the next swing she takes at me.

"Put down the branch and you won't get hurt," I say, keeping my arms raised.

Unexpectedly, the brunette takes a step back as she continues to hold the branch in a defensive position.

"Katy, run! Run into the woods!" she screams.

Run? What's she talking about? I don't dare to turn around because the bitch will clock me in the back of the head. Incredibly, I hear the sound of creaking metal behind me, the car's passenger side door opening. How the fuck did the blonde open it with her hands cuffed behind her back? She must be a contortionist.

This thing is going bad fast, so I start to back up toward the car. I don't dare turn around to check on the blonde because the brunette is coming at me with the branch like a mugger with a baseball bat. I figure there's not much the blonde could do to me anyway with her hands cuffed behind her back. Unless, she somehow slipped out of those too.

I hear feet crunching through leaves and undergrowth to my left. In my peripheral vision, I see a figure with its arms pinned behind its back darting into the forest. The blonde getting away. Fuck.

I hear another car coming from the direction of the neighborhood, so I continue to step backward toward my rental. The brunette comes at me again with her makeshift weapon, so I duck out of reach of a swing and use my momentum to turn and sprint toward the car. The car is still running and the driver's door is open, so all I have to do is slide into the seat.

I close the door as the branch slams into the window, creating a spider-web in the glass. Without bothering to close the passenger door, I press down on the gas pedal and watch the brunette become steadily smaller in my rearview mirror. She looks like some kind of amazon warrior as she continues to hold the branch in front of her like a heavy sword.

The wind slams the passenger door shut as I accelerate. In the rearview mirror, I watch a car pulling over to the side of the road as the brunette waves her arms to flag it down. Fucking bitch. I can't believe I let her sneak up on me like that. I press down on the pedal until the silhouettes of the figure and the car disappear from view.

CHAPTER 51

Sergeant Jim Conrad met Detective Marilyn Lombardi at her office in the Westfield police station.

"I thought you might want one of these." He held a large Dunkin Donuts ice coffee in each hand.

Reaching across the desk, he handed one to the detective.

"Just what the doctor ordered. Have a seat," Lombardi said, taking the ice coffee and gesturing to the chair across from her desk.

The sergeant sat down and took a sip through a straw.

"When did you get in?" Lombardi asked.

"About an hour ago," Conrad replied. "I can't believe how long I slept last night. It must have been eleven hours."

"That's what happens when you push yourself too hard. You have to make up for it eventually," Lombardi said, sipping her coffee. "I only got into work a half-hour before you did. I must have slept for over ten hours myself."

"I planned to start working on this case this morning, but I guess 2:15 in the afternoon will have to do," Conrad said.

"Maybe getting a good night's rest will give us a fresh perspective," Marilyn said, taking another sip of coffee.

"I hope so because I feel like we're losing time," Jim replied. "This creep is still out there planning God-knows-what violence."

"We'll get him before he strikes again."

"I wish I had your confidence. I just went over the incident report that Detective Johnson faxed over last night."

"Did you find anything interesting?"

"Other than the fact that our usually tightly-controlled killer went berserk, the red Ford that he used in the hit-and-run is worth noting. He went through the trouble to change cars because the car he used to kidnap Tracey Randall was a black Japanese-made vehicle."

"Do you think the most recent car is a rental?" Marilyn asked.

"It could be," Jim said, considering. "It could also be stolen. According to Johnson's incident report, witnesses were able to record the license plate number of the red Ford used in the hit-and-run last night. When Farmington ran the plate, it came back to one reported stolen last week from a Cadillac SUV in Westfield. But that doesn't mean the Ford isn't also stolen. He might have placed a different set of stolen plates on it to throw us off track."

"We should check all the local car rental agencies," Marilyn said.

"I agree. We could get lucky and find an employee who remembers a customer matching the perp's description."

"What else did we learn from the crime scene last night?" the detective asked.

"We know our boy is deviating from his usual MO and getting sloppy," the sergeant replied, leaning back in the office chair.

"I agree with you on the MO, but I'm not so sure about the sloppy part," Lombardi said, flashing Conrad a lopsided grin. "That psychotic piece-of-shit killed two women and severely injured another two in a Macys parking lot in front of numerous witnesses. That means he's still as efficient at dealing out death as he ever was."

"I'm not questioning the creep's efficiency at killing," Conrad said. "However, by deviating from his usually precise MO to go off the rails into random slaughter, I think he's losing it."

"Okay, I'll give you that," the detective said. "The bloody scene last night looked more like a random crime of opportunity."

"He's losing it and it's only a matter of time before he makes a vital mistake."

They jolted upright in their seats as the phone rang on the detective's desk. She picked it up and spoke into the receiver.

"Detective Lombardi," she said. "Sure, send him through."

Conrad waited as a brief pause ensued.

"Hi, Detective Johnson," she said. Her face turned pale. "You're kidding me. It just happened? Ten minutes ago? What kind of vehicle was he driving?" A pause. "Uh, huh. Okay, you put it out in a BOLO?" The detective frowned as her eyes met Conrad's. "You would like us to be present when you interview the witnesses? Sure, no problem." Another pause. "Okay, we're on our way."

Detective Lombardi hung up the phone, stood from her chair, and picked up her coffee from the desk.

"What's up?" Conrad asked, raising an eyebrow.

"Our perp attempted a kidnapping in broad daylight in a

residential neighborhood in Farmington. Detective Johnson invited us to attend the interview with the witnesses at the scene."

"I told you it was only a matter of time. Any fatalities?"

"None. He attempted a kidnapping, but his two would-be victims fought him off. According to Johnson, they beat him up pretty badly."

"That fucker is definitely getting sloppy. He can't even pull off his usual MO when he tries," Conrad said, feeling a rush of adrenaline.

"Maybe this is the break we've been waiting for," Lombardi said, as she headed for the door.

Conrad followed her into the hallway.

"Here's another fact you might be interested in," the detective told the sergeant as they walked side-by-side down the corridor. "Johnson informed me that the perp was driving a light green Hyundai during today's attempted kidnapping."

"That means he's using car rental agencies," Conrad replied. "I doubt he's that proficient at stealing cars or willing to take the risk of getting caught doing it."

"After the interview, we can check all the local rental places."

"I have an idea," Conrad said as they cut through the report-writing room. "Why don't we divide our labor so you attend the interview in Farmington while I check the car rental agencies starting with the ones in Westfield."

"We can cover a lot more ground – a lot quicker – that way," Lombardi said.

"Since time is a factor, it's our best option."

"Okay, I'll go to the interview in Farmington while you check the rental agencies," the detective said. "We'll meet back here when we're done."

Conrad halted next to the dispatch booth while Lombardi continued down the short corridor toward the front lobby.

"I'll catch you later," she said as she turned the handle on the security door and pushed it open.

"See ya," Conrad said, stepping into the dispatch office. "Hey, how's it going?"

Conrad didn't use the dispatcher's name because he had forgotten it. Was it Jenna? Jane? She had just been hired last month, so she was still fairly new.

"Not bad, how are you, Sarge?" the dispatcher replied.

"Terrific," Jim said. "I just wanted to drop in to check on the cruiser detail at the Randall house."

"Sarge? Didn't they tell you?"

"Tell me what?"

"The detail has been called off," the dispatcher said, looking uneasy.

"What!" Conrad exclaimed, feeling his face flush.

"The Chief called it off yesterday. He said it's too expensive to keep someone there twenty-four-seven, but he asked the officers on duty to do increased patrols of the area."

Conrad felt rage gush through his brain like a torrent of boiling water through a burst pipe. He closed his eyes and counted backward from ten.

"Are you all right?" the dispatcher asked.

When he was finished counting, Conrad replied, "Sure, I'm

fine. I need you to do something for me though."

"Sure, anything, Sarge."

"Check the police network for a BOLO out of Farmington."

BOLO was an acronym for "Be On the LookOut"; it was an informational bulletin that was sent out state-wide through the police computer network when inter-jurisdictional co-operation was required.

"Read it carefully, and tell the officers on duty to check the parking lots of the two apartment complexes in town for a light green Hyundai," Conrad instructed the dispatcher. "Also, give the officers any additional relevant information from the BOLO. Got it?"

"No problem, Sarge."

"Thanks. I'm heading out, so you can put me down as Signal Five."

Signal Five meant that a unit was clear from its last call and was now free to take new calls from the dispatcher. Conrad left the dispatch booth and backtracked through the report-writing room to the rear corridor. He followed the corri-dor, left through the back door, and headed for the closest marked cruiser.

CHAPTER 52

Conrad drove the cruiser out of the police parking lot and headed in the direction of the closest car rental agency in town: E-Z Car Rental. He arrived and met with an employee, a heavyset, middle-aged, gray-haired woman, standing behind the counter.

"Ma'am, I'm Sergeant Conrad with the Westfield PD." He shook her hand.

"I'm Linda Gray, the store manager," she replied.

"Nice to meet you. We're looking for a suspect who is wanted for several very serious crimes and we have reason to believe he may have been a customer recently in your store."

Conrad pulled out the photograph of the suspect he obtained from the mall security camera, and held it in front of the manager.

"I don't recognize him," the manager said, as she squinted at the picture. "But another employee could have been at the desk when the person checked out a car."

"How many employees do you have?" Conrad asked.

"Only three. I supervise and fill in when needed."

"Can you to provide me with an employee work schedule?"

"Sure, I'll make a copy," the manager said.

She disappeared into a back room, returned a few minutes later, and handed a piece of paper to the sergeant.

"These are the last names of all the employees who work for you?" Conrad asked.

"Yes."

"Would it be possible for me to obtain their phone numbers as well?"

"I'm not sure if I'm allowed to give those out."

"Ma'am, I can't stress enough the importance of tracking down this suspect. Lives could be saved if I can find him quickly."

The manager let out a deep breath.

"All right. We usually don't give out confidential employee information, but if it could save lives, I would be remiss if I didn't help you."

The manager typed on a keyboard and Conrad heard a printer buzzing behind the counter. She pulled out a sheet of paper and handed it to him.

"Thank you, Ma'am. This will help a lot. I'm only going to show each employee the picture, ask if they recognize the individual, and the interview will be over."

"That doesn't sound too strenuous," Ms. Gray said, smiling.

Conrad checked the phone numbers and employee schedule.

"According to the schedule, a part-timer with the last name Fahey is supposed to come in at five PM today." Conrad glanced at his watch. "It's a little after three now, so is it all right if I come back after five to interview him?"

"Sure, that's not a problem," the manager said. "His name is

Michael and I'll tell him to be expecting you around five."

"Thank you for your help, Ma'am."

"No problem, officer," she replied, looking worried.

Conrad didn't bother to correct her that he was a sergeant, not an officer. The three blue stripes on his arm indicated his status, but most civilians didn't know the difference. He forced a smile, nodded his head, and headed for the door.

There was only one other car rental agency in town, Liberty Car Rental, and it was less than ten minutes away. He got there in eight and parked his car in an open spot near the front glass doors. A pretty blonde twenty-something was working behind the counter.

"Hi, I'm Sergeant Conrad with the Westfield PD," he said, extending his hand.

"Linda Atkins," the girl replied, shaking it.

"Linda, I'm looking for a suspect who is wanted for several serious offenses. It's possible that he might have rented a car from you recently. Do you recognize this person?"

He held up the picture and the girl's eyes widened.

"He was just here this morning!" she exclaimed.

Conrad felt a jolt of adrenaline travel through his body like an electric shock. He went instantly into crisis mode and paused for a moment to compose himself.

"Are you okay?" the girl asked upon witnessing his pallid complexion.

He forced a smile in an attempt to put the employee at ease.

"Sure, I'm fine. Could you please print me a copy of his rental paperwork?"

"Sure, officer. Can I ask what he did?"

"There are several assault and battery charges filed against him."

It wasn't a complete lie; In addition to killing various people, the psychopath had also assaulted and beaten them.

The blonde girl typed on a keyboard for several seconds before Conrad heard the buzzing of a printer.

Conrad could barely stand still as he waited for the employee to hand over the paperwork. He shifted from foot to foot to ease his nervous tension. Finally, after a seemingly endless wait, the girl handed the paper over the counter. Conrad focused on the name and address on the form; Brad Carlson, 262 Lydon Street, Westfield, Massachusetts.

The sergeant felt his body tremble like a car engine running in the red as another surge of adrenaline struck him as if he touched a high voltage wire. He felt like he could take off like a rocket, smash through the ceiling, and launch into the sky if he chose to.

Instead, he nodded at the girl behind the counter, mouthed the words "thank you," and jogged out the door. Dashing to the police cruiser, he slid into the front seat while holding the paper in front of him. As he started the engine, he suddenly felt hot, so he switched on the fan and pointed the vent toward his face. He waited a few moments to cool down before picking up the cruiser radio mike and depressing the "talk" button.

"Nine-thirty-five to Westfield Control," he spoke into the receiver. "I just received the name and address of an individual matching the description of our murder and kidnap suspect from an employee at Liberty Car Rental. Are you ready to take it down?"

There was a brief pause before the dispatcher replied, "Sarge, I'm ready for it."

Conrad read the name and address on the car rental form. He spelled the suspect's last name phonetically to make sure the dispatcher had it right. "That's Carlson as in charlie, alpha, romeo, lima, sierra, Oscar, November. Please do a BOP on the name and ask the Chief or Lieutenant to request a search warrant for the address."

"Received, Sarge."

A BOP was a Board of Probation report that would list all the misdemeanor and felony charges on an individual's court record from the age of eighteen onward. If the psycho had accumulated a criminal record, it might be easier to obtain a search warrant.

Conrad drove to the entrance and waited for a car to go by before pressing down on the accelerator to cut off the next vehicle in a line of cars. He heard screeching behind him as the driver hit his brakes. With his foot pressed down on the gas pedal, Conrad switched on the lights and siren as he headed toward Lydon Street.

CHAPTER 53

Sergeant Conrad watched a line of cars pull over to the curb to let him pass as he raced down the street with the lights and sirens blazing. He was wired. If he found the suspect at the address he was heading to, he would have to use all his restraint not to beat him senseless.

Conrad went into the zone that cops often went into during emergencies; it was a potent mixture of adrenaline and confidence that would give him an edge over any opponent.

Every detail on the road ahead became perfectly clear; he tracked each car as it moved toward the curb to the right, while also watching for oncoming traffic to the left. When a car was slow to move, he timed a swerve to the left to match a gap in the line of cars racing toward him. His movements were precise; he was in the zone.

His concentration was shattered by a disembodied voice on the cruiser radio: "Control to 935."

Conrad slowed only slightly as he picked up the mike and depressed the "talk" button.

"Nine-thirty-five," he replied.

"Sarge, you're not going to believe this, but the subject you asked us to check on, Bradley Carlson, is deceased. According to our records, he died of an apparent suicide nine years ago."

Conrad's concentration faltered as he attempted to process the conflicting information.

No, that can't be, he thought. *We have identified the killer. We know where he lives. It's over.*

Traffic cleared away as he entered a residential neighborhood with modest homes surrounded by finely-manicured lawns.

Conrad pressed the mike button and spoke into the receiver, "Control, did you say that the subject was deceased?" He placed a heavy accent on the word deceased as if it was a new word to him.

"That's right, Sarge. We have an incident report from 2013 that states he died of an apparent suicide at age seventeen."

My God, Conrad thought. *This psychopath is even cleverer than I thought. He's been using the identity of a dead teenager for years.*

"Received, Control," Conrad replied. He pulled over to the side of the road beside a wide lawn, and switched off the lights and siren.

The sudden silence felt surreal. How was this possible? He thought he had found the killer only to discover the killer had been using a stolen identity for nine years? It didn't seem possible, and yet there it was.

Conrad's adrenaline surge faded as the information sank in; the positive ID was a dead-end. All his energy, determination, and focus had been for nothing.

Conrad sat in his cruiser by the side of the road as he attempted to recalibrate his thoughts. In mere seconds, he felt like he had plunged from the height of the stratosphere to a deep abyss.

His thoughts turned dark. Why would God allow such a deadly psychopath to run amok kidnapping, torturing, and killing young women? Why didn't he just strike the fucker down with a bolt of lightning? Why was a Godless killer endowed with cleverness that allowed him to get away with murder and torture without being caught? Why was God allowing the good guys to run around in circles without giving them any help?

Everything the police had done so far had come to nothing. The sadistic psycho was still running around loose terrorizing the community. What difference did any of their efforts make? Why not just give up?

Because giving up would be un-American, he thought. *People are counting on us to do a job and not give up.*

Then, he thought of the answer to his own question: Perhaps God's gift to the good guys was the capacity to care for others, the ability to make logical deductions, and the strength to protect.

He thought of his own wife or daughter being stalked by a sick psychopath, and knew he had to continue to do everything he could possibly do to stop him.

Conrad took a deep breath as he picked up the radio mike, "Nine-thirty-five to nine-thirty-eight."

"Go ahead, Sarge," Officer Tannen replied from car four.

"Matt, any luck with finding that light green Hyundai at the apartment complexes?"

"Not yet, Sarge, but we still have some more parking lots to check out."

"Received, 938."

Conrad released the "talk" button and leaned back in his seat. An occasional car drove past him, but he ignored it and continued to stare ahead at the row of telephone poles lining the suburban street.

An idea came to him, so he depressed the button on the radio mike. "Nine-thirty-five to Control."

"Control's on. Go ahead, Sarge," the dispatcher replied.

"Aborting from previous destination, I'll be signal five."

"Received, Sarge."

Conrad flicked on his left blinker, looked left, and pulled out when he saw the way was clear. He headed in the direction of Tracey Randall's house. Even if all his other leads were falling through, he could still check on the safety of the courageous teenage girl who found the strength to fight back against the killer.

He drove to Tracey's neighborhood and circled the block. He saw two cars in her driveway: a red SUV and a blue Toyota. After doing a circle, he pulled his cruiser in behind the Toyota.

He pressed down on the cruiser mike. "Nine-thirty-five to Control."

"Go ahead, 35."

"You can put me off on a check of Tracey Randall's house. Also, as an FYI, I want the officers on duty on every shift to call in a check of the Randall house to dispatch every hour."

"Received, Sarge."

"Nine-thirty-eight copies," Officer Tannen's voice spoke from the radio.

"Nine-forty-two also copies," Officer Malloy chimed in.

"Thank you, thirty-eight and forty-two," Conrad said, hanging up the cruiser mike and switching on his portable radio.

He left the cruiser, followed the walkway to the house, and pressed the doorbell.

Seconds later, Mrs. Randall answered the door.

"Hello, Sergeant Conrad. How may I help you?"

"Actually, it's how I can help you. Is Tracey home?"

"Sure, come in," Mrs. Randall said, holding the door open.

Conrad stepped into the living room.

"Would you like something to drink?" the plain, brunette, middle-aged woman asked.

"If you have bottled water, it would be great."

"No problem."

She returned with a bottled water and handed it to him. He unscrewed the cap and took a sip.

"I'll get Tracey," Mrs. Randall said, disappearing down the hallway.

Tracey returned with her mother to the living room.

"Hello, Sergeant Conrad," Tracey said, shyly. "I'm sorry I didn't hear you pull up or ring the doorbell. I was listening to my Ipod."

"No problem, Tracey," Conrad said, smiling. "I just wanted to drop by and see how you're doing. I wanted to find out if you had any luck buying pepper spray on-line. I'm not trying to worry you, but I want to take every available precaution to make sure you can defend yourself if anything happens."

"I tried ordering police-strength pepper-spray on amazon, but they said they couldn't deliver it to my location," Tracey replied, rolling her eyes.

"That's disappointing," Conrad said. "They just passed a law two years ago that allows Massachusetts residents to carry pepper-spray legally without an FID card or LTC, so I don't know why you're not able to get it on-line. You will have to get it at a sporting goods store. The closest is probably Dick's in Farmington."

Tracey's face turned pale at the thought of driving to Farmington, parking her car in a parking lot that may or may not have security cameras, and then walking through a big store alone and unprotected.

"I'm not sure if I want to go out in public this soon until the kidnapper is caught," Tracey said, looking down at her feet as if she felt embarassed for being fearful.

Conrad realized that it wasn't a reasonable risk to take for Tracey to drive alone to a store in another town.

"No, you're right, Tracey. You shouldn't have to," Conrad said as he reached down to his police belt, unclipped the leather holster containing his pepper spray, and handled the bottle to Tracey.

"Here, take mine. I can just get another one from the armory."

"Really?" Tracey asked as her eyes widened, color came back to her cheeks, and any trace of fear or apprehension appeared to evaporate as she took the pepper spray in hand and practiced aiming it at a picture of a sailboat on the wall. "This is awesome."

"All you have to do is point, flip up the safety cap, and press down on the trigger," Conrad said, grinning as Tracey aimed the pepper spray bottle around the room as if she was defending herself against a horde of invisible attackers.

"Oh yeah, I like this," she said, smiling for the first time since Conrad arrived.

"It has a twenty-foot range, but you want to be careful if you use it outside when its windy to make sure you're not down-wind so it blows back in your face."

"Yeah, that would be a bummer," Tracey said, laughing as she placed the bottle in her front jeans pocket.

"Okay, great. I feel better now," Conrad said, raising an eye-brow.

"So do I," Tracey replied.

"Don't be afraid to use it if you have to."

"Don't worry, I won't."

"Tracey, have you had a chance to think of anything else that might help us in our investigation?" Conrad asked.

"I don't want to sound paranoid, but I don't think he's going to let me go. I'm sure he's going to try to come after me." Tracey's smile disappeared as quickly as it had formed as the color drained from her cheeks.

"What makes you say that?"

"Part of it was the way he treated me as if I was a prized possession that he didn't want to lose. I got the feeling that he thought I belonged to him, and if I got away, he wouldn't stop until he got me again."

"Understood. That's why I gave you something to fight back with, but let's hope it doesn't come to that. It's law enforce-ment strength, so it's the best you can get. It's a lot stronger than the crap you can get online."

"Thank you," Tracey said.

"No problem, "Conrad replied. "Do you have any more concerns that I can help you with?"

"Actually, there is one," Tracey said, looking down as if she was embarrassed to say.

"What is it?" Conrad asked, raising his eyebrows.

"There's a window in the basement that would be easy for someone to break and get inside the house."

"Show it to me," he said, eyes narrowing.

CHAPTER 54

My throat burns as I take another swig of Jack Daniels from the bottle. I alternate between chugging mouthfuls of whiskey and sucking in lungfuls of nicotine. After several hours of stewing in my own misery like a fly drowning in poisoned soup, my attempt to self-medicate is finally starting to take the edge off.

With the exception of my recliner, TV, and DVD player, all the breakables in my apartment are scattered across the worn carpet in pieces. When I returned home after my failed mission, I went into a rage and tore apart everything that wasn't nailed down.

It's amazing how easily wooden chairs come apart when you smash them against the floor to loosen up the nails and then use brute strength to tear off the legs. Also, I will have to get used to sitting in the dark because all my table lamps have been smashed to pieces.

As I lean back in my recliner, I look at my upside-down couch, which is overturned like a capsized boat. Since I didn't have the means to destroy the frame, I had to be satisfied with overturning it, slashing the cushions, and distributing what was left around the apartment.

I'm surprised none of my neighbors called the cops when

they heard the sounds of destruction. My downstairs neighbors must be out, because otherwise they would have come upstairs and complained to me in person as they had done once before when I played music too loud. At the time, I wanted to kill the middle-aged couple, but I'm too smart to put myself at risk by targeting anyone in my building.

If I want to eat anytime soon, I will have to make a trip to the grocery store because I tore all my cereal boxes to pieces and scattered the contents. I even created a disgusting milky gray lake – with thick white chunks floating in it – on the kitchen floor by dumping all the milk and soda from the fridge.

However, I did have the presence of mind not to destroy the essentials in my kitchen; I left the quart of Jack Daniels in the cabinet intact and the collection of bottled waters in my fridge. Even then, I knew I would need the Jack to relax and the water as a chaser.

In the midst of the devastation, I'm watching the remake of Friday the Thirteenth for perhaps the two-hundredth time. I love the remakes because they're more graphic than the originals. The same goes for the remake of the Texas Chainsaw massacre. Horror movies relax me. They always have since I was a kid.

As I mentioned before, my nanny used to make me sit in front of the home entertainment center when she didn't want to be bothered with me, which was pretty much all the time. As an eight-year-old in complete control of a remote control, I naturally gravitated toward movies that had the greatest emotional impact – horror movies. The first time I saw blood and guts on the screen, I had nightmares for weeks, but over time I became used to it.

I turn down the sound on the TV because the images are just as effective at soothing me as the screams of the victims. Besides, I don't want to give myself a headache. As I watch, I imagine that I'm the one wearing the hockey mask and each one of the two-legged vermin being exterminated are either Tracey Randall or the branch-wielding bitch.

When I'm done with my cigarette, I drop it on the carpet next to the recliner without stamping it out. I can smell the carpet smoldering, but I don't care. If the carpet catches fire, I'll dump one of my bottled waters on it, but it hasn't caught fire yet. Anyway, I like to watch things burn – even for a short while.

How did I end up in such a wretched condition? My plan to stalk, kidnap, torture, and kill Tracey Randall was perfect. What was the probability of a fucking unmarked state police cruiser cutting me off from my prey at the instant I was going to run her down? Pretty low, I would imagine, but it happened.

After that, I deviated from my usual careful planning to grab the first bitch I saw on the street. I saw her, I wanted her, and I grabbed her. How was I supposed to know her bitch friend was going to run away and come back – when my back was turned – to ambush me with a tree branch?

I try to console myself by remembering all the times my plans came to fruition. I flash back to images of the terrified faces of my victims – all the sluts I made into art in my parents' snowmobile cabin up north.

Then, my mood lifts again as I realize how much smarter I am than the cops. Although the cops may eventually discover my false identity, they'll never get close to discovering my real identity.

Due to my recent carelessness, it's almost inevitable that the cops will figure out that I'm renting various vehicles to carry out my snatch-and-grabs. This line of reasoning will lead them to the rental agency and my fake identity.

Unfortunately for the cops, I already disposed of the tainted rental vehicle. After the incident, I drove the car out to the lake, put it in neutral, and rolled it down a boat ramp into the water. The first moron who tries to put a boat in the lake will discover it resting on the bottom, but that could take days. Until then, the cops will search uselessly for the puke-green car.

I feel a rush of excitement as I imagine the cops discovering my alternate identity. Wait until they find out the individual who rented the car has been dead for nine years! That will fuck with their minds.

Ironically, my first victim wasn't even a female; it was just a loser in my class during my senior year at high school, who I knew no one would miss. I secretly befriended a social misfit without any friends with the sole intention of killing him and stealing his identity. One day, I lured him out to the woods behind his house to drink a pint of Jack that I stole from my parent's liquor cabinet.

When the moron wasn't looking, I spiked his drink with a crushed sleeping tablet that I stole from my mother's bathroom medicine cabinet. About twenty minutes later, he was lying on the ground snoring. I wrapped a noose around his neck and threw the rest of the rope over a thick tree branch. Then, I placed a sawed-off tree stump next to him, which I could slide under his feet when the time was right.

Getting him into position was difficult because he was dead weight, but I figured out a way to do it by using the rope as a lever. I leaned all my body weight against the rope on the opposite side of the branch, and pulled down with all my might.

The fucker was skinnier than me, so I lifted him until his feet were dangling in the air. That's when I heard him gasping for breath. I figured he must have woke up at that moment.

After tying off the rope with difficulty, I walked over to him so I could look at his face. His bulging eyes stared at me with disbelief as his cheeks turned red, then blue, then purple. His body and limbs twitched and jerked as if someone was controlling him like a puppet by pulling on his strings.

Finally, after several minutes, his eyes rolled up so only the whites were showing and his tongue dangled out of his mouth like a drooling dog's. Soon, the twitching and jerking diminished until it was barely noticeable. I slid the sawed-off tree stump behind him so it looked like he climbed it and jumped off. It was the perfect height; it was only slightly higher than his dangling feet.

Staring into the loser's bloated, purple face, I felt *the rush* for the first time. Using my cunning and strength, I had demonstrated my absolute power over another human being by taking his miserable life. He wasn't the target I wanted to go after, but I needed his identity to protect myself while I stalked the targets I wanted to go after.

While he dangled from the tree like a chunk of meat in a butcher's shop, I reached into his back pocket and took out his wallet. His body was still twitching as I grabbed it. Inside the wallet were eight crumpled dollars, a bunch of queer family pictures, and most importantly, his social security card and driver's license. That was all I needed to assume his identity.

For nine years, I've used his name and social security number to create fake credit card and bank accounts. The extra money comes in handy to purchase supplies that I might not otherwise be able to afford on my measly security guard paycheck.

After my recent failed snatch-and-grab, I have to assume that my fake identity is now compromised. That means I will eventually need to obtain the identification of a male around my age: twenty-eight years old. However, there's no rush. I figure that I can lie low for a while to wait for the heat to die down. After a month or so, the cops will forget all about me and I'll be free to resume my reign of terror.

CHAPTER 55

Conrad slid into the cruiser seat, started the engine, and hesitated as he stared at the small ranch house. It looked secure, but he knew there were always weak spots that could be exploited.

He couldn't think about that angle though. He had done everything he could to keep Tracey safe and that's all that mattered. Looking over his shoulder, he backed out of the driveway and pulled onto the street to continue his patrol.

Tracey was right. The basement window was a concern. It was close to the ground and large enough for a person to crawl through. The glass wasn't particularly strong and a well-placed kick would have shattered it easily. The window was concealed from view under the porch, and it would have been an ideal place for an intruder to break in unseen.

Not anymore. Conrad had limited options, but he figured out a way. He couldn't board up the window because nails wouldn't pound into concrete. He would have to innovate. There was a twin-bed mattress and wooden frame stored in the basement, which he figured he could use to block the window.

He propped the mattress and frame against the wall so it would cover the window opening. Then, he asked Tracey and her Mom to carry one side of an old dresser stored in the corner, while he carried the other. They leaned the dresser against the mattress frame to hold it in place. The dresser was heavy; no amount of force would budge it.

After sealing the basement window, the only remaining weaknesses in the house consisted of two small panes of glass in the back door and two panes in the wall next to the front door. It would have been child's play for an intruder to smash the windows, reach in, and open either door.

Tracey's father had a tool bench and several two-by-fours propped against the wall in the basement. Mrs. Randall made a call to her husband at work to ask if Conrad could borrow his tools and wood to block the windows. Aware of the danger to his daughter, Mr. Randall consented - despite the lack of aestheticism inherent in the improvised carpentry work. It wasn't going to look great, but it had to be done.

Conrad used a saw to cut the two-by-fours into sections and nailed them into place over the small windows. He also checked the rest of the windows in the house. Mrs. Randall informed him they were recently-installed, heat-saving windows constructed of thick glass. Someone could smash through with a heavy steel object like a tire iron, but the resulting noise would alert the entire household to an intruder.

Conrad knew that Mr. Randall had his License to Carry and owned a handgun, so anyone foolish enough to make a lot of noise breaking in would receive a 22-caliber bullet welcome.

Conrad rechecked his work in the basement, double-checked the solidness of the wood covering the windows, and determined the house was as secure as possible without installing an alarm system.

Conrad had tried to convince Mr. and Mrs. Randall to install a home security system, but Mr. Randall was adamant that he couldn't afford it. Conrad repeated the suggestion to Mrs. Randall when he was finished with his improvised carpentry work. He confronted her in the living room after Tracey returned to her room.

"I've taken care of the most glaring security concerns, but I'd feel a lot better if you installed an electronic security system."

Mrs. Randall shook her head. "We can't afford it. Since Jack's hours were cut, we can barely afford to pay our bills."

"I could give you a loan."

"Jack would never accept it. He's too proud to borrow money."

"What good will his pride be if he ends up burying his daughter because this psychopath got to her?"

Mrs. Randall buried her face in her hands and sobbed. Conrad placed his hand on her shoulder.

"Look, I didn't mean to upset you. I just want to make sure we do everything possible to protect Tracey."

She removed her hands from her face. "Okay, I'll talk to him again."

As Conrad drove away, he felt better after making an effort to protect the teenager and her family. The feeling was probably an illusion, but taking steps to improve the security of the home gave him a feeling of control over an uncontrollable situation. While he moved heavy objects and nailed wood into place, he was doing something concrete to protect the family – despite the fact the killer was still on the loose.

Conrad drove to the first apartment complex, Westfield Gardens, to begin a systematic check of the parking lots. He was certain the killer had disposed of his latest rental car, the light green sedan, so he concentrated on locating the black, four-door Japanese-manufactured vehicle that Tracey had described during her interview at the hospital.

He wrote down the license plate numbers of each vehicle that matched the general description. After checking the apartment complexes, he had a list of eighty-six cars. When he was finished, it was 6:20 PM. It was getting dark already, which wasn't a surprise as it was mid-October.

Conrad picked up the radio mike. "Nine-thirty-five to Control."

"Westfield Control," the dispatcher replied.

"Has Detective Lombardi returned to the station yet?"

"Yes, sir, she just walked in."

"Okay, then I'll be 10-19." The sergeant gave the code that he was returning to the station as he pulled over to the side of the road.

After checking for oncoming cars, Conrad headed in the direction of the police station. He considered what their next move should be as he drove through an ordinary neighborhood toward the downtown area.

He thought they were on the right track by checking out the local apartment complexes; he needed to check the residence lists when he returned to the station. The renters that matched the profile of the killer had to be recorded and investigated.

As he pulled into the station parking lot, Conrad spotted Lombardi's blue unmarked cruiser parked next to the front doors. He parked next to her, entered the lobby, and got buzzed in through the security door. He met the detective in her office.

"How did the interview go?" he asked, as he sat in the chair across from her desk.

The detective sighed as she rested her cheek on her palm in a classic pose of frustration. "It went okay. They looked at the photo of the suspect taken by the mall security camera, and confirmed it was the same perp. Of course, that was no big surprise. Other than that, they didn't have any useful information other than the fact that the killer/kidnapper is losing his touch – which we already suspected."

"Did anyone tell you about what happened on my end?" the sergeant asked.

Lombardi sighed again. "I heard that slippery bastard rented a car by using the stolen identity of a suicide victim. The Lieutenant told me you were on your way to the victim's residence when the dispatcher informed you the owner of the ID was deceased. That must have been a downer."

"It was disappointing, but I shouldn't have been surprised. Our boy is a planner and no matter how much deterioration he's showing, he never would have taken the risk of using his real name to rent a car. "

"Jim, you should have known this scumbag wasn't going to make it that easy for us." Marilyn said, raising an eyebrow.

Jim gave her a lopsided smile. "That's a good point."

"What now?" the detective asked.

"We check the apartment complex resident lists. We should be able to narrow down our suspects to all the male renters between the ages of twenty and thirty. Then, we interview each person who fits the profile, apply some pressure, and let the psycho reveal himself."

CHAPTER 56

I don't know how long I passed out for. All I know is when I wake up, I have no idea what time it is. My smashed clock isn't going to help me. I see thin lines of light along the edges of the window shade, so it's daytime at least. When I passed out, it was just getting dark, so it must be the next day.

Not surprisingly, I feel as if the back of my head has been struck by a sledgehammer. I'm hung-over and I need to eat something to recover.

To add insult to injury, I had a vivid nightmare flash-back; I flashed back to my second year of college at Farmington State University. By some miracle, I had made it to my sophomore year by barely scraping by in all my freshman year classes – despite all the curvy distractions shaking their shapely asses around campus. Somehow, I was able to tune out the sluts and focus on completing the minimal amount of work to pass. It helped that I was able to smoke a lot of weed.

In my flashback, I had just worked up the courage to ask out a girl who lived down the hall from me in my dorm. After my horrific experiences in middle school, I never dated in high school, so it was quite a milestone when I overcame my fears during my sophomore year of college.

It happened like this: I made friends with a couple of stoners in my college dormitory. One of them, Robbie Evans, was my roommate, and he was part of a social clique that included some freaky – but attractive – gothic girls, who dressed all in black and wore pale makeup. Despite their vampiric appearance, I found them intriguing because I always felt like an outcast myself.

Everyone in the clique smoked weed, so it was easy to fit in by pretending to get high. Passing a joint around, I inhaled when they were looking, but faked it when they weren't looking.

I don't like to lose control because it makes me feel vulnerable and the same was true then. I wanted all my senses to remain intact so I never got blindsided like I was in middle school. My plan didn't always work because sometimes I inhaled when I was being watched closely, and sometimes I breathed in the lingering second-hand smoke.

However, I went with the flow so I could fit in. Besides, the weed actually helped me to relax and concentrate on being sociable. Unexpectedly, I discovered that I had a sarcastic sense of humor that made everyone laugh. It was the first time in my life since grade school that I had any real friends to hang out with.

Anyway, this one chick in our group, Adrienne Danforth, thought I was funny and used to laugh at all my sarcastic comments. One day, Robbie told me that she liked me and wanted me to ask her out.

At first, I was shocked. Was it another set-up like the one in middle school? After bothering me about it for a couple weeks, Robbie finally convinced me. For the second time in my life, I set up a date with a girl. I figured there was no way this was going to be as bad as the first one.

It wasn't. We took a train into Boston to grab some dinner and catch a movie. It was great. Being with Adrienne felt as natural as breathing. I was laughing and joking with Adrienne over dinner. Then, the image altered to an unfortunate event that happened several weeks later.

After three successful dates, Adrienne complained to Robbie that I was too possessive. I always wanted to know who she was with, where she was going, and what she was doing. Could you blame me? She was precious to me. She was the first girl I kissed and felt up.

Worried, I began spying on her. I followed her to and from class. When she was in her dorm, I set up a stakeout in the second floor of the library so I could watch her come and go from the front door of her residence hall.

One of her bitch friends must have caught me staring out the library window because Adrienne confronted me about it a few days later. I told her that her friend was mistaken and it was just a coincidence. She didn't believe me. She said she was breaking up with me. It had only been a month since our first date.

Obsessed, I couldn't stop following her. One day, I saw her laughing and joking with one of the jocks on the football team. That did it.

Enraged, I confronted her in her dorm room.

"What the fuck were you doing talking to that jock piece-of-shit?" I asked, fists clenching.

"I can talk to whoever I want, Eric," she said. "We're not going out anymore. I think it was a mistake for me to lead you on, and for that I apologize."

My eyes scanned her voluptuous body; she looked hot wearing form-fitting white shorts and a tight blue t-shirt that showed off her modest, plum-sized breasts. I couldn't believe that only a few weeks earlier she had offered that body to me.

"I thought you didn't like jocks. You said they always treated you badly in high school."

"They did, but college is different," she replied. "People change in college."

"So all that stuff you said about hating jocks when we were smoking weed was all a lie?" I asked.

"It wasn't a lie. At the time, I thought I did. But, people change."

"So you're going to start dating jocks now?"

"If I want to."

My hands clenched into fists as a red haze clouded my vision. I flashed back to multiple images of the abuse I suffered in middle school at the hands of jocks. I thought back to the image of Michelle laughing in my face as she watched me being pounded by her jock boyfriend.

Before I knew what I was doing, I lashed out and struck Adrienne in the cheek with a closed fist. I must have hit her hard because she screamed as she went down. Horrified, I ran out of her room and returned to my dorm. Laying low, I was reading a book in my room when there was a knock on the door.

"Campus Police," a gruff voice spoke outside the door.

Fuck! That bitch told on me!

Opening the door, I saw two uniformed cops. One of them told me to turn around and place my hands behind my back. I was too stunned to fight so I did what they said. They put me in the back of a cruiser and transferred me to a cell at the Farmington Police Station because they didn't have anywhere to keep prisoners at the college.

I spent half the night in a cell before my father bailed me out. When he faced me through the bars, he became wild-eyed like the mad scientist from the old black-and-white Hollywood movie, *Frankenstein*.

He informed me they had kicked me out of school and I was never allowed to go back. He went on and on about how I had disgraced the family and ruined my life. At that point, I felt so low that I didn't have the strength to argue with him, so I just stood there and took it.

"You're lucky she's not going to press charges," my father said as we drove home.

"Dad, I didn't mean to do it. I lost my temper," I said, staring straight ahead.

"You mean like this?" my Dad snarled as he lashed out at me with a vicious backhand that struck my left cheek.

My cheek stung as if I was attacked by a swarm of bees. I sat there, humiliated, as we drove the rest of the way home in silence. He continued to give me the silent treatment when we reached the house.

The next morning, he woke me up early and told me to start looking for a job because my college career was over. He repeated that I was lucky Adrienne didn't press charges because then I'd be a convicted felon and I'd never get hired by anyone.

I spent the day driving around in my parents' back-up SUV smoking cigarettes and listening to rock music on the radio. I was in no mood to look for a job. Violent images flashed through my mind of murdering my father in a thousand different bloody ways. Someday, I would kill the old man.

But for now, it was a slut who brought me down and it was sluts who were going to pay. I began planning how I was going to get my revenge on the little demons.

I thought about returning to Farmington State and killing Adrienne, but the idea didn't feel right. Sure, she wrecked my life by getting me kicked out of school, but for a while at least she treated me like a real person. I had enjoyed myself more during that one wonderful month of dating her than I had in my entire life.

Inexplicably, it felt wrong to kill her despite her getting me kicked out of school. However, this unusual sentiment didn't apply to the rest of the demonic sluts inhabiting the earth. They would be the ones to pay.

I feel sick to my stomach as I think about what happened during my final night at college. Eventually, I motivate myself to stand up and trudge to the kitchen. The putrid feeling in my stomach spreads outward when I see food scattered across the kitchen floor like the contents of hundreds of trays from my middle school cafeteria. Pieces of cereal float in a blackish-gray puddle like debris from a tiny fleet of wrecked ships. Checking the fridge, the only items I find left are four bottled waters.

Opening one, I consume most of it in one swig. I feel a little better, but I still need food. In addition to my pounding head, my stomach is gurgling as if I just drank a cup of acid. Also, the bottom of my throat is burning and pouring water down my gullet doesn't help.

I light a cigarette and smoke it, but it doesn't help my throat or stomach feel better. Actually, it makes the acid burning worse. I look in the bathroom mirror; my disheveled hair appears as if I've slept on it for a week and my pale face looks like it belongs to a homeless drug addict; I need to get myself together.

I turn on the shower, strip off my clothing, and step in. The hot water feels soothing on my aching body. As the spray massages my scalp, the pain in my head and stomach stops pulsing as hard. I stand beneath the soothing stream for a while before bothering to use soap and shampoo.

I feel a lot better after showering. I run a comb through my hair, add some gel, and stare at my reflection in the mirror. I look presentable enough to appear in public. The bruise on the side of my head feels a little tender, but it's healing nicely.

I need to look clean-cut if I'm going to ply my trade unhindered. Disheveled persons get noticed and attract unwanted attention, so I always make sure I'm neat and clean.

I put on a light-blue dress-shirt, black dress-pants, and black shoes. I find dressing nicely puts people at ease. It makes them think I'm a harmless drone taking a break from whatever retail job I'm wasting my time at. The light blue color also seems to help. People hardly give me a second look.

I gulp down three Ibuprofen pills, and hope they go to work fast. Lighting a cigarette, I leave my apartment and head down the hall. I don't want to run into anyone because of the "no smoking indoors" rule and the trail of smoke. Taking the elevator down to the first floor, I leave the building. I still feel like hell, but at least I look presentable.

I go to my car and check the time on the dashboard. It's 10:20 AM. I think they serve breakfast at Mickey D's until 10:30. I don't bother to turn on the radio because it's a waste of time until the pain in my head subsides.

I drive to McDonalds and order a number one combo: egg Mcmuffin and hash brown. I also order a large coffee and one of those parfait things. Drive-throughs might be our country's greatest invention. When you're hung-over, the last thing you want to deal with is a crowded restaurant.

I park in an open space between two cars in the back of the lot to eat my meal. I take my time to let my stomach handle the intake of food. The parfait tastes better than I thought it would, and even settles my stomach a bit. After I eat, I light a cigarette so I can think about my next move.

Last night I had the idea of lying low until the heat wore off, but I'm not so sure now. Sipping a coffee and smoking, I'm starting to feel like there could be possibilities.

I called in sick yesterday to go on my failed snatch-and-grab mission, so it's not ideal if I call in sick again, but I hate to let the day go to waste by working. I make just as much money, if not more, by using stolen identities.

I feel a sudden cramp in my stomach as I think about the unmarked police cruiser that came between me and my prey in the parking lot yesterday. All is not lost, however. I still have a few hours to go before I have to be in for my 3-11 shift, so I figure I'll take a cruise through the slut's neighborhood.

I'll do a harmless drive-by. I can't risk doing another stakeout this soon in case a cop comes along and sees me hanging out by the side of the road. It will look suspicious and they'll probably stop and question me. Since there's no cruiser detail, there's no reason for a cop to pull me over if I'm just driving through the neighborhood. I'll check out the situation to see if the slut is home alone, and make a decision about what to do next.

I take a dry-run through the slut's neighborhood and notice one car in the driveway. It's the same blue Toyota she was driving when I stalked her yesterday.

I cruise over to the patch of woods I parked across from before to spy on her. I check the chain gate blocking the conservation land trail and notice a lock hanging on the end of the chain, but it's not snapped shut.

I park and get out of the car. Moving quickly, I pull the lock off, unhook the chain, and drop it to the ground. I dart back to my vehicle and drive it onto the trail. I drive down the dirt path until I'm certain my car isn't visible from the street. What a stroke of luck!

Returning to the chain gate, I replace the dummy-lock so it doesn't look suspicious. Feeling confident, I make my way through the woods toward the bitch's house.

The first house I come to is a red Cape with no cars in the driveway. I stay behind the trees at the edge of the yard as I cut through the woods toward my prey's house.

Soon, I'm crouching behind a clump of bushes at the edge of the woods, observing her backyard. I feel a sense of deja vu because the rear of the house and yard appear just as they did in my dream. I spot a ground-level window under the porch that should be easy to break into.

It's broad daylight, but she's home alone. There's no one at the neighbor's house I passed. A line of trees is blocking her yard from the other neighbor's yard. I make an immediate decision; I will get the bitch now.

Crouching like a commando, I dart across the back lawn toward the porch. When I reach the porch, I dive underneath it and crawl on my belly toward the window in the foundation. I feel a rush as I contemplate the things I'll do when I get my hands on her.

I shift my body so my legs are facing the window and draw my foot back. Lashing out, I smash the window with the sole of my sneaker. At this point, I don't care if she hears me. By the time the cops get here, it will all be over. I kick out the remaining glass shards and crawl backward so my feet go through the opening.

Then, something goes wrong. My feet strike a hard, unyielding object. What the hell? I kick the object and it doesn't budge. The window is blocked. I try one last kick and realize it's a waste of time. Rage boils in my brain like a reactor in meltdown. That fucking bitch knew I would come for her!

Without thinking, I scramble out from under the porch and dart across the lawn. I ascend three short steps to the porch and cross it to the back door. Staying low, I prepare to smash out the glass panel above the doorknob with my elbow. With one smooth motion, I raise my arm, draw it back, and launch it into the glass. I hear the sound of tinkling glass.

Smashing out the remaining glass shards with my elbow, I reach in. My hand slams against a piece of wood. They boarded up the window! I was in such a rush I didn't even notice it. I feel like yelling and screaming, but remain silent. Turning, I sprint toward the woods.

Disappearing into the forest behind the house, I weave in and out past trunks and duck under branches as if I'm running an obstacle course. The leaves become a blur. Seconds later, I reach my car and pause to catch my breath.

Remembering the dummy-locked chain, I unhook the lock on the gate and drop the chain. Returning to my car, I slide into the driver's seat and start the engine. I shift into reverse and press down on the gas pedal.

I hear tires ripping up dirt as my car launches down the trail toward the street. As I reach the street, I pause to squint through gaps in the trees to check for cars coming, and press my foot down on the gas pedal when I see it's clear.

Tires shriek as my car shoots onto the street like a train off its tracks. Before I even stop, I shift the car into drive and press down on the gas pedal again. More screeching as I race away from the house.

All my caution evaporates as I speed down the street. When I reach the main road, I skid to a stop, look both ways, and head away from the town of Westfield. For all I know, the bitch saw everything I did and the cops are on their way right now.

CHAPTER 57

Sergeant Jim Conrad sat at a desk in the common area reading incident reports faxed to the station from other towns. Meanwhile, Marilyn Lombardi was in her office checking over tenant data.

Conrad and Lombardi had arrived at the station early; he got in at 6:45 AM and she arrived at 7:15. It was Wednesday, October 18. The time in the lower right-hand corner of Conrad's computer screen read 10:15 AM.

They divided the labor; Conrad read the incident reports detailing every known crime in the area with the killer's modus operandi, while Lombardi cross-checked the lists of apartment tenants between the ages of twenty and thirty with tenants who owned black, Japanese manufactured cars.

Conrad focused on a police report written on April 13 that documented a teenager disappearing from the Greendale Mall in Worcester; it was the most recent incident since the kidnapping of Tracey Randall at the Westfield Pond Mall.

It happened on a Saturday night at 8:45 PM: fifteen-year-old Rebecca Thornton went to a restroom in a corridor at the rear of the Food Court, while her friends waited for her at a table in front of a nearby Thai restaurant. Her friends saw her enter the back corridor and never saw her again.

There was an *Employees Only* door at the end of the corridor that led to a maintenance/janitorial area with a rear exit stairwell. It was believed the perpetrator grabbed her in the rear corridor as she was coming out of the restroom, incapacitated her, dragged her into the maintenance area, descended the stairwell, and left by the exit door. The exit led to an isolated back alley.

The next earliest incident occurred in Westfield in February; a sixteen-year-old female disappeared from the parking lot of a 24-hour Honey Farms convenience store. Conrad remembered the incident clearly; he wanted to investigate the incident as a kidnapping, while the Chief and Lieutenant maintained the theory that the missing girl was a runaway – despite the existing facts to the contrary.

Sixteen-year-old, Rachel Steinberg, was known to have had arguments with her parents – like any normal teenager – but the arguments never reached a severity that would induce her to run away from home. In addition, it made no sense that she would drive to the convenience store parking lot, leave her car there, and run away on foot. The lieutenant formulated the preposterous theory that a friend met her at the parking lot, and drove her out of town in a different vehicle. The theory made no sense, but Conrad's logical deductions were ignored.

The sergeant shook his head, disgustedly. If they had started an investigation back then, maybe they would have caught the psychopath by now. They would at least be further along.

Still, all was not lost; Conrad was discovering distinct patterns in the incident reports. In all the previous incidents, the suspect always struck between the hours of 8:30 PM and midnight. Eighty-five percent of the time he made his move on a Thursday night. The other ten percent were on various weekdays and the final five on Fridays. His hunting grounds were mall, store, and school parking lots. Despite the two-month gap between last year's incidents, the average cooling off period between kidnappings during the past four years, which they had records for, was six months.

The suspect had obviously deviated from his six-month routine by committing two additional murders only days after kidnapping Tracey Randall. Then, only a day later, he attempted another kidnapping. The killer's impulsive actions over the past week reminded Conrad of Ted Bundy's rampage shortly before he was captured. Like Bundy, their local psychopath was losing his self-control and Conrad was sure he would make a fatal mistake soon.

When Detective Lombardi had completed her analysis, the list of suspects would be narrowed down so they could interview the remaining tenants who fit the profile, and look for suspicious behavior. Conrad thought he would be able to spot the suspect during an interview; he was certain the psychopath would do or say something that would send up a red flag.

Conrad closed out the incident report from February, and began searching the archived files; he was looking for the report relating to the suicide of the person who the killer was using as his alternate identity. He typed in the date: March 18, 2013. A filed popped up, so he clicked on it and started reading.

The teenager had been reported missing on the evening of Friday, March 17, 2013. After a brief search, they found his body in the woods a short distance behind his house the next day. The death had been ruled a suicide, but Conrad was sure there was more to it. It seemed more likely that the killer lured the teenage boy into the woods and murdered him to steal his identity.

Conrad looked up from the computer as he saw Detective Lombardi enter the room. She didn't waste any time.

"Jimmy, I cross-checked all the lists and found thirteen tenants who are males between the ages of twenty and thirty, and also own black-colored, Japanese-manufactured vehicles."

"Only thirteen? If we rush, we could complete all the interviews in a single day." Conrad felt a shiver crawl up his spine; maybe they were even closer than he had thought. "Let's track down the tenants right now." Conrad stood up, adjusted his police belt, and rested his palm on the handle of his holstered forty-caliber pistol.

"Okay, let's do it," Lombardi agreed.

They cut across the common room and headed down the hallway toward the front of the building where Lombardi's unmarked cruiser was parked. As they passed the dispatch center, the dispatcher shouted to Conrad.

"Sarge, I just received a 9-1-1 call from the Randall residence! Tracey Randall said someone is trying to break into her house!"

Conrad noticed the dispatcher still held the phone to his ear as if he still had a person on the line.

"Is she okay?" Conrad asked.

"Sarge, she's fine. I have her on the phone right now," the dispatcher said.

"Keep her on the line."

The sergeant glanced at the detective and turned back to the dispatcher. "Send all units and contact the Shrewsbury police; the Randall house is close to the town line; tell them to be on the lookout for a black, Japanese-made vehicle. Did you get a vehicle description or license plate number?"

"Negative, Sarge. She says she can hear him breaking a window."

"Right now?" Conrad asked.

"Right now," the dispatcher confirmed.

Conrad's mood darkened as an electric charge ran up his spine. He felt an adrenaline surge kick in, and sprinted toward the front lobby. He heard Lombardi's footsteps following him. Passing through the security door, he swept through the lobby, shot out the front doors, and ran for the marked cruiser parked next to Lombardi's vehicle. He was too wired to be a passenger with the detective.

Unlocking the door, he slid into the seat and started the engine. Looking to his left, he saw Lombardi was already in her cruiser. He threw his cruiser into reverse and pressed down on the gas pedal; the rear tires screeched as he shot out of the parking space and turned the wheel so he spun to face the street. Throwing the car into drive, he pressed the gas pedal again. The tires squealed again as he raced across the parking lot.

Conrad slowed, but never came to a complete stop as he reached the street. He saw Lombardi's unmarked following him in his rearview mirror.

Conrad flipped on the lights and siren; he went into the zone; the road and cars ahead came into perfect focus. He drove as if he was possessed by the spirit of a long-dead racecar driver, swerving into the opposite lane when cars were slow to pull over and swerving back when the way ahead was clear.

Conrad didn't slow as he picked up the cruiser radio. "Nine-thirty-five to nine-twenty-six."

"Twenty-six, Baker street," Officer Malloy replied.

"Jack, head for the Shrewsbury town line and try to cut him off if he goes that way. You're looking for a black, Japanese-made vehicle – probably exceeding the speed limit."

"Received, Sarge."

"Nine-thirty-five to nine-twenty-eight."

"Twenty-eight, Russell Street."

"Twenty-eight, head toward Exeter street and try to cut him off if he turns back toward town."

"Received, Sarge."

"Control, I'm heading for the residence."

He made it to the Randall house in record time; a fifteen-minute journey was reduced to a mere eight minutes. The tires shrieked as he swerved into the driveway behind the parked blue Toyota. He sprang out of the car and sprinted toward the front door.

Conrad felt relieved as he spotted Tracey Randall's pale, frightened face in the small crescent window at the top of the door. Her eyes widened as she recognized him, and he saw the doorknob turn. Conrad pulled the door open and stood face-to-face with Tracey.

"Are you okay?"

"Yes, I'm fine, but he was just here. I heard him break two windows in back. Then, when I looked out my bedroom window, I saw him running toward the woods. He was dressed in black pants and a light blue shirt."

Conrad heard footsteps on the walkway behind him and turned to see Detective Lombardi.

"Marilyn, stay with her while I check around back," the sergeant said as he began circling the house.

He found the smashed ground-level window first. A few seconds later, he found the smashed glass in the rear door. The hairs on the back of his neck stood on end; if he had not reinforced both windows yesterday, Tracey Randall would be dead.

Conrad backed away from the damaged windows and checked the wood-line; it was clear. He clicked on the shoulder mike on his portable radio.

"Nine-thirty-five to Control."

"Westfield Control."

"You can put Detective Lombardi and myself off at the Randall residence. We found Ms. Randall unharmed, but there are two smashed windows in the back from an attempted break-in. Call the state police and have them send a forensics team."

CHAPTER 58

I tap the brakes as I approach the Shrewsbury town line. If I were one of the Westfield cops, the first thing I would do is contact the police in the adjacent town – closest to the Randall residence – and tell them to be on the lookout for a fast-moving vehicle. Therefore, I must not be that fast-moving vehicle. However, I don't want to call attention to myself by going too slow either.

I pass a sign with the posted speed limit: 35 mph. I slow to 34 mph and maintain it.

Still, if the slut saw me run away from the house after my failed attempt to break in, she could have saw me drive away in my vehicle. I was in such a rush to get away that I didn't bother to use the rearview mirror to look behind me as I pulled out of the conservation trail. She could have been standing at the edge of her yard writing down my plate number. It's a good thing I placed a stolen one on my car.

I feel sweat forming on my brow as I contemplate this potential pitfall. If the slut took down my plate number and/or car description, then the Westfield cops and the Shrewsbury cops will be on the lookout for me. That means I have to get off the road – pronto.

I try to think of a place where I can park and lay low for

a while. I remember there's a mini-mall about a half-mile ahead on the right; it contains a Shaws Supermarket, a pizza joint, a Dunkin Donuts, a laundromat, an H and R Block office, and a Karate studio.

It's too early to go for pizza, but I could grab coffee and a donut from Dunkins and then go next door to the supermarket and push a shopping basket around for an hour or so to kill some time. Besides, I have to replace all the food and drinks I dumped on my kitchen floor anyway. There's an ATM in the Shaws that I can use to take out money to pay for groceries.

The cops will be on the lookout for a vehicle on the road, but they won't be on the lookout for a vehicle parked within a line of cars in a supermarket parking lot. In addition, there are few things that appear less suspicious than a car in a lot or a person pushing a shopping basket around a supermarket. I just have to take my time.

Even better, I can spend fifteen minutes drinking my coffee and eating my donut at Dunkins, spend forty-five minutes grocery shopping, and by then it will be noon and I can order a pizza at the pizza joint. If I eat slowly, I could kill another forty-five minutes. By then, the heat should be off and I can hit the road again.

The sweat on my forehead dissipates as I contemplate my new plan of action. There's a good chance it will actually work and I will never see a prison from the inside. Prison is the last place I want to be. For one thing, there are no teenage girls there.

I slow down as I approach the mini-mall. The parking lot isn't packed with cars, but there are enough to blend in. I pull into the lot and head for the largest cluster of cars near the front entrance to Shaws. I park between two large SUVs, which block both sides of my car.

SHAWN WILLIAM DAVIS

A cruiser would have to drive down the aisle directly behind my car or in front of my car to see it. In addition, the cop would also have to be looking toward my vehicle at the precise moment he passed. The mathematical probabilities are on my side.

After turning off the engine, I take a moment to sit quietly and ruminate. Sometimes, I'm amazed by my own ingenuity. There were days when I came close to being caught by the cops, but each time I made a slick move that enabled me to get away.

If what I'm doing is wrong, then why would I be endowed with the intelligence to elude the police? This is one of the reasons I know what I'm doing is right. God put me on earth to punish all the sinful whores who reveal their bodies in public. By carving them up, I punish them and create art from their sin.

This leads me to wonder if I would do what I do if I lived in one of those Islamic Republics in the Middle East where all the women are covered from head-to-toe in black robes. In a society like that, would my services even be necessary like they are here? Being covered, I would not be able to distinguish between the brazen sinners, who deserve to die, and ordinary people. How would I choose an art project if I couldn't view the original clay I was working with?

Then I realize that my activities would be the same in a Middle Eastern society because I would see a covered girl and have to know what lay beneath the girl's concealing clothing. I would want to see the body that went with the eyes showing through the small slit in the facemask.

After stripping off her clothing, I could tell from the shape of her body whether she was a sinful whore who deserved to die or not. I'll bet that beneath those black robes most of foreign women have voluptuous, whorish bodies like the women in this country. If they did, I would have to kill them.

These thoughts kill some time, but now I need to get moving if I don't want to look suspicious.

Leaving the car, I light a cigarette. Inhaling, I blow out a thin stream of smoke. Then, I walk through the gaps in the parked cars to head in the direction of the Dunkin Donuts, which is located to the left of the supermarket. When I reach the entrance, I stamp out my cigarette on the sidewalk and go in.

My plan goes just as I envisioned it; I kill a couple hours by drinking coffee, grocery shopping, and eating pizza. When I'm done wasting time on purpose, I return to my car and check the dashboard clock; it's now 12:30 PM and the heat should be off by now. The way ahead of me is open, so I start the car and cruise out of my parking space. I turn left toward the entrance.

When I reach the street, I decide to take the long way back through Shrewsbury toward my apartment. I stay a few miles below the speed limit so I don't call attention to myself. A Shrewsbury police cruiser passes me going the other way, but he doesn't notice me. I feel relieved as I cross over the Westfield town line; it looks like I'm going to make it.

As I drive through a neighborhood on Chestnut Street, I see something that sets all my nerves on fire; a teenage girl wearing high-cut jean shorts and an orange halter top is walking a small dog along the sidewalk. It looks like she has curves in all the right places. I glance around for potential witnesses. Except for the girl and her dog, the neighborhood is clear.

I make a split-second decision. Turning the wheel, I pull onto the sidewalk in front of her. Looking in the rearview mirror, I see her halted on the walkway behind my car – unsure of what to do. Her mouth is formed into a surprised "O" expression, and she appears to be frozen in place. I feel slightly disappointed because she looks younger than the girls I usually grab, maybe fourteen years old, but beggars can't be choosers.

Getting out of my vehicle, I try to appear casual and force a smile.

"Hi miss, I'm lost and I'm wondering if you know where Daniels Street is?" I ask.

The girl hesitates as she looks me up and down; I must look harmless with my neat hair, dress-pants, and dress- shirt because the girl doesn't turn to run. The little dog starts barking at me, so the girl pulls on the leash to make him stop.

"Yes, sir, Daniels Street is just ahead on the right. If you keep going straight, you can't miss – "

I lunge at the girl before she can finish her sentence. The time for subtlety is over; I punch her in the left temple before she can react and she goes down. I wrap my arm around her neck and pull her to her feet before she drops to the pavement.

"Do exactly as I say and you won't get hurt," I whisper in her ear.

She released the leash when I struck her, but I can hear the pitter-patter of the dog's tiny feet near my feet. The dog starts yapping at me, so I kick it in the ribs and it runs away yelping.

"What do you – "

"Shut up and do what I say. Walk toward the car."

I loosen my grip around her neck so she can move, and she shuffles toward the car like a zombie. I glance around as we walk together. The lawns and houses appear pristine and untouched like a painting of an ideal neighborhood. There's no one in sight.

I almost panic when I hear the sound of a car engine coming

up behind me. However, instead of panicking, a jolt of adrenaline kicks in and I shove her hard toward the passenger door.

Keeping my right hand clamped firmly on the back of her neck, I open the passenger door with my free hand. I release her and shove her into the seat as the approaching car drives by. Looking over the roof of my car, I watch the car drive away down the street; the uncurious driver never even glanced in our direction.

Reaching down, I grab the slut's right arm and snap a handcuff around her wrist. Then, I grab her left wrist, drag it toward her right, and cuff them together. I slam the door, click the door-lock button on my key remote, and circle around to the driver's side.

Sliding into the seat, I make sure the girl hasn't moved and then pull away. The tires squeal, but I'm not worried because I don't see anyone around. The girl looks miserable, but she isn't struggling or making any sounds. Feeling exultant, I drive away with my prize. My next stop is my parents snowmobile cabin in New Hampshire. We're going to have so much fun together.

CHAPTER 59

Sergeant Conrad drummed his fingers on the steering wheel as he sat in his cruiser, which was parked behind a dumpster on the left side of the 149 building at the Westfield Gardens Apartment Complex. From this angle, he could stake out the main entrance without being seen by cars entering from the street. It was 12:45 PM and so far he had seen no cars matching the description of the suspect's vehicle.

A massive, state-wide police manhunt was underway. Conrad had assigned Officer Malloy to stake out a similar position at the town's other apartment complex in case the perpetrator went there.

Conrad assigned the remaining officer on duty to conduct an extensive search of all the streets, neighborhoods, and parks in town. Then, he called in two more off-duty officers – for overtime – to assist with the search. The streets of Westfield were being scoured by patrols, and yet so far there was no sign of the suspect or his vehicle.

In addition to the Westfield officers, the police departments in the bordering towns of Shrewsbury, Northfield, Marlboro, and Southfield had been alerted to search for a vehicle matching the description of the perpetrator's. Finally, a BOLO (Be On the Look-Out) bulletin was sent out to all the police departments statewide. A BOLO involving a serial killer was rare, so it had generated a lot of attention.

With every cop in the state looking for a black, four-door, Japanese-manufactured sedan, Conrad could not comprehend how a search of this magnitude could fail to locate the killer's vehicle.

There had been several false alarms; cars fitting the description of the suspect's vehicle were pulled over, but it turned out the drivers were soccer moms taking their kids to games or middle-aged businessmen on lunch-breaks. Conrad was beginning to wonder if the suspect was actually a diabolical spirit that could materialize and dematerialize at will.

He felt like he was wasting his time doing surveillance, but he also felt better knowing that Detective Lombardi was attacking the problem from a different angle. While most of the cops in the state attempted to locate the suspect's vehicle, she had begun interviewing the tenants on the apartment list who matched the suspect's profile.

The sergeant and detective had begun to refer to the thirteen single male tenants on the list as the "Lucky Thirteen." Conrad had agreed that Lombardi should start the interviews right away because if one of the Thirteen was conspicuously absent, they could narrow down the suspect list even more.

A twenty-two year-old tenant from apartment eight in building one-forty-nine, a full-time veterinary student who matched the profile, had agreed to come down to the station to speak with her. She was talking to him right now in the station's interrogation room.

Lombardi had a copy of the photo captured from the surveillance camera at the mall to compare the interviewee against. The facial features of the psychopath were partially pixilated because of the low quality of the mall cameras, so they couldn't make a solid identification.

However, they could at least rule out underweight or overweight individuals, who didn't fit the body type or facial structure of the suspect. Unfortunately, they couldn't rule out suspects with blond hair because the killer could have used hair dye. The photo was helpful, but they would still need to engage in face-to-face interviews to identify the killer.

A state police forensics team had investigated the scene at the Randall house, but found no smoking gun. However, they had discovered what kind of tires were on the killer's vehicle from tracks they found on the nearby Conservation Land trail. Also, the crime scene technicians discovered a shoe-print in the dirt that was unlike the killer's usual choice of sneaker. Conrad thought the detail only revealed that the killer possessed more than one choice of footwear.

The techs also discovered a drop of blood and a scrap of blue polyester material clinging to the sharp edge of a glass shard found beneath one of the smashed windows at the rear of the house. Not surprisingly, the blood matched the unidentified blood sample found at the scene of the recent abduction at the Westfield mall. The polyester belonged to a light-blue dress-shirt.

Conrad felt like they were all wasting their time banging their heads against a wall. The slick psychopath never left anything crucial behind. Again, the sergeant was reminded of a supernatural wraith that came and went from an alternate dimension – at will – to wreak havoc on our plane of existence.

The sergeant decided to use his down-time productively by checking in with the Randall family. He dialed the number and recognized Tracey's voice when she picked up.

"Hello?" she said, tentatively.

"Hi, Tracey, it's Sergeant Conrad. How are you holding up?"

"I'm a little shaken up, but I'm all right," she said.

"That's good. Hang in there. We're making progress. Is your father home from work yet?"

"Yes, he came home early when he heard what happened."

"Can I talk to him?"

"Sure, just a minute."

Conrad fidgeted as he waited; it felt like long minutes were dragging by, but he knew it was probably just seconds.

"Hello?" Mr. Randall's voice emanated from the earpiece.

"Mr. Randall, it's Sergeant Conrad with the Westfield Police. How's everyone doing there?"

"We're a bit tense after what happened, but we're okay," Mr. Randall said.

"Mr. Randall, with the suspect on the loose, I wanted to call to advise you to stay at a hotel with your family for the next couple of nights until we catch him."

Conrad waited in silence for a response as the seconds seemed to tick by at an interminably slow pace.

"Sergeant, with all due respect, I know it's your job to make recommendations, but there's no way in hell some piss-ant loser is going to scare me or my family out of my own house. I have guns and I know how to use them, so if the little bastard makes the mistake of coming back, I'll fill him with lead."

Conrad was taken aback by Randall's aggressive response.

"Mr. Randall, the problem is that this killer is highly motivated and highly dangerous. It's likely that he will make another attempt to break into your house."

"I appreciate your concern, sergeant, but I think I can defend my family. I own several high-powered hunting rifles and a .22 pistol. Besides, I scheduled an alarm company to come out to the house tomorrow morning to put in a new alarm system."

"A home alarm system is good, but I still think it would be a wise precaution to stay at a hotel for at least a couple of nights."

"Sergeant, I can take care of my family."

"Okay, fair enough, Mr. Randall. It sounds like you've made up your mind. Just be aware that this psychopath might try to contact your daughter again at the house."

"Sergeant, if that piece of shit makes any attempt to break into this house, it will be the last thing he does. I'll blow his head off."

"Okay, Mr. Randall, then I won't waste any more of your time. Please stay alert and keep her safe."

"I will, sergeant. I appreciate your concern."

"I'll give you a call if I have any new information."

"Thank you, sergeant."

"Okay, then stay safe," Conrad said.

"Goodbye."

Well, that could have gone better, Conrad thought. Apparently, Tracey's father had an old-school survivalist mentality; he thought he could handle any further break-in attempts with guns. Conrad hoped that Randall wasn't underestimating the killer, but he didn't have time to argue because he still had leads to pursue.

Conrad still felt fidgety; he couldn't sit still any longer. He picked up the cruiser radio mike and depressed the "talk" button.

"Nine-thirty-five to nine-forty-two," he said.

"Forty-two is on," Officer Tannen replied.

"Forty-two, can you meet me at the Westfield Garden Apartments? I'm parked on the left side of the one-forty-nine building."

"Sure, Sarge."

A short time later, Conrad saw Tannen's cruiser turn into the main entrance of the complex. The sergeant backed away from the dumpster and headed across the lot to meet the officer. They pulled alongside each other in an aisle between two rows of cars in front of the one-forty-nine building.

"Rich, I need you to park next to the dumpster on the far side of the building so you have a good view of the main entrance. Keep your eye out for the suspect's vehicle. I'm going to meet the detective at the station."

"No problem, Sarge," Tannen replied.

"Thanks, Rich."

Conrad pulled away and drove toward the exit. As he headed for the station, he felt himself go into the zone; everything became perfectly clear; if they could find out which of the thirteen suspects was not available for the interview, they might have their man.

Then, came the doubts. Would it really be that easy? What if more than one tenant on the list was unavailable for an interview? What if the perp drove back to his apartment in yet another stolen vehicle? They were searching for a very specific vehicle, so any other car he was driving would make it past the police gauntlet. The psycho could be relaxing in his apartment right now. As slick as he was, maybe he could even fool them into thinking he was normal during an interview.

Conrad pushed these doubts aside as he turned into the police station parking lot. He parked next to Lombardi's unmarked vehicle in front of the building. He got out of the car and encountered a young blond-haired man leaving through the front doors of the station. He was in his early twenties, clean-cut, dressed in a collared shirt and plaid shorts. The young man passed by the sergeant without meeting his eyes. Conrad continued into the lobby and the dispatcher buzzed him through the security door.

He figured the young man must have been the veterinary student Lombardi was interviewing. He met the detective in her office.

"What was he like?" Conrad asked without preamble.

"He's clean," the detective replied. "If he's a serial killer, then I'm a genocidal maniac. The kid loves animals, for God's sake."

"Good, that's one down and twelve to go. Who's next on the list?"

"A kid named Chris Burton; he's a manager at Dunkin Donuts. According to the tenant info, he works second shift, so he should be there right now."

"Good, I could use a coffee. Ready to go?"

"You bet."

Conrad glanced at his watch as he and Lombardi left the office. It was a little after five PM. He didn't want to waste any time; he wanted to interview all twelve men on the tenant list today. He didn't want to give the psycho a chance to make it home, become comfortable, and think about how to pretend to act innocent during an interview. They needed to keep the pressure on.

They drove to the local Dunkin Donuts in Lombardi's unmarked cruiser; it was only a half-mile down the street. The skinny blond teenager working behind the counter widened his eyes when he saw Conrad's police uniform.

"We're looking for Chris Burton," Conrad said.

"Sure, Mr. Burton is in back. I'll get him," the teenager said, as he headed for a doorway behind the counter.

Thirty seconds later, he returned with a tall, well-dressed, dark-haired man who appeared to be in his late twenties. Conrad recognized him from his many visits. Like the kid at the counter, the man's eyes widened upon viewing Conrad's uniform.

"Chris Burton?" Conrad asked.

"Yes, how may I help you officer?" the man asked, appearing surprised.

"We need you to come down to the station to ask you some questions," Lombardi said. "You're not in any trouble. We're just looking for information."

"May I ask what this is about?"

"It's confidential, and extremely important. Lives are at stake. We could really use your help. Can you get someone to cover for you for a half-hour?" the detective asked.

Burton paused to think about it for a moment and then replied. "I think Matt can handle the store by himself for a half-hour," he gestured to the teenager behind the counter. "You all set to handle it?

"Sure, boss," the teenager replied.

"Okay, then I can go," Burton said, circling around the counter to the customer side.

"That's great," Conrad said, shaking Burton's hand as he came around. "But first we need two large ice coffees to go."

CHAPTER 60

I'm making good time in my journey north; I'm halfway to the cabin already. Glancing right, I see the little slut is crying, but she's not making a sound, so I leave her alone.

Lighting another cigarette, I offer her a drag; I'm not a savage. Ignoring the cigarette, she continues to stare straight ahead through the windshield as if in a catatonic trance. However, I notice her shoulders trembling. It's like deja vu. I pull the cigarette away, take a drag, and blow the smoke out through a crack in the window.

I have the music on my favorite rock station turned down low so I don't get a headache. I can't believe how young this bitch is; she doesn't look any older than fourteen years old; she's definitely not my type; I'm no pedophile; I like them at least sixteen. Her tiny breasts are no bigger than a pair of plums. She has short, straight blonde hair, while I prefer long, straight-haired brunettes. But, it doesn't matter. I will be imagining her as a brunette when I go to work on her. I will imagine that she is Tracey Randall.

I concentrate on the road so I won't become distracted by picturing what I am going to do to this little slut later. I feel a tremor of excitement shudder through my body. I'm going to use her unripe body to create a modern art masterpiece. It will be my best work yet. My parents' basement will be transformed into a sanguine modern art gallery.

I concentrate on sucking smoke down my throat and blowing it out. I can't allow myself to become overexcited. When I'm overexcited, I don't think clearly; when I don't think clearly, I make mistakes. Case in point: when I tried to pull the snatch-and-grab on that little bitch yesterday. I thought her friend had run away, but instead she came back and beat the hell out of me with a tree branch. It wasn't my finest moment.

But, this will be different. This little slut will be my modern art masterpiece; I will carve her up in new ways that will make my old work resemble a layman's pencil scribbling on office paper. This time, I will take off her fingers and toes one-at-a-time, string them into a necklace, and make her wear it while I'm slicing and dicing her. I'll bet I can keep her alive if I use the blowtorch creatively and keep feeding her Oxycontins.

I go into a zone where if feels like an outside force has taken control of my body and mind. I see my hands gripping the wheel, but they feel like they belong to someone else. The highway shoots toward me in a linear perspective as if someone else is viewing it.

After an unknown amount of time goes by, I realize it has become dark without me noticing it. The streetlights cast pale illumination down on the highway. I snap out of it and check the clock: it's after seven PM. I'm almost there.

I hit the brakes as my exit comes out of nowhere. The tires shriek and some idiot behind me beeps his horn as I decelerate rapidly to swerve onto the ramp.

Checking my passenger, I see her glaring at me with wide, horrified eyes. I frown at her as if to say, "What are you looking at?" and she stares ahead again. For a while, I forgot she was even with me. A lightning bolt of excitement crashes through my brain as I realize that she IS with me.

Tapping the brake, I concentrate on steering around the curving ramp at a reasonable thirty-five miles-per-hour. At the end of the ramp, I halt briefly at a stop sign and look both ways. Seeing no traffic, I pull onto route 64. A little over twenty minutes more and we'll be there. I can't wait.

The twenty-plus minute drive feels like it takes forever. I'm relieved as I finally pull onto the dirt road that leads up the mountainside to the cabin. I enjoy the rollercoaster feel of the curves, dips, and ascents as I drive. The sound of the tires grinding over pebbles and small rocks is comforting because I know I'm almost there.

As we pull alongside the cabin, I glance over at the slut, and become annoyed when I realize she's nodding off to sleep. I turn the volume up suddenly on the rock station and she wakes up, startled. I enjoy the panicked expression on her face as she realizes it wasn't a bad dream and she is really here.

The loud music ceases as I turn off the engine. The girl's pale, wide-eyed face looks terrified. I smile at her as I watch a single tear flow down her right cheek.

Laughing, I turn away and slide out of the car seat. I open the passenger door and seize her right forearm in an iron grip. She winces with pain, so I apply more pressure. The tears are really flowing now. I drag her roughly out of the car, and she whimpers like a wounded animal.

Adrenaline pulses through my brain as I shove her across the walkway toward the front door. She stumbles. When she recovers, I shove her again. I hear her gasp as she tries not to lose her balance. It's difficult for her to keep steady with her arms secured behind her back. Her instinct is to hold out her arms to catch her balance, but it's no longer an option.

I grab her shoulders to halt her forward momentum as we reach the front door. Guiding her out of the way of the door, I slide my house key into the lock. I turn the key, apply some pressure, and watch the door to the mudroom swing open. Seizing her shoulders, I shove her inside. I steer her like a sheepdog guiding an unruly flock and halt when I reach the set of steps leading to the inner door.

I ascend the steps first and use another key to open the inner door. My back is turned, but I can see her frozen in my peripheral vision, unsure of what to do. Come on, bitch. Run. I dare you to.

She doesn't.

Descending, I grab her skinny arm in a vise-grip and drag her up the steps. I pull her through the open doorway into the kitchen, guide her to the left, and shove her down on one of the dining room chairs. She sits. What other choice does she have?

"Don't move," I command as I walk over to the fridge and open it.

I take out a bottled water, unscrew the cap, and take a long, satisfying swill. I wipe my lips and stare at her as if daring her to say something. She is watching me, expectantly, like a grade-schooler awaiting a command from a god-like teacher. I savor my power over her and take another sip of water. She looks thirsty, so I'll make her wait a while before I let her drink.

"What are you going to - " she begins to ask, and then stops as I glare at her, furiously.

I calmly place the water bottle down on the counter and lunge at her without warning. As I move, I bring my right arm back and smash her left cheek with a vicious back-hand. She whimpers in response. Leaning down, I glare into her frightened eyes.

"You will only speak when I say you can," I growl at her in an ominous tone. "If you do exactly what I say when I say it, you won't get hurt. Do you understand?"

She merely nods because she's apparently too afraid to speak again. I smile as I notice the red welt on her cheek. I got her good. She will think twice before opening her mouth again.

CHAPTER 61

After the interview, Conrad and Lombardi escorted the Dunkin Donuts manager out of the police station. They stood next to the front doors and watched him cross the lot toward his parked light-blue BMW SUV.

"If that guy is a serial killer, then I'm Osama bin Laden," Conrad said.

"Isn't Bin Laden dead?"

"You know what I mean."

"Actually, I agree with you. He resembled the perp in the photo, but you pressed him pretty hard and his responses didn't send up any red flags. I think we can cross him off the list," Lombardi said.

"Who's next?" Conrad asked.

Lombardi scrutinized the list of the *Lucky Thirteen*.

"Some kid named Derek Connor. It says here that he's a campus police officer at Farmington State College."

"Does it say how long he's been there?"

"Six years."

"That doesn't sound very promising. Serial killers usually

can't hold high-stress jobs with a high level of interaction with the public. Especially, jobs where power is involved. Inevitably, a crack in the killer's psyche will show through and he's terminated. I think we can eliminate him from the list. Who's next?"

"The next kid is a student at Westfield State College."

"What year is he?"

"He's a senior."

"Psychopaths usually don't make it that far in college. I think Bundy completed less than one year of law school when he quit – although he did earn an Undergraduate Degree in psychology. There are usually too many distractions at a college campus for a psychopath to thrive; it's tough to focus on studying when you're surrounded by potential victims."

"Do you think we can skip him?"

"We'll interview him later. He's not a priority candidate. Next?"

"The next young man works at Sears at the Westfield Pond Mall. His name is Nicholas Freeman and he drives a forklift in the stockroom."

"Bingo," Conrad said. "He works an unskilled job out of the view of the public, but he also has heightened access to the mall and plenty of opportunities to find victims. We know our killer likes to hunt in malls. Where does he live?"

"Apartment eight in the one-forty-six Building at the Westfield Gardens complex."

"Do you want to take your car or mine?" Conrad asked.

"Let's take mine so we can keep a low profile," Lombardi said.

"Let's go then."

The sergeant followed the detective across the parking lot to her unmarked cruiser. They got in and she backed out of the parking spot.

They made it to Westfield Gardens in under ten minutes. Lombardi parked in a guest space on the right side of the one-forty-six building, and they walked over to the front doors. Entering the vestibule, Conrad checked the resident panel and pushed the button for N Freeman. When there was no response, he pressed it again. Ten seconds later, a hesitant male voice emanated from the speaker.

"Hello? Can I help you?"

"Mr. Freeman?" Conrad asked.

"Yes, who's asking?"

"Sergeant Conrad and Detective Lombardi with the West-field Police. Are you free to answer some questions? Don't worry, you're not in any trouble. You may have information about a case we're working on."

"The police? Why do you want to talk to me?" Freeman replied, sounding defensive.

"Let me try," Lombardi said. "He may respond better to a female voice."

"Hi, Mr. Freeman, it's Detective Lombardi. I just wanted to sit down and speak with you for a few moments about whether or not you witnessed a crime at your place of work."

"I haven't witnessed any crime."

Lombardi rolled her eyes at Conrad as she pressed the "talk" button again.

"Nicholas, if you buzz me in real quick, I'll just take up a brief moment of your time."

Conrad smiled as he realized that Lombardi had made her voice breathier – sexier – for Mr. Freeman's benefit. He figured that it must have worked because the door buzzed open a moment later.

"Nice job, Marilyn," Conrad said, holding the glass door open for her. "That's something they don't teach you at the police academy."

Lombardi raised her eyebrows as if to say, "I'm full of surprises." Conrad was impressed. It was clear that he had severely underestimated the detective in the past.

They ascended a stairwell to the third level and paused outside the door marked with the number eight. The sergeant stepped aside to let the detective take over. She obviously had a better rapport with the subject.

Lombardi knocked lightly on the door. "Mr. Freeman? Are you there? It's Detective Lombardi."

Conrad smiled again as he realized she was using the same seductive voice of her alter-ego that she used before.

"I'll be right there!" a muffled male voice shouted from the other side.

After twenty seconds of anxious waiting, the door finally opened and a freckled, pale face that didn't look any older than seventeen peered out of the doorway. His black hair was wet as if he just combed it and his shirt was un-tucked as if he just put it on.

Conrad mentally compared Freeman to the suspect in the photo and decided they couldn't rule him out. He and Lombardi couldn't seem to catch a break with an underweight or overweight suspect with a different facial structure, who they could rule out right away.

Marilyn placed one hand on her hip in a pose she had seen a model do on a cover of a magazine, and extended her other hand out to the young man. "Mr. Freeman?"

"Yep, that's me," the young-looking man replied, shaking her hand as he looked her up and down.

Conrad had to admit that she did look attractive wearing a medium-length gray skirt, white dress-shirt, and gray suit jacket.

"Can we come in real quick and ask you a few questions?" Lombardi asked when she saw the twenty-something was hesitant about opening the door.

"Yeah, sure, I guess," the young man said as he opened the door another foot.

Lombardi took over by pushing the door open the rest of the way and walking in past the timid resident. She pointed to an empty recliner placed in the corner across from a large couch.

"Have a seat, Nick, and we'll only be a few minutes."

Nick did as instructed and sat down. The detective sat across from him on the couch while Conrad tactfully shut the door, and remained standing by it with his arms folded.

"Nick, how long have you worked at Sears?" Lombardi asked. She already knew he had worked there almost three years.

"Two and a half years," Freeman replied, clasping his hands together nervously as he stared at the detective with wide eyes as if she was the first attractive woman in a business suit that he had ever laid eyes on.

"Okay, that's a good start, Nick," Lombardi said, shooting him a smile with just a hint of seduction. "How long have you lived at this apartment complex?"

"For a little over a year," Freeman said, glancing up at the intimidating uniformed figure by the door. Conrad stared back at him, expressionless.

"Where did you live before here?" the detective followed up

"I lived in Farmington for about a year and a half, but it was too far from my Dad's place. I moved up here from Atlanta to be near my Dad. My Mom lives in Marietta, a small town outside of Atlanta, and we weren't really getting along. My Dad fixed me up with a job at Sears, while I take part-time classes at Westfield State. I'm studying Criminal Justice there."

Nick Freeman glanced up expectantly at the uniformed sergeant as if expecting an "atta-boy" from him. Conrad didn't alter his expression because he was thinking that if the kid went into the criminal justice field, he would need a lot more confidence.

Then, something about what the kid said struck Conrad as relevant and he became animated. "Nick, when did you say you moved here?"

"About two-and-a-half years ago."

Conrad shot an intense glance at Lombardi. "It will be easy to check his residency status."

Then, turning back to Nick Freeman. "Nick, what was your address in Georgia?"

"Three-thirty-nine Little Pond Lane in Marietta. It's a twenty minute drive from the city."

"Nick, what's your date of birth?" the sergeant asked, glancing over at the detective, who had a knowing glint in her green eyes.

"September twentieth, nineteen-ninety six."

"Okay, good enough. I'm going to step outside for a moment while the Detective stays and asks you some more questions." Conrad opened the door, stepped into the hallway, and keyed his radio mike. "Nine-thirty-five to Control."

"Control's on," the dispatcher replied from the station.

"Can you check the status of an out-of-state resident for me?"

"Sure, Sarge, what do you need?"

"I need you to confirm that a Nicholas Freeman, date of birth 9/20/86, lived in Marietta, Georgia two-and-a-half years ago."

"Sure, Sarge, I'll get right back to ya."

Conrad began pacing in the hallway outside the apartment as he waited. He had already done three laps when the dispatcher called back.

"Sarge, that's affirmative. I have a Nicholas Freeman, date of birth 9/20/96, residing in Marietta, Georgia until April of 2017."

"Thank you, Control. I appreciate your help." Conrad pressed the button on his radio shoulder-mike.

"No problem, Sarge."

Conrad burst into the apartment like an avalanche, startling the already nervous young man and earning him a raised eyebrow from Lombardi.

"Marilyn, let's go. This kid checks out."

When the detective hesitated, he elaborated. "The situation we're dealing with has been going on for at least four years, and this kid just moved here a little over two years ago."

"Okay then," Lombardi replied, standing. She turned toward the anxious young man. "Mr. Freeman, thank you for your cooperation and good luck in your CJ classes."

"No problem. I was happy to be able to - "

The young man never got to finish his sentence as the detective followed the sergeant into the hallway and closed the door quietly behind her.

CHAPTER 62

I feel nothing but contempt for my pathetic captive as she sits, trembling, on the dining room chair. An immense wave of satisfaction washes over me like floodwater bursting through a smashed dam as I realize that every muscle of her body is quivering from head-to-toe. She is right to be afraid. If she knew what I was going to do to her later, she would be screaming with fright.

I see tears streaming down her cheeks, but I'll let her leak as long as she stays quiet. She appears to be frightened enough to follow my every order.

"Get up," I command her.

My captive's shaking becomes more pronounced as she tries to stand. She can barely make it off the chair without toppling over. She's about a foot shorter than I am, so I can easily look down at her with a feeling of superiority.

Reaching into my pocket, I take out my folding knife and flip it open. I hold it in front of her face as I glare down at her with a feral intensity.

"I'm going to take the handcuffs off now," I tell her. "If you disobey me or try to escape, I will slit your throat and you will bleed out until you die."

She lets out a gasp as her already pale face loses all its remaining color. Her shoulders start to quiver as if she's having a seizure. If she's too scared, she won't be able to follow my instructions. I flip the knife closed and put it away.

"Look, you need to calm down," I say, removing the harsh edge from my voice. "What's your name?"

"E-elizabeth," she stammers, as tears stream down her face like a downpour and her body shakes as if she's having a grand mal seizure.

"Look, Elizabeth, if you do what I say, I won't hurt you. We're just going to take some modeling pictures together and then I'm going to let you go. Do you understand?"

She nods at me and the shaking subsides slightly, but the flow of tears doesn't diminish.

"Elizabeth, I'm not a bad guy. I'm going to let you go soon. You need to stop crying now." I imitate the sickly sweet voice I've heard parents use with anxious toddlers.

She blinks rapidly as if she is trying to halt her tears, but they keep flowing. I give up.

"Elizabeth, turn around so I can take the handcuffs off. After you do some modeling for me, I will let you go."

She hesitates for a moment as if she doesn't comprehend what I'm saying, and then slowly rotates until her back is facing me. I take out the handcuff key and slide it into the slot in the right cuff. I turn it, hear a click, and pull the cuff off her wrist. I do the same for the second cuff. Dropping the cuffs on the floor, I hear the clanking sound of metal striking wood.

"Okay, Elizabeth, you can turn around and face me again."

Slowly, as if walking on eggshells, she rotates to face me. The tears are still flowing, but they have gone from a rain-shower to a drizzle.

"Okay, Elizabeth, I need you to take your t-shirt off for me. Can you do that?" I ask her in the same sickly sweet voice.

After a moment of typical hesitation, she raises her arms and slides the t-shirt off over her head. My eyes lock onto the small, plum-sized breasts poking out from beneath her bra. I feel myself getting hard.

"Okay, Elizabeth, now I need you to unbuckle your belt, un-zip your zipper, and drop your pants."

She stares right through me as if she is focusing on a point a thousand yards away, but she does what I say.

"Step out of them now."

She complies until she is standing in front of me wearing only a bra and panties. Her body is not fully developed yet, so I use my imagination to fill it out until it matches Tracey Randall's superb curves. Her skin is also much paler than Tracey's, so I picture it darker as I scan her up and down.

I almost become distracted as I stare at her body, but then I remember that I have to get the lingerie and digital camera from the trunk of my car. Leading her through the living room, I cuff her wrist to the stairway banister.

I retrieve the skimpy, red, two-piece ensemble and model-ing camera from a suitcase in the trunk of the car, and carry the items back to the scrawny, quivering thing cuffed to the banister. I become angry for a moment when I realize it's not Tracey Randall standing before me, but then my imagin-ation kicks in and I see what I want to see.

Without saying a word, I un-cuff the little slut from the ban-ister and hand her the two-piece lingerie.

"Take off what you're wearing and put this on," I tell her.

My body trembles with anticipation as I feel heat enter my loins. Her scrawny, pale naked body makes me angry as I watch her strip out of her underwear. She is not the one I want. But then, she starts to slide on the red bra and panties from Victoria's Secret, so I imagine Tracey Randall's voluptuous body filling out the clothing.

"Okay, now I'm going to pose you."

CHAPTER 63

"Who's next on the list?" Conrad asked Lombardi as they crossed the parking lot toward the unmarked cruiser.

The detective narrowed her eyes as she scrutinized the printout of the *Lucky Thirteen*.

"Douglas Reynolds is a twenty-eight-year-old who works for the Westfield Fire Department."

"How long has he worked for the department?"

"Seven years."

"There's no way in hell an unstable serial could hold a high-stress job like that for six years. We'll interview him last. Who's next?"

"Richard Evans. He's unemployed and lives in the one-forty-nine building."

"Unemployed? We need to talk to him. Which building is one-forty-nine?"

The Detective pointed to a building on the far side of the parking lot. "That one."

"Let's walk then."

They hurried across the lot to the front glass door of the

one-forty-nine building. Entering the vestibule, Lombardi scanned the names on the mailbox panel.

"He's in apartment three on the first floor," she said.

"Ring it."

Lombardi pushed the button. A few seconds later, the electronic lock buzzed on the inner door.

Conrad raised his eyebrows. "This kid is so trusting that he doesn't even ask who it is?"

"Works for me," the detective said, pulling the door open and going in.

Conrad followed her to the end of the hallway where they found apartment three.

"It's all you," Conrad said, grinning as he stood back and folded his arms.

The detective rolled her eyes as she reached out and knocked on the door three times.

"Open up! It's the police!" she shouted.

"Hey, don't scare him by shouting," the sergeant said, raising an eyebrow. "Use the voice."

Lombardi paused for a moment to get into character. She took a deep breath and said, "Greetings young man, it's the police." This time, she utilized her patented breathy, seductive voice.

"That's better."

They heard footsteps within and the door was flung open by a skinny young man wearing immaculately pressed black dress pants and a dark purple dress shirt. His black hair was perfectly combed and slicked back with gel. Incongruous to the rest of his appearance, Conrad noticed his feet were bare.

Except for the feet, he looked like he was ready to go on a job interview

"Oh, wow, it really is the cops," the resident said, smiling a wide, goofy grin as if he had just won the lottery.

Conrad's eyes darted to the interior of the apartment, which appeared to be an ideal exhibit from *Better Homes and Gardens* magazine. The apartment was spotless and all the wood furniture appeared to shine as if it was recently polished. Magazines were arranged in perfect rows on a gleaming coffee table placed parallel to a long, black leather couch. There was a state-of-the-art wide-screen plasma television in the corner with a comfortable-looking black leather recliner placed in front of it like a miniature movie theatre. Conrad noticed at least two video game console systems on the shelves below the television.

Conrad made a quick study of Evans and decided they couldn't rule him out. Apparently, the world was full of men in their twenties, who were medium height and medium build with black hair and no prominent, easily-recognizable facial features.

"Are you Richard Evans?" Lombardi asked, reverting to her normal voice.

"Are you a policewoman?" the perfectly-groomed young man asked without missing a beat.

Conrad stepped closer to the eccentric-looking resident and frowned down at him. He had at least a foot on the little guy. "Just answer the detective's question."

"You're kind of scary," Evans said, widening his eyes.

Conrad was losing his patience. He leaned in close and shouted in the kid's face like a drill instructor. "Are you Evans or not?"

The young man raised his arms in a defensive gesture as he cowered back. "I'm him! Don't hurt me!"

Conrad felt badly that he had scared the little guy. "Thank you, Richard," Conrad said, stepping back to give the nervous man some space. "Sorry to scare you."

"Why are you yelling at me? What did I do?" Evans asked, sounding perplexed and scared.

Conrad was taken aback for a moment; the resident's genuine confusion evinced a child-like quality. He decided to try a different track.

"Richard, do you live here by yourself?"

Richard bit his upper lip as he paused to think about the question.

"Yep, I live by myself now, but I still have to check in with my doctor once a week. I moved out of my halfway-house about a year ago."

"What's your doctor's name, Richard?"

"His name is Dr. Ernest Mendel."

"Do you know what kind of doctor he is?"

"He's a psychiatrist, I think."

"Have you been seeing him long?"

"I've only been seeing him for about three years, but before that I saw another one named Dr. Alvin Long."

"Do you know why you see a psychiatrist, Richard?"

"My first doctor diagnosed me with something called schizophrenia. I used to have problems when I didn't take my medicine, but now I take it every day, feel really good, and can live by myself."

"Richard, do you know how you pay for your rent?"

"I get a disability check every week, and Section Eight."

Conrad shot a glance at Lombardi. "We can check this easily. If it checks, we can move on."

"I know, but do you really think we should cross him off the list?"

"I'm getting an innocent vibe from this kid," Conrad said.

"I don't know. Maybe we should question him just to be sure," the detective said. "In a way, he does fit the profile."

A voice squawked suddenly from Conrad's portable radio. "Control to all units."

It was the station dispatcher. Conrad waited for the other patrol officers to respond before he pressed his shoulder mike button and replied. "Nine-thirty-five."

"Be advised that we just received a report of a teenager reported missing from 229 Chestnut Street in town. Thirteen-year-old named Elizabeth Benton went out to walk her dog several hours ago and she hasn't been seen since. When she didn't return a short time later, her parents assumed she was visiting a friend's house down the street, but when they called the friend, the friend said she never came by. Her parents said the dog trotted into the yard a few minutes ago dragging its leash, but there's no sign of her."

Conrad's forehead creased into a frown as he locked eyes with the detective. Her expression hardened as if her face had turned to granite.

Conrad waited for Malloy and Tannen to check in with the dispatcher before he replied. "Nine-thirty-five copies. Either myself or the detective will be en route."

Conrad looked at his watch; it was seven-fifteen. He saw that it was getting dark outside the windows.

"What do you think happened?" Lombardi asked.

"It sounds like another victim," Conrad said, as he felt a rush of adrenaline.

"Am I in trouble?" Richard Evans asked as his eyes darted back and forth between Conrad and Lombardi's frowning faces.

"No, Richard, you've been very helpful. We're sorry for bothering you," the detective said, softening her expression.

She figured that unless he could be two places at once, they could cross him off the list.

"Oh, it was no bother," Evans replied, smiling.

"Thank you for your time, Mr. Evans. You helped us out a lot." Conrad said.

"Are you going to chase bad guys?" Evans asked.

"You got it, buddy," Conrad said, winking at the young man as he turned and followed his partner down the hallway.

CHAPTER 64

I've only been taking pictures for a half-hour, but I'm beginning to feel tired already. How many provocative poses can I put this little bitch in?

Looking at the clock on the wall above the TV, I notice it's only 7:15 PM. The night is still young, but I've had a busy day. At this point, I'm beat.

Part of me wants to go to work on this slut right away, but another part of me wants to wait, take my time, and savor it. Right now I'm exhausted from the day's activities, so I'm not sure if I'll be able to enjoy the experience to the fullest. If I wait until tomorrow morning after a good night's rest, I could make the session last all day and maybe even into the night.

I feel a twinge of paranoia. If I wait until tomorrow to start taking her apart, she could escape – just like Tracey Randall did. However, I'm not going to make the same mistake I made last time. This time, I'm going to wait until she has no arms and legs before I have sex with her. That way, she can't fight back.

Usually, I like to sample the girls when they are whole, but this time I can't afford that luxury. I can't risk another escape; that would put me over the edge.

The blonde slut is looking at me, expectantly, as if she is waiting for me to put her in another pose. Miraculously, she appears to be more confident and less scared after the modeling session. She probably thinks that if she continues to cooperate, I'm going to let her go, but that's not going to happen. There's no way I'm going to relinquish my prize.

"Okay, Elizabeth, we're done now, so I need you to turn around and put your hands behind your back so I can put the cuffs back on."

She raises an eyebrow and hesitates, as if this instruction doesn't conform to her expectations. She must have figured that I would let her go after taking the pictures.

"Don't worry, Elizabeth. I'm going to let you go soon," I tell her in a placating tone of voice. "We should wait until the morning when it's light. It's too late to drive all the way back now. It will be easier to take you back to your house when it's light out. Okay?"

She nods her head as she complies by turning around and placing her arms behind her back. She hasn't dared to speak since I cracked her across the face the last time she said something.

I snap the cuffs on and escort her to the downstairs bathroom.

"If you have to go, then now's the time because this is your last chance," I tell her as I point toward the bathroom doorway.

Without replying, she enters the bathroom and shuts the door awkwardly behind her. I'm sure it will be challenging for her to do it with her hands cuffed behind her back, but that's her problem. I'm not taking the risk.

When she's done, I escort her upstairs. Leading her to the master bedroom, I un-cuff her left wrist, and attach the cuff to the bed leg. She has room to either lie on her back or her stomach.

Despite her excessive thinness, she looks enticing in her lingerie as she lies sideways on the hard-wood floor at the foot of the bed. However, I don't have time for that because I have to start my preparations; I need to set everything up just right so I can get started right away tomorrow morning.

"Elizabeth, you should get some rest because you're going to be here until morning." I tell her. "If you have to go to the bathroom during the night, then hold it. Whatever you do, don't wake me up at any time or you will regret it. Do you understand?"

She nods at me as she lies sideways on the floor with her elbow on the floor and her cheek resting on a palm. Again, she appears seductive in this pose, but I don't have time to mess around.

"I'll be back in about an hour," I tell her as I leave the room. I cut across the short hallway between the upstairs bedrooms, and bolt down the stairs two-at-a-time.

Sprinting across the living room and kitchen, I reach the mud-room door. Flinging it open, I descend four steps and jog the short distance to the exterior door. As I throw open the exterior door, I feel like an animal breaking out of its cage as I emerge into the cool twilight mountain air.

I head in the direction of the shed where I store my primary art tool: a well-oiled chainsaw. During my art project, I will also utilize a sharp knife for certain details, but only a chainsaw can cut easily through bone.

I cross the driveway to the shed and open the side door with my key. Pushing it open, I step into the darkness and flip the light switch on the wall.

CHAPTER 65

Detective Lombardi handed Sergeant Conrad the suspect list as she drove the unmarked cruiser toward the station. Conrad flicked on the interior light so he could scrutinize it. He counted the names the detective had crossed out before arriving at the next suspect on the list; so far, they had either interviewed or discounted eight suspects. Suspect nine's name was Eric Blackburn.

Conrad reviewed the information on the tenant form. Blackburn worked as a full-time mall security guard at the Farmington Mall.

Immediately, a red flag went up. One of the kidnappings and two of the murders had occurred at the Farmington Mall. The perpetrator obviously felt comfortable using malls as hunting grounds; working full-time as a mall security guard would account for his familiarity with malls as a place to track prey. As mall security, the perp would be able to access areas that ordinary shoppers would not be allowed to access. He would be familiar with mall layouts and security routines in general.

"Marilyn, have you seen this next guy on the list, Blackburn?" Conrad asked.

"No, why?" she replied.

"He works as a full time security guard at the Farmington Mall. That would explain the perp's comfort level using malls as hunting grounds."

"He sounds promising," Lombardi agreed. "In addition, mall security is a low-skill job. It requires little education or training, and is generally low-stress. A psychopath could probably blend in without attracting notice if he was careful."

"Excellent point," Conrad agreed. "A psychopath working mall security could check out potential female targets walking around, and yet still be able to make his rounds and unlock doors. The job doesn't require a high level of concentration, so he could still go through the motions despite all the distractions surrounding him."

"I would check him out ASAP," the detective said, as she pulled into the station parking lot.

"Absolutely," Conrad agreed.

Lombardi drove around back and parked next to Conrad's marked cruiser.

"So I'll track down this Blackburn guy while you respond to the missing person call on Chestnut Street?" the sergeant asked.

"Sounds good," Lombardi agreed. "Let me know if you find any more red flags on this guy."

"He's already sending up red flags," Conrad said.

"I mean, during the interview."

"You'll be the first to know," the sergeant said, opening the passenger door and stepping out. "I'll catch up with you after I interview him."

"Okay, fair enough."

As he turned his back, Conrad heard Lombardi's engine rev as she stepped on the gas pedal and peeled out. Without looking back, he took out his key and opened the driver's side door of the marked cruiser. Sliding in, he started it up.

"Inspector Lombardi to Control," the detective's voice spoke from Conrad's cruiser radio.

"Westfield Control," the dispatcher replied.

"I'm en route to Chestnut Street," she said.

"Received, En route to Chestnut Street at 19:25 hours."

Conrad backed out of his parking spot and took off. He enjoyed the satisfying sound of screeching tires as he shot across the lot toward the exit.

When he reached the street, he picked up his radio mike and depressed the button. "Nine-thirty-five to Control."

"Control's on."

"I'm returning to the Westfield Garden apartments to conduct another interview."

"Received. 19:26 hours."

The sergeant waited for several cars to pass before pulling out. Pressing his foot down on the gas pedal, he enjoyed the feeling of rapid acceleration as the cruiser picked up speed. There really was nothing like driving a police interceptor.

Conrad made it to Westfield Gardens in record time. Several times, he had flashed his blue lights to inspire slow-moving cars to get out of the way. The dashboard clock read 7:33 as he pulled into the apartment complex parking lot.

He drove around the lots until he found the one-forty-eight building, and parked in one of the guest spots. Springing out of the cruiser, he felt an electrical charge shoot through his body. He had a strange feeling about this one. He didn't want to jump to any conclusions, but it would make perfect sense for the killer to be a mall security guard. Especially, at the Farmington Mall where so many of the crimes occurred.

Entering the vestibule, the sergeant pressed the button for apartment six: Blackburn. Even the name sounded ominous to him. The buzzer rang, but there was no response. He pressed it again. Still, no response. A chill crawled up his spine like icy fingers.

If the missing person call that Lombardi was responding to was the killer's latest victim, then it would make sense that he wasn't at his apartment. If he was following his usual routine, he would be taking her up north to the isolated snowmobile cabin where he brought Tracey Randall.

A feeling of helplessness suddenly assailed him. If Blackburn wasn't home, then what were his options? Simply being a mall security guard didn't give him probable cause to obtain a search warrant to check his apartment. On the application, he couldn't write down that he had a bad feeling about the guy.

He pressed the buzzer several more times and finally gave up.

Staring at the name BLACKBURN on the mailbox, his mind raced for a solution. Then, he thought of something. There was no way that Blackburn could afford to own a cabin in the mountains on a security guard's salary. Being a fairly young guy, it was more likely that his parents owned it and he only had access to it. All Conrad had to do was look up Blackburn's parents, talk to them, and find out if they owned a cabin in the mountains. If they did, that would throw up another giant red flag.

Conrad depressed the button on his portable radio's shoulder mike and leaned his mouth toward it.

"Nine-thirty-five to Control."

"Westfield Control."

"I need you to look up a name for me in the directory. The name is Blackburn. Let me know how many results you get."

"Received, Sarge."

Conrad exited the vestibule, descended a short flight of steps, and stepped onto the asphalt surface of the lot. He was overflowing with nervous energy, so he began pacing the length of the parking lot. He sped up his pace; he knew it was irrational, but he felt that if he didn't keep moving, he would freeze up.

He had already made three laps by the time the dispatcher called back.

"Control to nine-thirty-five."

"Thirty-five's on."

"I found five Blackburns listed in the local directory. One resides at the one-forty-eight building at the Westfield Garden apartments in town, another lives on Laurel Street in town, the next one resides in Northfield, another in Southfield, and the final one in Farmington."

"Give me the address of the Blackburn residing on Laurel Street in town."

"One-twenty-six Laurel Street."

"Thank you, Control. I'll be heading to that location."

"Received, Sarge."

Conrad shivered as a jolt of adrenaline surged through his body. He felt like he was close. For some inexplicable reason, he was sure that the address in town was the right one.

The sergeant bolted to his cruiser, flung the driver's door

open, and slid into the seat. In seconds, he was racing across the lot toward the street.

Again, Conrad made record time by utilizing the lights and sirens when necessary. He knew the Chief and lieutenant wouldn't approve because technically he was not responding to an emergency call, but he felt more urgency now than at any time in the past.

As he pulled onto Laurel Street, he noticed the houses were very large – almost mansions – accompanied by wide, spacious lawns that reminded Conrad of the vast estates of the British aristocracy. Thick forest surrounded the immense lawns like green battlements. No doubt this was the richest section of town, and one of the neighborhoods Conrad knew the least about because the only time he responded here was for a rare burglar alarm – usually set off by a nanny, housecleaner, or handyman.

The first house he passed was too far away to spot a number, but the second house had a number inscribed on the mailbox: 220. Calculating that he still had a distance to go, he sped down the twisting, turning road for a mile until he thought he was in the vicinity. Sure enough, the house on the right was labeled one-thirty-three. He slowed down and began checking more carefully.

The next house on the right was one-thirty-one, the next – one-twenty-nine, one-twenty seven, and after an intervening stretch of forest, one-twenty-five. Conrad checked the house across the street and saw it was one-twenty-four. He had to backtrack. He did a smooth three-point-turn and slowed down when he came to the first house on the right. Sure enough, it was one-twenty-six.

The house was set very far back at the end of a long, straight driveway. The lawn surrounding the driveway and house was relatively flat, but the rest of the yard contained many small hills and dips like a restless ocean. Clusters of trees were scattered across the uneven terrain like green ships' sails floating on ocean swells.

Conrad descended a slight dip and punched it on a long straightaway that went for almost a hundred yards until it reached a rectangular asphalt area that resembled a small parking lot in front of a four-car garage. A curving path struck out from the edge of the driveway for about a hundred feet across the lawn until it reached a set of steps leading up to a set of fancy wooden doors that resembled the doors of a cathedral more than a residence.

There were no cars parked in the driveway, so Conrad hoped they were out of sight in the garage rather than the residents being away on vacation. Conrad parked next to the path, turned off the engine, and got out.

CHAPTER 66

Sergeant Conrad followed the walkway across the lawn until he reached the double-doors at the front of the impressive residence. From far away, the house had seemed large, but up close it was immense. It was only two levels high, but the right wall stretched away into a distant linear perspective. He couldn't tell from this angle how far across the lawn the house extended; it seemed to go on forever. From the street, the right side of the house had been partially obscured by trees.

An elaborate chime sounded within as the sergeant rang the doorbell. Twenty seconds later, a well-groomed young man in an impeccably tailored suit answered the door.

"May I help you?" he asked.

"I'm Sergeant Jim Conrad with the Westfield Police. I'm investigating a kidnapping and it's vital that I speak with Mr. or Mrs. Blackburn as soon as possible."

The suited man gestured for Conrad to step into a great hall beyond the doors. "Wait here a moment while I relay your request to Mr. Blackburn."

As the young man turned his back and walked toward the rear of the hall, the sergeant looked around. The hall was incredibly spacious; beneath the two-story, cathedral-like ceiling, an elaborate winding staircase curved upward around the far wall to a second floor balcony that over-looked the entire hall.

To the right, he saw a large opening leading to a living room equipped with sumptuous, expensive-looking furniture. To the left was a dining room with a long table that looked like it could seat at least twenty. At the rear of the hall, where the young man had gone, a wide hallway disappeared into the depths of the house. Conrad was not used to such opulence, and he hated to admit that he felt slightly intimidated.

A short time later, the man in the suit appeared from the corridor at the rear of the hall and motioned for the sergeant to follow him. Conrad tried to psych himself up as he crossed the wide marble floor. This interview was crucial and he wasn't going to let anyone talk down to him.

He followed the suited man to the end of the hallway and caught a glance of an immense kitchen area to the left as they took a right into a side corridor. Walking to the end of the corridor, they passed through an open doorway into a large study with an oversized mahogany desk placed in front of a massive fireplace. The walls were lined with bookcases as if the room was actually a well-stocked mini-library.

Seated behind the desk was a tan, robust, gray-haired man with a slight receding hairline who looked to be in his mid-to-late fifties. He was wearing a white dress shirt, which appeared casual when contrasted with the formal study and the impeccable suit of the assistant.

The gray-haired man stood and came around the desk to offer his hand to the sergeant. Conrad shook it.

"I'm Ray Blackburn. Please have a seat, sergeant," the man said, gesturing to one of a pair of comfortable-looking leather chairs placed in front of the large desk.

This guy is sharp, Conrad thought. *He noticed the sergeant's stripes right away.*

As Conrad sat, Blackburn circled the desk to sit at a high-backed, black, leather executive chair. He leaned forward attentively while he folded his hands on the desk. "Thank you, Tom," Blackburn said, nodding at his assistant, who immediately turned and left the room. "How may I help you, sergeant?"

"Sir, I'm investigating an exigent case involving a young woman in town who has been kidnapped. I believe it's possible that your son may have encountered the suspect while working as a security guard at the Farmington Mall."

"Then why aren't you speaking to my son?" Blackburn asked, furrowing his brows.

"Sir, I went to your son's apartment and he wasn't there. However, this case is serious enough for me to follow up with you in an attempt to locate him right away."

"Did you check his work? You obviously already know that he works security at the Farmington Mall."

Conrad noticed that Blackburn mentioned the word "security" with a tone of contempt as if his son had let the family down by sinking to a menial job.

"I did call his work, and they told me he had called in sick today," Conrad said. "I'm wondering if you might know where I can find him? Is there another residence he might be at?"

Blackburn thought for a moment, and replied. "We have a vacation home at West Palm Beach, Florida, but there's no reason for him to be there now."

"Do you have any other vacation homes that are more local?" Conrad asked, hoping he would get the response that

SHAWN WILLIAM DAVIS

he urgently needed.

"We have a snowmobile cabin in Dolebrook, New Hampshire, but it's not the right season for him to be there either," Blackburn said, matter-of-factly. His tone changed to one of pained regret. "I'm afraid that Eric doesn't maintain consistent communication with us, so he could be anywhere. He's so secretive that we know very little about his friends or social life. He keeps mostly to himself. Other than his apartment and place of work, I wouldn't know where to find him."

Sir, you just helped me more than you could possibly know, Conrad thought as he felt a charge of adrenaline shoot through his body like a bolt of lightning.

"When is the last time you heard from him?" Conrad asked, attempting to conceal his excitement with a question.

"My son called us about two weeks ago to say he wouldn't be able to come to dinner because he had to work an overtime shift. That's the last time he called us. However, I did reach him on the phone a day or so ago at his apartment. I wish he would call more, but it's something I've learned to accept. Why do you think he may be able to help you out?"

Conrad paused to formulate an adequate lie. "Mr. Blackburn, we have surveillance footage of our kidnapping suspect being escorted out of one of the stores at the Farmington Mall for shoplifting by your son in his security uniform. I wanted to check with your son to see if he could give us any more information about the shoplifter."

"Wouldn't that information be written in an incident report?" Blackburn asked.

"We checked the incident report generated by the security department, but the suspect gave a fake name and address, so I wanted to speak to your son directly to see if he noticed any distinguishing characteristics like scars or tattoos."

404

"I wish I could help you more, sergeant, but I'm afraid I'm at a loss as to where my son is. He's very independent and does his own thing."

"Does your son have a cell phone?" Conrad asked.

"Unfortunately, he doesn't have one anymore," Blackburn said. "He used to have one, but he's very private, and when he found out his location could be tracked by GPS, he got rid of it. In order to contact him, we have to call his apartment number, and he's rarely home. If you were just there, it would be a waste of time to call him. I'm sorry that I can't help you out more with your case. Where did the most recent kidnapping occur?" Blackburn asked.

"It happened earlier today on Chestnut Street in town. A thirteen-year-old girl was snatched while she was walking her dog in her neighborhood."

"That's terrible. I read about the murder and kidnapping at the Westfield Pond Mall last week," Blackburn's brow furrowed with what appeared to be genuine concern. "It was amazing that the victim was able to escape. Do you think the two cases are related?"

"Most definitely," Conrad replied. "We're positive that we're dealing with the same suspect."

"Then, I wish you luck, sergeant. I hope you find him."

That may not be entirely true if it turns out to be who I think it is, Conrad thought.

"Thank you for your time, Mr. Blackburn. We will do our best." Conrad stood up and Blackburn followed his lead. Again, the older gentleman circled the large desk and shook hands with the sergeant.

"Good luck, and I'm sorry I couldn't be more help," Blackburn said.

"I appreciate that you took the time to talk to me," Conrad said. "If you do hear from your son, would you please ask him to call the Westfield Police Department?"

Not that he ever would, Conrad thought.

"I don't know when he's going to call next, but I will let him know if he does."

"I appreciate it." Conrad said as he headed for the doorway.

Blackburn fell into step beside him and escorted him to the hallway. "Can you find your way out from here, sergeant?"

"I think I can manage." Conrad nodded at the older man as he headed down the corridor.

CHAPTER 67

Conrad tried to maintain his composure as he felt adrenaline surge through his veins like liquid fire. His body quivered with energy as he hurried away down the hallway. He didn't want to start running because he didn't know if Blackburn was still watching him from the study.

The Blackburns owned a snowmobile cabin in Dolebrook, New Hampshire; Dolebrook was the town located directly adjacent to West Brookfield, the town next to East Brookfield where the trucker brought Tracey Randall to the police station after he rescued her on the highway. Tracey Randall had been tormented by the kidnapper in a similar cabin in the mountains. It had to be more than mere coincidence. The mathematical probabilities pointed to a correlation.

Conrad broke into a run as he turned a corner in the hallway. He sprinted until he emerged into the spacious front hall. Like a lightning bolt, he dashed across the marble floor and hurtled out the front door. Descending the steps two-at-a-time, he picked up speed when he hit the walkway.

Conrad felt another burst of energy as he ran full-tilt toward the parked cruiser at the end of the walkway. He was certain that he knew exactly where to find the killer and his latest victim: Dolebrook, NH. All he had to do was drive to that town and obtain the address of the cabin from the local police.

During the interview with Blackburn, Conrad thought about asking the older man what the address of the cabin was, but he was worried that it might raise suspicions. Blackburn was smart, and that question may have helped him to come to the conclusion that his son hadn't witnessed the suspect, but WAS the suspect. The last thing Conrad needed at this point in the investigation was interference from a wealthy and powerful town resident.

The police sergeant got in his car and spun around in the parking lot in front of the quadruple garage until he was facing the long driveway. Seeing the way was clear, he pressed down on the gas pedal like a racecar driver at the starting line.

The tires shrieked like a tortured ghost as a long, black mark formed on the gray surface of the driveway. At this point, Conrad didn't care. He would never be able to live with himself if he wasted a single moment and arrived at the scene in Dolebrook too late. The Blackburns could complain about the skid mark to the Chief if they didn't like it.

When he reached the street, he stopped for a moment to look for traffic and pressed down on the gas pedal when he didn't see any.

He was pretty sure he had left a longer mark on the street than the one on the driveway. Again, he didn't care. He was in the zone and nothing was going to stop him.

As he headed toward the station, Conrad steered through the town roads on psychic autopilot, while he thought about how he was going to present the latest information to the Chief and the lieutenant. As excited as he was about the latest development, he acknowledged that he was in a delicate and potentially compromising situation.

First, Dolebrook was not his jurisdiction and he had no arrest powers there. Secondly, owning a snowmobile cabin in the same area where a psychopathic kidnapper also happened to have access to a cabin did not create Probable Cause to apply for a search warrant. Thirdly, he would have to rely on the Dolebrook police to check the cabin for the kidnapped girl under the cover of a general well-being check.

Conrad couldn't tell the local police about his theory that Eric Blackburn was a killer/kidnapper, who had possession of a female captive, because he didn't have Probable Cause. He barely even had Reasonable Suspicion, which didn't meet the legal standard to obtain a search warrant.

The local police could chalk up his theories to coincidence, and decide that checking on Blackburn without Probable Cause was a violation of his Constitutional right to privacy. If the Dolebrook Police were anything like the East Brookfield Police, they could even make the situation worse by alerting the kidnapper that the police were looking for him, which would then enable the killer to murder or escape with his victim.

The bottom line was that calling the Dolebrook police and sending them to the cabin was a potential legal minefield, and could make the situation worse. Then again, if the psychopath was going to murder his female captive within the next several hours, it might be her only chance for survival. Conrad estimated that it would take at least four hours to drive to Dolebrook. Four hours could mean the difference between life and death.

Conrad felt sweat forming on his forehead as he pulled into the police station parking lot. He could imagine a worst-case scenario where the chief or lieutenant would hear his flimsy evidence and order him not to travel to Dolebrook because of jurisdictional issues. Then, the local police would botch a check of the cabin and enable the killer to escape.

As Conrad parked in the rear of the lot, he realized that the only person he trusted was Detective Lombardi. Turning off the engine, he stared at the brick wall of the station as he considered the situation.

Detective Lombardi was the only person in the department who would agree with him that it was worth it to take the risk to travel all the way to Dolebrook, and make the check on the cabin without Probable Cause or jurisdictional authority. He was facing a dilemma that he never foresaw; it could cost him his job to track down the killer in a jurisdiction where he had no authority.

After several moments of rumination, he knew what he had to do. Without leaving the cruiser, he picked up the radio mike and depressed the talk button.

"Nine-thirty-five direct to Inspector Lombardi," he said.

After what seemed like an interminable amount of time, she replied. "This is Lombardi." She was obviously not expecting his call and had answered on her portable radio at the crime scene.

"Where can I meet up with you?"

"I'm at the crime scene on Chestnut street. Could you meet me here?"

"Sure, I'll be there in ten."

Conrad wanted to speak to Lombardi in person. He didn't want to relay any information over the airwaves in case the chief or lieutenant was listening. It was best to keep them in the dark for now. Conrad thought it was ironic that his former rival was now the only one he trusted in the department.

Satisfied with his decision, Conrad started the cruiser and backed out of the parking space at the rear of the station.

When he reached the road, he pointed the reinforced nose of the vehicle in the direction of Chestnut Street and drove that way.

CHAPTER 68

Arriving at the crime scene, Conrad spotted Detective Lombardi at the edge of a perimeter of caution tape, which had been strung up around a sizable section of the sidewalk on Chestnut Street. He saw two white-uniformed crime scene techs working within the rectangular barrier.

The sergeant pulled up next to the curb where the detective stood outside the tape. She saw him, walked over to the cruiser, and leaned down as the passenger window rolled down.

"We need to talk," he said.

"What's up?"

"I know who and where the killer is, but we have a problem with jurisdiction."

"We can't talk here," Lombardi said, glancing over at Officer Tannen standing by the caution tape several feet away. "I've learned everything I can from the scene, so I'll follow you back to the station."

Without further explanation, Lombardi walked over to Officer Tannen and said something out of Conrad's earshot. Conrad saw Tannen nod his head as Lombardi turned and walked down the sidewalk toward her parked cruiser. In his rearview mirror, he watched her get into her car.

He gave her a few seconds to start up her vehicle, looked left to check for traffic, and pulled away from the curb when he saw it was clear. As his cruiser shot down the street, he saw Lombardi's unmarked following him in his rearview mirror. She quickly matched his excessive speed and followed his lead by utilizing her lights and sirens when slower cars got in the way.

They made good time and arrived at the station less than ten minutes later. Conrad pulled up next to Lombardi in the rear parking lot and got out. She remained in the driver's seat as he walked over to her car. Her window was already down.

"You have me intrigued," she said. "Are you serious about knowing who this psychopath is?"

"It's Blackburn," Conrad said. "I'm not only going by the fact that he works as a security guard at the Farmington Mall. He wasn't at his apartment, so I visited his father's house in town. The father confirmed that the family owns a snow-mobiling cabin in Dolebrook, which is one town away from where the truck driver picked up Tracey Randall after she escaped. There's no way it's just coincidence."

The detective paused for a moment; she placed her hand on her chin as she appeared to memorize the pattern of the brick wall at the rear of the station.

"I agree," she said. "It can't be a coincidence. Blackburn is our man. But if he's in New Hampshire, how the hell do we get him?"

"That's why I'm talking to you – so we can formulate a plan. I'm sure I don't need to remind you about what's at stake."

"I know what's at stake – a young woman's life," Lombardi said, her green eyes flashing. "All the evidence at the crime scene on Chestnut Street points to the same psychopath. If he's not at his apartment, he must have taken her to the parents' cabin in New Hampshire."

"That's what I think."

"Then we need to call the Dolebrook Police and ask them to do a well-being check on the girl at the cabin," the detective said.

"That's also what I was thinking at first," Conrad said. "But what happens if the local cops show up at the cabin, Blackburn answers the door, and then convinces them there is no girl with him. They don't have any Probable Cause to search inside, so they will have to take his word for it. When they leave, he will either escape with the girl or he will kill her and escape with the body. Either way, the girl dies."

"I'll tell you what," Lombardi said. "Get in the car so we can start driving north. We can iron out the details of our strategy as we go."

"You're right," Conrad said, as he circled around the hood of the car and slid into the passenger's seat.

Lombardi had the car on the road before Conrad could put on his seatbelt.

"What would you have done if I didn't agree to drive north with you?" Lombardi asked, as she headed toward the highway.

"I would have taken my own vehicle and gone alone."

"That's what I thought," she said, flashing him a mischievous grin. "This way – if we both go – it won't look like you're going rogue. If we catch hell for it, we can say we're following a lead."

"We can tell the chief and your father that Blackburn's father told me that his son was probably at the cabin, and we're going there to conduct an interview."

"The only problem with that is – what will we do if psycho-boy meets us at the door of the cabin and tells us to fuck off?"

"I don't know about you, but I'm not taking no for an answer," Conrad said. "No matter what this punk says, I'm going inside the cabin to look around. I'm sure we'll find the girl. We can get our stories straight about it later."

"If I have to, I'll say I saw blood on his shirt," the detective said.

"That's a good idea because if we're right and Blackburn does have the girl, he will end up having plenty of blood on his shirt after he inevitably resists arrest."

"I'm glad we're on the same page."

As Lombardi pulled onto the entrance ramp to the highway, Conrad agonized over whether or not to call the Dolebrook police to ask them to check the cabin. Sweat beaded on his forehead as he realized the significance of his decision; his choice had the potential to save or cost the young woman her life.

If the local police took the killer's word for it that the victim was not there and didn't search the cabin, then she would most certainly die or be brought to another location to die because the killer would be alerted they were on to him. But if Conrad didn't call and waited until they arrived in roughly four hours, while the psychopath killed her before that time elapsed, then it was possible she might be murdered before they reached her.

"I know what you're thinking," Lombardi said.

She glanced sideways at her partner as she steered into the

fast-lane and accelerated past slower-moving cars until the speedometer read 95 mph.

"You do?" Conrad was taken aback.

"You're thinking the same thing I am. Should we call the local police and ask them to do a well-being check or not?"

"You're right," Conrad agreed. A feeling of relief washed over him as he realized his partner was so in tune with him. "What do you think?"

"I'm thinking that making the decision to call could cause her death and not making the decision to call could cause her death. Either way, we're responsible for her death," Lombardi said, gravely.

"Or responsible for saving her – if we make the right decision," Conrad said.

Conrad had never been religious, but he was thinking now might be the right moment to pray to God for guidance. Maybe it would make the difference. He leaned back in the seat and closed his eyes.

Please, God, I know I've tried to do things on my own and I haven't sought your guidance in the past, but I need help with this decision in order to save a young woman's life. Do I trust the local police to intervene or do I follow my instincts and wait?

No answer came. Conrad kept expecting to hear a deep, male voice speak to him in his mind: "Make the call" or "Don't make the call." However, all he heard was the rumbling of the car engine and the sound of the wind racing by on the highway.

"Did you get an answer?" Lombardi asked.

"What?"

"Did you get an answer to your prayer?"

Conrad felt unnerved. "How did you know what I was doing?" he asked.

"I know because I'm silently doing the same thing," she said.

CHAPTER 69

The dashboard clock read 8:48 PM. Conrad and Lombardi had only been on the road for an hour, but it had seemed like many hours. They still had over three hours to go before they got close to their destination.

"I just thought of something," Lombardi said, as Conrad heard the engine rev and saw the speedometer climb to 100 mph.

The cars to the right appeared to be crawling as the unmarked police car left them behind in its wake. So far, the fast lane was clear.

"What?" Conrad replied.

"What if he's torturing her?" Lombardi asked, eyebrows knitting together.

"I've thought of that too. I don't know what we can do unless we make the call to the Dolebrook police," Conrad said, feeling a rush of anxiety.

It was a situation he had considered, but he was trying not to dwell on it. He didn't want to waste time and energy second-guessing.

"What if making the call could save the victim from being

tortured?" Lombardi asked.

"Then, obviously it would be worth it to make the call," Conrad replied.

"Then we have to make the call," Lombardi said, glancing at her partner.

"Are you sure?" Conrad asked. "What if the cops talk to the perp, but they don't check the house and he gets away with the victim. Then, he brings her to another location, kills her, and goes after more victims."

"That would be horrific, but at least her pain would be ended. We have to consider the possibility that the victim is enduring pain at this moment."

"I agree that we have to think of the victim. But what if he's not torturing her now, but then decides to torture her after the cops show up and alert him that we're on his trail?" Conrad asked.

"If the cops show up, the perp will probably panic and make a run for it after they leave."

"Sure, then he brings her to another location, tortures her, and kills her. Our best chance to capture the perp and prevent him from killing again is to handle this situation ourselves without getting the locals involved."

"It's our best chance for capturing the perp, but we also have a moral obligation to prevent the victim from experiencing severe pain. If I was the victim, I would just want the pain to stop," the detective said.

Conrad imagined his own daughter writhing in horrific pain as she was tortured with a razor-sharp blade. That did it.

"Okay, I'll make the call," Conrad said, as he took his cell phone out of his pocket. He dialed information.

"Can I help you?" a male operator asked.

"Dolebrook, New Hampshire. The police department."

"One moment," the operator replied.

The operator recited the number and Conrad hung up. Conrad felt his heart pounding as if it was about to burst like an overfilled water balloon. His sweaty fingers punched the numbered buttons on the cell phone, and when it finally rang, it seemed to take forever to be picked up.

"Dolebrook Police. This call is recorded," a female dispatcher answered.

"Ma'am, I'm Sergeant Conrad with the police from Westfield, Massachusetts. We're pursuing a dangerous serial killer and we believe he may be in your town. Can I speak to the supervisor or OIC on duty?"

"A serial killer?" the dispatcher asked, sounding skeptical.

"We believe he has a thirteen-year-old victim from our town with him right now. He's going to kill her unless we stop him."

"One moment please," the dispatcher said, pressing the hold button.

Conrad listened to dead air for what seemed like an endless amount of time. Finally, he heard the dispatcher's voice again.

"Sir, I called the shift supervisor back to the station. Do you have a number he can reach you at?"

"Sure," Conrad said, fidgeting impatiently. "It's 508-236-6224."

"I'll have him call you as soon as he gets in."

"Thank you."

Conrad felt his heart hammering in his chest as if it was a piece of meat being pounded by a mallet.

"What did they say?" Lombardi asked.

"The supervisor is going to call me back."

"You don't look so good," she said. "Your face just went white."

"I don't feel so good," he said.

Conrad's vision wavered as if he was viewing the highway underwater. He heard ringing in his ears.

"Lean your seat back and try to relax." Lombardi said. "When's the last time you drank any water?"

"Don't remember," Conrad said, as his concentration started to waver like a radio station losing its signal.

"You look like you're about to pass out. Do you want me to pull over?"

"No, keep going. I'll be fine," Conrad said, reaching down for the lever that reclined the passenger seat.

Pulling the lever, he felt pressure lift from his chest as the seat descended until he was staring at the car roof. He closed his eyes and tried to clear his mind. He couldn't get the images of his daughter being tortured out of his mind. He thought he understood how people could drive themselves insane.

"Feeling better?" Lombardi asked.

"I'm getting there," Conrad said.

Conrad had forgotten that he was still holding his cell phone in his hand until it rang.

As he lifted it toward his ear, Lombardi said, "Jim, hand the phone to me. I'll do the talking."

Conrad felt his concentration faltering, so he handed the phone to her. Closing his eyes again, he listened to the one-sided conversation.

"Hi, it's Detective Lombardi with the Westfield Police."

A pause.

"I wish we could be speaking under better circumstances, Sergeant Layton, but we have a serious problem that can't wait."

Another pause.

"We've tracked a serial killer to a snowmobile cabin in your town. We believe he has a thirteen-year-old victim from our town with him."

A longer pause.

"The cabin belongs to the Blackburn family. The killer is the twenty-eight-year-old son, Eric."

Lombardi glanced over at Conrad as an even longer pause ensued. Opening his eyes, Conrad saw her forehead crease into a worried expression.

"Yes, we're positive it's him," she said, turning back toward the oncoming highway.

Conrad felt a slight decline in speed as Lombardi let up on the gas pedal to concentrate on the conversation. The speedometer dropped to 90 mph.

"The evidence is compelling – we discovered that Eric Blackburn was the killer after creating a geographical profile."

A pause.

"Yes, a geographical profile. We created it by mapping out the locations of the killer's crimes."

A longer pause.

"No, it's a proven method the F.B.I uses."

She glanced at Conrad again as there was another pause.

She's not convincing him, Conrad thought. He reached down for the lever and brought his seat up. He was feeling less dizzy now, so he gestured for Lombardi to hand him the phone.

"I'm going to hand you off to Sergeant Conrad," Lombardi said.

Reaching out, she appeared relieved to hand the phone to Conrad. He hesitated for a moment as he brought the phone to his ear.

Do I put my career in jeopardy by inventing a plausible lie that will convince him for sure? Or do I tell the truth and risk him not believing I have enough evidence?

"Sergeant, Layton, I'm Jim Conrad, a sergeant with the Westfield Police. We have more than just a geographical profile to go on. Blackburn's vehicle matches the car described by witnesses at multiple crime scenes. Blackburn is a security guard at the Farmington Mall where two murders occurred recently on a night when he called in sick to work. The mall job explains the killer's preference for stalking his victims at area malls." He paused to take a breath and continued. "Blackburn's physical appearance matches the video image of the perpetrator recorded on a Westfield Pond mall video camera – taken during the night of a murder and kidnapping at the mall last week. Blackburn's last victim escaped and described a cabin identical to the one owned by the Blackburn family. I've been in police work for eleven years and I can honestly say this kid is as guilty as sin."

Layton replied in a gruff voice. "Sergeant Conrad, I'm not doubting your word, but I'm going to need corroboration before I start kicking in doors. I'll need to speak to your chief before I can check out the Blackburn's cabin."

"Sergeant, we don't have time to waste. We know Blackburn is at the cabin. To make matters worse, he just grabbed a thirteen-year-old girl from Westfield and he has her with him. You may be able to stop him before he kills her."

"I understand what you're telling me, but I can't start violating the town residents' civil rights without at least minimal confirmation," Layton said. "For all I know, you're a prank caller with a grudge who's trying to get the young man in trouble with an outlandish story."

"Sergeant, we don't have time for this back and forth," Conrad said, becoming impatient. "You need to go to the Blackburns' cabin and stop him before he kills her."

"Sergeant Conrad, you know the protocol. I can't just take your word for it. I don't know who the hell you are. I'll call your chief at the Westfield Police station, obtain his confirmation, and get back to you."

Conrad glanced at Lombardi as he wracked his brain about how to get around this obstacle. The chief was in the dark as much as Layton was. A call to the chief would hurt rather than help his argument. He noticed that Lombardi had brought the vehicle's speed back up to 110 mph.

"He wants to call the chief for confirmation," Conrad said to Lombardi.

"The Chief?" the detective asked, her green eyes widening. "He doesn't know anything because we didn't tell him anything!"

Conrad gritted his teeth in frustration as he tried to think of a way out of the predicament.

"Sergeant Conrad? Are you still there?" Layton asked.

After cursing under his breath, Conrad replied, "I'm still here, sergeant, but we have a problem. The detective and I haven't had time to update our chief about the evidence we recently uncovered."

CHAPTER 70

Conrad's body tensed as he waited for Sergeant Layton's reaction. Layton was quiet for an awkward amount of time before he finally spoke.

"Sergeant Conrad, I can't do anything until you notify your chief."

Conrad grimaced. "Okay, that's fine. I'll call my chief and get back to you."

"I'll be waiting for your call-back," Layton said.

Conrad hung up and unleashed a string of profanity. When he got himself under control, he turned toward Lombardi.

"Marilyn, we have to notify the chief if we want any cooperation from Layton."

"I was afraid of that," Lombardi said. "But I have a better idea. I'll notify my father, the lieutenant, and he'll notify the chief. If I can convince my father, he'll do our job for us and convince the chief."

"Okay, it's worth a try," Conrad replied. "Do you need to borrow my cell?"

"No, I have my own," Lombardi said, reaching into her pocket. She took out her phone and dialed with her right hand while she steered with her left. The phone rang four times before it was picked up.

"Hello?" her father's voice came on the line – sounding tired.

"Dad? I hope I didn't wake you," she said, glancing down at the dashboard clock. It was only 9:25 PM, but her father sometimes went to bed early.

"I was just getting into bed. What's up?" the lieutenant asked.

"Dad, Jim and I have uncovered new evidence. We know who and where the serial murderer-kidnapper is."

"You're kidding me. What's your evidence?"

Lombardi glanced at Conrad and took a deep breath.

"Okay, Dad, here it is. The perpetrator is Eric Blackburn, a twenty-eight-year-old resident of Westfield." She hesitated for a moment as she recalled the information that Conrad relayed to Layton. Then, she imperfectly repeated Conrad's explanation to Layton and awaited a response

"That still sounds pretty thin," the lieutenant said. "I don't think it's enough to obtain a warrant even if it occurred in our jurisdiction. You also said you knew where the perp was."

"He's at his parents snowmobile cabin in New Hampshire."

"How do you know?"

Lombardi hesitated as she thought for a moment. "He wasn't at his apartment, so that's the only other place he could have taken the victim."

"What evidence do you have that he's the one responsible for kidnapping the victim?" Lieutenant Lombardi asked.

This wasn't going well. She couldn't even get him to accept their basic assertion that the psychopath had brought the teenage girl to the Blackburn family's mountain cabin.

"Give me the phone," Conrad said, extending his hand.

She handed it to him.

"LT, it's Jim," Conrad said.

"Jimmy, please tell me you have more evidence than what my daughter told me."

"LT, it's him. Blackburn is the killer. I'd stake my life on it. All we need from you is to ask the chief to call the Dolebrook PD and ask them to do a well-being check on the Blackburn cabin. I agree that we don't have enough for a warrant, but there's enough for a simple well-being check."

"Are you willing to stake your career on it?" the lieutenant asked.

"Absolutely," Conrad replied without hesitation. "If I'm wrong, I'll turn in my badge."

"Okay, good enough. I'll call the chief and ask him to call the Dolebrook PD. Do you have the number?"

Conrad had to contain his excitement as he recited the number slow enough so the lieutenant would have time to write it down.

"Okay, I'll make the call."

"Thanks, LT. You won't regret it. We're right about this."

Conrad heard a dial tone as the lieutenant hung up the phone.

"He's making the call to the chief."

"Thank God," Lombardi said, keeping her foot pressed down on the gas pedal. "We have to do something. I wouldn't be able to live with myself if we show up at the cabin three hours from now and all we find is the teenager's corpse."

"That's not going to happen," Conrad said, wiping sweat from his brow. "The perp is too smart to leave the body behind. If this doesn't work, he'll make a clean getaway with the victim. We just have to hope the knock-on-the-door by the cops spooks him enough so he does or says something suspicious that will warrant a check of the interior of the cabin. If not, there's a high probability that he will make a run for it and kill the victim at another location."

CHAPTER 71

The sound of tires scraping on gravel wakes me from an enjoyable dream. In my mind, I was slicing off the slut's hand at the wrist when the annoying sound interrupted my fun. Opening my eyes, I notice the glare of headlights reflecting off the ceiling above me. A car in the driveway? But no one knows I'm here!

My body starts to tremble; I feel paralyzed. Sweat breaks out on my forehead as I imagine two cops getting out of a police car parked in front of the cabin. I can picture them moving up the walkway to the door of the mud-room. As if on cue, I hear someone's fist knocking on the door at ground level. Clutching my chest, I feel like my heart is going seize up like a car engine with no oil.

Damn it, I'm too young to have a heart attack! I need to get myself under control. Maybe I can sneak out through a back window on the ground floor?

Then, I remember my victim lying at the foot of the bed, and shove the covers off me. Scrambling toward the base of the mattress, I slide off the bed and land on the floor beside her.

As my eyes adjust to the darkness, I see her wide eyes glaring back at me. Her mouth is open as if she is about to scream, so I press my palm firmly against her lips. Apparently, it was just in time because I feel a vibration on my hand and hear a muffled noise.

I hold my hand in place until the vibration stops and whisper a threat to her, "Make another noise and I'll slit your throat."

She shuts up long enough so I have a chance to remove my hand and devise an improvised gag from a sock to shove in her mouth. Once again, my quick thinking and actions have allowed me to avoid discovery. I can do this. I will just get rid of whoever is at the door and continue with my plan.

Feeling more confident, I leave the bedroom and descend the stairs to the living room. The muffled knocking sound on the mud-room door becomes more insistent, but I don't let it get to me. I just want to get this next part over with.

If it's the cops, there's no way they can know anything. Maybe they're just checking on me because they saw a car parked in front of the cabin off-season. Then again, maybe it's just someone who got lost and looking for directions. Either way, I'll get rid of them.

Cutting across the kitchen and mud-room, I reach the front door. The knocking pauses as whoever is standing outside contemplates whether to leave or continue annoying me. I'm still feeling good about my timely stifling of the bitch's scream, so a smile is not difficult to manufacture.

I turn the knob and open the door to find two cops standing outside in the dark.

"Eric Blackburn?" One of the cops, a balding, middle-aged man with a slight potbelly, asks.

"Yep, that's me," I say, flashing them what I hope is a convincing smile.

"Eric, we saw your car parked out here, so we're just doing

a well-being check on you to make sure everything is okay," the middle-aged cop says.

I notice sergeant's stripes on the sleeves of his dark-blue uniform. The cop standing behind him is a muscular kid in his twenties with a Marine buzz-cut. He looks uncomfortable as he shifts back and forth from foot-to-foot.

"Sure, everything is fine, sergeant," I say without any trace of annoyance. "I had some time off, so I came up to the cabin for a few days to get away from the rat-race. The colors on the trees are very beautiful at this time of year. I figured I could catch up on my reading."

"Do you have anyone else here with you?" the sergeant asks.

What? Why would he ask that? I try to rack my brain for an answer.

"No, sir, I came up here alone."

The cop peers over my shoulder into the interior of the mudroom as if expecting to find someone standing behind me.

"Are you sure, son?" the cop asks.

"Of course I'm sure," I say, laughing. "I think I would know if I wasn't alone."

The cop continues to peer over my shoulder into the interior. I get the feeling that he is listening for any sounds from within.

"Do you mind if we come in and look around?" the cop asks.

"Actually, sir, it's very late and I have an early start tomorrow. I would just like to go to sleep and get some rest. Is there some kind of problem?"

Now I'm becoming suspicious. Why are they so intent on searching the cabin? Is it possible that I drove past them earlier while they were parked on the side of the road in their cruiser, and passed them on my way here? Did they see the silhouette of my teenage captive in the passenger seat? Or is it something else? Are the cops from Westfield on my trail? I can't comprehend how those idiots could have figured anything out yet.

"We'll just take a quick look around and be on our way," the sergeant says.

The blond cop appears to be getting increasingly anxious as he speeds up his foot-to-foot shifting. Like the older cop, the younger one also peers over my shoulder at intervals as if he expects to see someone inside. As he fidgets, he reminds me of a greyhound chomping at the bit to get started in a race.

"Sergeant, I know my rights pretty well," I say. "If you want to search my house, then you will have to get a search warrant. Did you receive a report of any wrongdoing? I thought you said this was just a well-being check?"

The sergeant's eyebrows knit together as he appears to think. Then, he smiles at me and says, "No, there haven't been any reports. I thought I heard a noise upstairs when we arrived and we just like to be thorough."

"Sir, that was just me moving around. I appreciate your concern, sir, but my father has assured me that no one would bother me if I came up here for a couple days to relax."

"No problem, Eric," the cop says, holding his smile in place as if it was molded in plastic. "You can go back to doing whatever you're doing. Have a good night."

"You too, sergeant," I say as I watch the cops turn their backs to me and head toward their parked cruiser.

Waiting at the door, I watch them get into the cruiser. I don't want to appear too anxious by slamming the door and disappearing within. After all, I don't have anything to hide, right? The young blond cop glances over at me from the passenger seat, so I smile and wave at him. He doesn't wave back, but only stares at me, expressionless.

I hear the sergeant fire up the engine and watch him do a careful three-point-turn in the wide driveway before pulling away. Tires crunch on gravel as taillights disappear into darkness.

Grinning, I shut the door. That was easy. They probably saw me drive by earlier, and thought they saw someone sitting in my passenger seat. Now that I've convinced them they're wrong, they've gone on their way. I continue into the house, cross the living room, and ascend the stairs.

The unexpected arrival of the local cops has caused a burst of adrenaline to flood my system. There's no way I can go back to sleep now. I don't need to wait until tomorrow morning to go to work on this little bitch because I'm ready now.

Grinning like the Joker from the Batman comics, I enter the bedroom and gaze down at my helpless prey. She looks pathetic lying on the floor at the foot of the bed with a sock-gag in her mouth. She will look even more pathetic when I'm done with her.

CHAPTER 72

Conrad kept his mind occupied by watching the almost imperceptible climb of the cruiser speedometer from 105 mph to 110 mph as the minutes went by. He didn't know if it was a conscious or subconscious decision on Lombardi's part.

Whenever they encountered a rare vehicle on the highway in the right lane, they closed in on its taillights, and seconds later he was watching the headlights recede in the passenger side mirror. A split-second rush of wind was the only evidence that another vehicle had shared the highway. He felt like he was skimming over the earth in a low-flying rocket.

It was almost 10 PM. About forty minutes had gone by since his partner, Lombardi, had called her father, the lieutenant. Had her father even called the chief and had the chief even called Sergeant Layton in West Brookfield? How long did it take to relay a message to do a well-being check at a cabin?

Conrad watched the speedometer's barely-perceptible, but inevitable climb from 110 mph to 111 mph as he tapped the palms of his hands on his knees. He stopped when Lombardi glanced over at him with her eyebrows knitted together. Then, he began tapping his right foot. He stopped when he received another glance from his partner.

While Lombardi's tension apparently manifested itself in

a steady increase in the velocity of the cruiser, Conrad's manifested itself by producing annoying physical ticks. He needed to find something to do that wouldn't distract his partner because she needed to concentrate on driving at 111 mph. He began counting the streetlights they passed on the median strip between the northbound and southbound sections of the highway.

Conrad was shocked out of his trance when the cell phone rang in his right hand. It took him a moment to pull his eyes away from the unending line of streetlights so he could focus on the phone, which he had almost forgotten about. He clicked the green button and held it to his ear.

"Conrad," he said.

"Sergeant Conrad, it's Sergeant Layton with the West Brookfield PD."

"Hello, sergeant," Conrad replied.

"We made a check of the cabin and Mr. Blackburn met us at the front door. After explaining that we were just there to check on his well-being, I asked if he wouldn't mind if we took a walkthrough of the house. Predictably, he said no. However, at that moment I saw a change in his facial expression. For a few seconds, his confidence faded and I saw panic in his features. He recovered quickly and started going off about his rights, but it was already too late. I knew he was hiding something. However, despite my personal suspicions, we still don't have enough Probable Cause to kick in his door."

Conrad felt an unexpected tidal wave of rage blast through his mind like a rogue tsunami.

"If you can't do anything, why the fuck are you bothering to call me back?" Conrad exclaimed, raising his voice.

Conrad felt a sudden deceleration in the cruiser as Detective

Lombardi's foot came off the gas pedal; she glared at him with wide eyes and raised eyebrows. Ignoring her, he waited for a response from Layton. There was only silence at the other end of the line.

After several seconds elapsed, Layton's voice returned. "Look, sergeant, I understand you are frustrated and I realize your motives are good, but you know the law. Our actions are limited by legal guidelines that are contingent on the information we possess. That being said, we're not going to just drive away. I'm going to position myself a short way down the road from the cabin so if Blackburn looks out a window, he won't see me, but we can still see the cabin through the trees. If we notice anything suspicious, we're moving in. If he tries to make a move in his car, we'll follow him. The bottom line is that he's on our radar. He's not getting away."

Conrad felt his rage dissipating like a massive wave breaking on a sandy shore. Layton's continued surveillance was certainly better than just walking away.

"Okay, sergeant, I'm sorry I snapped at you. The situation is rather tense, to say the least," Conrad said.

"No worries, sergeant," Layton replied. "We'll keep an eye on the cabin to make sure Blackburn doesn't make any sudden moves."

"I appreciate that," Conrad said. "However, if you see a light go on somewhere in the house, you should check it out – especially if it's on the ground floor. At this time of night, there's no reason for Blackburn to making the rounds. I would argue that if you start seeing lights going on in different areas of the cabin, it constitutes suspicious behavior worth investigating."

"Okay, fair enough," Layton replied. "We'll keep our eyes open. I just hope to God you're wrong about this."

"I'm not wrong about this," Conrad said. "Maybe you can't break down the door, but there's still enough reasonable suspicion to search the yard around the cabin and look in a window if the lights come on."

"Okay, we'll do that," Layton said.

"Thank you, sergeant," Conrad said. "I appreciate anything you can do. I'm not wrong. She's there and he's going to kill her if we don't stop him."

CHAPTER 73

This time, I'm not taking any chances. I get my knife from the drawer in the bedside table before I even think about un-cuffing the teenager's wrist from the bed leg.

Holding the blade to her throat, I whisper in her ear, "Make a sudden move and you die. Do you understand?"

She gives me the merest nod in response, so she doesn't slit her own throat. Keeping the knife blade millimeters from her skin, I take the handcuff key and slip it into the slot on the cuff fastened to the bed leg. I turn the key, hear a click, and open the metal pincers. Carefully, I slip the tiny key into my pocket and grab the open cuff. Seizing the cuff in a firm grip, I move the knife several inches away from her throat so I can control her better.

"Lean forward," I command.

She does as I tell her. I drag her restrained wrist painfully around her back, and cuff it to her naked wrist. With both hands secured, she's not a threat. Tossing the knife on the bed, I stand up and reach down for her. She lets out a yelp of pain as I seize the handcuff chain and drag her roughly to her feet.

"Move," I say, shoving her toward the hallway.

I grab her by the back of the neck like a cat grabs its errant kittens with its teeth, and guide her through the hallway and down the stairs. When I want her to turn, I apply pressure to the side of her neck in the direction I want her to go. The system works well as I guide her through the living room, kitchen, and hallway until I reach the basement door.

I feel a thrill of excitement as I push the door open to reveal the wooden stairwell leading into the depths of my secret art studio. Flicking on the light switch, I guide her down the stairs. I am very careful with her because I don't want her to trip, fall, and break her neck on the narrow stairs. That would be too quick.

She lets out a gasp as her bare foot touches the cold concrete at the base of the stairwell. I don't know if her gasp is from feeling the cold or the sight of the clear plastic tarp spread across the center of the floor. If she has any intelligence whatsoever, that certainly won't bode well in her mind.

The tarp is positioned on an almost imperceptible slant, so blood and other bodily fluids will flow down into the drain at the center of the floor. Ropes are fastened onto objects at the four corners of the tarp. We're almost ready to start.

I hesitate as I realize I don't have any white roses; my routine is to soak five white roses in the victims' blood and bury each dripping red rose with a body part.

Fuck it, I'll just have to wait until morning to buy roses at the flower joint in town, and place them with the body parts post-mortem. There should still be enough blood pooling on the tarp to make the roses turn red.

I instruct her to lie face-down in the center of the tarp, and she complies.

"Stay there and don't move," I tell her as I cross the floor and ascend the stairs.

I return to the upstairs bedroom to obtain my combat knife and re-descend to the ground floor. My eyes focus on the gun cabinet next to the stairs. A knife is good, but a hunting rifle with a scope is better. If the improbable chance occurs that she somehow gets away and makes a run for it, I can train the scope on her and hit her from a distance of a hundred yards or more. My Dad took me hunting in these woods many times and I'm an excellent shot. Why not be extra sure?

I find the key to the gun cabinet in a kitchen drawer and bring it over. Staring at the glass panel on the cabinet, I have a flashback to the time when that bitch Tracey Randall smashed the glass and grabbed a rifle. She thought she was going to blow me away, and she was sorely disappointed when she found out it wasn't loaded. Stupid bitch. No one keeps loaded weapons lying around. The ammunition is stored on a shelf above the work bench in the basement.

Opening the cabinet, I take out the best hunting rifle we have. I can hit a deer between the eyes at two hundred yards with this one. I practice aiming and looking down the sight. I focus on a picture of my smiling father and mother on the table next to the couch. Bang. I only wish I could get away with it. Then, I would inherit all their wealth and I could really go to work. With their vast resources at my disposal, I would be unstoppable.

I bring the rifle and knife to the basement. Placing the knife on the work bench, I reach up to the shelf to grab a box of the proper ammunition. I take the bullets out of the box and load up the rifle. Then, I throw several spares in my right pocket. I don't know why I'm even bothering. She can't get away.

However, the cops, who dropped by earlier, convinced me to take extra precautions. What if they come back and catch me engaging in my socially questionable activities? At least with the rifle, I'll be able to defend myself.

Placing the rifle against the wall next to the work bench, I glance up at the single, ground-level basement window above me. The window consists of a dirty square pane of glass covering a space that is barely large enough for a person to squeeze through if opened. I think about covering it up, but someone on the outside would have to drop down to the ground level to look into the basement. The cops don't have any probable cause to come onto my property. If they did, my father would sue their asses.

Time to go to work. I have art to make.

The chainsaw resting on the work bench is covered with a dirty gray towel so she doesn't see it and freak out. That will come later. I have to begin slowly. First, I will use the knife. Wielding it like a painter's brush, I will create a work of art that will surpass all the others.

CHAPTER 74

Sergeant Layton saw a window in the cabin light up through a crack in the barrier of leaves, as his partner, Officer Sean Thorpe, fidgeted in the seat beside him. They had parked the cruiser at an ideal location for surveillance; the car was hidden from view from the cabin, but the cabin was clearly visible through strategically positioned gaps in the trees lining the dirt road.

"Another light just went on," Thorpe said, tapping his foot faster on the floor mat.

"I can see that," Layton said, glancing irritably at his partner.

"Shouldn't we check it out?" Thorpe asked.

Layton sighed. "Despite what Sergeant Conrad says, a light coming on in a cabin doesn't give us Probable Cause to search the property."

"I'll go by myself," Thorpe said. "That way, I'll take the heat if something goes wrong."

Layton glared at his subordinate. "We both go, or neither goes."

"Okay, we both go then."

Layton sighed again. "This could end up blowing up in our faces. Blackburn's father is rich and he has a lot of influence in town."

"Sarge, that guy, Blackburn, gives me the creeps. It seemed like he was hiding something when we talked to him."

Layton blew out a stream of air as if he was blowing out smoke from a cigarette. Actually, he had quit several years ago and he was craving one now.

"I'm not sure," the sergeant said, rubbing his forehead.

"Sarge, what if Blackburn DOES have that girl and he's torturing or killing her right now?" Thorpe asked.

Layton noticed that in addition to general fidgeting, both of Thorpe's feet were now tapping on the floor-mat like unsynchronized drum sticks.

"Okay, we'll take a quick walk-through of the property," Layton said, hoping he wouldn't regret the decision.

Thorpe yanked on the passenger door handle and left the cruiser before Layton could blink. Layton followed his lead without hurrying.

I hope this doesn't end my career, he thought.

Thorpe placed his right hand on the butt of his holstered pistol as he took the lead. Layton followed the younger officer a short way down the dirt road and then up a grassy hill toward the right side of the cabin where a single downstairs window glowed with light.

"Don't get too close," Layton said. "Stay on the perimeter."

"Sure, Sarge," Thorpe whispered as he stayed near the tree-line as he advanced.

The lighted window was about two hundred feet away, but no discernible forms were visible behind the glass. Thorpe scanned the three remaining darkened windows as they cut across the side yard toward the back. He didn't see any movement.

Thorpe remained near the wood-line as they circled the house. He could see the back of the house now; one lower and one upper window glowed with light. The remaining two windows on the lower level and one on the upper level were dark. A single basement window was also dark.

Thorpe halted as he saw the basement window suddenly glow orange.

"Sarge, the basement light just went on."

"Despite my advanced age, my eyes still work," Layton said, as he continued past Thorpe along the perimeter of the yard. He estimated that the rear of the cabin was about three hundred feet away, so they were far enough to blend into the dark forest backdrop if anyone looked out a window.

"Shouldn't we check it out?" Thorpe asked. "What's he doing in the cellar at this time of night?"

"I couldn't tell you," Layton said. "Maybe they have a Jacuzzi in the basement."

"A Jacuzzi?" Thorpe asked, puzzled, as he moved toward the cabin with his hand on the butt of his holstered weapon.

"I didn't say you could move in," Layton said, as he halted near the woods a short distance from Thorpe.

"I didn't ask," Thorpe said, as he continued across the back yard toward the glowing rectangle in the foundation of the cabin.

"Fuck," Layton said, sighing as he veered off his pre-determined course around the perimeter to intercept Thorpe.

Layton caught up with the younger officer and they walked side-by-side toward the basement window. They remained silent as they approached. Thorpe strained his eyes, but he couldn't see into the interior of the cellar from this particular angle. Even when they stood above it, all he could see was a small section of gray concrete floor below.

"I can't see shit from here," Thorpe whispered. "I'm getting closer."

"Hey, wait a minute - " Layton began to speak, but then cut himself off as he watched Thorpe drop to his hands and knees.

"You're going to get grass stains on your uniform," Layton said.

Ignoring his boss, Thorpe moved across the grass on his hands and knees like a four-legged animal. Layton remained standing as he followed him to the window.

"Can you see anything?" Layton whispered.

"I see Blackburn, but I can't tell what he's doing," Thorpe said, as he spotted the young man's upper body framed by the window. Blackburn stood with his hands on his hips looking down at something on the floor.

"What's he looking at on the floor?" Thorpe whispered as he moved to within inches of the dirty glass pane. He still couldn't see the section of the floor Blackburn was staring at. From this angle, he couldn't see anything below Blackburn's knees. Thorpe crawled to the left to try to get a clearer view.

CHAPTER 75

I gaze down to survey my handiwork. The bitch lies spread-eagled on top of the clear plastic tarp covering the center of the concrete floor; her body forms an "X" shape. She is tied so her arms and legs are stretched to their utmost as if she has been laid out on a Medieval torture rack.

Her eyes are wide with fear; she stares up at me like a human sacrifice in awe of a pagan god. She still hasn't seen the chainsaw; for now it lies on the work bench – covered by an opaque tarp. I don't want to start the terror too soon; I want to prolong her agony.

I'm not sure if I should start working on her with the knife or if I should have sex with her right away in her current pristine condition. Wearing the red lingerie, her smooth, pale, young body looks enticing. Her firm, plum-sized breasts move up and down as she sucks in desperate breaths; she appears to be close to hyperventilating.

My eyes dart over to the combat knife resting on the work bench next to the green tarp covering the chainsaw. I decide that I will wait to go to work on her after I've sampled the merchandise. I begin to unbutton my shirt.

Suddenly, I halt my actions as the short hairs prickle up on the back of my neck; I have an overpowering feeling that

I'm being watched. My eyes dart up to the basement's single, ground-level window. A chill crawls up my spine like icy spider legs as I see two eyes staring back at me from the other side of the dirty glass pane.

I dart my eyes away as if I didn't notice the intruder. I couldn't tell who it was; I don't' know if it's a nosy teenage neighbor or one of the cops who came by earlier. Either way, they will have to be dealt with. I just need to remain calm; they haven't made a move yet. The interloper may not have seen the girl on the floor yet due to the severe angle from the window.

Pretending I didn't notice the eyes staring back at me from the other side of the dirty glass, I look away from the window, step over the girl's body, and walk without hurrying toward the back wall beneath the window.

Now, I'm out of sight of the person crouching at the window. I reach down for the hunting rifle. Picking it up, I adjust my grip. Holding it upright in front of me, I turn my body away from the window; the intruder will not be able to see the weapon from this angle.

I proceed forward, stepping over the girl's body again. I am now in position. I place my right index finger on the trigger as I continue to hold the rifle barrel upright. I feel adrenaline pumping through my veins like liquefied plutonium.

Spinning around, I aim the rifle at the window and fire. The explosion is deafening in the confines of the basement; my ears ring like a clanging bell. I realize that it's a cop at the window as he awkwardly brandishes a pistol with the tip of the barrel pointed toward the glass.

However, he won't be shooting anyone anytime soon as a bloody red hole appears in the center of his forehead. The pistol slides from his twitching hand as his shattered face drops into the dirt. Despite my victory, I don't have time to waste because there could be more; I remember two cops came to the door earlier.

Turning, I head for the stairwell. Bolting across the cellar floor, I ascend the stairs two-at-a-time. As I move, I hold the rifle in a combat grip with my finger hovering over the trigger. If there's another cop out there, I have to be ready.

Reaching the top of the stairs, I aim my rifle ahead and sweep it across the kitchen area. Empty. Keeping the rifle barrel pointed ahead, I move in a combat stance toward the mud-room door. I switch to a one-handed grip so I can open the door with my free hand. Flinging the door open, I descend the stairs into the mud-room.

I stare down the rifle sights as I move toward the exterior door. Arriving at the door, I keep my finger brushing the trigger as I lower the rifle and turn the knob. I open the door with my free hand while I hold the rifle aloft. I revert to a two-handed hunting grip as I lunge through the doorway.

Sweeping the rifle across the driveway from right to left, I spot the blue uniformed back of a police officer as he runs toward a cruiser parked behind a cluster of trees. The coward never even drew his weapon. I don't need to use the scope at this distance; I aim down the sight and fire.

The cop halts in mid-stride as he convulses as if hit with an electric shock. Stiffening, his body goes down. I hit him square in the back between the shoulder-blades.

I scan the area for more opponents and I don't see any. It makes sense because there were only two cops here before. Lowering the rifle, I observe the crumpled body of the cop. I notice yellow sergeant stripes on the right sleeve of his uniform. Moving closer, I prod the body with the barrel of the rifle. It doesn't move. I feel myself coming down from an adrenaline high.

I pause to contemplate my options. Do I run or finish the job? I think of the half-naked girl lying spread-eagled on the cellar floor, and I realize I need to finish the job. I don't have time to play, so I'll just slit her throat and be gone. I head back to the cabin.

Returning to the basement, I gaze down at my teenage victim. Her eyes are closed as if she's sleeping. Prodding her shoulder with the rifle barrel, she still doesn't move. She must have hyperventilated and passed out. It would be a waste of time to kill her while she's unconscious; I have to wake her up so she feels it.

Stepping over her body, I return the rifle to its former place against the wall beneath the shattered window. I head over to the work bench, pick up the combat knife, and return to hover over her half-nude form. I bend down as I lower the knife tip toward her smooth belly. She'll wake up screaming when I rip out her intestines. Her eyes will fly open as her mouth emits an ear-piercing shriek; I'll savor her pain for a few moments before I slit her throat. Lowering the razor-sharp blade, I prepare to plunge it into her abdomen.

Suddenly, I halt when I hear a muffled sound in the distance. Pausing, I realize it's the wail of police sirens. I can't tell how far away they are because the mountain range sometimes amplifies echoes. The sergeant must have had time to radio dispatch before I shot him.

If I kill her and they catch me, it will be another murder charge. I can argue self-defense with the cops because one of them had his gun drawn. Right now, all they can get me for with the girl is kidnapping; I'll be out in ten years. They're not smart enough to tie me to all the other murders.

Cursing, I raise the gleaming knife blade from the unconscious teenager's pale, smooth belly. Listening, I hear the wailing sirens, but I can't tell if they're getting louder or not. I need to move now.

Changing my grip on the knife so I don't stab myself, I dart across the cellar floor and ascend the stairs. I left the door to the mud-room open, so I bolt across the kitchen and fly out the doorway. Sprinting, I make it outside.

I shiver in the cold. I was so wired before that I didn't even notice it. Now I have goose-bumps popping out on my skin. The sirens sound very far away, but it's hard to tell in the mountains.

Gazing down the sloping dirt driveway, I spot the gleam of metal from the hood of the police car poking out from behind the trees. The police car is much faster than my vehicle, but it's also more conspicuous. Hesitating, I contemplate whether to search the sergeant's body for the cruiser key or walk a few steps to the driver's side door of my Honda.

They will spot me easily in the cruiser, but with the Honda I could slip away unnoticed. Reaching into my pocket for the keys, I go for the Honda. Throwing the combat knife on the passenger seat, I slide into the driver's side. I insert the key in the ignition and fire up the engine. The rear tires spit out dirt and gravel as I press down on the accelerator.

CHAPTER 76

The roar of my car engine drowns out the wailing sirens as I shoot down a steep incline in the long, winding, dirt driveway. Despite my anxiety about the oncoming pursuit, I feel a visceral thrill as the incline bottoms out and I begin a sharp ascent as if I'm on a roller-coaster track.

Ascending rapidly, I feel my body lift in the driver's seat as I race over the crest of a hill to begin another steep descent. I'm driving much faster than is prudent on the unfinished road, but I know every twist and turn after taking many practice runs over the years, so I maintain control around all the sharp corners and sudden dips.

As I near the intersection, I think it's a good sign that I don't see any flashing blue lights yet. If I take a right, I'll pass my neighbor's house on the left until I reach the paved road leading to the highway. If I turn left, I'll reach the clearing where we dispose of excess leaves, grass, and tree branches. It's an obvious choice; I turn left.

It's only a short distance to the clearing – about two hundred feet. Swinging around in it, I park on the right side behind a line of trees. Checking my rearview mirror, I see a decaying mound of moldering leaves and grass piled high behind me. A patchwork array of tree leaves camouflage me from the front. In this position, I'm hidden from anyone driving through the intersection, but I can still see whoever turns into the driveway through openings in the leaves.

Waiting anxiously, I hear the sirens grow louder. Lowering my window a crack, the sirens blast my ears as if they're right on top of me. The mountain range amplifies the noise; it sounds like an air raid siren echoing among skyscrapers.

Now I can see the faint glow of flashing blue lights at the far end of the dirt road. Sweat breaks out on my forehead. If the cops overshoot the driveway and end up in the clearing, then I'm done for.

However, that scenario isn't likely because there's a large mailbox at the end of the driveway, which is clearly marked with reflective letters spelling BLACKBURN. I doubt the responding cops have the confidence to drive fast enough on the winding dirt road to miss seeing the silver reflection.

My prediction pans out; through the gaps, I watch a pair of state police cruisers slow at the intersection and make a sharp left turn into the cabin's driveway. I'm not surprised to see the state police markings on the sides of the vehicles because I killed off all the local law enforcers on duty.

Now, for the next gamble. Are more cruisers coming, or are the ones pulling into the driveway the only ones in the area? In this isolated region, I know that a single cruiser covers a massive amount of territory, so I doubt that any more cruisers will reach this area anytime soon.

Listening carefully, I hear the sirens moving away from me up the driveway. After several seconds, they go silent. The state cops have arrived in front of the cabin. Listening, I only hear the sound of wind through the trees. I shift the Honda into drive and press down lightly on the accelerator so I don't peel out.

Steering out of the cul de sac, I coast past the entrance to the driveway and continue past my neighbor's house toward the main road. When I reach the main road, I have to decide whether to turn right toward the highway or left toward the back roads that wind their way through the narrow valleys intersecting the vast mountain range. If I turn left and take the indirect route, it will take me an extra two hours to reach Massachusetts.

Checking the gas gauge, I notice that it's three-quarters full. This is the very reason why I purchased a fuel-efficient, Japanese-made car; I can easily drive for six hours on three-quarters of a tank.

There really is no choice; I take a left to follow the poorly-lit back roads that twist and turn their way deeper and deeper into the narrow valleys intersecting the mountain range; gradually, the route will become a paved version of the dirt roller-coaster leading to my parents' cabin. I've made many practice runs on this route for just such a contingency as this one.

Confidently, I negotiate the familiar curves, dips, and ascents in the road. As I travel deeper into the bowels of the mountain range, steep rock cliffs loom above me on all sides. Occasionally, a massive lumber truck rumbles past me, but at this time of night, that's the only traffic I encounter. It's now past midnight.

More and more, I realize that I made the right decision. The state police barracks are located close to the highway in the opposite direction. There are several penny-ante towns clustered within the mountain range, but most don't have police forces containing more than a few officers. The state police wouldn't bother to call them for back-up, so I should be home-free for the rest of the way.

Now that I'm free and clear, I need to formulate a plan. When they find the half-naked girl bound with ropes in the basement of the cabin, the jig is up; the police will know who I am and what I do. My freedom to wreak havoc on teenage girls in this region will be at an end.

I'm not stupid; the state-wide manhunt underway will turn the mathematical probabilities of escape against me. I could conceivably be captured. Being captured isn't part of my plans, so I want to go out with a flourish. As my last artistic act, I will visit the home of the girl that got away, Tracey Randall; I will make her my final masterpiece.

CHAPTER 77

It was after midnight and Lombardi's steady acceleration had finally maxed out at 115 mph. The cars in the slow lanes looked like metallic blurs as the police cruiser blew past them.

Occasionally, Lombardi and Conrad encountered a clueless driver crawling at a mere 75 mph ahead of them in the fast lane. At these times, Lombardi decelerated rapidly as she swerved into the middle lane to pass on the right. She didn't want to draw attention by using the flashing lights outside her jurisdiction.

They repeated a similar pattern whenever they encountered a vehicle blocking them. Conrad spotted the vehicle's twin red taillights and said, "Car." Lombardi replied, "Okay." Then, she let up on the gas pedal, pressed down on the brake if necessary, and swerved into the middle lane if it was clear.

"How long has it been since you talked to Sergeant Layton?" Lombardi asked.

"It's been a while," Conrad replied. "Almost an hour ago."

"He should have called back by now."

A chill went up Conrad's spine as he thought of the sergeant and officer meeting with foul play at the hands of the psychopath, Blackburn.

"I hope to God they just forgot to call back and nothing has happened," Conrad said.

"Try calling," Lombardi suggested.

Without replying, Conrad pulled his phone out of his pocket and dialed Layton's cell phone number. It rang four times before the voicemail picked up.

Conrad waited for the beep and left a message. "Sergeant, it's Jim Conrad. We're getting worried. Please call me back with a status update."

"Something's wrong," Lombardi said, glancing at her partner.

"I agree," Conrad said.

"Try calling the station. They must know what's going on."

"Sure." Conrad dialed the number for the Dolebrook Police; the dispatcher picked up on the first ring.

"Dolebrook Police. This call is recorded," she said.

"This is Sergeant Conrad. I called earlier and spoke with Sergeant Layton about doing a well-being check on the Blackburn cabin. I'm getting worried because it's been a while and I haven't heard back from him yet."

Several seconds of silence ensued before she finally replied. "Sergeant Layton is dead. The state police found him and Officer Thorpe shot to death at the cabin."

Conrad was stunned into silence as a sharp pain radiated outwards in his chest. He breathed deeply several times and the pain faded away.

Finally, he asked, "Did the state police find anyone else at the cabin?"

"They found a teenage girl tied up in the basement, but she's okay."

Conrad breathed out a deep sigh. "Thank God. She must be the young lady from our town who was kidnapped. Did you get her name?"

"They didn't give me a name," the dispatcher replied. "They just said she was a thirteen-year-old female. The ambulance is en route to the cabin to transport her to the hospital."

"Can you give me the number for the state police?"

"Certainly. Hold on a moment."

Conrad heard fingers clicking on a keyboard, and she replied with the number.

"That's the cell number of the lieutenant at the scene," she said.

"Thank you for your help," Conrad replied. "I'm sorry to hear about Sergeant Layton and Officer Thorpe."

"So am I," the dispatcher said. "Call me if you need anything else."

Conrad hung up when he heard a dial tone.

"What?" Lombardi asked as she noticed the ashen pallor of Conrad's face.

"Blackburn killed the Dolebrook cops when they made the well-being check on the cabin."

"Oh my God," Lombardi said, easing up on the gas pedal. "What happened?"

"He ambushed and shot them. I'm going to call the state police to see if I can get more details."

Conrad dialed the number the dispatcher gave him, and it picked up after one ring.

"Lieutenant Reynolds," an older male voice answered.

"Lieutenant, it's Sergeant Jim Conrad with the Westfield Police."

"Hello, sergeant."

"I've been in contact with the Dolebrook Sergeant, Layton, but the dispatcher just informed me he's been shot."

"Why were you in contact with him?" Reynolds asked.

"Eric Blackburn is our chief suspect in a series of unsolved murders and kidnappings in Massachusetts. We tracked him to his parents' snowmobile cabin in Dolebrook, New Hampshire. We asked Sergeant Layton to do a well-being check about an hour ago."

"It looks like you have the right suspect. From the evidence at the scene, Blackburn shot two local police officers when they discovered he had a female captive tied up in his basement."

"The female is a teenager from our town: Westfield, Massachusetts." Conrad said. "We suspected that she was being held captive at the cabin, so we were on our way there when we called Layton."

"It sounds like you already know a lot more about this case than I do," the lieutenant said. "How far away are you?"

"We're still a few hours away."

"An ambulance is en route to pick up the victim, but we'll still be here processing the crime scene when you arrive," the lieutenant said. "When you get here, we can trade information."

"What happened to Blackburn?"

"He got away. We've activated a statewide manhunt, but we believe he's using rural back-roads to avoid the police."

"That sounds like him. He's a slippery bastard," Conrad said. "He's been getting away with these crimes for years with impunity. It wasn't until the murder and kidnapping happened in our town a week ago that we realized we had a serial killer operating in our area for the last four years."

"How many victims do your estimate?" Reynolds asked.

"I don't have an exact count, but I would guess more than ten over four years. We had a breakthrough several days ago when Blackburn's kidnap victim, Tracey Randall, escaped. She described being held in a cabin like the one at your crime scene. Based on the information she gave us and a geographical profile, we narrowed down a list of suspects. Yesterday, when a local teenager was kidnapped, we knew it was the work of our boy. Today, we narrowed down our list until only Blackburn remained. We suspected he was holding the victim at his parents' cabin."

"It sounds like you possess a wealth of information about the perpetrator," Reynolds said. "I look forward to speaking with you when you get here."

"Okay, lieutenant, I'll let you get back to your crime scene and we'll see you soon."

"We'll be here," Reynolds said, ending the call.

CHAPTER 78

I'm making excellent time; I crossed the Massachusetts border at 3 AM despite taking back-roads all the way. It helped that I encountered almost no traffic on the twisting mountain roads. It's now almost 4 AM and I will be at Tracey Randall's house in less than an hour; it will still be dark when I get there.

My successful evasion of the police has sparked a new idea: maybe I can kill the bitch and still get away. How impressive would it be if I achieve vengeance on the one that escaped, and I'm still able to elude the state-wide police gauntlet?

I'm smart enough to do it. I've proved it with my annihilation of the Dolebrook cops. It's true what they say: success breeds success. I'm on a roll and I don't want to stop.

As I leave the mountain roads and enter civilization, I make sure I drive the speed limit. It's bad enough they have a state-wide BOLO out on me; I don't want to bring more attention to myself. I try to blend in with whatever 4 AM traffic I can find. Mostly, I encounter trucks hauling loads of consumer merchandise, so I fall in behind one whenever I can.

As I approach a clearing on the side of the highway that looks like it could conceal a police cruiser, I casually change lanes and place a truck between myself and the potential cop hideout. I repeat this pattern whenever necessary. The only time I come close to panicking is when there are no trucks or cars around, and I have the highway to myself. It would be too easy for a cop parked on the side of the road to single me out.

At times like these, I curse myself for forgetting to grab my hunting rifle before I left the cabin. It would have taken mere seconds to pick up the rifle and stash it in the back seat. What will I do if I encounter any overzealous police officers? With the rifle, I had a fighting chance. My knife won't do me any good in a gunfight.

I force myself away from this line of thinking because it isn't getting me anywhere. Without the rifle, I will have to depend on stealth, and stealth is my specialty. It's the age-old rule of violent conflict: when you possess inferior weapons, you have to rely on guerilla warfare. Sneaking up on my opponents will have to get me through this.

I turn up the radio to distract myself from my nervousness. The closer I get to her house, the more amped up I become. My hands are starting to tremble on the steering wheel. It isn't fear, but barely-contained excitement. Images of my knife sliding into Tracey Randall's bare midriff fill my mind, and cause my body to quake with adrenaline. I try to light a cigarette, but my hands are shaking too badly. I concentrate on the rock music -Ozzy Osbourne's Hellraiser is playing-in an effort to distract myself from the exciting images running through my mind like a speeded-up movie.

****

As they crested the top of a steep hill, Conrad spotted reflections from multiple sets of flashing blue lights shimmering on the Fall leaves like colorful apparitions. They were nearing the end of their long journey to the Blackburn cabin.

Rounding the next curve, the trees gave way to blue lights beaming into their eyes point-blank. Conrad saw three state police cruisers and one white crime scene van in the driveway. Lombardi parked behind one of the cruisers.

Conrad's legs felt stiff as he got out of the cruiser. He stood on his tiptoes to stretch them. The trip had taken longer than he expected: over 5 hours. Sighing, Conrad followed Lombardi up the short walkway toward the front door of the cabin where a state police trooper stood guard.

The trooper stood with perfectly straight posture and his uniform was meticulously pressed; Conrad thought he looked like the poster boy for the New Hampshire state police. The trooper addressed Conrad first because he saw he was wearing a police uniform.

"Can I help you, sir?"

"I'm Sergeant Conrad and this is Detective Lombardi with the Westfield, Massachusetts police. We're here to meet Lieutenant Reynolds."

"One second, sir," the trooper said, as he reached across his chest for his shoulder mike. He depressed a button and spoke into the receiver. "Thirteen-forty-two to Thirteen-oh-one."

"Thirteen-oh-one," an older man's voice responded.

"I have a Sergeant Conrad and Detective Lombardi here to meet you."

"I'll be there momentarily," Reynolds said.

"The lieutenant is on his way," the trooper said.

"Thank you," Lombardi replied.

Conrad and Lombardi used the free moment to survey the yard around the cabin. To the right of the structure was a grassy expanse that led downward at a slight incline to the edge of the shadowy woods. Slicing through the woods to the right of this area was the dirt road leading up the hill to the gravel driveway. Another wide expanse of grass separated the driveway from more thick woods, which appeared ominous and mysterious in the dark.

Scanning right, Conrad saw the driveway led to a small garage/storage shed. There was a vehicle-sized door at the front of the shed and a person-sized door on the side. A short stretch of grass separated the garage from the cabin.

Looming beyond the garage were the black, ever-present forest leviathans reaching up toward the stars like the grasping fingers of giants. Conrad noted that the yard was surrounded on all sides by these gigantic wood sentinels. It gave him a feeling of being trapped. The only gap in the forest existed where the narrow dirt road cut through the trees.

Squeaking hinges signaled Conrad to turn toward the cabin. He saw a man in his fifties sporting a gray, Marine-style haircut push open the front door and make his way down the short walkway toward himself and Detective Lombardi.

"Good to meet you both," the lieutenant said, shaking Lombardi's hand and then Conrad's.

"Likewise," Conrad replied. "How are the techs doing with the crime scene?"

"They're doing fine."

"Can we take a look around?" Lombardi asked.

"I'm sorry, but I can't risk contaminating the scene," Reynolds said, and then changed the subject. "A state-wide manhunt for Eric Blackburn is underway. Detective, I understand that you and the sergeant have been tracking this perp for at least a week. Based on your profile, where do you think this psycho will go next?"

Conrad and Lombardi glanced at each other, and Lombardi raised her eyebrow as if to signal Conrad to speculate first. Conrad was tired from the late hour and long drive, but he had a ready answer.

"Obviously, no matter where he goes, he will be trying to put as much distance between this crime scene and himself. Based on his past behavior, I believe he will go after the first victim who escaped, Tracey Randall. He has been obsessed with her from the beginning."

"Where is the victim now?" Reynolds asked.

"She's at her home in Westfield."

"We already have every trooper between here and Massachusetts patrolling the highways looking for this psychopath, but if he hasn't been located yet, my guess is that he's taking back roads to reach his destination," the lieutenant said.

"It took us slightly over five hours to get here," Conrad said. "How much of a head-start do you think he has?"

"I received a call from the Dolebrook dispatcher at 12:21 AM after she lost contact with her officers. She told me she called after only a few minutes of attempting to make contact with them. So, I would say shortly before that time – maybe around 12:10."

"It's four-fifteen now, so that means he could be almost there by now!" Lombardi exclaimed.

"She's right," Conrad said, as his face turned pale.

He reached into his pocket for his cell phone and took it out. He speed-dialed the Westfield Police station.

"Westfield Police, your call is recorded," a male voice answered on the first ring.

Conrad recognized the dispatcher as a reliable twenty-something who had been working for the department for several years.

"Jack, I need you to order a patrol car out to Tracey Randall's address immediately. We have reason to believe our suspect is en route to her location right now. The suspect's name is Eric Blackburn and he's driving a black 2016 Honda Civic. Instruct the officer who is not responding to make a systematic check of all the roads between the highway and Ms. Randall's neighborhood. Make sure you warn the officers that the suspect may have a firearm, and he's not afraid to use it. He's killed two cops already. Got it?"

"I have that, Sarge," the dispatcher replied. "I'll put that out right away."

"Okay, I'm trusting you to get this out fast."

"No problem, Sarge."

"I'll talk to you later then," Conrad said, hanging up.

Conrad's eyes locked with Lombardi's and then Reynolds's.

"A cruiser is on the way. I hope to God that our officer beats the perp to her house because when he's under pressure, he's more dangerous than ever."

CHAPTER 79

I feel a rush of excitement as I cross over the border into the town of Westfield. At this point in my journey, I can't afford to make a mistake; the police are most likely on the look-out for my vehicle. There may even be a cruiser guarding the Randall House. However, it won't matter because I'm in the zone. If I can make it to her house unmolested, my blade will take it from there. I just need to get there.

Fifteen minutes later, I pull onto the adjacent street that swings around in a circle to connect to her street; that way I can approach her house discreetly. I will park in the small clearing hidden by a cluster of trees across from the chain entrance to the town Conservation Land; I can view her house through gaps in the leaves.

Cruising slowly through the neighborhood, I keep my eyes peeled for the little clearing across from the gate. When I spot it, I glide in behind the trees and shut off the engine. Eyes straining, I peer through the gaps in the leaves.

Because it's still very dark, I only see the faint glow from the light by the front door of the Randall house. The rest of the home is dark.

I need to get a better look, so I open the car door as silently as possible and get out. Creeping into the midst of the trees, I use the thick gray trunks for cover.

As I reach a better vantage point, I peer out toward the street. The sight ahead chills me to the bone; a police cruiser is parked next to the curb directly across from her house. I can see the back of the officer's head because the interior cruiser light is on. Damn! How did the cops know I would come here?

I shouldn't panic; it's probably just a precaution; they didn't know for sure I'd come here. I can figure out a way to get past this obstacle.

Turning my wristwatch toward a nearby street light, I see it is 5:08 AM. I don't have much time because it will start getting light around six o'clock. I need to come up with a plan. It's hard to concentrate because I feel tense with the anticipation of what I'm going to do to the slut when I get my hands on her.

However, if I'm going to get my hands on her, I have to make it past this cop. I could try to sneak by him, but if I cross the street and circle behind the house without being seen, the cop will hear me when I kick in the back door. He will certainly hear the screams of her mother and father as I slit their throats in preparation for some alone time with their teenage daughter. Then, he will come in guns blazing and it will be over. No, I have to take him out first so I can take my time with her.

Studying the parked cruiser from my place of cover, I try to think of a way around the obstacle. The cop has a gun, while I have a knife, which means I will have to utilize subterfuge to overcome his superior firepower.

He's sitting in the driver's seat with the interior light on, which means he's probably reading, using a laptop computer, or messing around with his cellphone. If he's right-handed like most cops, his gun will be pinned against his right hip while he's seated. He can only bring the gun into play if he exits the vehicle, and there's no way in hell he can draw and aim the weapon as he opens the latch on the door and climbs out of the cab. I know what I have to do now.

Returning to my vehicle, I pick up my knife from the passenger seat and slide it into the back of my belt within easy reach. I practice reaching behind my back and pulling it out. I can do it very quickly – a lot quicker than he can draw his pistol from its holster.

The cop will be at a disadvantage in a confrontation due to his seated position. As I approach the vehicle, I will make sure he can see my hands so he knows I'm not armed. If I knock on the driver's side window, his instinct will be to roll it down or exit the vehicle. Either way, it will take too long for him to reach down to his holster, draw his weapon, aim, and fire. As his fingers wrap around the handle of his service revolver, my knife will be in his throat.

Taking a deep breath, I step onto the street. Reaching around my back, I wrap my fingers around the handle of my knife, which is lodged diagonally inside my belt for easy access. I can have it out in a split-second. I'm ready.

I feel a rush of energy as a jolt of adrenaline kicks in. In spite of the energy surge, I feign a casual attitude as I saunter down the road toward the cruiser. I am only a concerned neighbor out for an early morning stroll.

As I advance, I see that the cop is looking down – scrutinizing something he's holding out of sight. His left hand is holding something – probably a clipboard – while his right hand moves a pen on a piece of paper. Catching up on his paperwork? He is completely immersed in what he is doing and doesn't even notice my approach.

Smiling with amusement at the cop's inferior position, I reach out and knock on the driver's side window. The cop jumps in his seat as his head whips around to face me. His face is pale and his eyes are wide. It takes a moment for him to focus.

"Excuse me, sir, may I ask what you're doing here in the neighborhood? Is there a problem I should know about?" I ask using my most innocent-sounding voice.

The cop rolls down the window a mere two inches – not enough space for me to plunge a knife through accurately. Damn! I didn't see that coming.

"Who're you?" the cop asks, eyes narrowing with suspicion.

"Oh me? I'm Rich Johnson. I live two houses down that way." I say, pointing toward the curve in the street.

"Do you have some ID I can see?" the cop asks, face hardening.

"ID? Why would I carry my ID when I'm just out for a morning walk in the neighborhood?" I ask as I make sure to keep my hands raised where the officer can see them.

The cop looks me up and down with suspicion, but there should be nothing suspicious about me. I'm wearing ordinary blue jeans, a light blue button-down shirt, and a black, unzipped leather jacket. The cop frowns as he continues his silent appraisal of my person.

"Which house do you live in?" the cop asks through the crack in the window.

I step back a few steps to make the cop feel safer and point again to the curve in the road.

"Sir, I live right around that corner," I say.

The cop's frown deepens as he glances in that direction and

sees nothing but trees.

"You say you live in this neighborhood?" he asks.

"That's right, officer. We can take a walk over to my house if you want."

The officer continues to look me up and down as he considers whether to vacate the safety of the cruiser. I see him glance down at the radio on the console as if he is considering calling for back-up. Raising my open-palmed hands in the air so he can see I'm unarmed, I widen my eyes as if I'm afraid and back up another few steps to give the cop more space.

"Officer, did I do something wrong?" I ask, innocently.

I can see the wheels turning in his head as he considers whether I'm a threat or not. He looks like he wants to pick up the radio and call for back-up, but he's probably thinking it would be embarrassing if I really was just a lone, unarmed neighbor out for an early-morning walk. How would he explain to his back-up that he was afraid to confront an unarmed man alone? I'm counting on his ego to influence him to make the wrong move.

Finally, after a seemingly endless wait, I hear a click as the cop pulls on the inner door handle. As the door swings open, my body tenses for action. His right hand disappears behind his body as he reaches for the handle of his holstered pistol.

Cautiously, he pokes his head out from the interior of the vehicle with his eyes glued on me. I judge the distance between him and me; only ten feet separates us – I can cover that space in a split-second. I still have my hands raised in the air, but I lower my right hand ever so slightly.

As the cop begins to stand with his right hand resting on the butt of his gun, I lunge. My right hand darts behind my back as I spring toward him. The cop appears startled by my sudden movement, and he freezes for a moment before he begins to pull his pistol out of its holster.

He has just slipped the gun out of the holster as my knife plunges into his neck. His mouth opens in an exaggerated "O" shape as blood spurts from a severed carotid artery. Sinking the knife to the hilt in his throat, more blood gushes. I savor the image of his surprised face for a moment before I yank the knife from the wound, and watch his body crumple to the pavement.

CHAPTER 80

I feel unstoppable as I loom, triumphantly, over the bloody corpse of the police officer. I imagine the rush must be what victorious gladiators felt in ancient Rome after skewering opponents in the arena. With this cop's quick demise, I've proved my superiority over law enforcement once again. I want to savor the moment, but I have work to do.

But first, I have to upgrade my weapon. Sliding my blood-slick blade into the back of my belt, I reach down toward the cop's fallen pistol. He has collapsed face-down on the pavement next to the cruiser with the pistol lying next to his lifeless right hand. I pick up the weapon and relish the feel of cold steel in my palm.

Grinning, I turn and face the front of the house. The small, ranch-style dwelling beyond the insignificant yard appears vulnerable as if it's constructed of cardboard. It may as well be. With the gun in my possession, I can blast out the lock on the back door without resorting to kicking it in.

Without hurrying, I cross the street to the short driveway. The only light I see on in the house is the exterior one by the front door. Veering left, I move toward the side yard, which will bring me into the shadows beyond the range of the feeble light. I feel like a stealthy assassin as my dark clothing blends into the blackness, and I glide like a shadow past the side wall.

Charged with adrenaline, I feel like I have the strength of ten men as I enter the backyard. There's no light on next to the back door beyond the small porch, so I continue on in darkness. In seconds, I'm staring at the doorknob. It would be fun to blast out the lock with my stolen pistol, but on second thought, it could bring unwanted attention my way. It's inevitable that a loud bang will sound if I kick in the door, but at least I can avoid the sharp metallic blast of a pistol shot.

Drawing back, I lower my center of gravity to prepare to strike the spot to the immediate right of the doorknob with the sole of my right sneaker. Winding up, I lunge forward and hear a crack like a gunshot as the door splinters. The door doesn't swing inward right away, so I give it a second kick to complete the job.

Scanning ahead with my pistol barrel, I enter the darkened kitchen. I remember the common layout of most ranch-style houses, so I sweep through an opening beyond the kitchen, which leads both to the living room to the right and a hallway to the left. I take a left down the hallway.

Holding the gun in front of me like a cop, I stalk down the corridor. The first doorway on the right is open, so I lead with the gun and peer into the darkness. By the dim light shining through the window, I see an unoccupied twin-bed that has been made-up neatly next to a small dresser, which indicates a guest bedroom. That means her room is ahead down the hallway to the left or right. I aim my gun down the corridor as I advance.

Suddenly, I hear a creaking sound as the right-hand door opens at the end of the hallway; I see a dark form emerge into the corridor, holding a shadowy object in its grasp. The form is far too large to be Tracey Randall, so I assume it's hostile and fire at it. Metallic thunder blasts my ears as the shot resounds in the narrow corridor.

My ears ring from the blast as I watch a human-shaped silhouette collapse in the darkness. The body hits the floor, and I hear a heavy metallic clanking noise that sounds like metal striking wood. It's a good thing that I have fast reflexes because whoever it was – probably the father – had a handgun in his grasp. Pointing downward, I fire another shot into the crumpled human form to be sure. This time, the blast doesn't bother me as much because my ears are already ringing.

Reaching down, I search the floor for the fallen weapon. After several seconds of frantic searching, my fingers wrap around the barrel of a small twenty-two caliber pistol. Standing, I change my grip on the pistol and slide it into my right pocket.

Stepping over the collapsed body, I swing my handgun toward the open doorway to my right to make sure no one else is there. My eyes have adjusted enough to the dark to see that the door on the left side of the hallway is closed. I figure the father emerged from the doorway to the right, so the one on the left must be Tracey's room.

I check the doorknob on the closed door and it doesn't turn: it's locked. Tracey either had time to get up and lock the door after she heard me kick in the back door, or the door was locked already due to her paranoia. It turns out she wasn't being paranoid!

This flimsy door will prove to be less of an obstacle than the exterior door. Lowering my body, I draw my leg back and launch it toward the spot to the left of the doorknob. There's a cracking sound as the wood splinters and the door swings inward. I don't see anyone in the doorway, so she must be hiding somewhere within.

SHAWN WILLIAM DAVIS

Checking the doorway to the right to make sure I'm not being out-flanked, I plunge into the room with my gun extended. From the dim light of a half-open shade on one of the windows, the room appears empty; the sheets are rumpled on a full-sized bed set against the far wall, but there's no one in it.

Looking around, I see both windows are closed, which means she didn't escape through one of them. The only remaining furniture is a small night-table next to the bed and a medium-size dresser set against the left wall.

Advancing further into the bedroom, I realize that she must be hiding in the closet or under the bed. I am only moments away from finding her.

CHAPTER 81

Tracey Randall slept fitfully as she experienced the same terrifying dream she had over and over since she escaped into the woods from the psychopath's cabin. In her nightmare, she ran headlong through the forest with the psycho close on her heels. She could hear his labored breathing as he got closer.

Sometimes, she was able to get away in the dream, while other times she was caught. At those times, the terror of being caught always woke her up. Tonight, she was steadily outdistancing her nightmare pursuer and was on the verge of leaving him behind. Suddenly, a tremendous crash like booming thunder exploded from somewhere far beyond the forest and she woke up with a start.

Somehow she knew right away that the crash had not occurred in her dream, but was real. Someone was breaking into the house. It was just as she imagined it. Sergeant Conrad had covered the windows at the most vulnerable points with wood in order to prevent a stealthy break-in. So, the psychopath had opted for a more direct route into the house by smashing down one of the exterior doors. From the direction of the crash, it sounded like the back door.

At least it was noisy enough to wake everyone in the household. She knew her father had a small pistol that he had bought years earlier for home defense. She couldn't remember the last time he had used it. He couldn't afford to practice at the gun club range after his hours were reduced.

Sgt. Conrad had recommended that they reinforce the exterior door frames with steel plates and install extra deadbolts. However, her father had said that it was too expensive and they couldn't afford it. Ditto for the alarm system the sergeant had recommended installing. Now the family was paying for that decision. She could only hope that her father had not slept through the crash and was even now preparing to blast the intruder with his pistol.

But Tracey was not going to count on that happening. She had imagined this scenario many times and she had prepared for it. Reaching toward the side of the bed, her fingers wrapped around the plastic grip of her titanium-reinforced tennis racket, which she kept within reach at all times. Sliding off the bed, she held the improvised weapon in front of her like a sword.

Sidestepping over to her bureau, she opened the top drawer and grabbed the can of pepper spray resting in the corner. She slid it into her PJ bottom's single rear pocket so it would be within easy reach. Sergeant Conrad told her that pepper spray didn't always incapacitate a person - especially if they were psychotic, so she planned to use it as a back-up if she had to.

Her bedroom door was locked, so he would have to break it down to get to her. This was another precaution she took every night before going to sleep. She figured that even a short delay would give her more time to get into position.

Tracey advanced toward the locked door and drew the racket back over her shoulder in preparation to strike. She positioned herself in the space between the closet door and the bedroom door, and waited.

Tracey was startled when an ear-piercing metallic blast thundered outside her bedroom door. Was that her father shooting the psycho or the psycho shooting her father? She had gone to the range several times with her father to learn to shoot, and she tried to remember the sound the 22-caliber gun made when fired. She didn't think it was as loud as the blast she heard in the corridor.

She had expected the killer to be armed with a knife, not a gun. He had not been armed with a gun the last time she dealt with him.

Tracey shuddered as a second blast rang out in the hallway outside her bedroom door. That was definitely not her father's gun; it sounded louder and more powerful. If the psycho kicked down the door and came in shooting, there was no way he would miss her as she was standing in ambush only slightly to the side of the door.

It was time for plan B. Holding the steel racket aloft, she reached over with her free hand and opened the closet door. Keeping her eyes glued on the bedroom door, she lowered the racket and retreated into the closet. Carefully, she closed the door without making any noise.

The closet extended far enough back so she could retreat into the corner behind the wall. If the psycho fired into the closet door, she would be sheltered by the wall.

There was enough space in the closet for her to slide in and pull on the clothing dangling from hangars until she was hidden from view, but she would still have a clear shot with the racket if someone stuck their head or appendage in. There was barely enough room to lift the racket above her shoulders before the top of it scraped against the ceiling. She wished she had more room to draw it back so she could bring it crashing down with greater impact.

She realized that she had slipped into the closet just in time as a loud crash indicated the door giving way to the psycho's boot. She imagined him hesitating for a moment on the threshold before entering with his gun drawn. At least he hadn't come in shooting. She was worried about her father though. Two shots had rung out in the hallway. She could only hope the psycho's aim was bad in the dark.

Sweat beaded on her forehead as she waited tensely with the racket raised high enough so the top of it scraped against the closet ceiling. Her muscles began to feel sore from tension as she waited for the closet door to open. After that, whatever poked inside – whether it be the psycho's hand or head – she was ready to strike with all her strength.

CHAPTER 82

The room appears to be empty, but that can't be right. Panic invades my brain like a charging battalion as I imagine the bitch has escaped from me again. But how could she get away with her bedroom door locked from the inside and all the windows closed? She must be hiding somewhere out-of-sight. Advancing toward the twin bed, I train my gun on the empty space beneath the mattress.

Ducking, I look under the bed. Nothing but bare floor. Turning, I move toward the closet.

Holding the gun in front of me, two-handed, like a cop drawing on a suspect, I place my index finger outside the trigger guard. Shooting to kill is not an option because I want to use the knife on her.

Keeping the gun pointed ahead, I reach down with my free hand to turn the closet doorknob. I yank the door open and see nothing but empty space inside. Not even a hangar dangles from the closet rack; all the clothing appears to have been pushed to the side. How far back does the closet go? Could she be hiding behind the clothing?

I don't want to fire into the closet for fear of killing her; then, all my plans would be for nothing. I don't want it to be fast; I want to take my time.

I hesitate, but how much damage can she do to me from inside a closet? She's not strong enough to overpower me – even without the weapons I'm holding. I need to be sure she's not hiding there so I can move on to searching the rest of the house.

Lowering the pistol, I move cautiously so I don't shoot her in the head by accident as I check the closet. I will reach in, easily, with my free hand and drag her out. Then, I'll pistol-whip her to stun her and go to work with the knife.

Holding the closet door open with my right shoulder, I peer inside. Suddenly, a sharp pain radiates from my forehead as a hard metal object strikes my skull. To make matters worse, an ear-piercing explosion blasts my ears as I stagger backwards.

Stumbling backward into the room, I can't tell if my ears are ringing from the blow to my head or the explosion. Instinctively, I raise my arms to protect myself against further attack.

Trying to focus my blurry vision, I realize the explosion must have resulted as I reflexively pressed down on the trigger when I was struck. So much for keeping my finger outside the trigger-guard.

Regaining my balance, I'm startled by the sight of a blurry figure lunging at me from the closet. The figure must be wielding some kind of weapon because sharp pains suddenly stab into my forearms like needles.

I hear a metallic clanking noise, and I feel a wave of panic as I realize I dropped the handgun on the hardwood floor. I couldn't maintain my grip on it. My arms are taking a beating, but at least she only got in one head-shot so far.

I back up to buy some time to go for my knife. The blows from the hard object are raining down fast and furiously on my raised arms; it's all a blur.

Risking a possible head-shot from her weapon, I lower one of my arms to reach around behind my back. A glancing blow strikes the side of my head, but I maintain my concentration.

Panic turns to instant elation as my fingers wrap around the knife handle protruding from my belt. Whipping it out, I stab violently upwards. A cry of pain emanates from my attacker, so I figure I must have hit something.

The barrage finally lets up so I have a free moment to concentrate on my opponent. She's breathing heavily and covered in sweat. There's a maniacal expression on her face that makes me think she has lost her mind. I notice that her weapon is a steel reinforced tennis racket – now that it's finally stopped moving. No wonder it hurt so much.

Blood streams down from her forearm near the elbow. Apparently, I got lucky and hit a vein. She tries to stifle the bleeding with her free hand, but only succeeds in slowing the flow.

She's distracted by the bleeding wound, so I lunge with the knife like a fencer trying to score a point. Apparently, she's not that distracted because she parries my knife lunge with her improvised weapon. My knife blade clangs off metal like a sword clashing off a shield.

I lunge again, but her adrenaline must be flowing because she intercepts my knife with her racket before I can bury it in her flesh. We glare at each other like gladiators facing off in an ancient arena. The pressure she's putting on her wound is bearing fruit because the wound has stopped gushing blood.

Holding the racket in front of her, one-handed, she reaches around with her free hand for something in the back pocket of her light-blue pajama bottoms. I guess what it might be, so I raise my left arm to shield my face while I bring the knife back to prepare for a lunge.

Sure enough, I hear a hissing sound as she points a small bottle of either mace or pepper spray at me. A split-second later, I know it's pepper spray as my forearm burns as if it's on fire. My forehead and chin also burn, but at least she missed my eyes. The pain is intense, so I figure one of the cops must have given her the 15% law-enforcement strength stuff.

Peering over my raised arm, I see her full lips contort into a vicious snarl. "Why are you doing this?" she asks. "Why can't you just leave me alone?"

My response is to lower my arm, smile, and lunge at her again. This time, my knife collides with the shaft of the re-inforced racket, but then slides off and slices her left hand holding the pepper spray. Blood gushes from a half-severed index finger as the bottle clatters to the floor; she won't last much longer unless she has an extra hand to stifle blood-flow from dual wounds.

I lunge several more times, but she continues to parry the blows as blood spurts from her mangled finger. I hear a clinking sound as her right foot collides with something on the hardwood floor.

Is it the pepper spray can or the gun? Glancing down, I feel a rush of fear as I realize it's my fallen handgun.

She holds the racket defensively as her eyes dart to the object on the floor. Bending at the knees, she transfers the racket to her left hand, which causes blood to gush from the wounds in her arm and finger. Ignoring the blood, she reaches for the gun.

I can't let her get it, so I make a lightning lunge with my knife. She gets lucky and deflects it with the racket as her bloody hand closes around the butt of the pistol. There's no time to stop her. It's time to get out of Dodge. Turning, I sprint toward the open bedroom door.

A peal of echoing thunder resounds in the small room as a vicious pain rips into my left shoulder. The bitch shot me! Sinking to my knees, I maintain the grip on my knife despite the pain radiating from my wound. In my peripheral vision, I see her positioning herself for another shot.

I spring upward with my outstretched knife as she takes aim with the gun. A second peal of thunder explodes as my knife buries itself in her left thigh. Blood spurts from her leg-wound as a sharp pain like a bee sting radiates from my right ear. It feels like my ear-lobe was torn away by a bullet.

The blade, lodged in her thigh, is ripped out of my grasp as she stumbles backward toward the twin bed. However, it doesn't matter because she's all done. I see her eyes roll up in her head so only the whites are showing as she collapses into a pool of blood.

I can't take any more chances; it's time to get up close and personal to finish her off.

CHAPTER 83

Elation turned to despair as Tracey missed the psycho with her second gunshot and felt a vicious pain rip into her thigh. Incredibly, her antagonist had lunged and stabbed her after being shot through the shoulder.

As she lost more blood, her vision became blurry and her equilibrium was disrupted. Her muscles gave out and she collapsed. Dropping to the floor, she felt herself blacking out. After all she had been through, she couldn't let it end like this.

Lying on her back, she tried to fight her way back to full consciousness. She felt fingers constricting around her throat.

"You fucking bitch." The psycho's words echoed in her mind as if spoken from miles away.

Her eyes closed instinctively as her body began to shut down. But, she couldn't let them close. She had to fight. Forcing her eyes open, all she could see was a dark blur that resembled the silhouette of a human being's head, neck, and shoulders. She thought she could see the features of a face staring down at her, but she couldn't be sure as her airway was cut-off.

Please, God, give me the strength to fight back, she thought. *You helped me before when I was lost in the woods. Please help me again.*

Her concentration wavered as she felt her mind blanking out like a fading radio signal.

Please, God.

A sharp pain in her chest made her eyes fly open. The psycho was slicing her left breast with his knife. But, he had relinquished his grip on her throat. The pain went through her body like a bolt of lightning – energizing her. Her eyes focused on the face leering down at her. She balled up her fists. She felt something cold and smooth rub against her right knuckle. It was steel.

Opening her right hand, she felt her fingers brush against the smooth, cool steel of the handgun barrel. The pain moved across her breast, causing another burst of energy to surge through her. Imagining what the gun looked like on the floor from an angle above, she guided her fingers over the barrel until they reached the handle.

Focusing all her concentration, she wrapped her fingers around the handle of the gun. Energy flowed through the muscles in her arm like an electrical wave – allowing her fingers to tighten around the handle. As if guided by an unseen force, her arm flew upwards and she heard a sharp crack as the pistol butt collided with the psycho's skull. The intense pain in her chest faded to a dull, throbbing soreness. With a final burst of energy, she aimed at the silhouette above her and fired. She heard a blast of thunder before her vision faded to black.

****

Sergeant Conrad and Detective Lombardi were taking a tour

of the crime scene at the Blackburn cabin in New Hampshire with Lieutenant Reynolds when Conrad received a call on his cell-phone from the Westfield Police Dispatcher.

"Excuse me for a moment. I have a call from the station." Conrad pressed the green button on his phone. "Hello?"

"Sarge, it's Jack at Dispatch."

"What's up, Jack?"

"Sarge, we have a serious problem down here."

Conrad felt static electricity prickle the hairs on the back of his neck as a chill ran down his spine.

Please don't tell me Blackburn has gotten to Tracey Randall, he thought.

"What's going on?" he asked.

"Neighbors reported a loud crash followed by several gun-shots at the Randall residence. I radioed the officer on the detail, but he's not answering. I dispatched the other duty officer to the scene, and I'm waiting for him to report in."

Conrad closed his eyes and gritted his teeth. It seemed as if his worst fears were being confirmed. Still, he needed to keep his head in the game because he had a job to do. He took a moment to organize his thoughts before issuing instructions.

"Jack, you need to call EMS and have them send an ambulance to the Randall house; there are going to be injuries – probably serious," Conrad instructed. "Then, call the Shrewsbury and Northfield Police for mutual -aid assistance. Tell them to send as many officers as they can spare; make sure you warn them how dangerous Blackburn is. Also, call the chief at home and let him know what's going on."

"Okay, Sarge, I'll take care of it," the dispatcher replied.

"Call me back when you have more information," Conrad said.

"You got it, Sarge."

Conrad pressed the red button on the phone and shoved it into his pocket.

"What's going on?" Reynolds asked.

Conrad sighed. "Neighbors reported gunshots coming from Tracey Randall's house in Westfield; she was the only victim to ever escape from Blackburn. It looks like Blackburn is trying to finish the job he started."

"I thought you said there was a police detail guarding her," Reynolds said.

"The dispatcher called on the radio and received no response from the detail officer."

Lombardi's eyes widened. "Who was on the detail?" she asked.

"Rick Malloy," Conrad replied.

"Oh my God," Lombardi said.

"Do you think Blackburn killed him?" Reynolds asked.

"You saw the set-up in the basement with the restraints, plastic tarp, and chainsaw," Conrad said. "You saw how efficiently he took out the two town police officers. This psychopath can't be underestimated. I should have given Malloy a stronger warning."

CHAPTER 84

Tracey opened her eyes a short time later to find herself staring into the eyes of a stranger. The stranger was a blonde woman; her face appeared angelic as a bright light shone behind her. Scanning downward, Tracey saw the woman was wearing a dark-blue EMT uniform.

Tracey tried to move her arms and felt leather straps pressing against her body; she realized she was strapped to a stretcher.

There was a sudden motion and the woman's face disappeared from view – replaced by a blank white ceiling. Tracey felt movement, which felt like flying, and the ceiling darted past her vision for a few seconds until it transformed into the dark blue of the dawn sky.

Tracey felt a jolt as the EMTs carried her down the front steps of her home. She heard the stretcher's plastic wheels scraping against asphalt as the EMTs pushed her across the front walkway toward a waiting ambulance.

When they reached the ambulance, Tracey's stomach fluttered as the EMTs lifted her into the back compartment. The blonde EMT secured the stretcher in place and started an IV. As the needle entered her vein, Tracey thought it felt like a pinprick compared to the knife stabbing her thigh. She smiled at the thought of how tough she had become in a mere week's time.

"What's so funny?" the blonde EMT asked.

"I was just thinking – my tolerance for pain has increased a lot recently," Tracey said, maintaining her smile despite the dull, throbbing pain she felt from various wounds.

"I don't doubt it," the blonde EMT said. "It took five bandages to cover all your cuts. How are you feeling now?"

"I feel light-headed, but the pain isn't as bad as before."

"That's because we gave you a shot of morphine. Otherwise, you would be feeling it. You're going to need a lot of stitches."

"I'm happy to still be breathing," Tracey said.

Then, she frowned as she remembered the final sequence of events. As she felt the knife tip slice across the surface of her breast, her fingers had closed around the handle of the gun. The last thing she remembered was striking his skull with the gun butt, and then taking aim at his head and firing.

"What happened to the psycho who almost killed me?"

The EMT frowned back. "Unfortunately, he's still alive," she said. "He had one bullet in his shoulder and half his ear missing, but he survived."

"I thought I shot him three times," Tracey said. "He should be dead."

"You must have missed one of the times."

Tracey's eyes widened. "But if I missed him, why didn't he kill me? He had a knife pressed against my chest when I fired at him. I thought I survived because I stopped him with a bullet."

"Actually, you can thank your mother for stopping him," the EMT said, raising an eyebrow. "She came up behind him and clocked him in the back of the head with a table lamp. She knocked him out. Then, she picked up the handgun, which you dropped when you passed out, and placed it in her bathrobe pocket in case your attacker recovered. She saw that you were bleeding severely from your thigh and finger, so she alternated pressure to your wounds with items of clothing she found in your dresser. We arrived a few minutes later and took over."

"Wow, I didn't know she had it in her," Tracey said. "Now I know where I get my toughness from. What about my Dad? I heard gunshots in the hallway before I was attacked."

"Your father was shot twice, but only one of the wounds was serious. The other shot only grazed him. He will need surgery, but he should recover no problem," The EMT said.

"Thank God," Tracey said. "When I heard the shots in the hallway, I feared the worst."

"He's going to be all right," the blonde EMT said, smiling reassuringly.

"You still haven't told me what happened to my attacker."

"The cops got here at the same time we did and despite seeing your attacker bleeding out, they cuffed his wrists to the sides of the stretcher. After what he did to you, they weren't taking any chances. He lost a lot of blood, but it looks like he's going to survive. I was hoping the bastard would bleed out and die."

"I was hoping the same thing," Tracey said. "I would feel a lot better if I knew he was out of commission – permanently."

"Don't worry, Tracey. After what he did to you and the police officer, he'll never see the outside of a jail cell for the rest of his life."

"What happened to the police officer?" Tracey asked, eyes widening.

"I'm sorry to tell you, honey, he was stabbed and killed," the EMT said.

Tracey felt a sick feeling in the pit of her stomach.

"Was it Sergeant Conrad?" she asked, dreading the EMT's response.

"No, dear, it was Officer Malloy."

Tracey couldn't help feeling relieved; Sergeant Conrad was the cop who had taken time to do a thorough walkthrough of her home to assess it for possible security breaches; he had most likely saved her life by reinforcing the back door and cellar window with wooden planks. Instead of simply breaking the window pane to gain access, the psycho had to make a lot of noise to kick the door in, and that gave her time to prepare with an improvised weapon.

"I'm sorry to hear that," Tracey said, feeling slightly guilty about feeling relieved. "What happened?"

"Oh, honey, you don't want to know the details," the EMT said.

"Was he guarding my house?" Tracey asked.

The EMT hesitated. "Yes, honey, he was."

"Then it's my fault?"

"No, it's only one person's fault: the one who did it. I need you to stop worrying and relax. You're going to be okay and your attacker is no longer a threat to anyone. Soon, he will be going away for a very, very long time."

CHAPTER 85

I try to move my arms, but my wrists are cuffed securely to the side-rail of a hospital-type stretcher. I feel like a trapped animal as my eyes dart around the claustrophobic rear compartment of an ambulance. I see various items of medical equipment bolted to the walls and two blue-uniformed EMTs seated next to me on the right. There's an IV stuck in my arm.

Glancing left, I feel sick when I see a police officer seated on a bench near the rear doors. He stares back at me without emotion as if he's observing a dull laboratory experiment. I still can't figure out how they got me. How did I get knocked out?

The last thing I remember was the bitch taking a pot-shot at me. She missed completely and then passed out. When I saw her eyes close and the gun slip out of her hand, I raised my knife high so I could plunge it through her heart.

Then, I felt a sharp stab of pain in the back of my head, which radiated throughout my skull like a toxic leak. Everything went black, and the next thing I knew I was lying on this stretcher in an ambulance. I can barely move my arms with these police-style metal cuffs confining my wrists. In addition to a throbbing headache, there's a dull, nagging pain in my left shoulder and right ear.

Somehow, I got caught. The worst part is that my career as an artist – using human canvases – is over. Unless I can exploit an opportunity to escape while they're checking me out at the hospital, the next stop is jail, and from there prison. There's no doubt I will be convicted; they will find a wealth of evidence in my apartment because I never thought I would be caught this soon. Actually, I never thought I would ever be caught.

To add insult to injury, the slut is still alive. I blacked out before I got a chance to deliver the final death-blow. It's still possible she could bleed to death, but I'll never have the satisfaction of knowing for sure. Unless, she testifies against me in court.

But she won't need to testify against me in court. In addition to the mountain of evidence contained in my apartment, all they need are a couple cadaver-sniffing dogs in the vicinity of my parents' cabin, and I'm all done. A virtual cemetery exists in the woods a mere fifty yards from the backyard of the cabin. I wanted to keep them close for inspiration. They're all dismembered; I buried the limbs, bodies, and heads separately.

If you leave through the cabin's back door and walk straight into the woods for about fifty yards, you will reach the area where I buried the torsos. Veer a hundred feet to the left and you'll find the skull graveyard. About a hundred-fifty feet to the right are the entombed limbs.

I buried all the remains, but I didn't have the patience to bury them deep; cadaver dogs will be able to sniff them out easily. There's no way out for me by beating the law; they have me cold.

However, I'm still smarter than they are. I can still out-think and out-plan them. Maybe this is just a temporary set-back and I'll emerge from this even stronger. Who was the philosopher who said what doesn't kill us makes us stronger? Maybe I'll be able to act out his philosophy after I escape. Next time, I won't make the same mistakes.

There's no doubt I underestimated my opponent; the one that got away put up more of a fight than I expected. She almost killed me a couple times. If only I could have had the satisfaction of skewering her before I was caught. At least I would have had pleasant memories to refer to while imprisoned.

Imprisoned. There's a reality check. I don't know how well I'll do in prison. I'll go insane if there are no women there. Men are too ugly a canvas to practice my art on.

Then, there's the possibility of being raped. I can't even imagine the ignominy of that sickening act. However, I'm resourceful and I'll bet I can make any would-be rapists wish they had never tried to violate me.

How will I continue to write my story if I'm locked up? Will I have access to a computer? Probably not. A pen and paper? I hope so. One of the most damning pieces of evidence in my apartment is the extensive diary that I saved on the harddrive of my laptop. In it, I describe my art projects in exquisite detail. Surely, they will confiscate my great work and it will never be released to the public as I had hoped. The world will never know my genius.

As I contemplate the horror of my situation, a faint trembling begins in the tips of my fingers. At first, it's just the tips that quiver as if they've been exposed to extreme cold. I try to control it, but it spreads through my hands until it reaches my arm. Like an infection, the relentless quaking continues up my arms until I can't keep them still. I hear the handcuff chain rattling on the metal rail.

The scourge of trembling travels through my torso like an electric shock until it reaches my head and legs. My teeth start to rattle as my head quivers on the stretcher like one of those ridiculous bobble-head dolls. In no time, my legs join the rebellion and my entire body is quaking as if I'm having a seizure.

The EMTs stare at me with wide eyes as I slide into an uncontrollable fit. I can't tell what the cop is doing as my vision becomes too blurry to see clearly.

Suddenly, a high-pitched scream rings out in the compartment; it sounds like a small animal being tortured. The scream increases in pitch and volume until I think I will go mad.

My ears start to ring from the increasing decibels reverberating in the confined space. The scream becomes increasingly shrill as if an army of alley-cats are all caterwauling at the same time.

My body rebels in a frenzy of motion as my eyes dart around the compartment – searching for the origin of the horrific scream. Where is it coming from? Then, reality hits me like a lightning-bolt to the brain. I know I'm doomed as I realize I'm the source of the shrill, inhuman shriek.

CHAPTER 86

Sgt. Jim Conrad and Detective Marilyn Lombardi walked, side-by-side, down the third floor corridor of the Farmington Union Hospital.

"Her room should be just ahead on the right," Conrad said.

"It's number 324," Lombardi added.

Sure enough, they saw the number 324 stenciled above the closed door of the next room on the right. Conrad knocked twice and a muffled female voice replied from inside, "Come in." He pushed the door open and entered to find the indomitable Tracey Randall seated upright on an adjustable hospital bed with an open paperback on her lap.

Conrad felt as if a bright light shined suddenly on his face as Tracey beamed a radiant smile at him. Apparently, his worry about her mental and physical health was misplaced; she looked like she was doing great.

"How's it going, Sarge?" Tracey asked.

"I'm doing better now that I see how well you're doing," Conrad replied, returning her smile.

"I'm doing great," she said. "For the first time this week I feel safe with that psycho behind bars."

"I understand," Conrad said, approaching the bed. "None of us could relax with that nutcase on the loose. What are you reading?" He pointed to the paperback book on her lap.

"*The Narrows* by Michael Connelly," she said, lifting the book so he could see the cover, which showed a raven in the foreground with lightning crackling above a bridge spanning a dark body of water in the background.

Conrad had read that one; it was about the hunt for a particularly deadly serial killer called *the Poet*, who had been once been the head of an FBI profiling unit.

"Are you sure a violent crime novel is the best choice after what you've been through?" Lombardi asked.

"Absolutely," she stated without hesitation. "I have to start studying now if I'm going to become a successful criminologist."

"It sounds like you have it all planned out," Conrad said.

"Yep, I want to hunt serial killers when I grow up," she said, lifting an eyebrow.

"Kid, I think you're more grown-up than you know," Conrad said. "You just helped to subdue the deadliest threat I've dealt with in my career."

"What can I say? I found out what I'm good at: fighting nut-jobs."

"You've proven yourself adroit at your calling; Blackburn barely survived his attack on you."

"I only wish I did a better job and hit him with my last shot."

"Kid, don't sell yourself short. You did a hell of a job kicking his ass," Conrad said.

"Thank you, Sarge."

"You can be my back-up anytime," Conrad said, winking.

"In a few years, I might just take you up on that," Tracey said.

"How's your father doing?" Lombardi asked.

"He's recovering well from surgery. The docs said he should be back on his feet in a couple weeks," Tracey said.

"That's great. Do you need anything?" Lombardi asked.

"I should be all set with my book," Tracey said, picking up the Connelly novel. "But I do have a couple questions I wanted to ask."

Conrad and Lombardi's eyes met, briefly, before returning to Tracey.

"Sure, what do you want to know?" Conrad asked.

"How many bodies did you find at the cabin?"

"Fifteen," Conrad replied without hesitation. He didn't see a reason to lie to her about the number.

"That many?"

"All the missing women have been accounted for, but we're still trying to identify some of the bodies. There are more victims than we thought there would be."

"I'm sorry to hear that," Tracey said.

"So were we," Conrad agreed.

"What kind of state were the bodies in?" Tracey asked.

Conrad and Lombardi's eyes met again, and returned to Tracey.

"I would rather not say," Conrad said.

This particular detail was something a lot different from a body count. Conrad thought the gruesome knowledge of the mutilated and dismembered bodies could negatively affect

Tracey's recovery.

"I need to know," Tracey said. "I need to know what would have happened to me if I didn't escape."

Conrad paused for a moment before replying. He knew the details would eventually come out at trial, but he was not going to burden Tracey with the knowledge at this time.

"They were all killed with a knife," Conrad said. It wasn't a complete lie; a knife was used on each victim in addition to a chainsaw.

"Were they tortured first?" Tracey asked.

"Why do you need to know that?" Lombardi asked.

"I need to know."

"They were stabbed. It was quick," Conrad lied. "Anything else?"

"How many years is he going to get?"

"He will get a life sentence for each murder," Lombardi said. "The bottom line is that he will never get out."

"What if he escapes?"

"Tracey, this guy is going to be locked in a super-max facility; he's in there for the long haul," Conrad interjected.

"What about parole?" Tracey asked.

"You don't get parole when you're sentenced to a thousand years."

"Okay, I'm satisfied then," Tracey said. "Now I can live my life."

CHAPTER 87

The guards lead me down a long, concrete corridor toward the cellblock entrance. I feel the steel handcuffs cutting into the circulation in my wrists. Why did they have to put them on so tight?

As I suspected, the case against me was rock solid. They found the photos of my art work inside the safe in my apartment. They found and identified all the bodies buried behind the cabin. They found my fingerprints on all the art tools.

The only defense my Public Defender could offer was Not Guilty by Reason of Insanity. Not surprisingly, the jury didn't buy it. It wasn't true anyway. I knew what I was doing.

So now I face society's retribution. Society will not allow anyone who is different like me to co-exist with all the brain-dead drones – even though the relationship of predator to prey is as natural as the changing of the seasons. Society can't allow an Alpha Predator like me to roam around free.

An odd event happened when I was thirteen years old that opened my eyes to the way of the world. It happened when I was visiting a zoo with my family while vacationing in Florida. I became instantly mesmerized when we encountered a large cage housing a magnificent orange and black Bengal Tiger. I was impressed by the tiger's confident stride and sinewy strength. The graceful undulations of the beast's corded, rippling muscles was like a natural work of art.

Then suddenly – out of nowhere – the tiger went berserk. He had been pacing the cage after cooling off in a pool of water when he suddenly charged toward the encircling bars and stood on his hind legs to paw against the steel rods holding him captive. He growled and roared as he pressed his entire body against the bars in a vain attempt to escape from the confines of the cage.

What had caused the tiger's aggressive behavior? I followed the tiger's gaze to the pedestrian path outside the cage. The tiger was staring at a teenage girl being pushed around in a wheelchair by a male, who could have been her boyfriend or brother. The girl in the wheelchair remarked that she didn't understand why the tiger was behaving like it was. As the male pushed the girl in the wheelchair out-of-sight around the corner, the tiger calmed down and resumed his normal pacing.

The scene affected me like a violent car accident people can't look away from. Why was the tiger so fixated on the girl in the wheelchair? Could it have been something else that set it off? While my parents left to visit the rest of the zoo, I remained by the tiger cage observing the magnificent beast pacing back and forth.

A short time later, the male pushed the girl in the wheelchair past the tiger cage again as they retraced their steps. Again, the tiger went berserk. It stood on its hind legs, roaring as it pawed at the bars of the cage as if it desperately wanted to get out. Then, I knew it was no coincidence.

What was different about the girl in the wheelchair that set the tiger off? The solution hit me like a lightning-bolt to the brain. The tiger became fixated on the wheelchair girl because she was weak; she was easy prey.

If the tiger attacked a normal adult human, the beast could no doubt tear him or her to pieces, but there was always the possibility that the human would fight back by using an improvised weapon. The girl in the wheelchair could not fight back. She could not run. She was tailor-made by the Creator to be killed and consumed as the tiger's sustenance.

That's when I knew what I had to do; I had to be the tiger. If it was natural for a tiger to go after a handicapped girl in a wheelchair because she was weak, then it was natural for me to use my skills to hunt weaker prey. Throughout middle school and high school, the attractive girls had treated me like a pariah. They considered me a loser because I was always picked on by the jocks. Now I knew that I could become the tiger and turn the tables on them.

So, I prepared, schemed, and disciplined myself to become the ultimate predator. I obtained the proper tools and made the proper plans. Because I'm a creative human being and not a mindless animal, I could also appreciate the aesthetics of the hunt and the kill; by carving up my beautiful prey, I could turn them into works of art.

I'm jolted out of my reverie as we arrive at an array of thick bars blocking our path. A guard, seated in a glass security booth next to the steel barrier, waves to the guards encircling me and they wave back. There is a buzzing noise and the bars slide into the wall.

When the bars have receded, rough hands push me forward into the cellblock. Immediately, there's a loud commotion that reminds me of a mob of unruly chattering monkeys. Gazing upward at the three-tiered cell-block, I see the faces of prisoners staring at me from their cells as they hoot and holler like crazed maniacs.

"Hey, whitey, are you ready to get punked!" One of the prisoners – a muscular African-American on the ground tier – shouts at me.

"Oh no you don't! I'm gonna make him my bitch!" a thin, scruffy white guy in the cell next to him says.

"Hey, pretty-boy, I got something for you!" A voice shouts from above.

The cacophony of noise continues as I listen to the boisterous inmates threaten to violate my body in all kinds of unique ways. I tune them out. I am the Alpha Predator – not them. If any of them fucks with me, I'll kill them with my bare hands if I have to.

As I think these thoughts, we arrive in front of what appears to be an empty cell. One of the guards takes out an old-fashioned set of keys and slides it into a lock on the bars. He turns the key, I hear a click, and he swings open the barred cell door.

At first, I think I'm going to have a cell to myself because I don't see anyone inside. Then, I realize that a bald white inmate – with the tattoo of a grinning skull painted on his muscular arm – is lying on the top bunk of a double-bunk-bed. He doesn't move as I'm pushed into the cell. He appears to be staring at the concrete ceiling above him as if he's reading invisible words that only he can see.

Shoved into the cell, I hear the door slam shut behind me and then a click as the locking mechanism fastens. Turning, I watch the guards saunter away as if they don't have a care in the world.

The cell is smaller than I imagined. Besides the double-bunk-bed placed against the wall, the only other objects consist of a tiny sink next to a metal toilet crammed into a corner, a plain wooden chair in the opposite corner, and two shelves – one containing a small TV and radio while the other is littered with magazines and framed photographs of smiling idiots.

Observing the bunk-bed, I notice an open foot-locker on the floor on each side that could potentially hold a few meager possessions. The walls appear to be uncomfortably close; I'm starting to feel claustrophobic already. This experience could be even worse than I thought.

"Welcome to hell, bitch." The muscular inmate lying on the top bunk growls at me without moving.

I can't let him intimidate me. I sit on the chair in the corner with my back to the wall and try to lean back as if I'm perfectly relaxed.

As the inmate turns his square-jawed face toward me, I notice a hideous red scar emblazoned across his right cheek. His face reminds me of an artist's rendering of a primitive Cro-Magnon man that I saw once in a anthropology textbook. The mangy scruff on his wide jaw indicates he hasn't shaved in at least a week.

With a lightning-quick motion, the inmate sits up on the bunk and faces me. I try not to be startled by the sudden movement, but I can't help wincing slightly. A leering smile stretches across the inmate's brutish face that reminds me of a chimpanzee's oversized grin. He leans forward and flexes his massive chest, shoulder, and arm muscles. If not for his ugly face and protruding pot belly, he could have been a bodybuilder.

The inmate slides off the bunk and lands on his feet like a cat. I attempt to stand to face him, but he lunges at me before I can move. Monstrous hands seize my shoulders and push me back onto the chair. Fingers like fat sausages tighten around my arms like a boa constrictor's coils. With apparently minimal effort, I feel oversized hands turn my body around, and pull me onto the floor. My knees scrape against hard concrete as I'm shoved down onto all fours.

The inmate's massive hand clamps onto the back of my neck like a steel vise as I feel my pants being yanked down around my ankles. Panic invades my brain like a swarm of killer bees as I realize what's happening. I thought I would be able to fight back, but I'm completely helpless.

Suddenly, an object that feels like a hot poker is shoved into my anus. The pain is intense; it's like my insides are on fire. Blood trickles down the back of my legs. Fresh waves of pain radiate outward as the inmate slams into me repeatedly. Where are the guards? How could they allow this to happen? It can't end like this! As searing pain shoots through my body like white-hot sparks, I realize that I am now the prey.

CHAPTER 88

Detective Randall steered her unmarked cruiser down Exchange Street in Farmington on her way to interview eyewitness, Katie Stanton. She couldn't believe it was ten years ago on this day that she had her final, bloody conflict with the serial killer, Eric Blackburn – who was later dubbed *The Artist* by the media. During the trial, observers had been shocked as the psychopath testified that he was not guilty of any crimes because he was creating great works of art with his hideous photographs of dismembered women.

Today, Blackburn was still rotting in prison where he belonged. Unfortunately, he had gained a notorious celebrity status by releasing a manuscript called *Diary of a Serial Killer*, which described his actions during the last week before he was caught.

Although it was illegal for a killer to profit from death by publishing a manuscript from prison, last year Blackburn smuggled a copy of his infamous work out with one of his sick groupies after a prison visit. Although Blackburn never made any money from the book, his sick fans were able to distribute it throughout the Internet by giving it to various recognition-hungry bloggers, who had no scruples about luring readers to their site with Blackburn's heinous recollections.

Most of the blogging sites that published the manuscript had been shut down, but not until many copies of the book were printed by prurient Internet users. It constantly popped up on new sites and was copied extensively by serial killer aficionados, and others who were merely curious to get inside the mind of a sick killer. The book described Blackburn's warped thoughts and twisted philosophies in his own words as he kidnapped and killed victims during that last deadly week before he was caught.

As the only victim who had ever escaped from Blackburn's clutches, Tracey Randall was contacted many times by various media outlets to tell her story. Her story was made more compelling by the unique role she played, which Blackburn described in detail in his manuscript. In his writing, he was painfully honest about her heroic actions – although he never described them as such.

Tracey had been careful to avoid most media interviews in order to maintain her privacy. She just wanted to be left alone so she could concentrate on her criminal justice studies.

However, one time she gave in when a famous female television reporter, who she admired, offered to do an interview. Tracey was so excited about meeting the famous reporter that she may have bragged a bit during the interview in order to impress her. Tracey suspected that it could have been that fateful TV interview, which brought her to the attention of the new killer.

Tracey was extremely unsettled by the glaring similarities of the kidnapping and murder at the Farmington Mall to the crimes of the infamous *Artist*, Eric Blackburn. The vicious murder of two of her fellow officers at the breaking and entering scene last night was even more unsettling. Despite her chief and lieutenant's doubts, she was sure the mall perpetrator and the B and E perpetrator were the same man.

Tracey took a break from her reflections as she spotted her witness's street coming up. She pulled onto an ordinary suburban road surrounded by middle-class houses that reminded her of the house she had grown up in – and also happened to be the scene of her final battle with the deranged psychopath, Blackburn. Slowing down, she scanned the neighborhood for the number of the house. When she saw it, she pulled into the driveway.

Thinking about the similarities of this neighborhood to her old neighborhood gave her an uneasy feeling. Especially, since she was investigating a kidnapping and murder that had a modus operandi disturbingly similar to the one used by Eric Blackburn. However, she had already decided that this new killer was more dangerous than Blackburn. A lot more dangerous.

Now, Tracey had arrived at the home of the most important of the pair of witnesses to the crime. The detective was particularly interested in this witness because of the bravery she had shown when she attempted to intervene to save the seventeen-year-old male kidnapping victim.

Getting out of her unmarked cruiser, Tracey followed a cement walkway to the front door of the split-level house. She paused before ringing the doorbell.

Thinking about her takedown of Blackburn ten years ago gave her a surge of confidence. Even if this killer was more dangerous than Blackburn, he had picked the wrong time to ply his trade because Tracey had taken out the last violent psychopath, and she was ready to do it again.

NOT THE END

(Continued in Diary of a Serial Killer II: Ice Man)

AUTHOR BIO

Shawn Davis grew up in the small town of Holliston, Massachusetts. He earned his Bachelor of Science Degree in Criminal Justice from Salem State University, and he works as a police officer in a small New England town. He also worked as a police lieutenant at a New England College for eleven years. Shawn's background in law enforcement lends authenticity to his crime thrillers.

Shawn is also the co-author of the real-life WW II adventure, Never Surrender, with his Great Uncle and protagonist of the story, Earl Anderson. Never Surrender is the true story of Earl's incredible experiences fighting the Japanese in the Philippines and then fighting for survival for three and a half years as a POW in Yokohama, Japan.

Shawn also co-authored the Sci-Fi Thriller, American Insurrection, with his friend from high school, Robert Moore. American Insurrection is a high-tech, adrenaline-fueled, action-adventure story about a violent future rebellion in the United States.

The edgy horror thriller, Blood Kiss, details the reign of terror of a gang of beautiful female vampires at a small New England college.

In addition, Shawn authored the gritty crime thriller, American Criminal, which describes a former cop's struggle to survive in prison after being set up by his corrupt partners on a drug force tactical team.

In the novel, Bounty Hunter, an indomitable anti-hero drives an armored battle-car through a post-apocalyptic wasteland, fighting a deadly array of post-nuke enemies.

In the horror novel, The Soulless, written with co-author Mark Mackey, an army of zombies and genetically engineered monsters is let loose on a tropical island by a female mad scientist working for the government.

In Diary of a Serial Killer II: Ice Man, Shawn follows up his first popular horror novel in the Serial Killer Series by introducing a deadlier psychopath based on the notorious Ice Man, Richard Kuklinski. The victim-turned-heroine in Book I, Tracey Randall, returns as an indomitable detective tracking the killer in Book II.

Finally, in Diary of a Serial Killer III: Reaper, the Ice Man has relocated to New York City where a pair of diabolical sex killers are kidnapping, torturing and killing NYC's most beautiful co-eds. When the Ice Man's beautiful daughter, Rachel, is kidnapped, it becomes a race pitting FBI profilers against the Ice Man to find Rachel before she is brutally murdered by her sadistic captors.

Thank you for taking time to read DIARY OF A SER-IAL KILLER. If you enjoyed it, please consider telling your friends or posting a short review on Amazon – it will take less than a minute if you keep it simple! Independent, self-published writers face a lot of challenges – including doing all our own editing, marketing, and promotions because we don't have a traditional publishing company to back us, so any help you can give us with a review will be much appreci-ated!

Made in the USA
Las Vegas, NV
07 May 2023

71719647R00282